CHANTAL ROOME

WHAT TO EXPECT IN TIT ME WITH YOUR BEST SHOT

A (Probably Incomplete) List of Tropes and Things

small town romance

he falls first

sworn off love

curvy girl

older main characters (mid to late thirties)

himbo/golden retriever vibes

grumpy/black cat vibes

meddling out-of-town family

an underwear stealing menace of a goat

approximately 876 bird puns (give or take)

the second largest collection of rubber duckies in North
America (at least in Nick's mind it is)

spicy, open door sexy times
takes place in the fictional small town of Tuft Swallow, a shared
world which functions as the setting for books by six other
authors

Chapters With Sexy Times To Skip Over (Or Skip *To* * wink wink *)

Chapter 12 (kind of)
Chapter 13
Chapter 14
Chapter 34

Please see the next page for some content warnings.

Content Warnings

This book discusses several difficult subjects with what can occasionally seem like callous disregard. I promise it's not because I don't think these are serious issues. Truthfully, it has more to do with being an adult child of an alcoholic who's never addressed my own trauma beyond adopting a dark-ish sense of humor and denying the existence of my own feelings for far too long. So when you read about how Carson and Jared feel about their relationships with their parents, for example? Some (but not all, because I was lucky enough to have an amazing mom) of that is based on my own history with my dad.

My dad isn't in my closet, though. He's on my grandmother's mantle.

Anyway, read on for the content warnings. And, in case it's not clear, most of these are only mentioned in passing, but better safe than sorry.

Death of parents; house fires; death of parents in house fires; alcoholism and drug addiction; underage drinking; past child neglect; child abandonment; foster care and the foster system (I've done my best to portray this as accurately as possible within the limited scope and time-frame of this book. Despite all the research I've done for this book, I am not an authority on foster care or the foster system, and should not be looked to as a reliable source of information on the subject); past criminal activities of bumbling mobsters; sex trafficking; potential SA; serial killers and their crimes; references to incels, red-pillers, alphamales, and alpha doms; body shaming and fat shaming; theft and consumption of underwear by a goat; testicle mashing by that same goat; the world's tiniest running shorts; so many rubber ducks (however many you're thinking, it's still more than that); what some may consider an excessive number of bird puns (but what the other Tuft Swallow authors and I have determined it to be the exact right number); and possibly more that I missed (if you come across something that you think should have made this list, please email admin@chantalroome.com and we'll do our best to add it)

If a loved one's alcoholism or drug use has affected you, al-anon.org or smartrecovery.org may have resources to help.

To my mom,
thank you for being the most amazing mother I could ever hope
for, and for also being an amazing dad when you needed to.

And to Matt,
Thanks for the title!

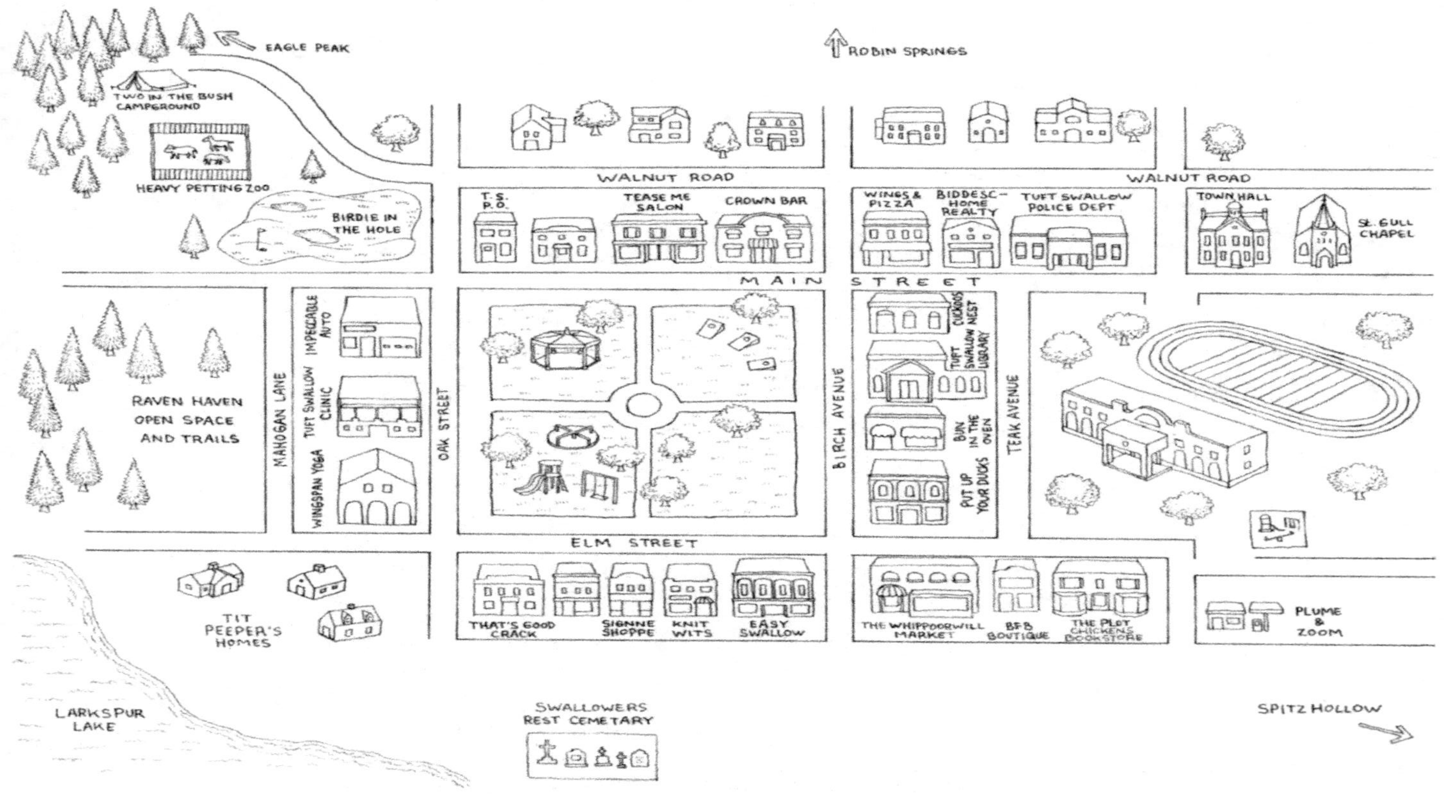

EAGLE PEAK

ROBIN SPRINGS

SPITZ HOLLOW

WALNUT ROAD

S. GULL CHAPEL

TOWN HALL

TUFT SWALLOW POLICE DEPT

BIDDESC-- HOME REALTY

WINGS & PIZZA

TEAK AVENUE

CUCKOO'S NEST

TUFT SWALLOW NEST LIBRARY

BUN IN THE OVEN

PUT UP YOUR DUCKS

THE WHIPPOORWILL MARKET

BFB BOUTIQUE

THE PLOT CHICKENS BOOKSTORE

PLUME & ZOOM

BIRCH AVENUE

MAIN STREET

CROWN BAR

TEASE ME SALON

WALNUT ROAD

T.S. P.O.

THAT'S GOOD CRACK

SIGNNE SHOPPE

KNIT WITS

EASY SWALLOW

ELM STREET

SWALLOWERS REST CEMETARY

OAK STREET

BIRDIE IN THE HOLE

HEAVY PETTING ZOO

TWO IN THE BUSH CAMPGROUND

IMPECCABLE AUTO

TUFT SWALLOW CLINIC

WINGSPAN YOGA

MAHOGAN LANE

RAVEN HAVEN OPEN SPACE AND TRAILS

TIT PEEPER'S HOMES

LARKSPUR LAKE

# Chapter 1

MOTHER KNOWS BEST

Tina

"Shit, shit, shit," I whisper under my breath, turning the knob on my gas range again, crossing my fingers that this time I'll hear the whoosh of the flame catching, instead of the click of the burner not lighting.

Click, click, click.

"Damn it!"

This can't be happening.

"What? What's wrong?" My mother's voice spills from the phone propped on the workstation next to me. "Should I call 911? Stan. STAN," she screeches at my father, in what I'm sure is a vain attempt to get his attention.

Stan Falcone is no doubt sitting in his recliner watching sports highlights from the last week, because if there's one thing my father loves, it's sports. Any sport, any time. If there's one thing he hates, it's my mom's tendency to overreact to any situation involving her children. He learned long ago, if he wanted any peace, he had to tune her out when her voice took on a certain tone.

Honestly, if it weren't for her belief in making us find our own way out of most messes we created, most people would consider Beatrice Falcone to be the original helicopter mom from back before helicopter parents were even a thing. It always drove my dad nuts, so he tended to ignore her when she started freaking out. Which is what he's most likely doing right now.

"Stan, turn that television off and call 911. Tina has an emergency."

Shit. That's the last thing I need. If a truck full of firefighters pulls up here because I can't get my gas range to light, I'll be the laughingstock of Tuft Swallow, and I barely fit in as it is.

Not that I leave the restaurant long enough to even make an attempt to fit in, but still.

"Ma! No," I yell at the screen where the top half of my mother's concern-wrinkled face is staring back at me. "It's nothing serious." I pick up the phone, turning the camera to take in the stove before pointing it at my face again. "See? The burner isn't lighting. I need to call a repairman. It's not an emergency." What will be an emergency is if I can't get the range fixed and I don't have the sauces I need to make it to closing tonight.

She pulls the phone away, getting most of her face on camera this time, and chides, "You know, if you had a husband, this kind of thing wouldn't happen."

It's a familiar refrain, and my eyes roll before I can stop them. Once a week for the last five years, I video chat with my mother, and once a week for the last five years, she's gotten on my case about finding a husband. In the Falcone family, all the women get married young. All the women except for me, that is. My mother has never forgiven me for choosing to follow the path of the Falcone men: moving to a new city and opening a pizza restaurant. That I was already a spinster at the ripe old age of thirty-one when I left? Well, that just added insult to injury. In her mind, I should have moved into her house and let her take care of me until she found me a husband, or until I died of loneliness, whichever came first.

Well, screw that. I'm fine being alone, gas range problems notwithstanding. I don't need to marry some overgrown man-child to feel fulfilled in my life. Don't get me wrong, I love my dad, but he's helpless without my mother. I have zero interest in taking care of a grown ass man like that for the rest of my life. I have my pizza place, my friends, my murder podcasts, and my creepy teapots. My life is perfect the way it is.

"Don't roll your eyes at me, young lady." Despite being all too aware of my advanced age, my mother sometimes forgets I am an independent thirty-six-year-old woman, and she scolds me like I'm a disobedient child. She means well, but she gets on my nerves when she does it. Usually I'm better at hiding it, though. "You know how I feel about eye rolling."

"Sorry, Ma. Tell me, what kind of insurance *exactly* would a husband be against a gas range breaking?" Okay, so maybe I would never come right out and tell her she was getting on my nerves, but the annoyance seeps into my voice when I'm not careful. Kind of like it is now.

"Valentina Violetta Falcone. You watch your tone when you're speaking to me."

Ah, shit. That stops me short. She middle named me. She only does that when she's truly upset. I suppose I didn't realize how worried she was before I explained about the stove, and now I've made it worse. Maybe I should text my aunts and send them over to talk her off the ledge. But not before shooting a warning text to my dad, of course. He'll want to be out of the house before all the aunts arrive with their loud voices and bottles of wine. He can ignore my mother without issue, but five loud, proud Italian women are more than even he dares to take on.

"Sorry, Ma. I'm frustrated with the stove. I shouldn't take that out on you."

She purses her lips before granting me one of her wide, toothy grins. "You're forgiven. I could never stay mad at my favorite unmarried daughter."

"I'm your only unmarried daughter." As the youngest of seven kids, and the only single one, my mom has turned all her matchmaking attentions on me as of late. Until recently, two of my brothers had been steadfast bachelors, but last year Tommy and Victor both met wonderful women and are now happily engaged and soon to be married. I don't begrudge them their happiness, but come on. Couldn't one of them have waited a while? Or at least given me some sort of heads up that I'd need to prepare for my mother's onslaught of dating advice?

"And if you'd give a man half a chance, you could be as happy as your brothers and sisters are. I don't understand why you insist on doing everything yourself. Your aunts and I know the type of man you need. You should let us be your matchmakers. We'll have you married by next year."

See what I mean? Just like that, we're back on the subject of finding me a husband. Luckily, I don't have time for this conversation today. If I can't get her off the phone soon, I'll never get the stove fixed, and if I don't get the stove fixed, it'll be another slow night at the restaurant. And despite my earlier assertion of having a perfect life, I can't afford many more slow nights at Wings and Pizza. Thank goodness my landlord shows up at least once a day. If it weren't for Wade charging me such low rent *and* buying food every day, I'd have been out of business long ago.

Sometimes I wonder if I'm in over my head, but then I remember I've been getting by just fine for the last five years. There's no reason to think I won't continue to do so for five more. If I can ever get off the phone and get the damn stove fixed, that is.

"Mom, I have to let you go. I need to call the handyman in to fix the stove. I'll talk to you next week, okay?"

"Oh no, that's too bad. Aunt Vera is on her way over to the house to visit with Nonna Mona, but I know she was also hoping to talk to you today. I suppose there's nothing to be done for it, though. It's not as though it's not her own fault. If that woman could ever be on time for anything, she wouldn't have missed you."

Nonna Mona is my grandmother on my father's side, and she's lived with my parents since my grandfather passed away almost thirty years ago. Despite living in the same house, my Nonna has never once questioned me about when I'll get married. She understands me better than my mom ever has.

"Okay, thanks Mom. Love you. Give my love to Dad, Nonna, and the aunts. Bye." I press the end call icon before she can continue the conversation. If there's one thing my mom is great at, it's extending a goodbye until you forget you were even trying to get off the phone. One time, I was supposed to meet a friend to see a movie, and my mom kept me on the phone so long that I wouldn't have even been able to catch the ending credits. Since then, I've learned to say a quick goodbye and hang up before she can suck me back in. Guilt pricks at my conscience, but it really is the only way to get her off the phone.

"Chloe? Can you come back here?" I yell to the front of the store, where Chloe is washing the windows and getting ready to paint a new mural. Besides being one of my closest friends, Chloe is my sole full-time employee, and in house art maiden.

While she's happy enough slinging pizza, what lights her up most is expressing her creativity. She paints the restaurant's windows for every season, sometimes even throwing in obscure holidays or sporting events just for the hell of it. When she isn't working with me at the pizza shop, she's using her artistic talents to paint murals and windows all around Tuft Swallow. But even though her heart isn't in the restaurant business like mine is, she's one of the most reliable people I know.

She pops into the kitchen, her wavy pink bob swinging just above her shoulders, a pair of her ever-present paint-covered overalls buckled on one side over a ratty white tank. It's impossible to look at her and not see an artist. "What's up?"

"Can you watch the store while I cook these sauces in my apartment? The stove won't light and we won't have enough sauce to make it through the day if I don't get these extra batches simmering."

Chloe wipes her hands on a towel and comes back to the stove. "Sure. I'll be here, anyway. Did you need me to call Wade for you?"

"Nah, we'd better get Thayer on this right away." Thayer Longspur, Tuft Swallow's resident reluctant handyman, is my first choice when it comes to restaurant repairs, because he's the best, despite how much he seems to hate doing it. My landlord may be responsible for fixing things, but he's not great at it, and I usually end up calling Thayer, anyway. If I want my stove fixed today, it's best to skip over the part where I let Wade make an attempt.

"I wouldn't mind if you could give me a hand bringing these pots up, though." I can carry a line of plates as long as my arm, but I've never figured out how to translate that skill to cooking pots.

"Sure thing."

I take the two largest pots and walk to the exit, leaving Chloe to take the remaining two. After years of doing grunt work in restaurant kitchens, I'm used to carrying more than seems possible for a woman of my size. I may be a little on the chubby side according to what you see in the media, but there is no denying the strength in my arms.

One of the best parts of living in an apartment above the restaurant I run is the commute. You can't beat being able to roll out of bed, walk down the stairs, and be at your workplace. It's been five years since I lived in the city and I can still vividly recall how soul-sucking it was taking public transit to and from work on top of the fourteen-hours I'd already worked in someone else's kitchen. Moving to Tuft Swallow was the best thing I ever could have done for my work life balance, and that's *with* still working fourteen-hour days more often than not. Being out of my mother's, and my four meddling aunts', reach is just a bonus. A peaceful, gloriously quiet bonus.

I make it to the top of the stairs on the side of the building and kick the partially open door of my apartment, letting it swing wide before making my way inside.

"You're still leaving your door open when you're in the store? That is so unsafe, Tina. You need to make sure it catches before you walk away, you know." Chloe follows me into the tiny apartment, stopping at the entrance to the kitchen while I set out each of my pots on a burner on the avocado green electric stove. "You can't keep leaving it open to the world."

"Here, pass me those." I ignore Chloe's speech and gesture for her to pass me the pots she carried, placing them on the remaining small burners.

"Don't avoid the question. How can you leave your door wide open like that? Anyone could come in here when you're at work."

I scoff. "It's Tuft Swallow. Who would come in? The worst thing that could happen is I'd find Winston in here eating the contents of my underwear drawer again. And I assure you, most of those underwear have seen better days. He'd be doing me a favor." I have a solid collection of cotton granny panties, but they can probably use updating soon. Working as much as I do doesn't leave a lot of time for shopping, though, so I make a mental note to order some panties online. Thank God for online shopping.

"How do goats even climb stairs?" Chloe chuckles before schooling her features. "No. Don't distract me. You need to start closing your door. And locking it, preferably. Tuft Swallow is small, sure, but that doesn't mean it's completely safe. You need to be more careful."

I wince at the note of concern in her voice. I suppose I've grown somewhat complacent since relocating to Tuft Swallow, but it's not as bad as Chloe is making it sound. So I leave my apartment door slightly ajar occasionally. It's not like it's wide open. A person would have to come up the stairs to even be able to tell. But despite how confident I am about my safety, the last thing I want is for Chloe to worry.

"Okay, okay. You're right," I say with a sigh. "I'll make more of an effort to remember."

She squints at me, hands on her hips, as though she's trying to parse the lie. Detecting none, she says, "Fine. I'll be checking on that from time to time. Think of it like...a surprise inspection from the health inspector. Except I'm a safety inspector. Your safety, to be precise."

I roll my eyes before turning to face her. "Yes. Fine. I will close my door from now on. Happy?"

"Immensely," she says, a smug smirk pulling at the corner of her mouth. "And if you don't do it, I'll call your mother and have her drive down here from Boston to straighten you out."

My eyes widen at the threat. "Don't you dare, Chloe. You know what she's like when she comes here. She'll take over my kitchen and before I know it, we'll be serving a full menu instead of just pizza, wings, and the occasional pasta special. Nobody wants that."

Except... maybe the people of Tuft Swallow do want that? Maybe that's why business has been so slow. Of course, it's always possible that opening a big city style walk up pizza place in such a tiny town wasn't a sound business decision. Maybe I really am in over my head.

Chapter 2

YOU'LL POKE AN EYE OUT

Nick

"No, no, no. Do it again. Tuck your arm in closer to your body and give me a nice underhanded lob. You're holding your arm out too far to the side. You look like a kid skipping rocks on the pond for the first time."

I take a deep breath, grip the bean bag, pull my arm back, and throw the damn thing the way my cornhole coach, Peter, is describing. At least, I attempt to throw it his way. As soon as it leaves my fingers, I can tell it won't be landing anywhere near the cornhole board. Again.

"This is why I told you to cut back on the workouts, you lunkhead. It's these things right here." He pokes at the latissimus dorsi muscle protruding from my torso under my arm. "This muscle is too damn big. You can't even put your arms down. You're like the little brother in that Christmas movie. You know, the one where the kid shoots his eye out?" Peter seems to take pleasure in berating me for my terrible cornhole skills. It reminds me of my childhood here in Tuft Swallow, before I left to become a professional MMA fighter.

Back then, the kids, and even some parents, couldn't wrap their heads around my complete lack of skill with the sport, and they gave me such shit for it. Hell, it's not like I can blame them. I couldn't even wrap my own head around it. I was like a duck to water with any martial art, but put a bean bag in my hand and I was... well, I was more of an odd duck. And trust me, it came as no surprise to me when they started calling me Odd Duck instead of Nick. I wasn't even bothered when the nickname stuck.

I kind of like ducks.

I have to chuckle at Peter's attitude, though. Throughout all my years fighting mixed martial arts, and out of all the coaches I've had in various fighting styles, none has ever been as frustrated with me as Peter is right now. But at least those coaches could say they helped me retire as an undefeated mixed martial arts champion. Who knew trying to learn how to play cornhole, my hometown's official sport and unofficial obsession, would be the thing that finally proves me uncoachable?

"Peter, I swear I rarely work out these days." I list items on my fingers. "I train my fighters, lead the seniors' physical activity group, and go for the occasional run. That's it. I never hit the weights. I don't know why that muscle is still so big." *I mean, sure, I trained hard every day for the last twenty-odd years, and I'm naturally a big guy, but besides that, I have no idea.*

Peter shakes his head, the disgust plain on his face. He slaps my stomach with the back of his hand and shakes his head. "And yet you've had no trouble letting your six-pack go."

Technically, he's both right *and* wrong. I still have a six-pack. It's hidden under a layer of well-deserved retirement fat, but it's there. Now that I no longer have to worry about making weight for upcoming fights, I'm eating everything that wasn't on my approved diet for all those years. So even though I've gained a little weight, all my muscle is still here.

"You're tall enough that you should be able to drop the damn bean bag into the hole," Peter continues. "With the wingspan you've got, you can lean forward and reach the board."

An exaggeration, obviously. Regulation competition distance for a cornhole board is twenty-seven feet. At six-four, I simply do not have that kind of reach.

"You're supposed to be some kind of undefeated champion and look at you. You can't even throw a damn bean bag straight enough to get it close to the target. Hell, after coaching you these last few months and seeing the shit aim you've got, I bet even if you did lean over and touch the board, you'd still never get your bag anywhere near the hole. Where did that last one go, anyway?" His head swivels in a half-hearted attempt to find the missing bean bag. "And don't you dare ask to use mine. You can't even keep track of your own bag, so you're nuts if you think I'd let you touch mine." He clears his throat with a grunt. "A man can't go sharing his bag with a guy who can't take care of what he's already got."

I fight to hold back the chuckle rising up the back of my throat. I know firsthand how Peter feels about me giggling at his talk of bags and holes, so I know he won't appreciate me calling out the unintentional dirtiness of his words. He takes the game of cornhole far too seriously for that. In fact, all of Tuft Swallow takes cornhole too seriously for that. It's kind of a sickness here.

Nevertheless, if I want to be taken seriously as an athlete by the people of my hometown, I need to up my cornhole game. That's why I hired Peter as my coach in the first place.

A former world cornhole champion, and somewhat of a local legend, Peter originally wanted to be left alone in his retirement, but money talks. And I have lots of money to spend on this endeavor. I accepted his first price without question. I probably could have put in a call to Shemar Moore for some cornhole tips, but despite his recent successes with the American Cornhole League and the Superhole Championship, he is still a working actor and doesn't have time to come to Tuft Swallow to coach the uncoachable. Besides, Shemar may be a champion cornholer, but he's no Peter Harrelson.

"That's what you get for leaving Tuft Swallow to pursue something as stupid as professional wrestling. You know that shit ain't real, right? Bunch of grown men in tights dancing around, pretending to hit each other." He scoffs. "And there isn't even any singing to make it palatable. It's like a Broadway show without the best part."

I scrub a hand down my face and fight back a grin. When Peter starts sharing his thoughts on how professional wrestling is simply a crappier version of Broadway instead of an actual sport, I know the cornhole lesson is over for the day. No matter how many times I explain to him I'm a retired MMA fighter, and that mixed martial arts are, in fact, real, he refuses to believe it. In addition to that, I've explained to him several times that professional wrestling, despite the scripts and pageantry, is incredibly hard on the body, and requires extremely high athleticism, a lesson I learned firsthand when I did a guest spot on one the biggest pay-per-view wrestling productions ever aired on television. He just doesn't want to hear it. If I've learned anything about my coach these last six months, it's that, like it is to most Tuft Swallowers, to Peter, cornhole is life.

That, and he really likes Broadway musicals.

"Alright, Peter. Let's call it a day. I've got a class this afternoon and I need to get out for a run before that. It has come to my attention that I need to lose some muscle, and some belly fat, if I ever want to improve my cornhole game."

Peter scoffs, a scowl forming amidst the bristles of his unkempt beard and overgrown eyebrows. "You can't even commit to a decent length practice. You'll never get your bag near any holes at this rate." Without a goodbye, Peter storms past my gym's front desk, completely ignoring everything around him while continuing to grumble about my poor work ethic. The trainer I have working the reception desk today, just shakes his head and smiles as Peter stomps past, already accustomed to his near daily habit of storming out of here in a huff. He says Peter reminds him of a grumpy grandpa, and he finds the stomping endearing. I guess I kind of do, too.

After gathering up the cornhole board and tracking down all the stray bags I'd misplaced during the lesson, I change into my running shorts, grab my headphones, and head to the door. I'm about to head out on my run when Rhett, the gym's manager, stops me.

"I know it's technically Spring, but don't you think it would be better if you wore a shirt on your run? It's barely above freezing out today," Rhett says with a pointed look at my naked torso. "And those shorts leave very little to the imagination. Are you trying to make the front page of the Town Flyer? Or maybe the Nosy Pecker?"

I shrug and shoot him a grin. "Sun's out, guns out, baby," I say, striking a bodybuilding pose. "Let them look." If the busybodies who run the town's official and unofficial newspapers want a picture of me in my little running shorts, who am I to deny them?

As I push open the gym doors, he yells after me, "It's not the guns I'm worried about, man. You'll poke an eye out with those nipples if you're not careful."

I bark a laugh as I pull my headphones on and run out the door.

MY RUN TAKES ME in a wide circle around Tuft Swallow proper, following the walking trails that are, as is usual for this time of year, packed with enthusiastic bird watchers. Despite Rhett's concern over my lack of a shirt, I poke no one's eyes out. Tourist season is starting, and some of the bird watchers recognize me, calling out "Odd Duck" and quacking as I run past. I'll never regret my decision to move back here. The people around town aren't impressed by me in the slightest, and the tourists aren't much different. I haven't been asked for my autograph once since I moved back six months ago. Sure, the bird-watching season is just getting started, and along with it, the influx of tourists, but if the people I've crossed paths with today are anything to go by, I'll be just fine here.

Which is perfect, because I'm in this for the long haul.

When I retired from fighting and moved back to the town I hadn't seen since I was fifteen years old, I did it with some very specific goals in mind. The first goal was to open my gym, which, I think we can all agree, is a goal I've met and exceeded. Put Up Your Ducks isn't the biggest training facility in the country, but I've already had several up and coming future champs expressing their desire to come and train with me. The second goal, learning to play cornhole without embarrassing myself, is off to a rocky start, but it's on track. I have a coach and

I'm confident he can turn me into a halfway decent player. The third, amassing the largest collection of rubber ducks the world has ever seen, is going better than I expected. If the numbers in the world record books are accurate, I'm firmly in second place, and gaining. I should pass the current record holder later this year, if everything goes according to plan. The last goal is where I'm having some problems. It turns out finding someone to settle down and have a family with is more difficult than I expected.

I never had issues finding a date when I lived in Las Vegas. The only problem was, my dates weren't really the kind of women who were looking to settle down with me. Don't get me wrong, they were nice enough women who would have been happy to marry me if I'd planned to stick around the bright lights of Vegas, but as soon as I mentioned moving to a town as small as Tuft Swallow to start my own fight academy, well, they couldn't move on to the next guy fast enough.

I don't know why I'm having an issue here in Tuft Swallow. The women in this little town are as good looking as any of the women I dated in Vegas, but they have no interest in me at all.

I suppose that's the downside to having the people of Tuft Swallow being so unimpressed by me. When they see my giant ass coming down the street, they turn the other way. Okay, it's not that bad, but I've had no luck meeting anyone I'd like to take out, let alone anyone who I'd consider spending my life with. Because that's what I'm looking for now: a partner.

I'm so distracted by my thoughts that when my run takes me off the trails and back into downtown Tuft Swallow, I'm momentarily lost. I slow down to take in my surroundings, and just as I get my bearings... I slam into something. Hard.

"Shit. What the hell just happened?" A woman's voice reaches my ears, her confusion palpable over the sounds of clattering metal. "Oh no. Mr. Landon. Are you alright?"

When I look down, I'm shocked to see I've landed in the middle of a crime scene. Splatters of viscous red liquid coat the sidewalk, and a metal pot stands upside down amid the carnage, with another pot rolling into the street. A man wearing what may have once been a brown suit is also covered in the red liquid, almost as though he's showered in it, and a woman in a white apron is fussing over him.

"Oh, Mr. Landon. I'm so sorry." The woman's curly black hair is tied in a knot on her head, splatters of the red liquid dotting the half-formed curls. "Promise you'll send me the bill when you have your suit cleaned."

Oh, that's right. Before I slammed into a short human wall, I'd realized I was near the pizza place Rhett hasn't shut up about for the last three months. I've been meaning to try it, but haven't had the chance yet. My stomach growls at the scent of tomato sauce in the air. Maybe I should stop in now, since I'm already here.

"And you!" The woman spins around and pokes me in the chest, leaving a bewildered, sauce-soaked Mr. Landon to wander off alone. "What the hell do you think you're doing running around on a busy sidewalk like that? You could have really hurt someone."

Holy shit. *Who is this?* She stares at me through thick glasses, the bright green frames smeared with the red sauce that I'm just now noticing is also dripping down the front of her shirt. She rests her fists on her wide hips and glares at me, her flushed face gorgeous despite her obvious anger. My mouth works silently, the words in my brain a jumble of mismatched questions and compliments, leaving me staring dumbly as her fury increases.

"Nothing to say for yourself? You ruined my sauce."

This woman is not scared of me in the slightest. I have at least a foot on her, not to mention probably a hundred pounds, and she's staring me down in the middle of the street better than any man I've ever faced in the ring. *She's fierce, and I love it.* Maybe my luck with women is finally changing. A grin creeps onto my face as a plan to ask this woman out forms in my mind, but before I can act on it, she throws her hands up and huffs out a breath.

"Never mind. I need to get my pots and figure out how to get this sauce off the street before it makes more of a mess." She turns her back on me and faces the mess on the sidewalk. "Now, where did that other pot go?"

"Let me get that for you," I mutter, finally finding my voice as I step into the street to grab the pot.

"Winston, don't you dare touch that. Shoo!" I spin around to see what would be a strange sight in any other town, but in Tuft Swallow, it's just another day. The woman has taken a defensive stance, arms spread wide in front of her, as she attempts to shoo a curious, fluffy, white-coated goat away from the red mess staining the sidewalk. "No! Bad Mr. Mayor. Gah…Your dad will kill me if you get sauce all in your pretty fleece. Never mind what deputy mayor Verona will do to both of us if you do anything to make yourself look less respectable. You know she's desperate to find any reason to impeach you. Now shoo. Go. Get going. Get!"

Seeing an opportunity to help, I place the pot I retrieved with the other, creep up behind the goat, wrap my arms around both sets of legs, and hoist him into the air. "Now what? Should I take him home?" I ask the woman. Despite his size, the goat is surprisingly easy to carry. He seems completely unfazed by my presence as he rests placidly in my arms. I would expect a farm animal to protest at least a little at being lifted into the air by a stranger, but then again, what do I know? I grew up in gyms and training facilities far away from any farm. This could be totally normal behavior for a goat. I have seen this one wandering around town a fair bit. Maybe he's more of a pet than a farm animal, after all. Remembering that she called him Mr. Mayor, I add, "Or would City Hall be better?"

"Uh, home?" The woman asks, before blowing out a relieved sounding breath. "Take him to his dad. Do you know where Impeckable Auto is? That's where he spends most of his day. Get him out of here before he gets into the sauce or I'll have hell to pay with his dad. It's almost shearing time, and I doubt he'll be happy to have Winston's angora soaked in red sauce and smelling like garlic."

"Yep. I'll bring him there now."

I'm halfway down the street with a two hundred pound goat in my arms before it dawns on me that I didn't even ask the woman her name. No matter. I'll be fixing that mistake as soon as I can get this goat back to his owner. Because whoever that woman was, she's the only woman I've met in Tuft Swallow who I want to know more about. And damn, am I ever excited about that.

But... What was she was saying about this goat being the mayor?

I thought that was just a joke in the Nosy Pecker. *Huh.* Would you look at that? It's not all unsubstantiated gossip, after all. Who knew?

Chapter 3

RETURN OF THE TRAMP STAMP

Tina

WHAT THE HELL WAS that? I think while staring up at the sky from a prone position on the cold sidewalk, muscles aching like I've been in a car crash. I was bringing my sauce back to the restaurant kitchen after the handyman got my gas range lit, and the next thing I know, I'm sprawled on the sidewalk. After being slammed into by a brick wall as I took the last step off the stairs from my apartment, I watched in horror as my hard work turned end over end in what looked like slow motion; the pots spilling their sauce in arcs of glistening red as they tumbled to the sidewalk with a crash. *It looks weirdly similar to the set of a slasher flick,* I thought as I watched the carnage unfold. *Or maybe like a crime scene from one of my podcasts.*

After confirming I have no broken bones or other horrible injuries, I force myself to my feet. "Shit," I mutter to myself. "What the hell just happened?"

Mr. Landon is on the ground in front of me, his appearance making it plain he's suffered the worst of the sauce spill. Where I have a few drops in my hair and on my clothes, Mr. Landon looks like he's just emerged from a tub full of the tomatoey goodness.

"Oh, no. Mr. Landon. Are you alright?" He takes my offered hand and allows me to help him off the ground. I untie my apron and wipe at his suit, smearing the sauce and making the mess worse. "I'm not sure what happened. It's a good thing it wasn't hot yet, huh? It would have been so much worse if it had been hot." I was thankful, if slightly irritated at having to turn around and come back down right away, when Thayer said he'd come and fix the range immediately, but now that I'd accosted a citizen with my cold sauce, I'm even happier. Poor Mr. Landon could have been seriously burned if the sauce had had any time to simmer.

"I bet that man knows something," he says, pointing behind me.

Glancing over my shoulder to where Mr. Landon points, I spot the brick wall that ran into me. Except, instead of a wall, it's a man. A giant blonde viking of a man in tiny running shorts. He stands there with his hands on hips, his shirtless chest distinctly, and unfairly (since he caused this mess), sauce free. It's barely above freezing today, so what's this guy doing out here nearly naked?

Not that I mind the view. He's an impressive sight with his tree trunk thighs, enormous chest, and tattooed biceps. The way he grins when he catches me staring sends a flush of heat to my belly, but I still can't tear my eyes away.

"In light of this unfortunate incident, I hope we can rain check today?" Mr. Landon finally drags my attention away from the shirtless giant. "I really need to get home to wash all this off."

"Huh? Oh, yeah. Sure. That's a good idea." I agree distractedly, stealing looks at the man in tiny shorts. "Have a nice day, Mr. Landon."

"And you!" I spin around and poke the man in the chest, as the sauce covered Mr. Landon wanders off alone. "What the hell do you think you're doing running around on a busy sidewalk like that? You could have really hurt someone." I tap my foot with irritation. "Nothing to say for yourself? You ruined my sauce."

Instead of offering any kind of explanation, the shirtless idiot just grins at me.

"Never mind. I need to get my pots and figure out how to get this sauce off the street before it makes more of a mess." I turn away from the silent giant and survey the mess on the sidewalk. "Now, where did that other pot go?"

"Let me get that for you," the man says, finally doing something useful by going to grab the pot I've just now noticed has made it all the way into the street. I'm gearing up to give him a piece of my mind, when a familiar bump to my butt warns of a visitor. A visitor who cannot be here right now.

I whirl around and point a finger at the offending butt bumper, who is inching closer to the worst of the saucy mess on the sidewalk. "Winston, don't you touch that. Shoo!" The Angora goat ignores me completely, taking another step toward the red mess, the look in his eye telling me he intends to partake in whatever delicacy this is. "No! Bad Mr. Mayor. Gah…Your dad will kill me if you get sauce all in your pretty fleece. Never mind what deputy mayor Verona will do to both of us if you do anything to make yourself look less respectable. You know she's desperate to find any reason to impeach you. Now shoo. Go. Get going. Get!" I'm looking around for something to lure him away from the mess when the shirtless guy steps between me and Winston.

Without preamble, he squats, wraps his arms around Winston's legs, and picks him up off the ground. My mouth drops open. That goat weighs at least two hundred pounds, and this man lifted him like he weighs no more than a bag of groceries. *Who is this guy?*

"Should I take him home?" he asks, his voice unstrained, as though holding a two hundred pound ruminant in his arms isn't a hardship. "Or would City Hall be better?"

I swallow roughly, the warmth I felt upon first seeing him rushing in again. Who knew a man lifting a goat could be such a turn on. This must be why some people have farmer fetishes. *Oh, shit. Do I have a farmer fetish now?*

"Uh, home?" I shake my head to clear it. One problem at a time. Right now, getting Winston away from this sauce needs to take priority. I can investigate my thoughts on farmers later. "Take him to his dad. Do you know where Impeckable Auto is? That's where he spends most of his day. Get him out of here before he gets into the sauce or I'll have hell to pay with his dad. It's almost shearing time, and I doubt he'll be happy to have Winston's angora soaked in red sauce and smelling like garlic."

He nods. "Yep. I'll bring him there now."

The man takes off at a slow jog and I can't stop myself from sneaking a peek at his backside, my curiosity about what his butt looks like in those little shorts suddenly all-consuming. It's as spectacular as you'd expect based on the rest of him. What I don't expect to see, though, is the tattoo across his lower back.

He has a tramp stamp? Who is this guy?

Even after getting Mr. Landon cleaned up and sending Winston on his way with the shirtless idiot who'd caused all the commotion, I'm still not out of the woods. With two of the four pots of sauce out of commission, we're dangerously close to not having enough to make it through the evening.

As soon as Mr. Landon and the giant viking left, and after I'd scraped up most of the mess, I came into the restaurant to start the new batches of sauce. Somehow, Thayer managed to sneak past me during the commotion and get the stove fixed before I noticed he'd even been here. So here I am standing at the stove, dotted with blobs of sauce from head to toe, instead of upstairs showering off the mess.

"This is why we should prepare some sauce in advance and keep it in the freezer." Chloe works at the prep station next to me, getting all the fresh vegetables chopped for tonight's pizza orders. "I know you want to do everything fresh every day, but a little back up sauce would have saved us this trouble. Heating it up takes less time than simmering it for hours."

"Yeah, yeah," I grumble, stirring a handful of spices into the sauce, the aroma of tomatoes, garlic, and onions thick in the air. "But it's better when it's fresh."

"I'm not saying it isn't. I'm just saying that if it comes down to frozen sauce, or no sauce, I'm picking frozen sauce every time."

She's right. Of course she is. But I grew up in a kitchen where if your sauce wasn't fresh, then it wasn't sauce. My mom routinely went out in the predawn light to pick fresh tomatoes, onions, and garlic from her garden, often starting her sauce for the evening meal before breakfast was even a thought. I can only imagine what she would think if she knew I was freezing sauce? Nothing good, I can guarantee you that. It makes me feel icky thinking about it. But I have to remember that restaurants differ from home kitchens, and sometimes, as long as I make it from scratch myself before I freeze it, frozen sauce is okay. But only in when it's an emergency.

And when a shirtless giant spills your sauce all over the sidewalk and innocent passersby? Yeah, I'd say that counts as an emergency.

Stupid viking giant. Where did he come from, anyway? And why was I focused on the rippling of his back muscles as he carried Winston back to his owner?

Okay, that's a lie. I wasn't so focused on his muscles that I didn't notice his lower back tattoo.

Now, I've never been a fan of tramp stamp tattoos, especially since all the examples I've seen have been butterflies, or poorly executed tribal art, but this one was special. I have never seen a lower back tattoo like it.

"Did you see that guy who carried off the mayor?" I ask Chloe. "You came out as he was walking off."

Chloe nods, putting the last of the prepped vegetables into the cooler. "I saw him. Isn't it a little cold out to be wearing nothing but tiny running shorts? It looked like he was wearing a bathing suit. I don't understand how he can be out like that and not freeze. I've got thermal underwear on under these overalls and cardigan, plus I'm inside in a hot kitchen, and I'm still cold."

I snort a laugh. They were very short shorts. They remind me of something they'd wear in old aerobics videos from the eighties. The ones where the men all dressed in tiny shorts and muscle shirts, and the women in dressed in leotards and tights. How could that be comfortable to run in? I'd prefer to be a little more covered up during a run. Not that you'd catch me running to begin with. Running is a little too athletic for me. I like my exercise to be slow and steady, like walking. Or standing on my feet for up to fourteen hours a day while I run my restaurant.

"Okay, but did you notice his back? Tell me that wasn't a rubber duck I saw tattooed right above his waistband."

Chloe chuckles, nodding vigorously. "It was. Wearing little shorts and gloves." She tilts her head. "You haven't met Nick yet?"

I shake my head, still laughing. "I haven't had the pleasure. You know how rarely I leave this place." I gesture to the surrounding restaurant. Chloe is the only employee who has keys to the restaurant, so if I need to be somewhere, then she's here taking care of business. She's fully aware of how little time I have to myself. "So, who is he?"

"Tina, if you'd read your Nosy Pecker, you'd already know this."

I give her a quick side-eye and turn back to my sauce.

The Nosy Pecker is Tuft Swallow's answer to a gossip rag. The information in it is suspect at best, and I avoid it whenever possible. I can't understand why a town full of mostly intelligent people would look to an anonymously written newsletter for all the latest information, especially when we have the Tit Peepers group of elderly bird watchers ready and willing to spread all the gossip you could ever want.

Actually, it wouldn't surprise me if one of Tit Peepers was also behind the Nosy Pecker. That would make so much sense.

"Okay, okay. I'll stop bugging you about it," Chloe says with a laugh, even though we both know she'll do no such thing. As soon as something else happens in this town, she'll be after me about reading that damn Nosy Pecker. "That's Nick D'Onofrio. He opened up that new gym down at the other end of the street. You know, *Put Up Your Ducks MMA*? He hired me to paint a weird duck mural on a wall there. You should go check it out. And not just for the mural. That man is single-handedly responsible for the increased availability of sexy man-meat in Tuft Swallow by at least sixty percent.”

“Sixty? He’s a big guy, but I wouldn’t give him that much credit.” Big guy is an understatement. The man is enormous.

Chloe shakes her head. “No, not because of him. It’s because of his gym. He’s running a fight academy. Young professional fighters move here to train with him. I’ve dated three of them already. You know, you could probably find someone to *service* you over there.” She waggles her eyebrows. “Lots of eligible men. And they’re all in excellent shape since all they do is work out. All that exercise leads to incredible stamina.”

A flush of heat runs through me at the thought of that large Nick fellow taking up space in my apartment, or my bed, but I shut that line of thinking down quickly. It’s ridiculous. He’s attractive and his body will feature in my future fantasies, but that’s where I have to draw the line.

“I’ll pass on that,” I say after clearing my throat. “You know I don’t date.”

Chloe rolls her eyes at me.

We talk about this almost as often as we talk about the Nosy Pecker. She doesn’t understand why I wouldn’t date casually, even if I’m not looking to get married and start pushing out kids like my family wants. I don’t understand why I should waste my time dating random guys when I know nothing will ever come of it. I refuse to give up my career, or my sense of self, just to have a man in my life.

“Plenty of women have successful careers and fulfilling relationships simultaneously, you know. You wouldn’t have to give up Wings and Pizza in order to have a man. Times have changed.”

“They have, but try telling that to my mother. She still thinks the only way I’ll be fulfilled as a woman is if I have a bunch of kids to fuss over and a husband to look after. I can't imagine anything worse." A shiver of disgust runs through me at the thought of having to take care of a grown ass man. "No, thank you. I'm happy alone. This restaurant is all I ever wanted. Now that I have it, I won't risk it by chasing after something I can get from my vibrator. And get it better at that."

A cough from the other side of the counter breaks me out of my rant before I can extol the benefits of battery operated boyfriends.

"Excuse me, ladies. I'm, uh, I'm here to pick up my date, Tina Falcone." The man looks at me expectantly. Wearing a short-sleeved button-up shirt tucked into pressed, pleated khaki pants, he reminds me of a kid whose mom dressed him up for picture day at school. The hair he's combed neatly to the side would give the same impression if it weren't blatantly obvious that he's attempting to hide a completely baldpate under those few strands.

Chloe bursts into laughter at what I can only assume is the stunned look on my face. Did this guy say he's here to pick me up on a date? That can't be right. I was literally *just* telling Chloe five seconds ago that I don't date.

"I'm sorry," I say, finally gathering my wits and putting on what I hope is a polite smile. "I think you're mistaken. I'm Tina, but I don't have a date tonight." *Or any night.* "Did you maybe get the name wrong?"

He shakes his head before I've finished asking the question. "No, look." He pulls his phone out of his pocket, pulling up a message on a popular dating app. "We made a date to go out for dinner today."

I take his phone to get a closer look and sure enough, there, plain as day, is a message from Tina Falcone confirming a date for this evening, and giving instructions for the man to pick her up at Wings and Pizza in Tuft Swallow. The only problem is,

I don't have a profile on any dating site, never mind one where I've communicated and made a date with this guy standing in front of me.

This is frigging weird. Who catfishes someone, then sends them to the actual person for a date?

"I'm sorry, Mr.?" I pause for him to say his name, but he doesn't catch on. Instead, he stares at me blankly, forcing me to forge on in ignorance. "Uh, yeah. Moving on. I don't know who you are, but I know I didn't make a date with you."

"Yes, you did," he says, stomping his foot and snatching his phone from my fingers. "I drove all the way from Spitz Hollow for this. You told me we would go for dinner. And I was hoping for *dessert,* too.*"* He waggles his eyebrows and drags his eyes down my body, smiling.

Ew. Hell no. This man-child is a prime example of why I don't date. He walked in here feeling entitled to my time and even after I politely explained he'd made a mistake, he's not taking no for an answer. But that shit won't fly here.

"Listen here, buddy—"

"No, you listen here. You can't make me drive all the way here, then take one look at me, and decide you don't want to date me after all. That's not fair. My mom says I'm a catch."

"Oh, now you've done it," Chloe says with a chuckle. "I would turn around and leave if I were you. This won't be pretty."

The man has the audacity to scoff. "What can she do?" He gestures to me. "I'll walk fast and be out of here before she gets out from behind the counter." He cackles cruelly, and there's no mistaking what he's saying. He's saying I'm too fat to chase him.

What he doesn't know is I don't need to chase anyone.

I grab the spoon I've been stirring with and whip it at his head, his laughter stopping when the spoon nails him right between the eyes. The small amount of sauce dripping down his nose makes me grin. "I don't have to chase you down, you little bitch. You're in my kitchen. I'll call the police chief and he'll be here before you can say boo." I'm bluffing, of course. Chief Woodcock is likely out patrolling at this time of the day. Despite the police station being two doors down, there's no way he'll be close enough to be of any help to me right now. "Why don't you head back to your car, drive home, then unmatch that fake-me on your dating app, and we can pretend none of this ever happened? Because if you continue to insult me, I can guarantee you won't like anything I have to say back to you. Let me give you a hint. I'll start with that oh-so-obvious comb over you're sporting and work my way down until I reach your dainty little feet."

"Hey, that's not very nice." The guy's pout rivals that of the child whose clothes he appears to be wearing. I'm sure I've seen the same quivering bottom lip when my nieces and nephews don't get their way, and the oldest one is only seven.

"No, it's not very nice. I tried being nice and you wouldn't listen. Remember when I politely explained that you were mistaken? That was your chance for a pleasant interaction with me. You blew it. Now, if you don't want a detailed description of exactly how much you're lacking in the appearance and, no doubt, personality departments, I suggest you turn around and march your sorry behind out that door right now."

Much to my surprise, the threat works. The man turns to leave, ducking out the door without another word.

"He must really love that comb-over if he doesn't want to hear you tell him about it," Chloe says with a laugh. "That's too bad. I kind of wanted to know what you would've said."

I tuck a sauce-sticky strand of hair back into my bun and huff a laugh. "I was lying. I didn't have much to say. Besides his scalp shining through the comb-over, and my observation about the size of his feet, I only had his clothes to comment on. If he didn't care about those things like I thought he did, we might never have gotten rid of him."

But now that he's gone, it's time to find out why a strange man thought he had a date with me at all. I wasn't lying when I said I don't have accounts on any dating apps, and I haven't set up dates with anyone. Because I don't date.

Just then, the chimes above the doorbell tinkle. "Welcome to Wings and Pizza," I say to the customer who walks in. When I look up, I see a familiar face attached to the man striding into the restaurant, and, for some reason, I can't stop the smile that crosses my face.

The giant from earlier today, Nick D'Onofrio, saunters in, a wide grin on his face when he sees me. Rather than shirtless and wearing tiny shorts, he sports jeans that stretch deliciously over his enormous thighs, and a t-shirt that hints at the muscle and slight belly I know is hiding underneath. His tattooed biceps test the seams on the sleeves of his shirt, and I find myself staring as I wonder whether he's ever worked in a restaurant kitchen. *How many pots can he carry with those pythons?* A flush of heat races through me.

"Like what you see?" he asks, grinning as he flexes his biceps, stretching the t-shirt sleeves even more. "I can take it off if you like. I'm not a big fan of shirts, but I figured I'd need to wear one to come in here. You know, the whole 'no shirt, no shoes, no service' thing? You know what I always wondered? Why are pants never mentioned? I'd be a lot more concerned about someone strolling into a restaurant sans pants than someone coming in shirtless, wouldn't you? Finding a strand of hair in my food doesn't bother me much unless it's short and curly." He turns his brilliant smile on Chloe, and my stomach drops uncomfortably. "Hey, Chloe. How are you?"

Chloe snorts a laugh. "Hey, Nick. Uh, I need to grab something from the fridge. I'll be right back."

I scrabble for her hand, attempting to drag her back to me, but she pulls away with a smirk and leaves me alone with the giant.

"So, hey," he says, running a hand over his soft-looking blond hair as he examines the restaurant. "I've been meaning to come here for a while now. I didn't think I'd have such an impact the first time, though. Heh." He forces a humorless laugh, but looks uncomfortable at his own joke. "I'm sorry I didn't ask you earlier; are you alright? I didn't hurt you, did I?"

Still stunned by the sight of him, it takes a moment before I can answer. "Other than the few spots of sauce in my hair turning it into a sticky mess, I'm okay. The sauce, on the other hand..."

He cringes, his shoulders crawling up. "Is there anything I can do to help? Do you need someone to stir for you?" He tips his head toward the pots behind me. "Maybe I can help clean up?"

An idea takes shape in my head, and giddiness builds in my chest. "Now that you mention it, there is something you can do. Come with me."

Chapter 4

OLD FOLKS AND DUCK JOKES

Nick

"I'm sorry. I don't think I heard that right. You did what?"

I sigh, pulling on my compression shorts and turning to face Rhett. "I scrubbed the sidewalk for her."

"The sidewalk? You scrubbed the sidewalk in this weather?"

Despite having lived in Alaska before moving to Tuft Swallow, Rhett is not a fan of the cold. He hates the cold so much he often thinks of mild spring temperatures as being as cold as a mid-winter freeze. Which is ridiculous.

It's beautiful outside.

"It's not even freezing out. I was warm enough." Never mind warm, I was damn near overheated. After watching how the woman, who I now know to call Tina, lit up as she ordered me to scrub the sidewalk, I haven't been able to get the thought of her out of my head. Something about the way her brown eyes seemed to glow from within when she set me what she clearly thought would be a terrible task sent blood rushing to my dick. I loved seeing her a little giddy with the excitement of making me pay for my mistake. What does *that* say about me?

"Hey, hello?" Rhett waves a hand in front of my face. "What's going on with you? I asked you a question. What did she say after you finished?"

I shake my head, forcing the image of Tina's smile from my mind. "Not much. By the time I finished, they were in the middle of the dinner rush. She was too busy to talk." Which sucks, because after I'd finished all the scrubbing, I was planning to ask her out. She intrigues me, and I want to know more. Any woman who isn't afraid of my size, and who is happy to put me to work, is a woman I want to know more about. "I wanted to place an order, but after I spilled her sauce all over the sidewalk, I didn't want to push my luck. I'll call in an order tomorrow." Or better yet, I'll go in and order. That way, I can see her again. "You wouldn't believe how good that place smells."

"Uh huh." Rhett eyes me with suspicion. "And that's why you were in a daze just now? Because their food smells good? If you recall, I've been telling you to go there for months now."

I shrug. "It might have something to do with the owner. When I nearly knocked her over earlier today, she had no problem giving me shit for it. She ordered me to bring that goat back to his owner. Oh, and he is the mayor, by the way. I asked Tina about him." We've both heard rumors of the goat mayor of Tuft Swallow, but with how busy we've been with getting the gym open, neither of us has had the time to confirm it.

"A goat? A goat is the mayor? The Nosy Pecker was telling the truth?" Rhett snorts in disbelief, shaking his head. "That's insane."

"Well, technically, yes, he is the mayor. He was voted in during the last election. But there is a woman acting as mayor in his stead. You know, because he's a goat."

Rhett shakes his head, and says with a laugh, "This town, man. I love it here."

"Me too."

Every day in Tuft Swallow is better than the last. Opening my gym here was a risk, but I'm so glad I took it. The guys who want to train with me aren't afraid of moving to a small town. They're coming to train with Odd Duck D'Onofrio, so the location doesn't matter. It helps that I have dorms upstairs for a few fighters, too. Having them live where they train has proven to be quite convenient in certain situations. Like now, when my fighters should be joining me for a training session with some of the local senior citizens. Instead of calling them, I send Rhett upstairs to bang on doors until they answer while I head into the room where I'm hosting the class.

Once in the main training classroom of the gym, I steel my nerves to greet the seniors. This group is feisty and inappropriate on the best of days. Not much will make me wear a shirt during a fitness class, but I wear one when the seniors are here. They all like to comment on, among other things, the state of my nipples in relation to the temperature in the room, and the comments occasionally border on sexual harassment.

"Hubba hubba, look at that fine hunk of man-meat. I'd like to get a big piece of that into my mouth. I bet he tastes absolutely delicious."

Correction. Their comments frequently careen wildly and land firmly in the territory of sexual harassment.

"Well, hello there, Miss Martha. You're looking lovely as ever." The elderly woman titters a laugh and her cheeks pinken, or they would, if she hadn't already coated them in a wide stripe of hot pink blush. "And hello to you, too, Miss Edith. How did I get so lucky as to have two of the most beautiful women in Tuft Swallow joining me in class today?"

Miss Edith grins salaciously and her gaze drops to the front of my shorts. "Well, I can't speak for everyone, but whatever you're smuggling in those shorts might have something to do with it."

Miss Martha nods. "And those tree trunks you call legs aren't too far behind. I love a man with big legs."

The ladies wander away to find their spots for the class as another voice gets my attention.

"Don't listen to those old birds. You look like a dumbass."

I can't hold back my laughter. "Hello to you, too, Peter. What brings you by? You don't normally join in with the seniors' class."

Peter's eyes slide to another of the elderly women, a newcomer named Sarah, before fixing me with a glare. "Never mind that. Just get to it. I'd like to see what you think makes a good class. Since you don't seem to be taking well to my coaching, that is," he adds in a whisper before strolling over to take the spot next to Sarah.

"Hey, Coach. Sorry I'm late." My newest fighter, Jared, jumps to a stop next to me, tying his long hair into a knot on his head while his eyes scan the room. "I fell asleep. It won't happen again."

My face screws up in concern.

This is Jared's first training camp, but not his first time away from home at only sixteen years old. He's bounced around foster homes for the last ten years, but this is his first time away from a home that he will go back to. He's not much older than

I was the first time I left home for training, and because of that, I may have a soft spot for him.

"Am I working you too hard? We can take longer to ease into it, if you need. I know you're not used to working out quite this much."

He looks at me sheepishly. "Nah. That's okay. It's my fault. I was up too late talking to my girlfriend. She was upset." He sighs. "She still doesn't like me being so far away. She thinks I'll meet someone else while I'm here."

I take a deep breath and choose my next words carefully. "You know yourself better than I do, kid. But you're here until the end of the school year. That can either be a really long time, or no time at all. That depends on you. But I'll tell you this; it'll seem a hell of a lot longer if you're not getting a proper night's sleep. You won't get the most out of it if you don't fully commit to the program. That includes a healthy sleep routine."

"Yeah, Coach. I know." He won't look me in the eye. I have a feeling he'll have a few more issues with his girlfriend before he figures out what it is he really wants. When you're first starting out, the life of a professional fighter doesn't leave much time for a love life. Ask me how I know. "I'll do better."

I clap a hand on his shoulder and give him a gentle push. "Good. Now go help these folks get set up for class." Jared joins a group of women and helps them get set up with the equipment we'll be using for their class today.

When I first approached the activity director of the seniors' home about hosting exercise classes for their residents, they were understandably hesitant. Having a six foot four muscle bound meathead tell you he wants to put on exercise classes for a group of people in their seventies and eighties at his MMA gym has got to be a scary experience for the average activity director. When she realized I had no intention of strapping the old folks into gloves and shoving them into the cage to battle to the death, she was all for it. Getting elderly people interested in physical activity can be difficult, especially here in Tuft Swallow, where the only sport anyone pays any attention to is cornhole. I surprised her with my detailed plan to get them involved, in a reduced capacity, in martial arts. I wasn't sure how popular it would be, but we have new students joining in every week, and watching them stream off the transport bus and into the gym is the best feeling.

Second best now, I suppose. Tina looking at me like she wants to eat me for dinner has moved way up to the top of my list. But I need to put those thoughts aside for later. I'm not wearing the right clothing to be getting turned on. Even more so than my running shorts, the compression shorts I'm wearing leave little to the imagination.

"Okay, are we all here?" I call out. An enthusiastic "yes" goes up from the group, followed by a grumpy "get on with it" from Peter. I chuckle and shake my head. At least he's consistent. "Okay, guys. Let's get warmed up."

After the warmup, I have Jared to lead the group through a modified Tai Chi program. While he demonstrates the movements, I talk to each of the seniors, helping them make further modifications as needed, and before I know it, class is over.

"Which one of these ducks is you?" Miss Martha yells at me from near the gym's entrance. She's pointing at the mural taking up the entire wall depicting a fight in progress, complete with a cheering crowd, refs in striped shirts, fighters, and various coaches and trainers. Chloe, who apparently also works with Tina, painted it before we opened. She was the second person I contracted for services when I moved to town, the first being Peter. He's the one who recommended her, in fact.

"You can't tell?" I yell back. "I'm the winner, of course."

Miss Martha pushes her glasses up on her nose and takes a closer look at the mural. There, in the center of the ring, is my likeness, in duck form of course, with my arm being held up in victory by the duck referee. How can you tell it's me? Duck me has the same haircut, buzzed on the sides and longer on top, the same tattooed arms, and even though you can barely see it because of the angle, the same rubber duck fighter tattoo on his lower back. Other than the fact that he's a duck, he looks just like me.

"You have a weird obsession with ducks." Peter is next to me, hands thrust into one of the many sets of pockets in his khaki cargo pants. "It's not normal for a grown man to have this many toys, you know." He gestures to the trophy case full of rubber duckies and championship belts near the reception desk. "That's supposed to be for trophies. Not toys."

My heart swells when I look at my babies, and by babies, I don't mean my championship belts. Sure, I'm proud of my belts. Being an undefeated heavyweight champion after so many years in the business is quite a feat. It's a hard life. Tough on the mind and tough on the body. The fact that I made it to thirty-eight years old, and retirement, without injury is something worth celebrating. Never losing was just icing on the cake. But either way, the belts are not what I'm most proud of in that case. No, that spot belongs to my babies.

My rubber duck family.

When I was a kid in Tuft Swallow, struggling to find my place as a martial artist in a town preoccupied with cornholers, my lack of cornhole prowess marked me as an outsider. An Odd Duck. A label I adopted as my own, becoming the odd duck both in and out of the ring.

I was one of those fighters who genuinely loved the sport. I loved being in the ring, and I loved my opponents. When I knocked a guy out, I was the first one checking to see if he was okay, a fact that many a ref took issue with until they learned that I actually was concerned. In post-fight interviews, I had nothing but nice things to say about my opponents, always expressing gratitude and humility that they'd given me the chance to go toe to toe with them, never mind that I was the champ. I always had compliments for my team, their team, and all the refs and announcers, too. On more than one occasion, I sent food to all the people involved in putting a fight on, from the director of the venue, to the people who worked the concession stands. I loved being a fighter, and I appreciated everyone who worked hard to allow me to do it as my job, and I had no problem showing it every chance I could.

And out of the ring? Well, out of the ring, I have amassed the second largest rubber duck collection in North America. It all started when a fan, a young kid, saw me out shopping for groceries a couple of days after one of my fights. He came up to me, held out his little hand, and gave me a rubber duck. He told me I was his favorite fighter, not because I was big, and not because I always won, but because I was so nice to the other fighters after. He said he wanted to grow up to be an odd duck like me. When I finally got the tears under control, his dad told me he'd insisted on bringing that duck everywhere since he first saw me fight.

That duck still has pride of place in my trophy case, above all the other ducks and every belt I've ever won. It's not something many people understand, but I'm lucky to be a big enough guy that few people have the guts to call me on it. Few people other than Peter, anyway.

"You know the story, Peter."

He scoffs. "Yeah, yeah. I know. A kid gave you a duck, then you cried. Doesn't mean you needed to keep it. And it certainly doesn't mean you needed to collect a bunch more of the ridiculous things, fill a trophy case, and make it your entire personality." Without waiting for an answer, he storms away to board the transport back to the seniors' home, leaving me shaking my head.

He's gruff, but I know he's not nearly as mean as he pretends to be. I'll get through to him one of these days. At least, I will if he doesn't drop me as a cornhole student first. And Peter dropping me is a distinct possibility, because in the six months he's been coaching me, I haven't improved at all. It might be time for me to admit that I am not made for cornhole. I wonder if I could take part in the cornhole league in some other capacity? Because at this rate, they won't let me *try out* for the team, never mind let me actually play for them.

Chapter 5

He's An Open Book, He Says

Tina

"Another one? Who was it this time?" Chloe asks. She's sitting at the counter, doodling in her ever present sketch book before the dinner rush starts. "And where the hell are they all coming from? Do you have an old account somewhere? Maybe you've been hacked."

I huff, pushing my glasses up my nose. "No. I don't. I've never used a dating app. Ever. Because I. Do. Not. Date." I enunciate each word deliberately, sending that information out into the world so these random men will stop showing up declaring we're going out for dinner, or bowling, or to a movie, or any number of other date night activities that I have no interest in doing with a stranger.

Chloe looks up from her book, her eyebrows raised. "Are you sure? Maybe something from back when you lived in the city?"

"When would I have had time to date? I worked in restaurants. The only people who would have understood my schedule were other restaurant staff, and I have zero interest in any of the egos floating around that industry." Between the chefs, bartenders, and wannabe actors working as waiters, the restaurant business is full of the worst types of toxic masculinity. Why women chase those men as much as they do, I'll never know. "Most of the guys I worked with over the years thought they were God's gift to women, never mind that we were working the same job. It was even worse when they reported to me. Nuh uh. No, thank you. Like I want to work that many hours in a day just to come home to a man who thinks I should take care of him because he has a penis."

"Hmmm." Chloe tapped the end of her pencil against her lower lip. "You have a point. You're not really giving off 'let's find the love of my life' vibes here. But if not an old account, then what?"

I shrug. "I have no idea. But that's every night this week that some random dude has shown up to take me on a date."

She snorts. "It's pretty funny when they get a look at you in your apron, with your hair a messy ball on your head, and still think they're here to take you out. I mean, wouldn't that give them a hint that maybe they've got something wrong? If not the fact that they have a date with you at all, then maybe the day? Because you don't look like you're trying to impress anyone."

I snort a laugh. "Thanks."

She rolls her eyes. "You know what I mean. Usually, when a woman has a date, she at least takes off her apron and brushes her hair. Maybe wears contact lenses and little makeup?"

She has a point. If I were to ever go on a date, I would probably at least attempt to wear contacts. My glasses may have me rocking the sexy librarian look, but the thickness of the lenses tells a different story. If I were to rip them off trying to be sexy, I'd likely slam into the nearest wall the moment I take a step. Because that's how blind I am without them. Never mind trying to wear my hair down. It's so curly and frizzy, I require at least six different products and some quality time with a straightener before I'll attempt anything like that. If I tried to do it spontaneously, it would look like I'd stuck my finger in an electrical socket.

"Fine. You're forgiven."

She grins. "I knew you loved me."

"Yeah, yeah. You're the wind beneath my wings," I deadpan. "It's time to call my parents. Can you hold down the fort for a few minutes?" She waves me off with a laugh.

It's Sunday, almost dinnertime, and I haven't talked to my mother yet. She's probably on the verge of having a conniption fit, if she hasn't already. I prop my phone on the counter as it rings and wait for her to answer.

While I wait, my mind wanders to Nick. He hasn't come by since last week, despite his promise to order dinner soon, and it's left me feeling...off? I don't know why, but I think I was looking forward to seeing him this week. After the way he took on the chore of scrubbing the sidewalk with such good humor, I want to know more about him. I can't figure out why he would come back after spilling all that sauce, let alone why he would scrub a sidewalk clean merely because I asked him to. It's strange.

Before I can think about it too hard, my mother's face fills the screen of my phone. "Honey, hi. It's so good to hear from you. When you didn't call this morning, I thought maybe you were too busy to talk today." The sounds of giggles and whispers come through the phone, and my mother turns her head, telling whoever it is to be quiet. Instead of silence, though, I hear my aunts yelling hello from off camera.

"Hi, Aunties," I say, smiling from ear to ear. For those unfamiliar with my family, my mother and the aunts look bizarrely similar, considering only two of them are my mother's actual sisters. One of the others is a close family friend, and the other is my father's sister. Despite not all being related, they are all short, voluptuous women with huge racks, tiny waists, and *all* the junk in their trunks. Add to that the medium length dark brown curly hair that they all wear teased to the Gods and they're virtually indistinguishable. That hair, though. I swear they keep their favorite brand of hairspray in business between the five of them. These ladies never met a bouffant hairdo they didn't love and aspire to. "So tell me, how many bottles of wine have you been through already?"

"Only one," my Aunt Vera says, squeezing onto the screen with my mother. Someone in the background yells "one each" and then cackles with laughter. Aunt Vera hushes them before facing me. "I missed you last weekend, honey. How are you doing? Ready to come home yet?"

I can barely stop my eyes from rolling all the way into the back of my skull. Aunt Vera has been after me to move home since my first week in Tuft Swallow. She agrees with my mother that I should have stayed home and let her look after me until I found a man to marry. Now that I think about that, it doesn't even make sense. If I were to let my mom look after me until I got married, how would I know how to look after a husband on my own? Nah. It's probably better for me to stick with my plan of being a successful restaurateur. Maybe one day, when I'm brave enough to withstand the scorn of my fellow Tuft Swallowers, I'll adopt a cat or six from the local rescue. I'm positive I would make an excellent crazy cat lady.

"So, Valentina. Did you have a pleasant week?" My mother asks. I catch a flash of something on the screen. That's weird. Is that a strange glint in her eye, or is that just a glare on the screen? I tilt my phone and it disappears. Must've been a glare, then. "Anything, or anyone, new and exciting in your life? Tell me everything."

"Uh, yeah. It was pretty okay. One exciting thing happened after I talked to you last week. Remember how my gas range wasn't working? Well, the handyman came by and fixed it almost right away. We brought the pots upstairs to my apartment, only to turn around and bring them back down shortly after."

My mother purses her lips, her eyebrows drawn. "I really wish you didn't live in that apartment. It must smell like a restaurant all the time. You can't bring a man home when it smells like fast food."

I nod, having heard this before. The thing she doesn't realize is that my apartment smells a lot like her house, since so many of my recipes are modified versions of hers. There's no fast food to be found at Wings and Pizza. "Yes, Ma. I know. But listen. I was bringing two pots down when I stepped off the last stair and BAM! Someone ran right into me, knocking the pots out of my hands and onto the sidewalk. It was such a mess, Mom. You should have seen it. Poor Mr. Landon. You remember I told you about him? He always seems to be on the receiving end of some misfortune or other? Well, wouldn't you know, he was walking by, right in the path of the flying sauce. It's a good thing they hadn't been on the stove for long, or he could have been seriously burned."

My mother gasps. "Oh, dear. Poor Mr. Landon. Is he alright? You should bring him something to apologize. What about some nice cannoli?"

"Sure, Ma. Maybe later."

Aunt Vera edges her way back onto the screen. "So who ran into you, sweetheart? Did they apologize?"

My heart quickens at the memory of Nick coming back into the restaurant that evening. I can't tell you how many times I've thought about his thighs in those jeans since that day. Somehow they looked even bigger than when they'd been completely exposed in his little shorts, almost as though by hiding them, he drew more attention to them. "He did. He came back later that day to help clean up. He spent an hour scrubbing the sidewalk clean."

Aunt Vera made an oh sound, her interest piqued. "He did, did he? And who was this nice young man?"

I can feel my cheeks warm like I'm some schoolgirl with a crush, which is silly. I don't have a crush on Nick. I can't help thinking it was nice of him to come back and clean up the way he did. Or that I really enjoyed the way he filled out those jeans. "Nobody," I say, despite everything inside me screaming otherwise. "Just some guy who opened a gym here. He was out for a jog and didn't see me step off my stairs. It's fine. No one was hurt."

"Ooh, out for a jog? Who doesn't love a man who looks after his physical fitness?" My mother pulls her lips in, stifling a grin. "And...was he cute?"

Of course that's where her mind goes. I mean, my mind was going there too, but I already know what Nick looks like, so it's hard for my mind not to go there. He's so big and sexy and cuddly looking, how could I not think about how cute he is? Not that I'll tell her that. I know better than to encourage my mother. If I admit to thinking he's cute, the next thing you know, she'll be planning our wedding.

"I don't know, Ma. I wasn't paying attention to that. I was more concerned about all the sauce that I lost. His looks didn't come into it at all."

"Sure, honey. You keep telling yourself that," Aunt Vera says with a wink. "I can't wait to hear what you have to say next week. Because from what I can see, that man looks pretty darn cute."

I whirl around to see none other than Nick from the gym standing behind me, a big grin on his face. "I hope I'm not interrupting?"

"Where'd you come from?" I blurt, my heart racing. "I didn't hear you come in."

He jerks a thumb to the front of the restaurant where I see Chloe waving. "Chloe told me to come straight back. I was hoping to talk to you."

"About what?" I ask.

"Yeah, about what?" Aunt Vera says, her grinning face filling the entire screen of the phone before my mother pulls her back.

"I would also like to know," my mother adds. "What do you want to talk to my Valentina about?"

I groan internally. This is about to become an interrogation. Poor Nick doesn't know what he's in for if I don't stop it right now. These women have zero respect for boundaries.

"Okay, Ma. I have to go now. Love to you and the aunties. Say hi to Dad and Nonna for me. Love you." I press the end call button before she can say anything else.

Nick snickers. "They seem nice."

I allow my eyes to roll finally, enjoying the stretch after holding them back so many times during tonight's conversation with my family. "They are nice, but they are also far too nosy for their own good. If I'd let them, they'd have grilled you for your life story and gotten all of your deep, dark secrets."

He shrugs. "I have no deep, dark secrets. I'm an open book. Go ahead. Ask me anything." He shoots me a wink and I melt a little inside. This is a bad idea.

"Okay. Fine. Why *are* you here?"

"Oh, that's an easy one. I'm here to take you out on a date."

 Chapter 6

LESS MURDER, MORE COOKING

Nick

"EXCUSE ME, WHAT?" TINA splutters and chokes, her eyes wide behind her glasses. Is it weird that I think the way she's choking on her own spit is adorable? Probably, but I don't care. Call me weird. "A date? Who says we're going on a date?"

"Ah..." I stall, rubbing a hand over the back of my head and trying to stuff down the swell of disappointment rising in my gut. "Okay, you caught me. We're not going on a date. I overheard you talking to your family about me and thought it would be funny." Would I be lying if I said I wasn't hoping she would let me take her out? Yes, I would be lying. It's obvious if I want to convince Tina to go out with me, it will take a lot more than a comment thrown out haphazardly when she's occupied in another conversation. Can't say that wasn't a bit of a long shot, but I couldn't resist. I needed to do something other than stand there like a creep waiting to see if she'd tell her family I'm cute. My self-esteem couldn't handle the blow if she didn't agree. I may be a giant, but that just means I have bigger feelings to hurt, damn it. "I'm guessing by how much you're choking, it wasn't as funny as I thought."

She shakes her head and grabs a rag from the counter, using it to wipe her mouth before throwing it into a laundry hamper in the corner. "You would be right. Maybe if I hadn't just been fending off the 'get Tina married no matter the cost' brigade, it would have been funnier. But now we'll never know."

I cringe, realizing how much she didn't like my joke. "Oh, shit. I'm sorry. I had no idea it would cause that much trouble. Do you want me to call them and explain that we're friends? Head them off at the pass." The look of horror that crosses her features is almost comical in its exaggeration. "Or would that make things worse?"

"Ha!" Tina's laugh is a sudden crack of thunder in the otherwise quiet restaurant. "Umm, I'll pass. That would make it so much worse."

"That bad?"

"Ugh." She heaves a sigh and looks up to the ceiling as though she's searching for her higher power. "No, it's not that bad. I mean, it's annoying, but I can usually handle it fine. It's been a long week, is all."

A long week? I don't like the sound of that, especially since I'm here to ask for a favor. I can't very well ask her for help when she's already at her limit. "Is there anything I can do?"

She turns a bright smile on me, but it doesn't quite reach her eyes. "Nah. I'm good."

I squint in disbelief and raise a questioning eyebrow, which earns me a genuine laugh. *Note to self: make faces at Tina to hear her laugh.*

"Really. It's nothing."

I continue to squint at her until she huffs another laugh.

"Okay, it's something. But I'll deal with it like I always deal with my problems. By listening to a murder podcast and crafting miniature cemeteries out of thrifted teapots. Let's move on from that. What brings you by? I know you didn't come here to catch me talking to my overbearing mother and aunts. Are you here for dinner, finally? Or do you need my help?"

The hint of irritation in her voice when she says "finally" doesn't escape my notice. I catch myself before I grin when I remember why I'm here. She might not like me grinning at her annoyance, and I can't risk making her angry right now. Not that I want her to be angry with me at all, but I don't want to risk making her so mad she refuses to help me.

"That's an understatement," I say, doing my best to sound apologetic. "Tina, I fucked up."

It's her turn to ask a question with her eyebrow, and I have to say, I can see the appeal. Watching her thick dark brow creep up over the frame of her glasses does something to me. Blood begins to creep its way south, much to my surprise. Who knew I was an eyebrow guy?

Who knew being an eyebrow guy was even a thing?

I force my attention to the matter at hand. "It's bad. I'm here throwing myself on your mercy, hoping you'll take pity on me."

"Oh my God, Nick. What did you do?" She rubs her hands together, her eyes taking on a sinister gleam. "I have freakishly strong arms from all my years working in restaurants so I can help with pretty much anything, but I draw the line at digging graves. It takes too long to get the dirt out from under my fingernails," she says, holding her hand up to show me her neatly trimmed nails. "A chef's cooking is only as good as her hands are clean."

I open my mouth, but words fail me. Digging graves? What? Who *is* this woman? Before I can gather my thoughts to give her a coherent answer, she continues.

"Anyway, you're in luck because I have excellent knife skills. Plus, I can butcher a full-grown hog solo in under an hour, and blood is easy to clean if you know what you're doing." She grins, and her face lighting up with a combination of glee and something a little more sinister.

The blood that was creeping south earlier picks up the pace. I'm well on my way to having a full-blown erection while standing in the middle of Tina's kitchen. After the turn our conversation has taken, I'm not entirely sure that's normal.

"So," she says, clapping her hands together. "How can I help?"

I clear my head with a shake, making a note to investigate Tina's blood-thirst another day. "Take it down a notch, Aileen. This has nothing to do with truck drivers."

She barks a laugh. "I listened to an amazing podcast series all about Aileen Wuornos just the other day. It's such a sad story. There are a lot of nuances there that deserve further exploration, the difference in how the public views violent acts performed by women and men being only one."

"I'd be interested in listening to that podcast sometime." That throwaway comment about Aileen Wuornos was the extent of my knowledge of that case, but Tina seems to be bursting with information about it, which I find fascinating. "But for today, my problem involves less murder, and more cooking."

"Well, why didn't you say so? You've come to the right place," she says with a sage nod and a sweep of her arm. "Welcome to Wings and Pizza, where we cook wings. And pizza."

The sarcasm in her voice would bother me if it came from anyone else, but coming from Tina, it's tolerable. Enjoyable, even. Okay, you caught me. I like her snarky attitude. A lot.

"Ha ha. Hilarious. Can I tell you my issue? Or do you want to tease me some more first?" Truthfully, I'm torn about what I'd prefer. I need her help, but the thought of her teasing me, then touching me, and kissing me, is pretty damn distracting. I sigh, drawing another of her epic eyebrow raises, which does little to improve my focus. My brain is suffering from a serious lack of blood flow right now, and it's making me stupid. *Come on, Odd Duck. Do what you came here to do.*

She gestures for me to go on.

"I have a gym full of trainers and athletes I promised to feed, but nothing to feed them," I blurt.

Two eyebrows go up, and somehow it's even hotter than when she raises just one. My dick presses painfully against the zipper of my jeans.

"That's it? No bodies to dispose of? No crimes to cover up?"

I nod distractedly, willing her not to look down. If she sees the situation in my pants right now, I can pretty much guarantee she'll never go out with me, let alone help me with the problem at hand. What kind of man gets hard talking about serial killers and ordering dinner? A weird one, that's who. "Yeah. I need to feed ten athletic men and women with enormous appetites, and I dropped the ball."

"So, what? You want to order a bunch of pizzas?"

"Well," I say, raising my shoulders in some sort of mega shrug, "I was looking online, and I saw that you sometimes do catering. Is there any way I could order some dishes from the catering menu?"

She chuckles and shakes her head. "You know, most people order catering in advance."

"I know, I know." I cringe. "I'm sorry to bother you with it, but my home kitchen is mostly out of commission, and the dorms above the gym don't have any of the equipment needed to make the quantity of food we'd need to feed all these people." The dorms have double burner induction cooktops, mini fridges, and microwaves. My house has the same equipment in triplicate, plus the ancient green fridge that came with the house.

"That sucks. What's wrong with your kitchen?"

When I moved here six months ago, I assumed I would live above the gym. I originally planned on making it into a loft style apartment. Imagine how short my commute would have been? But before long, I realized it made more sense to make that space into dorms for visiting athletes, which necessitated buying a house for myself instead. The problem arose when the house the realtor found for me was decorated exactly like it had been when it was built. In the seventies.

"It's been under renovation for months, and will be for the foreseeable future. The appliances I ordered have been delayed so many times I'm beginning to doubt they'll ever get here. And since I got rid of the avocado-colored stove when the company first issued a delivery date, I've been without a proper space to cook. When I put together this week-long retreat, I did so under the assumption that I would have a proper kitchen to work with. Sadly, that didn't pan out. I bought extra induction cooktops and microwaves for my house, where some of the out of towners are staying, but it's still not enough to cook a meal for more than a few people at once." And truthfully, I completely forgot about all of it until this morning when trainers and athletes began arriving at the gym. Who invites a bunch of people to a retreat then promptly forgets all about it? Someone who spent the last couple of months focusing on becoming certified as a foster guardian so an especially talented teenage fighter could come stay for an extended training camp, that's who. Or, if you listen to Rhett's opinion, someone who has some issues with organization.

"Uh huh, okay." Her head swivels before her gaze settles on the walk-in fridge at the back of the room. "Got it. Come with me," she says, turning away without waiting for me to follow.

I jog to catch up, her quick steps leading her away faster than I would expect. Her short legs eat up the ground, and I reach her as she opens the door and enters the fridge. "So... does this mean you'll help?" Without answering, she pulls bins from the shelves on either side of us and piles them in my arms. When she's loaded me up to my neck, she grabs her own stack of bins and guides me from the fridge.

"I will help. It'll cost you, though." She places her load on a stainless steel table and gestures for me to do the same. "There will be a surcharge for the rush job. I don't like sending out a catering order on such short notice." She pulls a stack of giant pots out from the lower shelf of the table and brings them to the sink. She turns on the tap and lets the water run into the first pot before facing me again. "Will you need help for the rest of the week? Because if you are, I can make up a menu and go to the wholesale store tomorrow morning for ingredients. If you want, I can break my personal rules and give you more than just pizza, wings, and pastas. Just don't tell the rest of the town. The less they know about my talents, the better. I run a pizza shop, not a full-blown restaurant. I'm not looking for Michelin stars here."

"How mad would you be if I said yes?" Coming here today was a last-minute stroke of genius, but I wasn't planning to impose on Tina for more than one night. Once I had tonight's dinner squared away, I was going to call around to other restaurants in the area and see what they could do for me. But, if Tina is offering... "I will love you forever if you can help me for the rest of the week."

A pink flush creeps onto her cheeks, and her gaze dips away as she switches the pots in the sink. Interesting. I'll add that to my list of things to investigate another day.

"I'll need dinner for the next five nights after tonight. Can you do them? Or some of them? I will take whatever you can give me. Honestly, I'm so grateful that you've agreed to help me tonight that expecting anything more from you seems wrong somehow."

"Oh, don't you worry about that." She laughs. "Your bill will more than make up for any inconvenience."

My head bobs rapidly. "Yes, yes. Absolutely. Whatever amount you think is fair. You're saving my ass by doing this." And I mean it. I should implement some sort of system to help me remember this kind of stuff, like writing it down or something. Which, if I'd listened to Rhett, I would have done when we first thought up the retreat. Don't tell him that, though. He's enough of a pain in the ass without telling him he was right all along. "What do you think? A thousand for each meal? Two?"

Tina chokes out a surprised, "Two thousand? Oh yeah, I think I can make something happen for that kind of money."

"Thank you so much, Tina." I breathe a relieved sigh. "You have no idea what this means to me. I'll pay you whatever you ask, but I still owe you one."

She waves me off, tightening the waist straps on her apron, calling attention to the delicious curves above and below her little waist. Curves that my hands are itching to squeeze. *I need to get out of here before my dick suffers irreversible damage.* I don't wear jeans often, and I may never do so again after today. I think the zipper imprint on my dick is permanent.

"Never mind that. Paying me is more than enough. Give me a couple of hours to get everything ready, then you can come pick it up. Sound good?"

"That's perfect. Thank you, thank you. You're my hero."

She fights to hide a grin, but her eyes betray her laughter. "Yeah, yeah. How about you get out of my kitchen and let me work?"

"Of course. I'll get out of your hair. See you in a couple of hours."

She nods, her attention already on the pots in the sink. As I turn to leave, she lifts a full pot to the stove, without so much as a grunt at the weight. The muscles in her arms even pop a little, a testament to how heavy the big stock pot actually is. She wasn't kidding about the strength in her arms.

I'm still not sure if she was serious with all that talk of butchering hogs and cleaning up blood, though. But damn, do I ever want to find out.

Chapter 7

IT REALLY IS ALL IN THE HIPS

Tina

"WINGS AND PIZZA. THIS is Tina. What can I get for you?"

"Tina? Hey. It's Nick. D'Onofrio. From earlier?"

He thinks I forgot who he is already? That's so adorable I have to scrub the grin from my face with a hand before I can answer. "Hi, Nick. Good timing. I'm bagging up the last of your order now. Everything is ready for you to pick up."

I hope these trainers Nick's feeding are ready for some carb loading. With Nick coming to me at the last minute, all I had available in my kitchen were the ingredients I normally have on hand. I pulled off lasagna and salad with garlic bread for tonight, but after I go to the wholesale store tomorrow, I'll be

58

able to provide more variety. I don't know exactly what training at Nick's gym would entail, but no matter what it is, I'm sure it's harder with a belly full of noodles and cheese.

"About that. My manager had to take the sixteen-year-old kid who's staying with me to the hospital. Seems his girlfriend broke up with him over text because he's here in training camp for a few more months and he tried to drown his sorrow in the bottom of a bottle of tequila."

My stomach drops at the thought of some sixteen-year-old boy, alone, away from home, drinking himself into a stupor. Poor kid. And Hawkthorne County General is in Spitz Hollow, so not even in the same town as his home away from home. That has to be scary. "Oh, shit. Is he okay?"

"I sure as shit hope so, or his caseworker will have my nuts in a vise. Luckily he was still talking when we found him, instead of passed out and unresponsive. If he drank as much as we think he did, though, he's in for a rough rest of the day. If we're really lucky, they'll monitor him and he won't need to have his stomach pumped. It's hard to say, though. It was a pretty big bottle. It didn't look like he'd gotten sick yet, either, but better safe than sorry. Especially with a kid who isn't mine."

My stomach roils in sympathy. I've never had my stomach pumped, but I've heard some horror stories of alcohol poisoning. It's not something I would wish on a kid. "What can I do?"

Nick's relieved breath blows a low note through the phone. *"I know I said I would come and pick up dinner, but is there any way you could deliver it? Or find someone to bring it to me. I wouldn't ask, but Rhett is the only other trainer who can run the class I'm hosting right now. I can't leave the, uh... gym goers, alone in the gym with trainers who don't have the correct first aid certification."*

He's still speaking when I reach behind my back and pull the string to undo the bow in my apron. I wrestle it over my head and drop it on the counter. "No problem, Nick. I can bring it now." I tuck the phone between my ear and shoulder and fill a small container with plain noodles. I add a side of sauce and some butter before adding the containers to a bag. With a sudden burst of insight, I make up a small container of regular lasagna, and add it to the bag.

"Are you sure? You must be in the middle of a dinner rush, or something. Can you afford to leave the restaurant?"

On a normal day I wouldn't dream of leaving Wings and Pizza before at least midnight, but with what Nick's paying me for tonight, never mind what I'll charge him for the rest of the week—which won't be two thousand dollars per meal, that's way too much—I'm comfortable stepping away for a little while. Truthfully, catering for Nick will keep my head above water for quite some time. He thinks he owes me, when in reality I'm the one who owes him.

"Totally sure. Chloe is here to watch the place until I get back. It's no problem."

"Tina, you're a lifesaver. If you keep coming to my rescue like this, I won't be able to stop myself from falling in love with you."

I feel my cheeks heat like they did earlier when Nick said he'd love me forever if I helped him. Stupid cheeks. Did they forget we don't care about silly things like men falling in love with us? Why would they burn when Nick says it?

"No need for that. I'll charge a delivery fee and we'll call it even."

He chuckles into the phone. *"Deal. Thank you, Tina. Now I really owe you."*

I mumble, "see you shortly," and hang up.

"Chloe? Can you handle being on your own for a bit? I need to run this food over to the gym for Nick. There's been an emergency and he can't leave right now."

Chloe looks up from where she's rolling silverware. "Yeah, of course. That's no problem. Is everything okay?"

I shake my head and shrug. "I'm not sure. He said some kid he's training drank himself silly and his manager, Rhett, took him to HCG to get checked out."

"Oh no. Poor Jared. He's such a good kid. I wouldn't have pictured him to be the kind of kid to go off and get drunk. It doesn't sound much like him."

"Nick said something about a girlfriend back home? Sounds like the poor kid was heartbroken."

Chloe nods. "That makes sense. When Jared isn't training or doing schoolwork, he's on his phone talking to his girlfriend. It always sounded like he was trying to convince her he was faithful. Seemed like a shitty situation for a kid to be in, if you ask me. Long distance is hard enough when you're old and settled. When you're a kid full of raging hormones, it has to be hell."

I slide my phone into my pocket and grab the bag and some boxes of food from the counter. "Yeah, I feel bad for him, and not just because of the girlfriend situation. That kid will have a killer hangover tomorrow."

Chloe doesn't wait for me to ask before grabbing the rest of Nick's order from the counter. "Maybe it will help him stay away from alcohol in the future?"

One glance at Chloe has us both laughing, remembering our own misspent youth. We didn't know each other then, but we've had enough conversations in the last five years that I know her teenage years resembled mine. Full of underage drinking, parties, and too many close calls. And hangovers. So. Many. Hangovers. None of which ever stopped us. At least not back then. These days if I have even one beer there's an excellent chance I'll have a hangover. Sometimes I'm really lucky and the hangover starts before I've finished the beer, which is always fun. These days I stick to tea and true crime for my entertainment, and it's not only because I work all day, every single day.

We leave the empty restaurant and bring our packages to my car, placing them carefully on the front seat. "Thanks, Chloe. I know you were hoping to leave early tonight." She'd been hinting at a hot date since she arrived this afternoon. It sounded like she was looking forward to it.

She shrugs. "Did I forget to tell you? We had to cancel."

"Oh, no. I'm sorry. But I'm glad that I'm not the one stopping you from going out."

"Yeah. It's great." She pulls her lips in and nods without meeting my eyes, failing to mask her disappointment. For a serial dater like Chloe, being visibly upset over a canceled date has my curiosity piqued. I'll be looking into this more later. Right now, I need to get this food to Nick while it's still hot.

"Call me if you need anything," I say as I get into my car. "I won't be long."

"Take your time." She gives me a wave. "It's not that busy. I might even repaint the window."

She walks back inside, leaving me shaking my head. One good thing about how often she paints the windows? I have the cleanest window sills in town because every time she washes off an old picture, she does a deep clean on the entire window. It's great.

I feel a little silly driving my car, since Put Up Your Ducks MMA is just down the street, but I'd never have been able to carry all the food otherwise. Usually, I can make deliveries on foot, because downtown Tuft Swallow surrounds a small square. Almost everything you need is in a one block radius, and the trail system connects everything else. If there's one great thing about living in a town obsessed with birdwatching, it's all the walking trails. I can get almost anywhere I want to go using the well-maintained trail system in and around town. Why drive when I can get some fresh air and exercise? If I didn't have so much food to deliver, I would probably be walking to the gym now, too.

I parallel park in a spot close to the door, behind the bus from the Spring Chickens senior living facility. *Are they here for the class Nick was talking about? Is there a special first aid certification needed for working with senior citizens?* I guess I'll find out when I get in there. I make my way out of the car and to the passenger side, where we've stacked the food. *Looks like I'll need to take two trips.*

"Hey!" A man in long skin tight shorts and not much else calls out in greeting. "Nick sent me out to help carry the food. I'm Demetrius." He thrusts a taped hand out for a shake, forcing me to drag my gaze away from the beads of sweat blazing a trail down his muscular chest. "Nice to meet you."

Is this what Chloe meant when she said the guys here are in shape? Because this is more than in shape. This man is chiseled. And chiseled is nice, I guess, but I'll take Nick's slightly fluffy body type over chiseled any day of the week. The little belly he sports over all those muscles puts me in a mood to cuddle.

"Hey," I say, grasping his hand in mine. "I'm Tina. Grab some boxes and let's get in there. You guys must be starving."

He laughs, his smile taking up most of his face. "You have no idea. I'm in the middle of training for my next fight and my diet has been pretty strict. One of the main reasons I love training with Nick is he makes sure my meal plan includes tasty food. Would you believe I've had plans that were nothing but dry chicken breast and broccoli for every meal? A man cannot live on chicken and broccoli. Not if he wants to have something to fight for." He reaches into my car and pulls out a stack of boxes. "But I can tell by how amazing this smells that you've brought us something delicious. My mouth is watering already."

It's my turn to laugh. "Nick gave me almost no notice, so you're getting what I already had in my restaurant. You'll probably want to call this your cheat meal, because if I had to guess, I'd say that extra cheesy lasagna, caesar salad, and garlic bread are not meal plan approved."

Demetrius licks his lips and makes a slurping noise. "Woman, you are speaking my love language. Marry me," he jokes. We get to the door and Demetrius kicks a foot out to hit the automatic door open button. "Marry me right now." He tips his chin, motioning for me to go in ahead of him.

A grin creeps over my face. I may not dream of getting married, but a good-natured fake proposal from a good looking man will always make me smile. "Aww, Demetrius. You're so sweet. I'm sorry, but despite that lovely proposal, I have to turn you down. Don't tell the native Tuft Swallowers, but I'm on the 'crazy cat lady' plan. As soon as I muster up enough courage, I'm adopting a dozen cats from The Great Catsby."

"The Great Catsby?"

"Local cat rescue. In a bird-loving community like Tuft Swallow, a place like that is anathema to the townspeople. If it weren't in the same building as the bookstore, I'm not sure I'd even know it existed."

"That sounds amaz..." Demetrius' words drift away as the wall beside us finally catches my attention.

Ducks.

Rubber ducks, to be precise.

Rubber ducks as far as the eye can see.

Chloe wasn't kidding about this thing. If there were ever such a thing as a weird duck mural, this is it. At the center of the wall-sized painting is a cage with little rubber ducks wearing shorts and gloves with one looking like he just beat the crap out of the other. I always knew she was a decent artist, but Chloe is *seriously* talented. She made their little duck faces complete masks of concentration, a feat on its own considering the eyes are just black circles and there's only so much you can do with a beak. I can almost see the killer instinct in their beady eyes. One little duck in the cage wears a striped referee shirt, and he's holding up the arm of the less beat up looking fighter ducky. Outside the cage are two teams of ducks in matching shirts. I'm guessing those are the coaches and support people for each of the duck fighters. And the crowd!

The amount of detail Chloe put into the crowd is astounding. Despite depicting an MMA fight arena, this entire mural is giving serious Sistine Chapel vibes. *This must have taken Chloe ages to paint. How did I not know she did this? Some friend I am.* I could stand here all day picking details out in the crowd. *Is that...?* I step closer, holding my packages out to the side. *Oh my God, it is!* Chloe painted Mr. Landon into Nick's mural. He's there in the aisle, wearing one of his boring brown suits, a drink being dumped over his head by a distracted and overly enthusiastic fan. I look closer. *She didn't. She did.* The overly enthusiastic fan is the serious woman from the library, Merethe. I've been on the receiving end of her epic shushes one too many times to not recognize her when I see her, even if it's as a duck. *Who else is in this thing?*

"It's really something, isn't it?"

The deep voice behind me ignites a fire in my belly and I know intuitively who it belongs to. My eyes glide to the ducky in the ring with his arm up in victory. Of course. It's so obvious I'm shocked I didn't realize it at first.

That's Nick, in duck form.

"When I hired Chloe to paint the mural, I asked her to paint an arena during a title fight, using rubber duckies in place of people. I had no idea she would paint me in rubber duck form."

"Nick," I say on a breath, forcing myself to ignore the flush of heat racing through me. Without turning, I add, "Where should I bring this stuff?"

"Who's your friend, kid?" A scratchy voice cuts through my thoughts. "You going to stand there like a creep, or are you going to take some of those boxes from her like a gentleman?"

On turning around, I'm greeted by the sight of an older man who I know only by reputation. Peter Harrelson, Tuft Swallow's own former world cornhole champion, and current grumpy curmudgeon. He tells the world he wants nothing to do with cornhole, but I've seen him sneaking around the field when the local team is practicing. Rumor has it he swore off the game when his nemesis from Spitz Hollow stole his championship and then his bride, but I don't know if that's true. No one in Tuft Swallow likes to relive the championship match of 1968. It's the last time we lost, and it's a bit of a sore subject for Tuft Swallowers.

This place is beyond serious about its cornhole.

"I *am* a gentleman, Peter. I was just getting to that. Why aren't you with the rest of the Spring Chickens working on your hip circles? You know how much the ladies love a man who has nimble hips." Nick swivels his hips in a way that reminds me of a sexy ballroom dance, making me burn all over again. "Tina, can I grab those from you?"

Mesmerized by the swaying of his hips, I can do nothing but nod dumbly and pass over the stack of boxes, thoughts of the mural, and Peter Harrelson, and decades old cornhole losses driven from my mind. Nick swivels away, his hips circling this way and that, and I follow without conscious thought, the tiny shorts covering his ample butt calling to me like a siren song.

How does such a large man move with such sensual grace? And, more importantly, does he employ the same fluidity of motion in the bedroom?

Chapter 8

"ARE YOU ALWAYS TOPLESS?"

Nick

I'M NOT NORMALLY MUCH of a dancer, but after the way Tina's eyes glazed over when she saw my hips in action, you can bet I danced all the way back to the staff room. Hell, if she keeps looking at me like that, I might dance everywhere I go from now on.

"Have you heard anything else about the kid yet?" Tina asks. "Have you talked to his parents?"

I shake my head. "No, I haven't. His biological parents aren't in the picture, and I haven't been in contact with his foster parents since a week after he got here." Which sucks, because he's a great kid. He does well in school, works hard at training, and helps around the house. He's basically the opposite of what people who don't know any better expect from a kid in the system, which makes it extra strange that I haven't been able to track down his foster parents. The way they talked about him when they first contacted me led me to believe they were on their way to adopting him. Something must have happened for them to have dropped from the face of the earth. Even Jared's caseworker hasn't been able to track them down.

"Oh, no. Poor kid."

I set the boxes on the table next to the stack Demetrius brought in. "At least Rhett is with him. It would really suck for Jared if he were in the hospital alone. I'll be heading over as soon as the Spring Chickens finish their cool down and get back on their bus."

"I thought that might be the case," she says, grabbing two smaller containers from a bag I hadn't noticed. "I packed up a couple of smaller takeout containers for you to bring. If Jared is okay and can eat, then maybe he can have some? I separated the noodles and sauce so he can eat them plain. There's a little butter in there, too. Buttered noodles always helped me feel better when I overdid it."

A warming feeling takes hold in my chest. *I can't believe she did that for me. Well, I suppose she did it for Jared. But still. It's so thoughtful. And that thoughtfulness makes me like her even more.* "That's really nice of you, Tina. Thank you."

She shrugs, her cheeks turning that shade of pink that is swiftly becoming my favorite color. *I wonder how far that blush goes.*

"It was nothing. I had extra lasagna noodles. Not the best kind of noodle to eat plain, but they'll do. If he's hungry, they'll be just what he needs to soak up some of the alcohol. Well, as long as the doctor says it's okay." As she rambles, I creep closer, unable to stop myself from closing the distance between us. If the curves on her body hadn't called to me when I first saw her, the kindness she's now showing some kid she's never met would have. This woman keeps getting more and more appealing.

I stop in front of where she stands with her back to the table, catching myself before I place my hands on either side of her body to box her in. *Dude, what are you doing?* I know how big I am. I know my size intimidates many women. Tina may not have shown any fear the first time we met, but that doesn't mean she invited me into her personal space. Not yet anyway. After this noodle incident, though, I'm damn sure going for that invite. For now, I take a step back and give her some breathing room. Room she appears to need as her breath quickens and her chest heaves, forcing her tits to stretch the limits of her tight black t-shirt. *Fuck, I hope I get that invite soon.*

"You... uh... you're not wearing a shirt again."

A giant grin creeps over my face.

"Do you always exercise topless?"

A snort of laughter forces its way out of me at that reddish tint her cheeks take on. Forget the pink. I think this red is my new favorite color.

"*Shirtless,*" she says with a heavy sigh. "I mean, do you always exercise shirtless?"

Taking pity on her, I answer rather than tease her about her mix up. "Most of the time, yes. I hate the feeling of peeling off a sweaty shirt, so if I'm going for a run, or think I'll be working especially hard, I leave off the shirt." She cocks an eyebrow and somehow I know she's asking about the senior citizens streaming into the room with my other trainers. "I usually wear a shirt when I run the Spring Chickens classes, but I lost a bet today."

"Damn right you did, you sexy beast. Now do that titty dance I like. I won the bet, and it's time to collect my winnings." The elderly woman's hands are reaching out as though to grab my pecs and move them for me when Tina steps between us and stops Miss Martha's advances.

"Hey! Granny Methuselah. Hands off the merchandise. Your old ass must know better than that. There's no way you've never been to a strip club before. Not at your *advanced* age."

A shocked silence falls over the gym.

I'm amazed when, instead of gasping in offense and clutching her non-existent pearls, Miss Martha cackles a dry laugh.

"Ooh, you're a firecracker, aren't you? I like this girl, Odd Duck. Don't let her get away."

I can't see Tina's face, but I hear her splutter, and I can imagine that her cheeks are taking on that lovely shade of pink again. For a woman who has no problem calling out an old lady's objectification of a man she barely knows, not to mention the way she ordered me to carry a goat across town the first time we met, she seems to have a shy streak.

"Well... Thank you, I guess?"

"What's your name, sweetheart? You look familiar." Miss Martha is laser focused on Tina now, giving me the opportunity to slip out from behind her and confirm the blush I suspected colored her face is in fact there.

She's such a contradiction.

"I'm Tina. I own Wings and Pizza downtown. Maybe you've seen me there."

"That's the place with the walk-up window, right?"

Tina nods, a smile creeping onto her lips. "That's the one."

Miss Martha shakes her head. "I never understood that. Why would anyone want to get their pizza through a window when you can order inside? Who wants to go walking around with a whole pizza?"

"See now, that's where you've gone wrong. The walk-up window isn't for whole pizzas. It's where we sell pizza by the slice. Sometimes people get really crazy and order some wings at the window, too. But you're right. Usually, the whole pizzas get ordered over the phone or inside the restaurant."

"By the slice, you say? Stephen, did you hear that? The pizza place in town sells their pie by the slice. Think we can stop there after our next nature walk? You know how spotting birds makes us all ravenous."

Stephen, the Spring Chickens' acne riddled bus driver, ambles over to Miss Martha. "Well, sure, Miss Martha. That's a wonderful idea. We'll have to check with the nutritionist first, of course. Some of y'all have special dietary restrictions, and we'll need approval before getting fast food."

"Excuse me," Tina interrupts, her voice balancing on the edge of anger. "I am up at the ass crack of dawn every day making things from scratch, so I would appreciate it if you didn't call it fast food. There is nothing fast about it."

"Pizza is hardly the most healthful food, though," Stephen says smugly. "There's a reason you look the way you do, after all."

White hot rage washes over me with such force I'm nearly thrown off my feet. *How dare he talk to Tina that way!* I'm gearing up to throw this asshole out on his ass, literally, when Tina barks a laugh.

"You're hardly the poster boy for healthy food." She gestures to Stephen's ever present tumbler full of neon green soda. "I'd hardly call soda healthy, but that toxic green sludge has to be the worst of it. Here's some free advice: Switch to water sometimes, and your skin might clear up."

Stephen's face reddens, and I snort a laugh. How funny is it that he looks like a splotchy mess when he gets embarrassed and Tina looks like a pink goddess?

"Well, at least I'm not fat," he sputters before storming from the room. "Bus leaves in five," he bellows as he stomps away. "Be on it or you'll be marching your old asses home."

Tina's shoulders shake as she watches him leave, and for a moment I worry she might be upset at what that asshole Stephen said. It's a very brief moment, though, because soon her raucous laughter echoes from the walls.

"I'm fat? Good one, dude. This ass is juicy, not fat." She punctuates her words by smacking a hand off the side of her butt, which sends a rush of blood straight to my dick, something that just should not happen when one is wearing shorts as tight as mine. "And my tits are outstanding." She smacks both of her breasts from underneath, one after the other, in rapid succession, making them jiggle deliciously.

I press my fist to my lips to fight back a groan. What I wouldn't give to get my hands on her body.

She's right, she's not fat. But she is curvy, and I am one hundred percent certain that her curves will fit perfectly in my hands. In fact, I'm pretty damn sure those curves were made for my hands. And I can't wait until I get to prove myself right.

"That guy is an idiot," I say, turning away so she doesn't see the effect she's having on me. "You're gorgeous."

I expect the compliment to throw her off, maybe bring a little of that cute pink back to her cheeks, but instead she turns a glare on me. "No one said I wasn't gorgeous, Nick. The guy said I was fat. Fat and gorgeous are not mutually exclusive, you know. Women can be fat, thin, gorgeous, ugly, and any combination of those descriptors or a million others. And you know what else?" She takes a step closer and jabs her finger into my chest. "None of that shit matters, anyway. What really matters is what a person is like on the inside, and that guy?" She jerks a thumb in the direction Stephen went when he left in a huff. "That guy's insides are hideous."

She busies herself with unpacking the rest of the food, cutting off that conversation cleanly. "I assume you have dishes. Can you show me where they are so your crew can start dishing up? They look like they're about to stage a revolt." Her head tips back to the door behind her, where a group of hungry looking trainers and a few seniors who stayed behind despite Stephen's threat linger. "You should probably get going, too, if you want to make it to the hospital before visiting hours are over."

I catch myself grinning again. Can this woman be any more thoughtful? First, she graciously made all this food at the last minute to help me out after I messed up, and now she's reminding me to get to the hospital so I can visit Jared. Not that visiting hours would stop me. I'm the closest thing Jared has to a parent right now, and I take that responsibility seriously.

"You're right. I should get going. Hey, Demetrius? Can you lock up after this? I'm heading out to see Jared."

Demetrius isn't with the group waiting patiently for plates and it takes a moment before I spot him sitting at the head of the table, hunched over a plate of lasagna. He's shoveling it into his mouth like someone's trying to steal it.

"Dude, seriously?" I ask with a laugh. "You couldn't show everyone else where the plates were before you sat down to eat?"

Tina laughs when Demetrius hunkers down further and pulls his plate closer. I'm pretty sure he snarls.

"Don't worry, Demetrius," she says. "There is more than enough food for everyone. My mother would die if she heard someone I cooked for went hungry. I brought enough to feed you all three times over."

Demetrius shoves the last bite into his mouth and finally relaxes his grip on the plate, leaning back in his chair with his hands behind his head. He swallows and says with a grin. "I knew I wanted to marry you for a reason."

Tina's answering laugh is a beautiful, tinkling thing, and it makes my stomach fall to my feet. *Am I too late? Is she interested in Demetrius?*

Chapter 9

I Peed Myself A Little

Tina

Nick seemed angry when he walked me to my car and I haven't stopped thinking about it. Did I do something wrong? Did I go too far when I gave that bus driver shit? Damn it. Men are so strange.

There's something else I'm even more curious about than Nick's sudden change of mood. I don't know why Demetrius was eating like a starving dog, but he didn't need to worry. I wasn't kidding when I said my mom would flip if she heard I didn't bring enough food for people I'd promised to feed. Never mind that, it's literally my job to make sure people have enough to eat. The shame my mother would experience at hearing about me not having enough food would destroy her, because she taught me better. Frankly, it would destroy me, too.

Growing up in what I assume was a typical Italian neighborhood, my mother drilled it into us kids how important it was to make sure everyone got enough to eat. That stereotype of Italian Nonnas plying people with seconds and thirds could have originated with my family. But it was never about force feeding anyone. It was always about making sure everyone in the neighborhood was looked after. No matter what happened, you could count on having a hot meal at almost any house on the street, and that included mine.

I run my restaurant the same way. Sure, it's not the most profitable business model, but if it's not good for my bank account, at least it's good for my soul. I'd rather have integrity than money any day.

I pull my car into my spot behind the restaurant and walk around to the stairs leading to my apartment. A quick peek at the restaurant window shows Chloe has indeed changed the painting again, a sure sign of another slow night. Thank goodness for Nick and his poor planning skills. The money he'll pay me for the next few days of catering will go a long way. Maybe he'll want to make it a regular thing? I don't know how often he hosts these retreats, but catering them could be the thing I need to get Wings and Pizza out of this slump we've been in. At the very least, it will get the word out. I've never put much thought into advertising, and it shows. That woman at Nick's gym didn't even understand the walk-up window.

It must be a common misunderstanding in Tuft Swallow, too. The only person who ever orders from the walk-up window is Wade Biddescombe, and he hardly counts. As the realtor who's renting me the place, he has a vested interest in the success of my business. If it weren't for Wade, I'd have no customers at all some days. Who would have guessed the mobster who used to show up in my neighborhood from time to time, the man all us kids called Uncle Gianni, would one day be my personal hero?

Not that I've ever let on that I know who he is, and he's never confirmed that he recognizes me, but that doesn't matter. I know it's him. Whatever brought him here, whatever made him change his name from Gianni to Wade, well, that's none of my business. He looks out for me by keeping the rent low and ordering enough food to keep my business afloat, and I look out for him by paying my rent on time and keeping his secret. I think that's a fair trade.

But if this thing with Nick becomes a regular gig, maybe I can do more than keep my head above water. It's something worth exploring, anyway.

My mind flashes to an image of Nick this evening, in his tight shorts and nothing else, and I can think of another thing I might like to explore. That man is the most perfect combination of muscle and fluff I've ever seen. People assume all women want a man like Demetrius, all hard angles with muscles that make it look like he's been cut from marble, when the truth is many women, like me, would be happier with a bigger man. A man with a little meat on his bones. A man who looks like he could rock your world in the bedroom and then cuddle the heck out of you for hours afterward. I can almost picture him hovering over me, looking down at me with lust-filled eyes, teasing me, ready to thrust into me and... Yeah, I wouldn't mind finding out if Nick is that kind of man, not at all. Not if the throbbing in my lady parts is anything to go by.

But that's a thought best saved for another day. I need to get back to the restaurant so Chloe can go home. If she's lucky, maybe she can convince her date to reschedule. First, though, I need to change my underwear. That brief fantasy of Nick above me has caused some serious flooding in my panties. If anything makes working long hours unbearable, it's wet undergarments.

The steps up the outside of the building to my apartment are dark, making it hard to pick out my steps. That's odd. I never turn that off. I guess the light must've finally burned out. After at least five years using the same light bulb, that makes sense. Even the best LED bulb on the market won't last forever, and I don't know how long that one had been there before I moved in. I'll see if Wade will help me change it tomorrow. He will be around at some point. His presence is the one thing I've been able to count on since I've moved here. For a former mobster, the guy is an excellent landlord.

My door swings open with a gentle touch, and I step into my tiny living room, shuck my shoes on the mat that serves as my entryway, and take the four steps to my bedroom. Tiny house living has nothing on this apartment. The only difference is my bed is in a tiny bedroom instead of a loft.

I reach out to flick the lights on so I can see what I'm doing, but the moment I do, an icy cold *something* grips my wrist, and I freeze in terror. You know how they say your life flashes before your eyes in times of extreme danger or physical stress? All I saw was pizza. And maybe a little Nick, but I'm sure that's because I was already thinking about him.

A hoarse voice whispers a warning. *"You're not safe here."*

My heart flops in my chest before careening off into an erratic rhythm as it tries to break through my ribs in some sort of prison break. I think I pee a little. *Oh my God. What do I do, what do I do?*

A whimper escapes my throat as the icy grasp releases me, and the lights in the room come on. My vision fills with a cloud of pink as Chloe's face comes into view, her disappointment plain in her eyes.

"Tina. You promised you would close your door. Imagine my surprise earlier when I went to take the garbage out, and it was hanging wide open. Again." She crosses her arms over her chest and watches as I drag in breath after relieved breath.

Holy shit. I was sure I was about to die. Or worse.

"You're lucky it was only me in here tonight. You know you had another date show up downstairs while you were gone? What if he took it upon himself to come up here and wait for you?"

My ragged breaths slow, and my heart stops thumping as hard, though it's still pounding a pretty impressive beat in my ears as I consider what she's saying. Another date? Where the hell are these guys coming from? And the door thing, too, of course.

"I'll try harder to remember the door. But, did you say another date? Who was it?"

She shrugs and steps around me, heading back to the living room slash kitchen area. "One of the douchebros from that new tech place in Spitz hollow. The guy looked like he'd fit right in as an extra in that old movie *American Psycho*. Between the weird suit and the slicked back hair, I half expected him to hand me an embossed business card before heading into the bathroom to do some coke."

"Oh my God, Chloe. Please tell me he didn't do that. We can't have customers doing cocaine in the bathrooms. Do you know how fast that would end up on the first page of the Nosy Pecker? That is the last thing this place needs. We'd never recover from that kind of press."

Chloe laughs and waves me off. "Of course not. He argued with me for a minute, insisting he made a date with you on that bumblebee dating app. When he realized you weren't about to materialize from thin air, he took off, grumbling about having his time wasted."

I sag, blowing out a breath. "That's a relief. Those old biddies who run the Nosy Pecker would have never let something like that go. It would get blown out of proportion until suddenly Wings and Pizza is a front for the mob, and we're giving our cocaine with our wing specials."

Chloe rolls her eyes at my tirade. "You don't even read the Nosy Pecker. They'd never write something like that. I'm sure they have some sense of journalistic integrity."

"Maybe we should put a sign in the bathroom to be sure nothing happens?" I rush ahead, ignoring her. "You know, take a proactive stance? I'm sure someone in town could make one of those cute cross stitches that read 'please don't do cocaine in our bathroom'. Do the Dirty Hookers do cross stitch, or are they strictly knitting and crochet?"

"Forget about the cocaine," Chloe huffs. "And leave that poor knitting club alone. Let's get back to the subject at hand. We're talking about you and your complete disregard for personal safety."

Chloe is like a dog with a bone when she cares about something, and as her friend, I am firmly on that last list. I know she won't drop this until I convince her I take my safety seriously. But I can't do that with wet underwear. Having serious conversations while wearing wet underwear is almost as bad as working extended hours in wet underwear. I reach up and tuck a stray strand of hair back into my bun. "I get it," I say with a nod. "Head back to the restaurant and I'll be right behind you. We can make a pot of coffee and talk until morning if we need to. But first, I need to change my underwear." She cocks an eyebrow and I grimace. "I think I peed myself a little when you grabbed me."

Chloe barks a laugh and shakes her head. "Okay, sounds good. You go ahead and change your pee pee pants while I make some coffee."

She's still chuckling to herself as she makes her way back out of my apartment and down the darkened stairs. After taking a quick shower and changing into clean clothes, I join her in the restaurant.

"I'm ready for my talking to," I say as I grab the coffee cup she holds out to me. She's already added the cream and sugar, so I take a deep drink and lick the sweet liquid from my lips. "Perfect, as always."

Chloe rolls her eyes and takes a sip of her own coffee. "Of course it's perfect. I made it. You know I don't mess around with coffee. A diligence I would love to see you take with your own safety."

I heave a sigh. So we're jumping right in then, are we?

"Don't you breathe heavily at me, young lady." Her mouth twitches with a snicker she doesn't allow to pass her lips. "You're my best friend, and I won't allow you to keep flouting your personal safety."

"Come on, you know that's not true. I care about my personal safety."

She scoffs and looks at me over her cup, her eyes steely. "Oh, really? So then, tell me. Did you close your door just now when you came down?"

Damn it! The sound of her frustrated laughter chases me out the door and up the stairs, where I pull the door shut until I hear it click. My walk back into the restaurant is the shortest, weirdest walk of shame ever. I'm not stumbling home barefoot wearing last night's dress with my heels in my hand, but it feels pretty similar. I can't believe I forgot to close the door minutes after Chloe scared me half to death. I will never live this down.

"What was that you were saying? You care about your personal safety?" Chloe asks when I push the door open.

"Shut up." I drop into the chair and take another drink of my coffee. "That was a practice run. I'll close it next time."

"Tina..." Chloe hangs her head and her shoulders rise as she takes a deep breath. "I'm not doing this to piss you off. I just want you to take care of yourself. This is no different from when I suggested you take a multivitamin to balance out all the pizza and pasta you eat."

I could argue, but as usual, Chloe is right. "Okay. I promise I will close my door."

"And lock it."

"Hey, that wasn't part of the deal."

Chloe reaches across the table and takes my hand, giving it a quick squeeze before dropping it again. "You've had a strange man here every day for the last week, all thinking they have a date with you, and we still don't know why. Something is going on, and I think it's best if you keep your door locked at all times. Either that, or you move in with me."

I can't stop the horrified look from jumping onto my face. "Oh, no. No way. Uh uh. Hard pass." She's laughing before I finish my refusal. "Do you know how early I'd have to get up to get here when I need to? I can't go back to having a long commute."

"I don't live that far away," she protests through a laugh. "It takes me five minutes to drive here on a bad day."

"Five minutes?! No way. I'll lock my door from now on."

"Excellent. Well, now that that's settled. Care to tell me why you were looking all hot and bothered before I grabbed you in the dark earlier? And how much did Nick have to do with it?"

I feel the blush creep onto my cheeks as I watch the knowing smile creep onto Chloe's face.

"Well, well, well. This is certainly an interesting development. Tina has a crush on the big, hunky fighter. I can't wait to see how this turns out."

Damn it. If I were different, I'd want to know how it could turn out too. But I'm not different. I don't date, so this little

crush, if that's even what it is, is going to stay right where it is.
With me. Alone.

Chapter 10

YOU HAD ME AT CRUSTY BREAD

Nick

"Hey, kid. How are you feeling?"

I've been with Jared since the hospital released him into my care last night. After getting him home and getting him into bed, I've just been sitting here listening to the kid breathe, of all the ridiculous things. I couldn't shake the feeling that something bad could still happen, so I sat up all night monitoring his breathing.

He was aware enough to help me get him from the hospital to the car, but I was on my own when I carried him inside and put him to bed. It would have been a little easier if Rhett had been there, but he had a date he was hoping he could salvage after having to cancel when he first brought Jared to the hospital. I didn't want to keep him from it any longer. The guy needs to get out more.

Besides, one of the great things about being a big guy is the ability to carry dudes who can't handle their liquor when necessary. And tonight it proved to be very necessary when I realized Jared had passed out in the passenger seat on our way home. I suppose I could have woken him up and made him walk into the house, but he looked so peaceful I couldn't bring myself to do it. And besides, he needed the rest.

Jared groans and sits up, his hand reaching for his head, which has to be absolutely throbbing right now. After his initial workup, the doctor declared Jared to be fine despite being drunk as a skunk, and discharged him from the hospital with orders to drink water, take an over-the-counter painkiller, and get some sleep. He also had some choice words for me and Rhett, that boiled down to needing to toughen up if we planned to raise a teenage boy. I can still hear him laughing at us for bringing the kid to the hospital for basic drunkenness. The dude even called me a mother hen. Me!

I mean, he's not wrong. But still. Imagine saying that to someone you just met.

"Ugh." Jared smacks his lips and rolls his tongue around his mouth. "Why is my mouth so dry? Did I eat glue?"

I grab the bottle of water from the nightstand, open it, and pass it to him. "Drink this. You're dehydrated." I watch as he chugs the contents of the bottle, ready with a bucket because I know from experience what comes next.

"I don't feel so good," Jared says, dropping the bottle as he covers his mouth. "I think I'm going to puke."

"Here." I pass him the bucket. "Go nuts."

To give him some privacy, I leave the room to get him some painkillers and another bottle of water for when he's done throwing his guts up. No one likes an audience when they're sick. When I get back to his room, he's sitting up with his legs over the side of his bed, feet on the floor, and head in his hands.

"She dumped me."

Ah, shit. I was hoping to have a little more time before we had to get into this conversation. Not that I didn't suspect this was coming for months already, but a little more time for Jared to sober up and get rid of his hangover would have been nice. Sadly, it looks like we don't have that luxury.

"I'm sorry, kid. Breakups are never easy."

"I don't understand why she couldn't wait for me. I'm only here for a few more months. We were supposed to be together when I went back home again. Maybe I should just go back now."

I heave a sigh and take a seat in the chair beside the bed. I've known this breakup has been coming since Jared moved to Tuft Swallow to stay with me, but that doesn't make this any easier. And as much as I wish I could take the kid's pain away, nothing heals this kind of heartbreak but time. Luckily, time is something we have in abundance. Because even if he wants to leave now, with both his biological parents and his foster parents missing, there's nowhere for him to go. And I'll be damned if I let him be shuffled off to some new foster parents when he can stay here with me.

"I don't know why she dumped you, kid. But I do know it's her loss. You're a good kid, last night's misadventure in tequila notwithstanding, and she was lucky to have you. I can't think of many other sixteen-year-old kids who would spend hours working out, doing homework, and working at the gym, all while trying to reassure their girlfriend that they wouldn't leave them for someone else. Most guys your age would have used this as an opportunity to play the field. See what a little town like Tuft Swallow had to offer. But not you. You're far too loyal to do a thing like that, something your girlfriend would have known, if she'd known you at all. You've shown impressive dedication to your career so far. Maybe you should focus on that for a while? Give her some time to cool off?"

Jared scoffs and reaches a hand out. "Water?"

"Take these, too," I say, handing him the painkillers first, then the water. "They'll help with that headache."

Jared pops the painkillers in his mouth then chugs the water. "Thanks."

We sit in silence for a few more minutes before Jared lays back in his bed and pulls the blanket up over his head. I'll let him rest for now, but this little act of rebellion won't go unanswered. Before that, though, I need to call Gloria, his caseworker, and report this incident. I just hope that she's as understanding about this as she has been about his parents and foster parents going missing. Because as much as I know having Jared here isn't a permanent thing, I'm not ready for him to leave yet. I care about the kid, and I enjoy having him around.

"Get some sleep, kid. We'll talk more about this later." Because even though I'm letting him rest right now, that doesn't mean I won't be addressing his underage drinking, or using alcohol to cope with his emotions. Those are both big no-nos in my house.

Jared's answering grunt tells me he's already half asleep. *Yeah, I like having him around,* I think as my heart warms with affection. He deserves so much better than the crap hand he's been dealt in his life. And while he's here, at least, I'll do everything in my power to make sure he gets it.

I leave his room and go directly to my home office. Time to rip off the proverbial bandage. Pulling up the contact information for Jared's caseworker, I settle into my office chair and hit send. Here goes nothing.

"Gloria Freeman."

Here goes nothing.

"NICK. HI." Is TINA's greeting the tiniest bit breathless, or is that wishful thinking on my part? "How did it go last night? Is Jared okay?"

My heart does that weird fluttery thing it did last night when she first showed me her thoughtful side. She's never even met the kid, and she's asking about his well-being. Why can't his parents and foster parents show the same concern? Jared deserves to have people in his life who care about him.

"He's sleeping it off right now. Thankfully, they let him come home last night." Rhett came over to check on Jared not long after my call with Gloria, so I took the opportunity to come visit Tina. I told Rhett I was confirming my dinner order, but mostly I wanted to see her. Despite all the reasons I had to think about Jared and his family life, last night while I was sitting up beside his bed, my mind kept wandering back to Tina.

Tina and her compassion. Tina and her concern. Tina and her curves. Oh man, did I think about Tina and her curves. My hands practically ache with the need to squeeze her ass. Even now, as she stands in front of me in her all black athleisure wear covered by a white apron, her curves call to me. Luckily, she's still too concerned about Jared to notice that my thoughts have taken a turn for the naughty.

Tension seeps from her body as she relaxes. "Oh, thank goodness. I looked up treatments for alcohol poisoning before I went to bed last night and it scared me so much I couldn't sleep afterward. I can't imagine what it would feel like to have your stomach pumped. The whole thing sounds terrible, honestly." Her face scrunches up in pain and I chuckle.

"You're not wrong about that. I wouldn't want to go through that, either. Luckily, the bottle from his friend's house only had a little left in it. That's what he told Rhett and the doctor last night, anyway. It makes sense, too. He threw up this morning, but no more than a normal hangover. So far, anyway. He may spend a little more time throwing up later, after I put him through his paces at the gym. I need to make sure he doesn't do something this stupid again any time soon."

Tina narrows her eyes. "Are you sure that's wise?"

I shrug. "An old guy I trained with when I was a kid did it to me and it helped me learn my lesson. I certainly never overdid it on the alcohol again. Not while I was underage, anyway." I've had a few stupid moments when I drank too much as an adult, but who hasn't? "Jared will figure out his priorities one way or another, but this way, he doesn't miss his workout. Plus, it should keep his mind off the girl who dumped him without needing to numb the pain with alcohol. The only real downside is the mess he'll make, but since he'll clean that as part of his punishment..." I trail off, leaving it unsaid that I think that part will be good for him, too.

Her face softens, then her lips turn down at the corners. "Ah man, that's really what it was? Poor kid. Everything feels so much bigger at that age, especially heartbreak. Is there anything I can do?"

Just when I think I can't like this woman any more, she not only shows concern for the kid currently in my care, but also offers to help. "Maybe there is something. I came to see what you were planning for tonight's dinner. I was hoping you'd be able to add some plain carbs for Jared like you did last night." She frowns. "I don't mean for you to make anything special, but if you could pull out a portion before adding any sauce. Or something like that. You're the chef, not me. I just thought it would be good to have something plain for him, in case his stomach isn't ready for whatever deliciousness you have planned for us."

"You're in for a treat tonight," she says with a grin. "I went shopping earlier and got everything I'll need for the rest of the week. And I wouldn't worry about Jared. The dinner I have planned for tonight will be perfect. Besides, he's a teenager. I doubt the hangover will hit him the same way as it does us old folks. It wouldn't surprise me one bit if he eats twice as much as the rest of you. I'm making a nice chicken piccata with mashed potatoes, some roasted asparagus, and a simple green salad. I also have a few loaves of crusty bread that I'll bake right before I bring everything over. Do you want me to make a small batch of noodles for Jared, too? Or do you think he'll be okay with what I have?"

Halfway through her description of the dinner she's planning, my mouth starts watering, and I have to swallow a bunch of extra saliva before I can answer. "You're baking bread? Fresh bread?"

She chuckles. "Of course. But don't get excited. It's a basic quick crusty bread, nothing fancy. It works perfectly for sopping up sauce, though. You can't let that lemony, buttery goodness go to waste."

"Stop," I say, my stomach grumbling at the mere thought of the dinner Tina has planned. "You had me at crusty bread. If you say any more, my stomach is will eat itself in anticipation."

She laughs and shakes her head. "Get out of here. I'll see you later."

I say my goodbyes and am halfway back to my house before I realize she said she would bring the food to the gym. With everything that's happening with Jared today, I'll take the help, but tomorrow I'm picking up my order myself. I'm thankful that she's willing to make an exception and do another delivery, but I can't keep taking her away from her restaurant this way. She has her own business to worry about. I can take care of the gym, and Jared, by myself. Well, by myself with some catering from the best restaurant in town, anyway. After all the messages the guys sent me about last night's feast, I know Tina's food is going to make the difference in this training retreat. And one week off meal plan won't hurt these guys. Not if I work them extra hard.

Look out Tuft Swallow. Tomorrow the trainers and fighters from Put Up Your Ducks MMA are taking over the walking trails. Twenty laps around town ought to do it.

 Chapter 11

Choking His Chicken

Tina

"This is the best thing I've ever eaten," Jared says without looking up from his plate. "I'm starving."

Nick raises an eyebrow at me and shrugs. I mouth the words "told you" and he grins. He's shirtless again, his powerful body on full display, the tiny shorts he's wearing doing nothing to hide his squeezable ass. I said a little prayer of thanks when he finally sat down to eat, because I couldn't take much more of that temptation. If I'd had to look at his butt for much longer, I'd have had to grab it with two hands. Or bite it. *Yeah, it's definitely biteable.*

"I'm glad to hear you're feeling better." I place a hand on Jared's shoulder as I drop two more slices of crusty bread onto his plate. "You had everyone pretty worried last night."

He swallows roughly and looks up at me. "I know. And I'm sorry. I won't let that happen again. And not just because Nick threatened to make me workout until I puke again. It wasn't even that fun being drunk. And it didn't help me forget about — it didn't help me forget about *her*." Then, in true teenage fashion, he shakes his head and goes back to his food. "This chicken is amazing."

"It is, isn't it?" Demetrius says from opposite Jared. He's just finished his food and is using the bread to wipe the plate clean. "You sure you don't want to marry me? Because this sauce tastes like a proposal."

I shake my head and laugh. "I'm sure. Besides, if this sauce was a proposal, then I would be asking you all to marry me, and I'm afraid I'm not interested in a reverse harem. There are way too many dicks involved, and I'm sorry, but those things are way more trouble than they're worth."

The sound of choking cuts through the chatter in the room, and we all turn to see the culprit. Nick's face turns red as he coughs into a napkin. "Wrong pipe," he says with another cough.

How is it that the man looks sexy even while he's choking? It's not fair. Here I am, hair frizzy and wild, my thick glasses smeared with fingerprints, my butt testing the stretch of my black leggings, and Nick still looks amazing even while doing his best not to choke on his chicken.

Heh, choke his chicken.

The crude joke jumps into my head unbidden accompanied with a not suitable for public consumption image of a naked Nick stroking himself, and my cheeks ignite with flame before I can stop them. Nick's eyes go hot as he looks at me, lit from within like he can see my thoughts, and suddenly it's a hundred degrees hotter in here. I grab the collar of my t-shirt and use it to fan myself. This attraction is becoming an inconvenience.

I should go.

"I should go. Chloe has a window to paint in town, so I need to get back. Not that I expect it to be busy. I'll probably only see Wade tonight."

"Wade?" Nick asks. "Wade Biddescombe, the realtor?"

I nod. "He's also my landlord. And my best customer. He comes in pretty much every day. I need to ask him to change the light over my apartment door so I can't miss him. You'd be surprised how dark those stairs are at night."

Nick nods, looking thoughtful. "If you don't see him, I could stop by and change it for you. Here, give me your phone." He takes my phone and adds his number. "Just let me know. I do owe you, after all."

As much as I don't want to admit it, Chloe scared me last night, and having that light out worries me. However, I remembered to close my door today, so peeing myself wasn't altogether in vain. So despite it going against all my independent instincts, I nod. "That would be nice, thank you. I'll let you know if I need your help."

Nick walks me to the gym's entrance, and again I'm impressed by Chloe's mural. I need to make some time to come by and find myself in it. I'm sure if she painted Mr. Landon and Merethe, she put me in there somewhere, too. I wonder what I look like as a duck?

"Thanks again for all of your help," Nick says. "I know I dropped the ball on the food for this retreat, but you're really saving my ass."

My cheeks flush again. I purposely walked ahead of Nick to keep his ass out of my line of sight, and now he's bringing it up?

Doesn't he know I'm three seconds away from using it to pull him against me?

"You're paying me," I say on a breath. "That's all the thanks I need."

"Nah. I owe you. Paying you and changing a light bulb won't be enough. Don't worry," he says with a wink that I feel in my core. "I'll think of something."

He places his hand on the small of my back and walks me outside, the heat from his palm burning through my shirt, then waits at the door until I'm in my car. With a wave, he turns and goes back inside, giving me a parting view of that amazing ass.

As soon as he's out of sight, I blow out a breath and melt into my seat.

It's been years since I've felt this level of attraction for a man. I've never had urges to grab one's ass like this, either.

What is Nick doing to me?

The only thing stopping me from acting on these impulses is knowing that despite the bit of flirting he's been doing, he's not actually interested in me. And thank goodness for that. Because if Nick gave me even the slightest hint that he was *really* interested, I'd be stripping off those tiny shorts of his and riding him into next week.

"THANKS FOR DINNER, VALENTINA." My landlord, Wade Biddescombe, waves his goodbye from the door of Wings and Pizza and heads out into the dark street. He always calls me Valentina, like everyone in the neighborhood did when I was a kid. It's one of the reasons I'm positive Wade Biddescombe is actually the man I used to call Uncle Gianni, despite neither of us ever broaching the subject.

"See you tomorrow," I yell as the door drifts shut behind him.

If you ask any person my age who grew up in my Boston neighborhood what their favorite memory is, nine times out of ten it features a visit from Uncle Gianni on a stiflingly hot summer's day and a fire hydrant that somehow spontaneously sprayed its ice cold water into the street shortly after he walked by. Not one kid or adult would ever admit to seeing him do it, but we all knew Uncle Gianni was the reason for that brief reprieve from the summer heat. Somehow, even though he was in town to attend to some mobster business that I was too young to understand, he always did something to help out the kids in the neighborhood.

So why am I letting him leave without asking for help with changing the light above my stairs? Because I'm weak, that's why.

Ever since I left Nick at the gym, he's the only thing I've thought about. Nick and that hot look he gave me right before I left. Nick enjoying my cooking. Nick in his tiny shorts. Nick's hand on my back as he walked me out. Nick naked and stroking himself. That last one has been an exceptionally persistent vision, much to my consternation. Do you know how hard it is to focus on cooking and cleaning when you have a sexy naked man in your head who won't stop waving (what I'm imagining is) his impressive dick at you? It's damn near impossible.

I allowed Wade to walk out of here without asking him about the light, so I can use the opportunity to call Nick and take him up on his offer to help change my light bulb. You see, throughout this evening of being tortured by fantasies of Nick, I came up with a brilliant plan. I'll get him over here under the guise of needing help with the light, seduce him, sleep with him, get him out of my system, and send him on his way. It will be your classic wham, bam, thank you sexy man situation. Then I'll finally be able to concentrate.

It's not that I mind having thoughts of a naked Nick running through my mind. Not really. But I would prefer if they would choose more appropriate times to pop into my head, like when I'm in bed, or in the shower. There's not much worse than being turned on and having to work another ten hours before you can do something about it.

I pull my phone out and open the contacts. *Here goes nothing.* I press the screen to initiate the call, holding my breath while it rings through in my ear.

"Hey, Tina. I was just thinking about you."

I release my breath. *He was thinking about me? That's a good sign, right? Maybe that hot look meant more than I thought.* Despite my earlier confidence when I came up with this plan, as soon as the phone started to ring, I had second thoughts. *What if I proposition him and he laughs in my face? What then?* I'm sure I can finish out the week of catering, but at what cost to my pride? If he shoots me down after I offer myself up to him on a platter, how will I ever be able to look him in the eye?

Fuck it. I'll never know if I don't try.

"Oh, really?" I ask in my sexiest voice. It's not all that sexy, but it's what I've got, so I go with it. "And what exactly have you been thinking?" That sounds flirty, right? I am so out of practice with this. Who would have guessed that swearing off dating would have such an adverse effect on my flirting skills?

"I was wondering if you would call me to help with your light. Did Wade not come in?"

Right. Of course that's what he was thinking. A guy like Nick wouldn't be having the same sexy fantasies about me as I was about him. I've seen pictures of the women he's dated in the past, and not a single one looks like me. Of them all, the closest would have to be the plus sized model he dated a few years back, and even she was a few sizes smaller than me, with much nicer hair. I *may* have internet-stalked him in between customers tonight. So what? My self-esteem can usually handle a little healthy competition, but I can't hold a candle when compared to his dating history full of literal models, actresses, and athletes. Still, I thought I sensed *something* when he was looking at me earlier. Maybe I should abandon my plans of seduction? I'm not sure I'm ready to seduce a man who has zero interest. I still need my light changed, though, and Wade is long gone. And besides, Nick *did* offer.

"Yup, that's why I'm calling. Can you still come by? I can change it myself if you will hold the ladder."

His chuckle echoes through the phone. *"I'll be right over. And I'll change it. You can hold the ladder for me."*

"Sounds good. Meet me at the restaurant. I need to finish cleaning, and then I can get out of here."

My plans of seduction officially set aside, I rush through my cleaning tasks and wait for Nick at the door of Wings and Pizza. I'd briefly entertained going upstairs to change into my one set of moderately sexy underwear before he arrived, but the thought of heading upstairs in the dark, alone, for a seduction that I've already determined has very little chance of success, has convinced me otherwise. Besides, my big cotton granny panties and comfortable bra should help keep my libido in check, no matter how many *looks* Nick throws my way.

Despite my deliberate choice of unsexy underwear, my mind runs off into dirty daydream-land as I wait, imagining what will happen when Nick finally gets here. Sexy fantasy Nick is hovering over me, poised at my entrance as I beg him to fill me, when real life Nick pushes his way into the store.

"Hey, Tina. You ready?"

I gasp at the interruption.

Nick looks me up and down, concern etched on his features even as his eyes darken with that same fiery look from before. "Is everything okay? You look a little flushed."

That look is the only thing in my brain when I lean forward, wrap my arms around Nick's neck, and drag him down to me for a kiss. Well, it's the only thing in there until my lips part and his tongue thrusts into my mouth, eagerly tangling with my own even as his arms wrap around me, his huge hands grabbing my ass and pulling me flush against his body. After that, my naughty daydreams take a backseat to a reality that's even better.

So much for skipping the seduction. I suppose I should have changed out of my granny panties after all.

# Chapter 12

The Sexiest Owl Noises You've Ever Heard

Nick

Well, that was… unexpected.

While I suspected Tina had been having less than pure thoughts about me off and on today, based on the way her eyes seemed to linger over my body, I did not expect her to jump me the second I walked through the door.

That was a fucking amazing surprise.

When I offered to help her with her light this evening, my only plan was to do just that. Change her lightbulb. Was I hoping to spend a little more time with her one on one, and maybe, just maybe, work up the courage to ask her out? Yes,

I was. But when I walked in to find her flushed and panting with that glazed look in her eyes, well, my dick responded with what was most probably misplaced enthusiasm, hardening in my running shorts.

Okay, so maybe my plan to change her lightbulb wasn't entirely innocent.

I've noticed the way Tina devours me with her eyes every time she sees me in my shorts, so of course I had to take this opportunity to wear them in front of her. I told myself if she didn't show interest after I got here, I would change the light bulb and go for a long, long run.

But she did more than show interest. She jumped me, then proceeded to kiss me silly. *Fuck.* She's still kissing me silly, and I'm here in my head instead of enjoying the experience. I should do something about that.

Don't fuck this up, Nick. Kiss her. Hold her.

I don't have to tell myself twice. My hands reach down, seemingly of their own volition, and I can't help but groan into Tina's mouth when I finally squeeze her ass. *The perfect fit for my hands, just as I thought.* I squeeze a little harder and pull her body flush to mine, grinding my erection into her stomach. *Fuck, that feels good.*

"Fuck, that feels good." Tina's words echo my thoughts perfectly as her hands scrabble to pull me closer. "I haven't been able to get you out of my head."

"Same," I grunt, running my hands under her thighs and lifting her off the ground. Her grip on me tightens, and her legs wrap around my hips. I spin and push her up against the window beside the door, using it to press myself against her, loving the feel of the heat pulsing between her legs. "Since the day we met, I've wanted you." I bend my knees and press up, grinding my dick into the apex of her thighs, sliding her up the window. "Just"—I drop an open-mouthed kiss to the left side of her throat—"like"—I nip the spot where her shoulder meets her neck—"this." I press my lips to hers, and revel in the way her breath comes in hot little pants against my mouth. Holding her body up with my own, I slide a hand from under her leg, running it up her side.

"Oh, fuck yes," she moans, thrusting her chest out, forcing her breast into my hand, the hard nipple tempting me through her shirt. "Touch me, Nick."

I bury my face in her neck, inhaling her scent. She smells of soap, and sweat, and... *pizza?* My dick gets harder than I knew was possible and I send up a silent prayer to whoever might be listening that I wore running shorts instead of something with a zipper. *Why is it so hot that she smells like pizza?*

One of her hands works its way up into my hair, grasping, gripping, pulling my face to hers. Soft lips press to my own before she pulls away and looks into my eyes. "Upstairs. Now," she demands, with more than a hint of desperation in her voice.

I hoist her higher on my waist, wrapping her around me even more, and step out the door. "Keys?" I grunt between kisses, my face once again buried in her neck. "You need to lock up."

"Ugh," she groans, tapping me on the shoulder until I let her scramble down from my grasp. I already miss the feel of her heat pressed against me. "You sound like Chloe. *Close the door, Tina. Lock the door, Tina.*" She pulls a set of keys out from a side pocket in her leggings, pushes the door open, turns off the lights, then pulls the door closed and locks it behind her. "Happy now?" she asks, shoving the keys back in her pocket and looking up at me from too far away.

Without hesitation, I step closer, wrapping my arms around her and hoisting her into the air until I can guide her legs around my waist again. *Fuuuck.* The feel of her heat pressed against me has me throbbing. "Almost," I say, pressing my lips to hers before I whisper directly in her ear. "But when I finally get you somewhere more private than the street in front of your restaurant so I can bury my face between those sweet thighs of yours?" I suck her earlobe into my mouth, giving it a meaningful flick with my tongue before staring into her dark eyes, and adding, "Well, that's when I'll be truly happy." The way her body shivers tells me she's happy with that plan, too.

She chases my mouth with her lips, kissing me hard, urging me to hurry with frenzied whispers of *"quick"* and *"faster"*. My cock is so hard it makes every step up the stairs to her apartment pure torture. The only thing keeping me from losing myself completely is Tina's body pressed hard against me, promising that sweet relief is near. One second we're on the stairs with Tina writhing in my arms, and the next we're inside her tiny apartment with her standing on the floor in front of me, pulling her shirt over her head.

Suddenly, her face drops, and she covers her bra with her hands while spinning around. "Wait. Hold on. Look away." She steps through a doorway, leaving me in the world's smallest living room, with a record breaking tent in my shorts. I overhear Tina muttering to herself amongst other bumps and bangs as she moves around the other room "Oh my God. I knew I shouldn't have talked myself out of changing. Crap!"

"Uh, Tina? I thought the idea was to get you out of your clothes, not change them?"

"Oh, um, yeah. Right. Just-just stay there for one minute. Don't come in he—Ahh!" her words cut off with a scream, followed by a loud thump.

That doesn't sound good. Ignoring her pleas for me to stay away, I take two big steps into what turns out to be her bedroom. "Tina?" I ask when I don't see her. "You okay?"

"Ow, shit. Fuck. Damn it." Her harsh whispers call my attention to the far side of the bed, where I hear more thumping sounds. "No, no, no. Not now. Ow, ow. Cramp. Cramp."

One more step brings me to the opposite side of the bed, where I'm met by a sight that is both so confoundingly sexy, and intensely hilarious, that I can't help but bark a short laugh.

Tina glares at me from the center of a human pretzel, her arms and legs tangled in a heap of black fabric, her tits exposed with their dark pink nipples pebbled and ready for my tongue. But she is in no shape for sexy times at this exact moment. She's somehow gotten one arm stuck in a pant leg with her bra wrapped around the back of her neck, keeping one leg trapped against her chest. She's rocking on her back like a turtle stuck shell side down, exposing more of her cotton panties with each rock of her hips. If it weren't for her obvious discomfort, I would be interested in exploring this position further. Her glare is more murderous than amorous, though, so I offer to help instead.

"Oh, baby. Let me help you."

Her leg kicks straight out, dragging an arm with it, as she yelps again. "Ow, ow, ow. Could there be a worse time for a leg cramp?"

"Let me get you out of those clothes." I kneel next to her on the floor and begin untangling her legs first, looping her foot back through the strap of her bra. "What the hell? This doesn't even make sense. Were you taking your pants off? Or your bra?"

"Ugh. Both," she huffs pitifully. "I didn't want you to see my ugly work bra. And now you see me like this, which is so much worse." She attempts to gesture with her arm, but it's still tangled in stretchy material. "Ow, ow, ow. Slow down. Cramp, cramp!"

I slide her pants the rest of the way off, then untangle her arms from her bra. Generous black cotton panties keep part of her shielded from my view, but she makes no further motion to hide herself from my eyes, choosing instead to rub furiously at the back of her leg, where I'm guessing the cramp is. "Here," I say, pulling her to her feet and guiding her to the bed. "Let me."

When she's face down on the bed, I take a deep breath, force myself to focus on the task at hand, then wrap my hands around her thigh and rub the hard muscles there, feeling the knot of tension melt beneath my fingers. Tina's smooth skin and soft flesh yield to my touch and before long she's writhing on the bed, emitting soft whimpers that do nothing to soothe the ache in my dick.

"Tina," I warn. "Are you sure that's what you want?" I drag a finger along the hem at the bottom of her panties, tracing her ass cheek, then dipping between her thighs before tracing a line back to her hip on the opposite side.

Face down in the pillow now, the only answer I get is a muffled "mmphhmphh" and a slight lifting of her hips. I continue tracing the hem of her panties, her legs widening and hips rising a little more with each pass. From my position next to her thigh, the sweet smell of her arousal threatens to overwhelm me.

"Damn, you smell good." I swipe my fingers into her panties, touching the inner edge of her thigh, my eyes focused on the ever-expanding wet spot in her panties.

From the corner of my eye, I see her head turn as she looks at me over her shoulder. "That's my apartment. It always smells like Italian food up here," she says before dropping her face back into the pillow.

The abrupt change of subject forces a chuckle from me. "No, honey. I'm pretty sure it's you." I slide a finger through her wetness, circling her clit and making her shiver. I wait until she shifts her face from the pillow and lifts her eyes to mine before sliding my finger into my mouth. I mean to tease her with this display, but the taste of Tina is too delicious. I can't stop the moan that escapes me the moment the salty-sweet taste of her hits my tongue. "And you taste even better."

Tina's eyes go liquid and her mouth parts. "Fuck, that's hot," she whispers. Her eyes burn down my chest and settle on my very tented shorts. "That's even hotter." Her pink tongue darts out to wet her lips, and my dick throbs. "I need to see it," she says, flipping over and scrambling to a sitting position. "Take those off." She surges toward me, grabbing for the elastic waistband of my shorts, but misses altogether. Instead, a clumsy, and surprisingly forceful punch to the gut shoves me off the bed.

I land on my back with a room shaking thump.

"*Hooo.*" The air rushes from my lungs in a whoosh and somewhere past the realm of strict consciousness, since I'm pretty sure I just saw my life flash before my eyes, I'm dimly aware that making owl impressions is not the sexiest thing I could do right this minute. Even so, that doesn't stop me from dragging in a shaky breath and forcing it out with another audible *"hooo"*.

"Oh my God, Nick. Are you okay?" Flailing arms and legs appear over the edge of the bed and materialize into Tina. She stands over me in only her underwear, breasts swaying with each frantic movement of her arms. "I'm so sorry. I didn't mean to push you."

I nod and force a smile. "I know," I say, holding a hand out, urging her closer. My breaths are coming steadily now, with no more owl noises to be heard, so I know what I need to do to fix this situation. "Come here." Her brows bunch in confusion. She hesitates, but eventually she takes a step, and then another. When she's close enough, I jackknife to a sitting position. "I'm fine. See?" I slide my hands up her legs, hook my fingers in her panties, and drag them down to the floor. "But you can still make it up to me, if you like." I guide her panties over her feet, then toss them aside before lifting one foot and dragging it over me so she's straddling my legs.

She shivers, and asks, "How can I make it up to you?"

"That's the best part," I say, wrapping my arms around her legs. "All you need to do is take a seat and I'll take care of the rest."

Chapter 13

WRESTLING WITH SWEATY DUDES

Tina

STANDING NAKED OVER NICK with my heart beating so hard I just saw my chest jump was not on my list of possible activities for this evening, but I can't say I'm disappointed with how things are turning out. Especially not now that his gigantic hands are squeezing my ass as he pulls me down to straddle his head. *God, I hope his tongue muscle works as well as the rest of his muscles seem to.* It's been so long since a man has had his face between my thighs. I don't think I could handle the disappointment of a poor oral performance tonight.

"And I better not hear any nonsense about suffocating me. I am a grown man. If a beautiful woman can't sit on my face without it killing me, then I deserve to die." He swipes a long slow lick over my sensitive clit and my eyes roll so far into my head I see stars. His arms wrap around my waist and he pulls me down hard against his face. "Yes, baby." His groan rumbles through my core, threatening to push me over the edge into ecstasy already. "I've been dreaming of this pussy since the day we met."

"Since you ran me over in the street, you mean?" I ask, my voice a breathy moan. He chuckles without easing up on his worship of me, circling my clit with the flat of his tongue even as he nods his reply. "Well, then," I gasp as he drives me higher, his tongue hot against my flesh. I reach down and grab his hair, forcing him to look at me. "I'm a giver, so I'll let you continue after that insult. But understand this." I grind against his face and grin at his answering groan. "I will never worry about suffocating a man after he's asked me to sit on his face. Because you're right." Another grind, and another groan from Nick, followed by his tongue making a slow circle of my clit. "If that man dies under me, he deserves it. And at least he died happy."

"So happy," Nick murmurs, the rumbling of his voice tickling me. "So *fucking* happy. Fuck, you taste good."

Without loosing my grip on his hair, I rock lazily against his mouth, loving the way he licks and flicks my clit with his tongue, the desire coiling in my belly until I'm panting with each breath. Nick's moans and groans spur me on, the mere sight of him as he devours me enough to drive my orgasm ever closer. When my rocking becomes more frenzied, Nick grabs my hips hard, sucks my clit into his mouth, and holds me against his face until finally I explode into a thousand sparkling pieces, clenching around nothing.

"Holy shit, that was amaz—" my words cut short when Nick slides me down his body as he sits up, presses me firmly to his waist, and stands with me in his arms all in one fluid motion. "What the hell? How did you do that?"

The kiss he presses to my lips is half grin. "Oh, kitten. I've wrestled with sweaty dudes three times your size. Picking you up off the floor is nothing."

My eyebrows rocket to my hairline. "Sweaty dudes, hey?"

Nick chuckles as he lays me across my bed. "Hazard of being a fighter. I've rolled around with a lot of sweaty dudes in my day. I have to say, though, it's way more fun rolling around with you." He drops a sucking kiss on my neck before settling his huge body between my legs, the weight of his erection heavy on my sensitive clit. "Not only that, you're a lot nicer to look at." He trails a hand up my side then palms my breast, rubbing his thumb over the hard tip, sending bolts of electricity through me. I tremble under his fingers. "And a hell of a lot nicer to touch."

He grinds his hips, pressing his length against me until I'm writhing beneath him, searching for more than the feel of him through his shorts. "Need you," I gasp between quick breaths. I slide my hands down his back and into the back of his shorts, digging my short nails into his ass cheeks and loving the way they flex in response as he presses into me harder. "Take these off," I say, releasing his ass and pushing at the waistband of his shorts. "Right now." When he doesn't immediately move, I add, "Don't make me punch you off this bed again."

Nick chuckles and presses a kiss to my lips, swiping his tongue against mine briefly before kneeling back and grinning down at me. He hooks his thumbs into the front of his shorts on either side of his erection, his blue eyes darkening. In one swift motion, he pulls the shorts up and over his cock, pushing the scrap of fabric to his knees before lowering himself over me once again. *And before I even got the chance to ogle him properly.* Which is unfortunate. Because from the glimpse I got, I know I'll need a much closer look, and soon.

"Shit," he whispers, wriggling against me awkwardly before bending his knee and reaching down to grab his shorts from his extended foot.

"Neat trick."

"You ain't seen nothing yet," he says with a wink as he drops the shorts next to me on the bed. "Just wait. I'm full of surprises." He laughs and pats a hand around the bed for a moment before sliding his body next to mine and turning to face me. He pushes the shorts off the side of the bed and drops something beside my head. The smile he gives me is tinged with guilt. "I need you to know that I didn't come here with this in mind. Not exactly, anyway. But I came prepared, because I was hopeful." He grabs the item he dropped by my head and shows me the strip of three condoms. "Very hopeful."

I grab the condoms and tear one off the strip, ripping it open with my teeth. "I have a confession to make," I whisper, taking Nick's erection in my empty hand and squeezing gently. The groan he makes when I stroke him deliberately is so sinful I have to bite back a groan of my own. *I could listen to that all day.* "I didn't tell Wade about the light tonight, because I wanted an excuse to call you. So I guess you could say I was hopeful, too."

Nick snaps a hand out, grabs the condom, rolls it on, and lowers himself over me, his now sheathed cock nudging my entrance. "Then I guess we're both getting what we wished for today." He pushes himself inside me, the wetness from my recent orgasm working to ease the way. Still, the stretch is just this side of painful, and my sharp intake of breath causes Nick to stop his momentum before he's fully seated.

"You okay?" His eyes full of concern, he looks down at me, holding the rest of his body still. "We can stop."

"Don't you dare stop," I hiss. "It's just been a while since anything that big has been in there. If I'd known you were moving to town, I'd have practiced with something a little bigger than old Solomon."

Nick pulls his cock away and I feel empty, hollow, like something is missing. "You're sleeping with an old guy named Solomon? I don't share, Tina."

I splutter a laugh. "What? No. Solomon is my dildo. I haven't slept with anyone in years."

He blows out a breath and lowers his head to my shoulder, covering me with his body as laughter rolls through him. "You named your dildo Solomon? What did you name your vibrator? Ezekial? Abraham?"

I grab his hair in a fist and pull his head away from my shoulder, growing irritated by his laughter. "No. His name is Robert." His eyes narrow in question. "Because he's my battery operated boyfriend."

His face lights with a grin when the information clicks. "Ha! I get it. Bob is short for Robert. Clever."

I shrug and give him a small smile. "I was running out of biblical names by the time I bought this one. Figured it was time to get traditional with it."

Nick settles into the cradle of my hips again, sliding his cock through my wetness, forcing a delicious shiver up my spine when he nudges my clit. He drops a soft kiss on my neck, then whispers, "I can't wait for you to tell me, in vivid detail, exactly how you burned through so many vibrators that you ran out of biblical names, but that'll have to wait. Because if I don't get inside you in the next three seconds—"

"Oh my God. Will you shut up and put your cock inside me alread—" Nick cuts me off by slamming his dick into me in one thrust, the force pushing me up the bed. I'm stretched wide and I love it. "Oh, fuck yes. Like that."

He pulls back, sliding out in slow motion before slamming back in roughly. "That's how you like it, Tina? You want me to be a little rough with you?"

I fist a hand in his hair and give a little tug. "I want to feel this tomorrow, Nick. So shut up and fuck me already. This isn't a tea party where we sit around gabbing and eating cucumber sandwiches."

His eyes darken as he stares down at me. "Yes, ma'am," he says as he hikes my leg over his shoulder, letting his hand drift down my thigh until he's hoisting me up by his grip on my ass. "Let me know if this gets to be too much." Nick thrusts into me again, this new position making him feel impossibly larger, and the snarky comment that was just on my lips melts away in the face of this new fullness.

He fucks me into the bed relentlessly, the sounds of my ragged breaths broken only by the slapping of his body against mine. Waves of pleasure tighten in my core, and tension coils in my belly as I fight to maintain some semblance of composure. *Another orgasm? Already? I'm not ready for this to be over.* My vibrators have never performed this well for me, hence the multitude I've burned through over the years. *Fuck.* Even the weight of him on top of me is perfect. Maybe I'll need more than one time to get him out of my system. Somehow, I don't think that would be so bad.

"Hey, where'd you go?" Nick grips my chin and turns my face to his. "I want you here with me for every moment."

Oh, shit. How'd I let my mind wander during this? It's too good to miss a second. "Sorry. I was... I was getting close, and I was thinking how I'm not ready for this to be over yet."

Nick's answering grin is full of wicked intent, yet still somehow adorably goofy. "Oh, honey. Don't worry about how close you are. This isn't over until I make you come at least three times." He slides out, then presses his length into me again, excruciatingly slowly this time, drawing a deep, rumbling moan from my throat. "Unless you have an objection to that?" Another slow retreat, followed by another long, slow thrust that has me moaning again. "No objections? Okay good." He presses a kiss to my lips. "Now be a good girl and come for me."

He slides his hand between us and with the barest brush of his thumb against my clit I come apart, my heart racing, my pulse pounding in my ears, my pussy squeezing around the thick length of him. I slam my eyes shut against the onslaught of fireworks—*Seriously? Fireworks? Who is this guy?*—and allow the ecstasy to roll over my body. A couple more of these orgasms, and I'll definitely feel this tomorrow. If I'm still alive, that is.

Before I can come down, Nick is flipping me over onto my stomach, grabbing my hips, and hoisting my ass in the air.

"Look at this gorgeous pussy," he whispers, his hot breath on my ass sending an involuntary shiver through me. "So fucking beautiful. I think I might need another taste." His tongue is hot on the sensitive flesh, but I don't get to enjoy it because as soon as it's there, it's gone again, replaced by his dick slipping into me. My arms give out and I collapse face down into the mattress. Nick's hands on my hips are the only thing keeping me from sprawling on my stomach in a heap of boneless limbs and quivering flesh. "That will have to be enough for now, though," he says, pushing his cock into me slowly, the angle of this position allowing him to get so much deeper. "You feel too damn good to spend another minute not buried inside you."

Nick sets a leisurely pace, pumping his hips with a speed that can only be described as suitable for a Sunday afternoon stroll in the park. Despite that, each thrust reaches the deepest parts of me, filling me like never before. The moans coming from my throat as I struggle to prop myself on my elbows sound foreign, the only familiar sound the rushing of the blood in my ears as it keeps time with Nick's relentless thrusting.

"Nothing has ever felt this good." I think I say.

"What's that, kitten?" Nick buries himself deep, pressing his hips to my ass, and waits for my answer.

"Nothing has ever felt this good," I repeat, loud enough for him to hear. "Do you have a magic penis or something?"

He chuckles, but doesn't reply, choosing instead to resume his thrusting. He leans over, pressing himself against my back, dropping a kiss on my shoulder, an act that's almost too intimate for the relationship I have with him. It's been a while, but fuck buddies, in my experience, don't spend a lot of time dropping kisses on body parts like shoulders. It's...nice.

"It's not magic, kitten. But it feels like it for me, too. I could stay inside you like this forever. The way you're gripping me, sucking me in, begging me for more. It's damn near perfection." His hand moves from my hip and settles between my legs. "The only thing better is the way you squeeze me so tight when you're coming all over my cock." He punctuates the last word by slamming into me while stroking my clit in a firm circle, forcing a wave of bliss to rush screaming up my body, showers of sparks lighting my eyelids from the back as spasms of ecstasy course through me. "Fuck, YES!" Nick's voice is distant, even as I feel him jerking and pulsing his release into me. "Tina..fuck...baby..."

Chapter 14

"XXL? That's Vanity Sizing. Right?"

Nick

My heart is still racing as I stumble out of Tina's bedroom, my legs shaking as I make this annoying trip to the bathroom. But, thanks to coming harder than I've ever come in my life, and nearly overflowing the condom currently tied off in my hand, I need to find a trash can. After that, though, I'm heading right back into that bedroom and curling myself around the woman I left snoring just a moment ago, after I let down her hair and took off her glasses.

Next time I get inside her, I want her undone from the start. Just the thought of her riding me, her hair a wild halo of dark curls around her head, has blood rushing back to my dick. But I'm not an animal. I can wait until Tina is ready. For now, I'll just relive the last hour of what will no doubt go down in history as the best sex of my life.

Fuck, that was amazing. I admit I was a little worried when she passed out after coming that last time, but when I heard the first little snore slip past her lips, I knew she would be okay. And I am definitely okay. More than okay, if a little wobbly. Somehow, I'm more worn out by this evening with Tina than I was during my last three fights combined. I'm a lot less beat up, though. And way more satisfied.

I stumble the rest of the way to the bathroom, which is mercifully only a few steps away, drop the condom in the trash, then make my way back to the bedroom to find that Tina in the same position as when I left her, she hasn't moved a muscle. The way the sheet drapes over her body, barely covering the delicious curves I know are underneath, causes a stirring in my still softening dick. If I weren't so invested in letting Tina get some rest, I'd be waking her for that third orgasm I promised. But after the way she passed out after the last one, I know she needs some sleep. I'll take care of number three in the morning. After switching off the overhead light, I crawl into bed behind her and gather her into my arms, burying my face in her mass of dark hair, inhaling the heady scent of her coconut shampoo mixed with the pizza smell from her restaurant. I blow out a breath and pull her closer, loving the way her ass cradles my dick as she presses into me.

Tina sighs and melts into my arms.

"I could get used to this," I whisper, squeezing her even closer. "You feel amazing."

She stirs, looking over her shoulder at me. "You don't feel so bad yourself." She wiggles her ass, the soft cushion of her cheeks settling on either side of my now mostly hard cock, forcing a groan from my lips.

I slide a hand up and palm her breast, pinching her nipple, rolling it between my thumb and finger until it's hard enough to cut glass. "You are so fucking sexy."

She splutters a laugh and spins in my arms, turning to face me. "Me? Have you seen me?" She gestures to her face and hair. "My hair is a frizzy nightmare, and I've got these chubby cheeks. You probably can't even see my eyes right now because I have to squint to see your face three inches away."

My stomach drops at the thought of this woman not understanding that she's the most beautiful woman on the planet. With the way she told off that idiot bus driver, and then me, the other day, I thought she must know exactly how gorgeous she is. How has she gotten this far in her life without realizing she's the literal embodiment of a goddess? It's unforgivable. Luckily, she has me now. I'll make it my life's work if I have to, but I will convince her she is the most beautiful woman on the planet.

"Tina, baby," I say, sliding a hand up underneath her hair. "Every damn thing about you is the most beautiful I've ever seen. Your hair is dark and luxurious, the curls just begging to be wrapped around my hand." I fist a hand in her hair and tilt her head back, loving the gasp that comes from her lips at the slight tug. "Your eyes are the most gorgeous brown I've ever seen, like rich coffee I'd be happy to drown in." Her eyes widen slightly, though admittedly she still squints in order to see me, and her breath catches. "And your cheeks may be a little chubby, but I wouldn't have it any other way. They make you look mischievous, like you're up to something, and I, for one, am dying to know what that is." I drop a kiss to her nose, then another on her lips. "That you have all that on top of a lush body? Ass cheeks that fit perfectly in my hands? Perfectly dimpled and creamy thighs? Tits that sway so enticingly when you're grinding your pussy on my face? Well, I'm sure you can understand why I've been obsessed with you since the day we met."

She surges forward, closing the distance between us, and kisses me greedily, thrusting her tongue in my mouth, grabbing my face in her hands. She pushes me to my back, her naked body straddling mine as she devours my lips. When slides her hips, rubbing her wetness over me, I groan at the contact. Apparently, Tina needed very little rest after all.

"Condom?" She pants against my mouth as she pats a hand over the bed. "Ugh. Where the hell did they go?"

I chuckle and lean to the side, grabbing a condom from the nightstand where I stashed them when I tucked Tina in a few minutes ago. "This what you're looking for?"

"Yes. Give it here." She snatches the condom from my hand and brings it close to her face, squinting to read the package. "XXL? You're joking."

I bring my hands up and fold them under my head, throwing her a cocky grin. "What's the matter, baby? We already know you can handle it." I pump my hips beneath her, loving the way my dick feels nestled next to her heat, but my enjoyment will need to wait. The way Tina squints her eyes while attempting to scowl forces another laugh from me.

"Why are you laughing? You're the one buying huge condoms to feed your ego."

My mouth drops open as I scoff, then laugh again. "Excuse me, kitten. You and I both know it's not for my ego." I pump my hips and relish the soft moan that falls from Tina's lips when my dick presses against her. I take my hands out from under my head and run them up her legs, letting them come to rest on her hips. "But honestly, getting the right size is important. I had a... uh... I had a few close calls in my younger years before I realized that with condoms, size does matter." After my second time fishing a lost condom out of a girl I barely knew, I learned to buy the proper size.

"But- but-" she stutters. "I've seen adults stick their entire arms in regular condoms for demonstration, for crying out loud. And as impressive as this is"—she wiggles on me, sliding her wet heat along my dick, and it's my turn to groan—"it's not as big as an arm." She cocks an eyebrow, as though daring me to disagree. I do her one better, sitting up and wrapping my arms around her, taking her mouth in a deep kiss, and making her melt in my arms.

"It might not be as big as an arm, but it should still do the trick." I pull the condom from her fingers and flick it in the air. "What do you think? Should we test it out? You know, for scientific purposes."

She purses her lips, making a show of thinking it over before she takes the condom back and rips it open. "I think we have to. For science, of course."

Tina makes quick work of rolling the condom down my length, her hot little hands teasing my length. With a hitch of her hips and her hands on my chest, she pushes me back onto the bed, lowering herself on my cock gradually, inch by inch, a mewling noise coming from her throat when she reaches the bottom. She rocks her hips, settling into an easy pace. Her hands press down on me, blunt nails digging into my pecs as she uses me for leverage, uses me for pleasure. Every muscle in my body is on fire, the feel of being buried inside her almost too good, too much. The way she moves is electric, her ecstasy clear on her face. Every roll of her hips makes my balls tighten, and it's all I can do to hold back the orgasm building at the base of my spine.

"Fuck, Tina. The feel of you sliding down my cock...it's... uhhhh, babe. I can't hold back much longer."

"Good," she says, lifting on her knees before slamming back down over me. "I want to watch you come apart. I want to see the look on your face when you're filling me." She lifts her hips again, then drops and makes a circle, forcing another groan from my throat. She tightens around me, her pussy clenching with every shift of her hips, pushing me closer to the point of no return. "Oh, fuck. I'm so close."

I strain to hold back, trying and failing to keep unsexy images in my mind long enough to stave off my orgasm for at least a minute. *Hungry puppies, sad clowns, that time I got a black eye so bad during a fight it busted open and I had to finish the fight blind.* Fuck, it's not working.

"Help me, Nick. Make me feel it."

I plant my feet on the bed, grab Tina's hips, and pump up into her, pushing in deep. Tingles shoot up my spine as Tina clamps down hard and screams her release. *Fuck, yes. Now I can come.* I fuck into her again and again, driving my hips until finally I explode. One last thrust has me burying myself balls deep, and I pull Tina down to my mouth, kissing the fuck out of her as my body threatens to overfill yet another condom.

Moments later, Tina is laying on my chest, her breath coming in little pants. Having her wrapped in my arms is nearly as good as the feel of the aftershocks of her orgasm as they squeeze my dick. *Just a few more minutes, then I'll get up and get rid of the condom. Just a little longer.*

Tina takes the initiative before I'm ready by disentangling from me herself, removing the condom and tying it off, then standing next to the bed. The light from the living room illuminates her from the back, highlighting her delicious curves, her hair a wild tangle of curls that I already want to sink my hands into again. She turns to open a dresser drawer, returning with a t-shirt that she pulls over her head. When it settles around her hips, leaving the bottom swell of her ass exposed, my dick stirs again. She leans past me and drops the condom in a trashcan I hadn't seen earlier, before grabbing her glasses from the nightstand and slipping them on her face.

"Oh, no," Tina says, wagging a finger when she catches sight of my growing erection. "Don't even think about it. I need some water, a snack, and possibly an ice bath before that guy gets near this little lady again." She points to the apex of her thighs. "I may have been a little too ambitious when I thought I could ride that bad boy twice in a row after such a long hiatus."

My stomach drops at the thought that I've hurt her. *Idiot. How could you be so stupid?* I throw myself out of the bed and wrap my arms around her.

"I am so sorry, Tina. What can I do? I can't believe I did this to you." I release her and spin around in a panic, looking for my shorts on the floor. "Let me get you some ice." I drop to my hands and knees and search the floor. I finally spy them just under the edge of the bed. Standing, I pull them up my legs and over my hips before reaching for Tina again. "I'm sorry."

She tangles her hands in my hair and pulls my face to hers, forcing me to look in her eyes. "You have nothing to be sorry for," she says against my mouth, before kissing my lower lip. "I'm a grown up, and I knew I would be sore afterward. I wanted it, remember?" She waits until I nod my understanding. I hear her, but I still feel awful about hurting her and I promise myself to be more gentle next time. "Good. Now that that's settled, let's talk about more important matters. For starters, I'm dying to know how you fit three condoms *and* your giant dick in those tiny shorts?"

Chapter 15

A Money Bin And An Ice Machine

Tina

"So..." Chloe leans over the counter, grinning like a Cheshire cat. I almost wonder what's got her looking so smug, but the soreness between my legs makes it hard to be curious. It's taking every ounce of brain power I've got to concentrate on the dough being kneaded in the industrial mixer and the sauce simmering on the stove. I don't have the mental capacity to guess what's going on in her head. Especially not when I suspect I already know. "I was grabbing breakfast at the Easy Swallow this morning, and I heard something very interesting."

"Oh?" I keep my reply short, hoping she'll drop it. I'm not sure I'm ready to talk about what happened with Nick last night. I'd like to keep that for myself for a little longer, if possible.

"Yeah. Some members of the Tit Peepers birdwatch group were fueling up before heading out in search of some rare bird that's been sighted near here and wouldn't you know, the Woodcocks caught sight of something even more interesting on their way to the diner? Care to guess what it was?"

"I'm surprised they can see anything at all past the glare coming off their brilliant turquoise windbreakers." Turning off the mixer, I heave the huge metal bowl from its cradle and dump the contents onto my prep station. "Never mind those bright orange sun visors. It's a miracle they can see at all wearing those eyesores."

Chloe laughs, heading over to turn on the tap in the hand wash sink. "I love their windbreakers. An army of elderly people in matching windbreakers is pretty much the most adorable thing I can think of." She scrubs her hands and arms thoroughly before drying them and joining me at the prep table. "But it sounds to me like you're trying to change the subject. Don't worry, though. I remember what we were talking about." Chloe grabs a stack of sheet pans and lines them up. "Care to share with the class why the Woodcocks saw a giant man in tiny shorts leaving your apartment early this morning?"

"Ugh. Those Woodcocks. I bet they're the ones behind that damn Nosy Pecker newsletter." I turn a syrupy smile on Chloe. "Would you believe me if I said he was here changing the lightbulb outside my apartment?"

She laughs. "I would if I believed you turned it off this morning before you came down. But I suspect, since you haven't turned it off once in the last five years, that it's still burned out. And, if it's still burned out, that means the giant man in the tiny shorts leaving your apartment at the crack of dawn this morning was up there for some other reason." She taps a finger to her lip. "I wonder what that reason could be?"

I ignore her questions, instead grabbing my bench scraper to separate the pile of dough into smaller pieces, which Chloe then forms into balls and places onto pans for proofing.

Chloe bumps me with her shoulder after a few minutes of silence and laughs. "So...? What's up with that? I could have sworn you were telling me all about how you don't date just the other day."

"I don't date." As much fun as I had with Nick last night, I still have no interest in dating.

"Oh really? What was last night, then?"

I dust the flour from my hands and turn to face Chloe. She's giving me that damn cat grin again, and I can't help but smile in return. *Fine, I guess I can share a little bit. It was pretty amazing, after all.* "Last night was sex. Some of the best sex I've ever had, but still... just sex."

She pinches her lips together. "Does he know that?"

I shake my head and hold back a laugh. "Of course he does. Have you seen the women he's dated? Trust me, Nick has no interest in me other than what we did last night."

Chloe cocks an eyebrow but says nothing, and I'm thankful to not have to explain any further. I'm content in my bigger body, but that doesn't mean I want to explain why other people might not be. Thankfully, she drops it.

Together, we finish placing the last of the dough balls on the trays, then take them to the walk-in fridge to store until we need them. When that's done, we prep all the vegetables for the workstation. All that's left now is to prepare tonight's menu for Nick and his trainers, but that can wait. Right now, I need coffee.

I pour us each a cup and take a seat at a table by the front window.

"What are you up to today?"

Every day, Chloe comes in to help with prep work before heading out to work on some of her art contracts for the afternoon. Even on nights when Carson is working, she comes back in time for the non-existent dinner rush, more to keep us company more than anything else. It's a good thing my rent is so low, or I'd never be able to afford to keep her on full-time. There's one more thing to thank Uncle Gianni slash Wade Biddescombe for. I'm pretty sure that man really is my guardian angel.

"What are you working on today?"

She cringes, her shoulders rising to meet her ears. "I'm heading over to Spitz to discuss painting a mural at their sportsplex," she says in a hushed voice.

Spitz Hollow, neighboring town and sworn enemy of Tuft Swallow. Telling a Swallower you're going there by choice usually leads to some serious side-eye, if not worse. I've seen some of the older folks around town spit at the mere mention of Spitz Hollow, as though they were warding off some ancient evil. I can understand why Chloe would want to keep her trip there under wraps. Still, she can't afford to turn down art jobs. I know she doesn't want to work for me at Wings and Pizza forever. She's an artist, not a chef.

"That's so exciting." I say, adding a little extra cheer to my voice, so she knows I'm on her side about her taking commissions wherever she can get them. "How did that come about?"

She shrugs. "Someone from that fancy new sports complex was in town for a meeting with Nick and saw my mural at the gym. They want *something that represents the Spitz-Shein spirit* or something like that. I'm presenting them with my proposal this afternoon."

"That's amazing. What do you have planned?" She groans and rolls her eyes. "Uh oh. That bad?"

"The guy couldn't tell me anything about the Spitz-Shein spirit that would actually make decent artwork. They're only interested in money." She grabs her portfolio and slips out a series of sketches, spreading them on the table in front of me. "I've been wracking my brain since they contacted me and this is the only thing I could come up with."

A rough sketch in charcoal, coins as far as the eye can see, stares back at me. "Is this... Is this the inside of the money bin? Like in *Duck Tales*?"

Chloe drops her head to the tabletop, a pained groan emanating from her lips. "Kind of. It's also partly based on the cave of wonders in *Aladdin*. See the jewels? And the statues?" She rests her chin on her hands and looks up at me. "After listening to that guy drone on for almost an hour, the only image I could conjure in my mind was of him trying to swim in piles of gold coins." She tips her chin at the papers. "It took me a week to come up with that."

I stifle a grin. "It's cute."

"It's shit."

I bark a laugh and Chloe holds back a smile. "It's not that bad. It looks very... *opulent*?" She releases her laugh at my questioning tone, and we both giggle until tears mark matching streams down our cheeks.

"Well, hopefully opulent is what they're going for," she says once we've finally calmed down. "Or maybe not. I don't know if I want to paint this mural. I mean, really. Gold coins and dollar bills? That's boring. I know I need to be willing to commercialize my art if I want to make a living from it, but at least with the mural at the gym and the windows around town, I had fun. This won't be fun."

"Then don't do it."

She slumps back in her chair and heaves a sigh. "I said I would present my proposal, so I will. Maybe they'll hate it."

"Or maybe they'll love it and you'll spend the next month painting Scrooge McDuck's wet dream on some rich asshole's ego project. I'm sorry, *charitable donation*."

"Ugh. That sounds awful." She pulls her phone from the front pocket of her paint stained overalls. "Damn it. I have to leave now if I want to make it in time." After gathering her sketches and putting them back into the leather portfolio, she chugs the rest of her coffee and stands. "I'll be back in time for you to deliver the order to the gym. And don't think I'm letting you off the hook. We will revisit the Nick conversation later. Before I read all about it in the Nosy Pecker, I hope."

I roll my eyes. "There's nothing to talk about. We had sex, he went home, the end. There's nothing more the Nosy Pecker could possibly report."

"Then what's that about?" she asks, pointing to the door.

Right then, Nick knocks on the glass door and waves, making my stomach drop into a fluttery mess of butterflies. He holds up the biggest bouquet I've ever seen, the blooms a riot of color.

"That doesn't look like a man who knows you don't date. That looks like a man who's here to *woo*."

Looking at Nick through the window, his smile adorably huge, I can see that Chloe isn't wrong. That is a man intent on wooing. He's wearing those snug jeans again, and the way they hug his thighs sends a flurry of not safe for work images flashing through my brain. A full body flush races through me as I mentally flip through some of the most memorable moments from last night.

"Uh huh. That's what I thought. Just sex, hey?" Chloe asks with a smirk. "We're *definitely* talking about this later. Right now, though, I need to go. Better gather your wits, and wipe up that drool"—she dabs a finger at the corner of her mouth — "because I'm letting him in."

She leaves me sitting at the table and lets Nick in as she goes. I'm still flushing hot all over when he sits across from me, laying the bunch of flowers on the table between us.

"Hey," he says, the grin on his face growing wider. "How are you feeling? I wasn't sure if I should bring flowers or ice. I settled on the flowers, since I'm pretty sure you have an ice machine around here somewhere."

An awkward giggle escapes my lips, and I try to tamp down this strange nervousness in my belly. *It was just sex, Tina. Calm down. You've had sex before without turning into a tittering schoolgirl.* But was it just sex? Can it be called that when it's with such an attentive lover?

This morning Nick woke me by cuddling up to my back while attempting to not stab me with his hard-on. While I appreciated the gesture, I had no interest in a chaste morning cuddle. I pushed him onto his back and put the third condom he brought last night to good use. Then he flipped me over and put his tongue to even better use. It was, by far, the best morning I've had in years. Not to mention, I slept like the dead following a night filled with the best sex I'd ever had.

But enough of that. It was just sex. Excellent sex. Still, just sex. I need to remember that. I can't go letting sex endorphins dick-notize me into a relationship where I'm responsible for looking after a grown ass man. Because look at him. With his floppy blonde hair, his brilliant smile, and the way he runs around in those tiny shorts half the time, he will no doubt need looking after at some point. And I sure as shit don't want to be the one who's doing the looking after.

"Thanks, Nick. You're right, I do have an ice machine. But I'm fine. You didn't need to come check on me."

He smiles again, that big stupid grin almost infectious enough to get me to smile back at him. "Well, to be fair, I didn't come here strictly to check on you. I actually wanted to ask you something."

Oh, shit.

Please don't say it. Please don't say it.

"I had an amazing time last night. And I'm pretty sure you did, too. Right?"

I nod, hoping this isn't going where I think it is. If he's already hoping for more, we won't be able to continue just having fun. It wouldn't be fair to him. "Yeah, it was fun."

He chuckles and shakes his head. "It was fun. And I would love to do it again sometime. But maybe next time I can take you out first?"

Nick looks so hopeful that it almost hurts when I blow out a breath and say, "I'm sorry, Nick. That won't be possible."

His face drops, and even though he's still handsome, I almost miss his big grin. "Not possible? What... uh... what do you mean?"

"Maybe I should have told you this before last night, but Nick? I don't date."

Chapter 16

NOT MADE FOR CORNHOLE

Nick

"AT ALL?"

"That's what she said."

I left Tina's restaurant with a fake smile on my face, and the crushing weight of disappointment slowing my steps. I'd needed to change and step into the ring with Rhett for some sparring before I'd calmed down enough to talk it through. I wasn't angry, but I was confused.

Scratch that. I *am* confused.

And it seems like Rhett is confused, too. "Like, *at all*, at all? Did she say why?"

I shrug, swiping a towel over my forehead. "No. All she said is that she doesn't date. Then she told me she had a bunch of work to do and said she'd see me around." She didn't even look at me when she rejected me, just waved me off and went back to work.

Rhett laughs, slapping me on the shoulder as he walks by me to his locker. "Shit, dude. You got dismissed. I guess you didn't live up to her expectations last night. Relying too much on boat size and not putting enough motion in the ocean?"

I throw my sweaty towel at him, hitting him squarely in the face, laughing at his splutter of outrage. "There's plenty of motion in my ocean. Don't you worry about that."

"So, what is it then? You were on cloud nine when you strolled out of here earlier with plans to ask her out. I can't imagine you're willing to throw in the towel"—he coughs a laugh and throws my towel back at me—"yet. So now what?"

"Right now, I need to grab a shower and get ready for my lesson with Peter. As for what I'll do about Tina? I'm not entirely sure. She said she doesn't date. I don't think pressuring her will change her mind."

Rhett laughs as he strips to head to the shower. "I didn't mean that you should pressure her. I was thinking more along the lines of wooing her a little. Charm her. Show her what it would be like to date you. I know you're a giant, but I also know underneath all that muscle there's a big-hearted guy looking for a woman to love and treat right." He leaves me with that thought and heads to the showers.

My stomach clenches in response to his words. He's right. I am looking for a woman I can love. The women I dated in the past weren't interested in settling in a small town like Tuft Swallow, and I knew if I wanted to build my gym and raise my family here, I'd probably have better luck finding a life partner in Tuft Swallow than I would in a city like Las Vegas. I could never live with myself if a woman agreed to move here to make me happy, and then she spent the rest of her life miserable and full of resentment.

But Tina seems to like it here.

But that's not the only reason I'm interested in her. She's amazing. If she's in the room, I have a hard time keeping my eyes off her. When she's not in the room, I have a hard time concentrating on anything else.

And then there's what happened last night. The way she pulled my hair and rode my face with such wild abandon? That was the sexiest thing I've ever seen. All I could think was she was right, and if any man died while she was on top of him like that, he *would* die a happy man.

And I better stop that line of thought right now, or I'll never get out of this change room. I can't go strolling up to Peter with a hard-on, saying I'm ready for my lesson. He would kill me, and not because he'd care if he were next to a man who had an erection. No, he'd kill me for not showing cornhole the respect it deserves.

To Peter, disrespecting the game of cornhole is the gravest of insults. One that will send him walking out of here in a huff, instead of sticking around to help me with my cornhole game like I pay him for. And I need the help. Badly.

There's also the fact that having a hard-on with no relief in sight can get more than a little uncomfortable. I hunch over on the bench and take deep breaths. *Puppies that are too skinny, lonely senior citizens buying a suspicious amount of canned cat food, parents who abandon their kids.* With a few minutes of focus on some of the more unpleasant things I've encountered in the world, my hard-on subsides, so I strip and take myself to the shower. As long as I don't dwell on thoughts of Tina, I'll make it through my day without much hardship.

With only minutes to spare, I get dressed and head out to set up for my lesson with Peter. I'm already setting up the board at the far end of the gym when he arrives.

"Ready to get this show on the road? I don't have all day to dilly dally."

I chuckle at his abruptness. You'd think I was making him clean toilets for how distasteful he finds it here. I mean, I know I suck at cornhole, but the gym is still nice. And he seems to enjoy the snacks we provide in the staff room. After my lesson, he usually finds a reason to stick around. There must be something big going on today if he's in a rush to get out of here. And figuring out what it is sounds like exactly what I need to distract me from the ever present thoughts of Tina.

"Oh? Why's that? You got a big date?"

Instead of the disgruntled protest I'm expecting, Peter gives a half-hearted laugh and looks away, but not before I catch the grin on his face. He clears his throat with a phlegmy cough. "Never you mind what I'm up to, you overgrown oaf. Better you concentrate on your throw than worry about what I'm doing with my time. I'm not the one who can't toss a bean bag to save his life."

"Oh, yeah. You bet," I say with an exaggerated nod. "So... what's her name?"

"I-I-I... Never mind. I've been waiting my whole life for this, and refuse to mess it up by telling tales now."

Holy shit. He can't be talking about... No. Not after all this time. Unless... "Peter? Is it *her?*"

Peter's head snaps in my direction and suddenly he can't keep the smile off his face. "Shhh." He puts a finger to his mouth to shush me. "Don't jinx it."

Impulsively, I pull Peter in for a hug. He clears his throat aggressively, and I pat his back before releasing him. "That's fantastic. But how?"

He shrugs, his smile back on his face. "She moved into Spring Chickens a couple of weeks ago. One thing led to another until the other night, when we were sharing a pot of tea after dinner, we talked. Nick," he says, his smile even bigger now, "it was like no time had passed."

"That's wonderful, Peter. But—and please tell me to piss off if I'm way out of line here—what about what happened after the championship? I thought she chose your rival after he beat you?"

The glare Peter sends my way could strip paint. But after a moment, he softens. "It was a different time," he says by way of explanation. "I won't go into details, because Sarah wouldn't want that, but suffice it to say, she had no other choice."

"Sarah? As in, Sarah from the seniors' class, Sarah?"

Peter nods. I was wondering why he'd started coming to the class. Looks like he was getting closer to the love of his life.

After the stories I'd heard, and from what I've learned about Peter these last few months, I wouldn't have expected he'd be the kind of man to forgive so readily. After all, he'd sworn off the sport he'd become a champion in and refused to marry at all after this Sarah woman had broken his heart. Whatever reason she had to up and leave him the way she did must've been a doozy. And whatever it was, it's none of my business. If Peter accepts it and has forgiven her, that's enough for me. I'm just happy he's found love finally.

"I'm thrilled for you, Peter."

"Thanks, kid." His eyes get misty as he looks off into the distance.

I watch him struggle to bring the grumpy look back to his face and barely manage to contain my laughter. If he needs to be a tough guy to coach, then let him be a tough guy.

"That's enough about me. Let's get to this lesson. I see you haven't shrunk those bat wings like I told you." He pokes me in the side. "I've been thinking, since you can't seem to do what I tell you, then we need to find a new way. You probably won't like it. And you'll look like more of an idiot than you already do, but I think it just might work."

For the next hour, Peter has me work on a two-handed throw. Over and over, I bend at the hips, swing my arms between my legs, and release the bean bag in the general direction of the board. And just like during every other cornhole lesson, I miss every time.

Every. Damn. Time.

"Damn it," I mutter after my latest throw flies wide and lands behind the reception desk. "I feel like a kid going bowling for the first time with this technique."

Peter's guffaw echoes across the near-empty gym. "While you might look like one, a kid going bowling for the first time at least gets the ball all the way down the lane once or twice. Your aim is even worse this way, if that's possible."

"Yeah, I think you're right. But how? I'm facing the board and swinging the bean bag through my legs. It shouldn't be possible for me to throw the bean bag this far in the wrong direction." I gesture to the bean bag on the floor behind the reception desk. "The only way I could get further from the board is if I throw the damn bag backward."

Peter rubs a thumb and forefinger over his stubbled chin. "I can't wrap my head around it. You've thwarted every method I've tried teaching you. Are you sure you ain't *trying* to miss?" He cocks a bushy gray eyebrow in question. "Because the only time I've ever seen anyone mess up this badly is when they were trying to throw a match."

I stoop to grab the bean bag and jog back to where Peter waits. "No way. No. Get that out of your head right now. I would never throw a match. I have too much integrity for that."

"How would you explain it, then? Because I'm stumped."

I scrub a hand through my hair in frustration. "I don't know what to tell you, Peter. I really am trying to get the bean bag in the hole. Why is this game so hard?"

Peter's grin takes up half his face, which would startle me if I hadn't already seen him smile a few times today. Whatever else this mysterious Sarah from the past has done, she's made him a happier man. "It takes a real athlete to play cornhole, kid. Some overgrown steroid freak in tights who gets paid to dance around without the courage to sing at the same time just ain't cut out for it, I guess."

It's a sign of my frustration level that I let Peter's usual anti-wrestling rant get to me. "Damn it, Peter. I was never a wrestler. I was a mixed martial arts fighter. A master of several fighting styles. An undefeated heavyweight champion. I did one stint on a professional wrestling program as a PR stunt. And I didn't wear tights, I wore wrestling jeans. Oh, and I am not now, nor have I ever been on steroids." I suck in a breath and continue. "Now, can we get back to the lesson? Because I have enough shit on my mind without listening to you whine about how wrestling is Broadway's crappy cousin."

Peter pats his hands in a placating manner. "Okay, okay. Don't get your tiny shorts in a twist, kid. We can get back to the lesson if you like. But first, you just gave me an idea."

"I'm not wearing tights and singing you something from *Wicked*, Peter. There will be no 'Defying Gravity' around here."

Peter scoffs. "Pshh, as if you could ever hold a candle to the incomparable Idina Menzel and Kristin Chenoweth."

"Maybe not, but I can lip sync with the best of them. Regardless, it's not Broadway night at Put Up Your Ducks MMA. Tell me your idea. I'll do pretty much anything if it helps my cornhole game."

Peter hobbles to a bench and sits down. "You'll hate it. But it might help. It probably would have helped me all those years ago."

I drop to the floor in front of him, elbows on my knees. "Okay, then I'm game. What'd you have in mind?"

"You need to talk about what's bothering you."

I stare at him, dumbfounded. *How does he know that?*

"Why would you think something's bothering me?"

He laughs. "Come on, kid. You've been distracted all day. I made you throw the bean bag from between your legs, for crying out loud. When have you ever seen a self-respecting cornholer do that? I was messing with you."

That son of a bitch. I bark a laugh. "You asshole. I thought that seemed weird."

He holds his phone up and shakes it at me. "Thanks to that nice girl from the reception desk, I also have video evidence of the whole thing. Now I'll never stop laughing."

I drop my head between my arms, chuckling until my shoulders shake. "I'm sure it made for some interesting footage."

"Indeed, it did." He chuckles as he slides his phone back into his pocket. "Now. Spill. What's your problem?"

I heave a sigh. "You're not going to drop this, are you?" I like Peter, but I'm not sure I want to share all my lady problems with him. Not after his cornhole lesson was somewhat effective at keeping thoughts of Tina from my mind. "Okay, fine. Here goes."

I spend some time detailing my reasons for moving back to Tuft Swallow, my history with dating, and finally, without getting into specifics, what happened with Tina last night and earlier today. He nods and makes noises in appropriate places, barely raising an eyebrow when I tell him I forgot to change the lightbulb so the entrance to Tina's apartment is still dark. When it's clear that I've stopped, Peter slaps his hands on his thighs and stands.

"Well. There's your answer."

My eyes betray my puzzlement. "What's my answer?"

"You need to convince that girl to give you a chance."

My heart swells inside my rib cage. What I wouldn't give for that to be possible. I shake my head and look at Peter. "She was pretty clear when she said that she doesn't date."

He rolls his eyes before shooting me a meaningful look. "And is that all you want? To *date* her?"

An idea takes shape in my brain, of Tina and me together, in my house, in my kitchen. She's teaching me to cook and laughing her ass off at every foolish mistake I make while sneaking peeks at the sparkling ring on her left ring finger. Jared's there, laughing right along with her, reminding me that in his years as an unsupervised child, he did all his own cooking, and the image both breaks my heart and makes me long to reach out and grab it with both hands.

"No, Peter. That's not all I want."

Peter grins from ear to ear. "That's what I like to hear. All that's left now is to figure out how to do it."

The more I think about it, the more I love the sound of it. But there's still one thing I'm curious about. "How's this supposed to help my cornhole game?"

Peter barks a laugh and shakes his head. "Oh, no. That's a lost cause. I wouldn't normally say this to anyone, but Nick? You're beyond hope. It's probably time you thought about giving up cornhole. Talk to the team and see if they'll let you be the water boy or something. Because mark my words, if they let you play, you all will lose every match. Every single one." He rubs his hands together, a gleam in his eye. "That's enough chatter. Let's spend the rest of our lesson time working out how you can convince your lady to want more with you. Because lord knows having you throw bean bags isn't getting us anywhere."

Chapter 17

CONVERSATIONAL NINJA WIZARD

Tina

"Was it weird? Tell me you didn't make it weird."

Chloe held off on grilling me until after we'd finished today's prep work, and I was hoping she'd be kind enough to drop the matter all together. After throwing out six dozen eggs that had spoiled well before their best by date, and arguing with my supplier about it over the phone for more than half an hour before he'd agree to refund me, I'm in no mood to talk about anything that happened yesterday.

Clearly, Chloe has no interest in letting me off the hook easily. She wants the dirt, and she wants it now.

Luckily, or unluckily for Chloe, I suppose, there isn't any dirt to tell her. Nick wasn't at the gym when I went to deliver the order.

"He wasn't there. Demetrius helped me set out the food, then I left. When I came back here to relieve Carson, I had another date waiting for me."

Chloe stifles a laugh. "Another one? I didn't realize there were that many men in Tuft Swallow trawling the dating sites looking for love. How did Carson handle being alone for a little while when you made the delivery? Sorry again that I didn't make it back to town in time."

I wave off her apology. "Carson was great, as always. More responsible than I ever was at his age, actually. Hiring him was the best business decision I've ever made. Besides hiring you, anyway." She rolls her eyes at my praise, the same as she always does. "But to answer your other question, I'm pretty sure there aren't that many men in Tuft Swallow. This was another finance guy from Spitz Hollow. He told me all about his *big important job* at Spitz-Shein before I could get a word in. The look on his face when I told him we didn't have a date was hilarious. He was all—" I screw my face up into an over the top rictus of confusion, garnering a snicker from Chloe. "He couldn't comprehend that even after his self-aggrandizing speech, I didn't want to date him. He called himself a 'high value man'. Can you believe that?"

Her mouth opens wide in shock. "Shut up. He did not."

I burst into laughter as I nod. "He really did. I promise."

She splutters through her laughter, "I thought only douchey podcasters said that. You know, as part of their alpha male schtick. I didn't think a real man would ever think that."

"I'm not sure finance bros count as real men, Chloe." I snicker again, thinking of the look on the guy's face as he repeated his claims. His indignation was palpable. If I didn't need to get started on an order, I'd have watched him cycle through all the shades of purple for a few more minutes. It was almost pretty, like watching the sky come alive when you can see the northern lights. "Luckily, when he realized he wasn't getting the reaction he wanted from me, he wandered away, still muttering about his high value status."

She slumps back in her seat, blowing out a long breath. "You're lucky he left on his own. What if he'd been dangerous? You need to sort this shit out, and the sooner, the better."

"Oh, come on. You can't be serious?" Instead of an answer, Chloe stares at me, a stony expression on her face. "Chloe, the guy smelled like cheese puffs and off-brand energy drinks. He probably lives in his mother's basement."

She gathers our coffee cups and stands. "You don't know anything about that guy. If he believed the high value thing, maybe he subscribes to other incel propaganda. He could think it's his right to date whomever he wants, and that he has the right to force you."

A shiver runs through me before I can catch myself. I honestly hadn't thought that much about it. But what if Chloe's right? How lucky have I been that all these dates have taken no for an answer? What happens if the next one doesn't? "I guess I'd better get to the bottom of this situation then," I say with a nervous laugh.

"Hmm." Chloe walks to the dish sink and sets our cups inside before turning to face me again. "What if I take tonight's delivery over to the gym, so you can stay here in case another date shows up? Maybe if he's not a complete idiot like the last guy, you can convince him to let you see the app where you're supposedly setting up these dates. You might be able to track down the perpetrator that way."

"Is that a good idea? I'll be alone here with some strange dude again." I'm not overly concerned, but what Chloe says makes some sense. I've listened to enough true crime podcasts to know that hanging around with a potentially dangerous person doesn't usually end well. There's something to be said for trusting your gut.

"I doubt anyone would be dumb enough to try anything here, not with the police station a couple of doors down." She shrugs. "But maybe get Carson to come in again, just in case. It's probably better if you're not alone. Plus, Carson can always use the hours."

Carson's parents, if you can call them that, barely provide the basic necessities for a kid of seventeen. I help him out as much as I can, but I can only do so much with how little money I bring in. Nick's catering orders mean I've been able to get Carson in for a few extra shifts. If I could do more, I would, but my hands are tied.

"He told me yesterday he's thinking of attending the summer basketball camp this year," Chloe says. "You know he'll need some of those fancy high-top sneakers all the kids are wearing these days."

I resolve to ferret out Carson's shoe size without sounding like a creep, so I can get him those shoes. I may not make enough at the restaurant to give him many shifts, but I have a credit card with enough room on it for sneakers. And a seventeen-year-old shouldn't have to go without because he had shitty luck in the parent lottery. Even if he manages to save enough for those shoes, I guarantee we will never see them on his feet. His parents will steal that money from him one way or another. Just like they always do.

Pushing those thoughts to the side, I nod. "You're right. I'll text him and see if he can come in after school."

"Thanks for the extra hours, boss." As usual, Carson was more than happy to come in for an extra shift. "And thanks again for the pizza. Even though you don't need to do that for me." Carson finishes cleaning up his dishes, washes his hands, and, now that I will allow it, gets to work.

When he confirmed he was coming in, I prepped his favorite pizza, so when he walked in to start his shift, I was pulling it out of the oven. His protest is merely a formality at this point. We both know that if he's working, I'll have something ready for him to eat as soon as he gets here. And we both know that I'll make him sit and enjoy it, on the clock, before I'll let him do any work. It's so routine that he was on autopilot when we went through the usual song and dance, and he didn't even hesitate to answer when I asked about his shoe size. I somehow even managed to get the brand and color of the shoe that he's been dreaming about worked into the conversation, like some sort of conversational ninja wizard. With the food distracting him, it was nothing for me to navigate to the website and order the shoes, all before he'd finished his third piece of pizza. Whether I'm that good at subterfuge, or he indulges me because he knows I'd do this stuff for him regardless of how much he protests, isn't really my concern. As long as I can get him fed, and help him do some things for himself instead of for his parents, then I don't care much about how it gets done and whether he knows about it. Then again, it is pretty fun when I catch him off guard. There's something special about the way his face lights up when he realizes someone is looking out for him for once. It makes me feel all warm and fuzzy. He's a good kid, and he deserves a better life than the one his parents provide for him.

"What time does the order need to go out for the gym?" Carson calls out over his shoulder. He's checking temperatures in the workstation cooler and marking them off in our food safety binder. See? Work ethic. "When should we start on it?"

"Chloe's taking it over at six."

He nods, then looks up when he hears the door chime, greeting Wade before I get the chance. This kid is seriously a great employee.

"Hey, Mr. Biddescombe, how're you doing tonight?"

"Hey, kid." The way Wade's eyes crinkle ever so slightly in the corners betrays the affection he feels for Carson, despite his gruff greeting, and I can't help but smile.

Three years ago, Wade was doing some maintenance work around the back of the building when he discovered Carson, barely fourteen at the time, rummaging in the restaurant's dumpster looking for something to eat. He marched Carson straight inside and bought him dinner. Then he pulled me aside and suggested I give the boy a job. My experience with Wade in the old neighborhood meant if he said this kid needed help, then he *really* needed it. I hired Carson on the spot and haven't regretted it for a single second.

"What'll you have today, Mr. Biddescombe?" Carson asks.

"Actually, I have some manicotti set aside for you, if you like? I made extra when I prepared the catering order because I thought you might like it."

He gives me the same crinkle-eyed non-smile as he gave Carson. "That sounds delicious, Valentina. Thanks."

Since Nick wasn't at the gym last night when I made the delivery, I asked Demetrius what kind of healthy meal he thought everyone would like me to make for today. The word "healthy" had barely escaped my lips before I was on the receiving end of an epic side-eye the likes of which I've never seen. Someone should crown Demetrius the king of the side-eye. He's that good at it. He convinced me to help him continue his cheat week as long as possible, practically begging me to make lasagna, like I did the first night. We settled on manicotti because there's no way I was going to repeat a dish twice in less than a week's worth of menus. I have standards, after all.

While I get Wade's food ready, Carson tells him all about the basketball camp that he's signing up for when he saves enough money. If Carson were anyone else, I'd think he was trying to guilt a customer into leaving a generous tip, but that's not how Carson is. He's genuinely excited about basketball camp, and so he's telling one of the few friendly adults in his life about it. If Wade tried to leave anything larger than a standard tip, I can guarantee Carson would chase him out the door to give it back. The kid prefers to work for what he gets, which makes it a lot harder to help him out, but it does make me admire him even more. I just wish there was more I could do for him.

"Here you go, Wade." I walk around to the front of the restaurant, setting Wade's food down at his usual table. "Soup's on."

Wade nods to Carson, leaving him to his work as he joins me at the table. "Thanks, Valentina. You always take such good care of me." He narrows his eyes at the vegetables I always try to sneak onto his plate. He rarely eats them, but putting them on his plate makes me feel better about his constant diet of wings, pizza, and pasta.

I scoff. "I think we both know who takes care of who in this relationship." I wave a finger between the two of us. "Don't think I don't know what market rate is on a building like this, even in a town as small as Tuft Swallow."

He shrugs and stuffs a forkful of cheesy pasta into his mouth. He chews thoughtfully, then swallows and says, "I got no idea what you're talking about," before turning back to his food, dismissing me. "Don't you have something better to do than bother me when I'm trying to eat?"

I drop a hand on Wade's shoulder, patting him twice before walking away. He'll never admit it, but I know this place is worth at least quadruple what I'm paying now. There's no way I could afford the rent on this place if Wade wasn't either subsidizing it himself, or giving it to me at a huge discount. So, regardless of what he says, I know he's looking out for me. And one day, I hope to repay the favor. For now, I'll cook for him.

The door chime sounds behind me and Carson calls out a greeting. "Welcome to Wings and Pizza. Are you looking for wings or a slice? Maybe a whole pie?"

"Neither," comes the reply, followed by a cough of disgust. "You couldn't pay me to eat here. Not that I need the money. I do very well for myself."

My stomach drops, and a sense of dread crawls over my flesh. This can't be happening. Not again.

"I'm here to pick up my date, Tina Falcone."

Fuck.

I spin toward him, pasting what I hope is a friendly smile on my face. "I'm afraid you're in the wrong place. There's no one here by that name."

The guy looks me up and down, making zero effort to hide his blatantly obvious appraisal of my body. A body he finds lacking, if the curl in his upper lip is anything to go on. "You look different from your pictures. You're so much... older."

Returning the favor, I take in the man's appearance. With short, dark hair, and a slight dusting of facial scruff, he's not altogether unattractive. At least, he's not ugly until you take in the twist of disdain on his lips and the hint of menace in his eyes. If I *were* on a dating site, I would never match with a man like this. There's something about the way he looks at me that makes my skin crawl.

"You caught me." I force a humorless laugh. "I'm Tina. We don't have a date, though. There's been some sort of mistake."

The man laughs cruelly. "You can say that again. You misrepresented yourself completely. Serves me right for lowering my standards such that I would use a dating site in the first place. You've really done it this time, Milton." He looks me up and down again, still not liking what he sees. "I suppose there's nothing to be done for it now. Put something nice on. I have dinner reservations at the hottest place in Spitz Hollow."

"We. Don't. Have. A. Date." I enunciate each word precisely, but it doesn't even phase him.

"Hurry along now. I don't want to be late. I called in a favor to get this reservation, so you better not ruin it for me."

What is this guy's deal? It's like he doesn't even hear me when I tell him we don't have a date. Either that, or he flat out doesn't care what I think.

"Don't stand there gawking, Tina. Go get dressed. A black dress, I think. Something that will cover your arms and legs." He looks me up and down, evaluating, judging. He heaves a sigh. "At least your body fat is distributed in a way that your waist looks small enough, but the rest of you leaves a lot to be desired. If I decide to continue seeing you, which I most likely won't, you would need to put in a *lot* more time at the gym before I would take you somewhere as public as Forked again. You're lucky I'm a man of high value, otherwise your appearance could reflect badly on me. Thankfully, I'm far too wealthy and respected for one woman's appearance to cause much harm. If I didn't need to show up with someone to teach my bitch of an ex a lesson, I would leave you here. Still, try to make yourself look pretty. And for the love of god, get rid of those terrible glasses. They make you look like a librarian, and not the sexy kind.”

With each word of his little speech, the rage bubbles up inside me until I can hold it in no longer. “Now you listen here, you self-absorbed little twat.” I take step after slow step toward him until I’m standing mere inches away. “The only thing ‘high’ around here is your blood alcohol level, because you have to be drunk if you think I would ever date you. I don’t understand how *anyone* would ever date you. In fact, I’d like to meet this ex of yours, maybe shake her hand. Sounds like she really dodged a bullet.” His face reddens, gradually turning the same angry purple as the last man who thought he had a date with me, ramping up the intense giddiness I feel in my belly. *Interesting. I wonder if turning purple is a common trait among these so-called “high value men”?* “And another thing, if you’d gotten your head out of your ass long enough to listen when I was talking, you would have known that we don’t have a date. I’m not on any dating sites. Someone catfished you.”

He splutters, his face nearing the color of a nice, ripe eggplant. *I wonder if Nick likes eggplant parmigiana?* I think to myself as the guy in front of me rages on. *Maybe he’d like that for tomorrow’s dinner.*

“No one catfishes Milton Maguire. I’m too smart for that. No, I know what’s happening here. Who are you to think you can fuck me around like this? No one treats Milton Maguire this way.” He takes a step closer, pressing his chest to mine, trying to crowd me, attempting to intimidate me with the few inches of height he has on me. “You need to learn not to fuck with your betters.”

“I think that’s enough.” Wade’s voice comes from behind Milton before he jerks him away from me, leaving a space where an angry eggplant previously stood. Wade is holding Milton’s arm twisted up high behind his back, and he’s using his leverage to move him to the exit. "It's time you left, Milton." He tips his chin toward the door. "Carson, my boy. Can you get that for me? It appears Milton here needs some help finding the door."

"You got it, Mr. Biddescombe." Carson wipes his hands on his apron as he rushes out from behind the counter. He slides to a stop by the door before pulling it open, the chime sounding as cheerful as ever. "There you go, guy. The door's right here. That wasn't so hard, was it?"

I watch in amazement as my middle-aged landlord and my teen-aged sous-chef frog march my would-be date out of the restaurant and force him into the driver's seat of what must be his car, then stand there and watch as he drives away. It's a good thing they took care of it, too, because I was a breath away from ripping that asshole's arms off. Who does he think he is, coming to my restaurant and talking to me that way?

Chloe is right. I really need to find out where all these guys are coming from, because this shit's getting ridiculous.

Chapter 18

I Wear The Required Uniform

Nick

"Ahhhhhhh!"

Tina's scream echoes down the street, and I instantly break into a sprint. *Why didn't I come sooner?* I knew that light needed changing, and I did nothing about it. *How could you be so stupid, Nick? You did this. She's getting hurt because of you.*

I'd started walking to the restaurant tonight, hoping to see Tina before she closed, but I got lost in my thoughts and wound up wandering a little. I'm at the end of the block on the other side of the square when I hear the first scream, and it takes a minute before I reach her building, where I'm met by another, even louder scream. Yet another scream echoes down the darkened stairs to her apartment and I launch myself up them two at a time, not stopping until I'm in her bedroom.

"Tina! What's wrong, baby? What happened?" She's standing at the foot of her bed facing away, screaming gibberish, fists on her luscious hips as she vibrates with fury. If my heart weren't beating hard enough to jump out of my chest, this would be incredibly sexy.

"That.. sonofa... Gah! Not again. God damn it, Winston. I'll turn you into a lampshade. I don't give a shit what your hot daddy has to say about it, either."

I finally take my eyes off of her and look past her to see what she's screaming at.

There, in all his mayoral glory, is Winston, the town goat.

He looks almost regal with a sash that reads "Mayor Winston" draped around his neck, even while grinding something that looks a lot like the pair of panties Tina was wearing the other night between his teeth. The sight of him chewing away on her panties as she screams about turning him into progressively more ridiculous pieces of furniture, including couch cushions, a coat rack, a hatbox, a journal, and the Necronomicon ex-mortis book of the dead, is too much to handle. I erupt into laughter, huge braying guffaws bursting out of me without a pause for a breath. "I can't—hatbox... book of the dead..."

Tina spins, her glare doing nothing to quell the hysteria, especially when I look at Winston again, and he's chewing away like we're not even here, his rectangular slitted pupils taking in nothing and everything all at once. He could not care less about my laughing or her screaming, which is what makes this situation so much funnier.

"Laugh it up, Chuckles. Hilarious." She leans back and wiggles her fingers in the air, jazz-hands style. "I hope you're enjoying the show."

I snort another laugh and bend to clutch my stomach. *Jazz hands. She jazz hands-ed me.* "Oh, God. I can't breathe." I suck in a deep shuddering a breath and squeeze my eyes shut against the sight of Winston's lazy chewing and Tina's frenzied anger, attempting to block out the hilarity and get myself under control.

"Oh, for fuck's sake." Tina huffs and takes a few stomping steps. "You need to leave. *Hmmph.*" Her grunt is followed by some shuffling and bumping sounds. I should probably open my eyes to see what she's up to now, but I'm not sure I can hold back my laughter if I do. The situation is beyond ridiculous. "You stupid goat. If you don't get out of here right now, I'll turn you into a ragu then use your skin to make menu covers for the restaurant." Some more shuffling and grunting noises follow, and I can't take the suspense any longer. I open my eyes.

Tina has Winston's sash wrapped around her hands, and she's pulling it like a leash, squatting down to get more leverage as she tries to get Winston to budge. For his part, Winston has sucked more of the pair of panties into his mouth, with only the smallest scrap hanging out now, and he's giving the impression that he's looking around for more to snack on without moving his head. *Goat eyes are so weird.*

"Move, you useless lump of flesh. I don't care if you are the mayor. I'm about to call animal control. Get"—she leans farther back, putting all of her weight behind pulling the sash—"out!" Winston doesn't budge when Tina gives one last heave backward, snapping the sash, and stumbling to the floor with a thud, her gorgeous ass taking the brunt of the impact. "Ouch. Shit," she whispers, getting to her feet as she rubs her butt. "That hurt."

Winston takes her distraction as an opportunity to dip his head into a dresser drawer, from which he emerges with another pair of panties between his teeth, and a bra snagged on one of his curling horns. He must decide he's had enough of this apartment because before Tina notices the contraband he's carrying, he clomps out of the room and out the door.

Tina rouses from her stupor and bolts from the room. I spin and follow as she flies down the steps to the street, making it to the sidewalk in time to see Winston trotting toward Impeckable Auto, his stolen undergarments waving in the wind.

"Yeah, you better run," Tina yells, shaking her fist in the air on the empty sidewalk. "And don't expect me to vote for you in the next election after this stunt, either. You're dead to me, Winston. Do you hear me? Dead to me."

By some miracle, I force down my laughter, so when Tina turns to face me, I'm as straight-faced as someone who'd spent the last several minutes laughing his ass off could be. So hardly straight-faced at all. It doesn't surprise me at all that Tina does not appear to be a fan of my face at the moment.

"Thanks for the help," she says, sarcasm dripping from each word. "It would be a shame if a giant man who heard me screaming for help ran to my apartment, then did nothing but cackle like a hyena and roll around the floor."

Her face is flushed, and her breaths come in great heaves, reminding me of our night together when she was breathless on top of me. I wish I could forget it for one minute, but the truth is, I've thought of little else since I left her apartment that morning. It felt like something real to me. Something permanent. Peter was right. I don't just want to date Tina. I want so much more than that. So I guess now all that's left is to convince her to take a chance on me.

And for that to happen, I should probably apologize for laughing instead of helping when Winston was stealing her panties. Now that I have a moment to consider the situation, I can't help but think how strange it is that Winston had the opportunity to steal her underwear at all. Why would she bring Winston into her apartment? As far as I know, he lives on a goat farm outside of town, so what brought him to Tina's underwear drawer?

"What was Winston doing in your apartment?" I ask, curiosity getting the better of me.

Tina clears her throat and her eyes slide away from mine. "Ileftmydooropenandhewalkedrightin." The words come out in a rush, so jumbled together that I can't make sense of them.

"I'm sorry. I didn't quite hear you. Can you repeat that?"

"Ileftmydooropenandhewalkedrightin." She slows down this time, but seems to mumble more. I think I heard the word door, but I still need more clarification.

"One more time?"

"I left my door open, and he walked right in," she says, finally lifting her eyes to mine. "Okay? It's my fault that an evil ruminant creature strolled into my apartment and helped himself to the contents of my underwear drawer. I came up here after I closed the restaurant, only to discover the damn goat helping himself to a selection of my finest undergarments."

Wait. What did she just say? What *the hell* did she just say? Please tell me I didn't hear what I think I heard.

"You left your door open?"

"Yes."

"When you got home from work?"

She cringes before muttering, "Not exactly."

My chest tightens. I can tell where this is going, even while hoping to God I'm mistaken. "What do you mean 'not exactly'?"

She blows out a breath and crosses her arms over her chest, looking away again. "I think I forgot to close it when I left this morning." She raises her eyes in challenge, then shrugs. "I had a lot on my mind."

My stomach drops even as I feel my frustration build. *She left her door open all day? How could she do that? Doesn't she have any concern for her own personal safety?* My mind fills with images suitable for the most bloodcurdling horror movie: scary clowns wielding chainsaws, black-robed wraiths with sadistic smiles staring from the shadows, creepy possessed dolls coming to life, Republicans. Anything could have been waiting for Tina in her apartment when she got home tonight. She's lucky it was only Winston.

"A lot on your mind?" I say, keeping the hysteria from my voice, but only just. "A lot on your mind?" Okay, the hysteria crept in a little on that last one. "You left your door open all day, Tina. Do you have any idea how unsafe that is?"

She rolls her eyes. "Yes, I do. Chloe and I have had this exact conversation several times. But we're in Tuft Swallow. What's the worst that could happen?"

Rage burns a fire through me, and I fight to moderate the volume of my voice. "Several times? And yet you still left your door open? You're lucky it was only a goat in your underwear drawer, Tina. Even with how small it is, I'm sure Tuft Swallow has its share of creeps. *That's* the worst that could happen. You come home from work to find some creep waiting for you in your apartment. If you're lucky, all he'll do is eat some of your underwear, then leave." She snickers when I mention a creep eating her underwear, and I narrow my eyes at her because it's not fucking funny. "If you're not lucky, though..." Fuck. If she's not lucky...

"I know, I know. It was an accident. I've been doing better. Somehow, I just...forgot today."

I pinch the bridge of my nose and blow out of breath, forcing my heart rate to slow by sheer force of will. "You forgot?"

She nods, the hair from her bun flopping down over her forehead. "I'm working on it."

"Work harder," I yell, my frustration getting the better of me. Why can't she understand? "If anything happened to you..."

"Now you wait a damn minute. You don't get to talk to me this way." She looks up with fire in her eyes and I know I've gone too far. "I am a grown woman who can take care of myself. You don't get to come around here telling me what to do just because I let you into my pants one time."

How can she be mad at me for this? For wanting her to be safe?

"You can take care of yourself, can you? Really? So it wasn't you I heard screaming bloody murder a few minutes ago because she found a goat in her apartment eating her panties? Was it someone else who fell on her ass while trying to extract a goat intruder from her bedroom, then, too?"

Her face flushes a deep red as she stomps over to me. If I weren't furious with her, it would be cute.

"Now listen here," she says, poking a finger into my chest. "I will scream about goat intruders if I want to. That's my prerogative, as it's my apartment Winston was intruding on. And, if you didn't notice, I got him out of here just fine on my own. I don't need you here looking after me."

"He left because he got bored," I yell, throwing my hands up. "You fell on your ass when you tried to move him, then he left on his own. He probably had somewhere to be. A ribbon cutting ceremony, or some other mayoral task he needed to attend to, judging by the sash he was wearing. You'd still be here watching him eat your underwear if he hadn't taken it upon himself to leave."

She scoffs, rolling her eyes again, crossing her arms over her chest. "Either way, he left. Everything is fine, so you can calm down now, *Dad*."

Dad? Dad? Does she really think I'm acting like a dad? My rage teeters over the edge into hysteria, and I bark a laugh. "Dad? Do I look like your dad?"

She snickers, the smile coming back to her face now that the tension between us has broken. "No," she says with a laugh. "Stan Falcone isn't a viking god come to earth to torment me. That, and he rarely leaves his recliner these days. Once he got those dedicated sports channels, that chair molded itself to his ass."

"He sounds like a fun guy." I take a small step toward her, my body craving closeness after feeling such intense worry for her. As hilarious as it was watching Winston eat her unmentionables, it's still terrifying to think that something much worse could have been waiting for her when she got home. "I'd like to meet him one day." *Like, maybe when you introduce me as your fiancé.* I think before catching myself. *Stop, Nick. Too soon.*

She snorts. "Oh, he'd love that. All he does is watch sports, so I'm sure he's seen you before. I don't know how often he watches fighting sports, though. Unless you count professional wrestling. He loves that shit. Calls it his 'stories'."

"Oh, yeah?" Hesitantly, I slide my palm up her arm, the feel of her skin working to finally calm my racing heart. "Did you know I did a stint in professional wrestling a couple of years ago?"

Her eyes widen as she searches mine, turning to bring her body into me. "Seriously?"

With a deep breath, I take a chance and place my hands on her hips, waiting for her to push me away. When she doesn't, I wrap my arms around her and pull her close, resting my chin on her head. The warmth of her arms wrapping around my waist is immediate, and so welcome.

"Seriously," I say, not really wanting to talk more, but also not wanting this moment to end. "It was a PR stunt, of course.

Something my publicist dreamed up for me leading up to the training camp for my last title fight. I was hesitant at first, but it wound up being one of the best experiences of my life."

"Really?" Tina's breath is hot on my skin as she buries her face in my chest, the heat reaching me straight through my shirt. Despite her earlier protests, I'm sure she was more scared to find someone in her apartment than she let on. Even if it turned out to be Winston. "It seems like a lot of... drama."

I chuckle, and her hair tickles my nose. "It can be. But it's also a lot of fun."

She squeezes me, running her hands up my back, and my breath catches. "I would love to see you running around in a pair of tights and knee-high wrestling boots."

I drop a kiss onto the top of her bun, loving how tightly she's letting me hold her, but still a little worried that she's going to pull away at any moment. "Sorry to burst your bubble, sweetheart. I wore a specially made pair of athletic jeans and wrestling boots that looked like regular sneakers."

She leans back and looks up at me, her eyebrows cocked in question. "What the hell are 'athletic jeans'?"

I shrug. "Regular jeans with more stretch, I guess."

She unwinds her hands from my back and places them on my chest, a smile teasing the corners of her lips. "So, like..." She stifles a snort and I can tell she's holding back a laugh. "You're talking about jeggings? You wrestled in jeggings?" The laugh she was holding back breaks free, and suddenly she's laughing as hysterically as I was when I walked in on her screaming at a goat eating her underwear.

"I wore a version of the required uniform," I say with a huff.

She barks another laugh. "You wore jeggings. Admit it."

Her laughter is contagious, and soon I'm laughing right along with her, huge gasping laughs that leave me struggling to catch my breath. I wrap my arms around her again and pull her flush against my body, loving the way she feels as she laughs in my arms. It's such a relief after the fear I felt earlier that my laughter stops in its tracks, with hers drifting away not long after.

"Tina," I whisper, tilting her chin until I can look into her eyes. Such a rich brown. The heat I feel is reflected back to me in her gaze.

"Yes?" Her voice is barely a breath. She moves a fraction of an inch closer.

"I'm going to kiss you now." Her eyes drift close, her chin tipping up in assent. "Good." I close the distance between us, her breath hot, then press a kiss to her closed mouth. When she opens her lips to me, her tongue poking out and seeming to seek my own, I can't hold back any longer. I open and kiss her fully, deeply, groaning when she kisses me just as eagerly, loving the way she melts in my arms.

Tina wraps her arms around my neck, squeezing even closer, until I run my hands to the back of her thighs, squeezing the soft flesh before picking her off the ground and wrapping her legs around me. "Take me upstairs," she demands, her lips not leaving mine. "Right now."

"Yes, ma'am," I say with a chuckle, kissing her right back. "But we'll be revisiting this *you don't date* thing soon."

She huffs, carding her hands through my hair. "Whatever. Fine. All I want to know right now is, how many condoms did you stuff into these jeans?"

Chapter 19

WHO LET THOSE DUCKS IN HERE?

Tina

FIVE.

The answer was five. Nick had five condoms in his jeans. And over the last few hours, we used every single one.

I reach over my head, my hands wrapping around the spindles of my headboard, and I turn my body, the stretch in my most intimate parts threatening to overwhelm. I love how sore I am after being with Nick. I can't get over how perfectly he fills me every time.

When we first came upstairs, I wasted no time stripping Nick out of his clothes. He'd scarcely set me down before I started shoving at his t-shirt, forcing it up and over his head. It's possible I broke his zipper with how roughly I ripped open his jeans and shoved them down. I didn't wait to push his boxers down before shoving my hand in and grabbing him roughly, and even now I can almost feel the weight of him in my hand. Thick and impossibly hard, with skin so smooth and hot wrapped in my fingers. And the way he moaned as I worked my palm up his flesh, as I ran my thumb over the thick head of his cock? *Oh my God!* I honestly think I could have come from touching him, from hearing the sounds he made, if he hadn't pulled my hand away. "Too close," he'd whispered harshly as he feverishly pulled my clothes off. My apron strings confounded him, and I know he would have left it on if I hadn't reached around and untied the knot.

As each item of clothing dropped to the floor, his eyes lit up even more, until I stood before him naked. I can still feel the heat that rushed through me as he devoured me with his eyes, licking his lips like he was about to enjoy a tasty meal after starving for weeks.

I liked it.

I shiver at the memory of Nick's tongue sliding through my wetness, and the movement causes him to stir awake beside me.

"You cold?" he asks, throwing a big arm around my waist and pulling my back flush to his front. "Let me warm you up."

I lay my arm over his, absently tracing the designs inked into his skin. "I'm not cold, but you can warm me up."

"Hmmm." He hums into my hair, and I can sense his lips turning up at the corners. "It's the sweat cooling on your skin. We had quite the workout the last few hours."

I chuckle. "You can say that again. I'll never have to exercise again if we keep this up. Not that I exercise much as it is, but still...I'm sore in muscles I never knew I had."

"Happy to be of service. I'll work you out anytime." Nick drops a hot kiss to my shoulder before rolling away from me. "I need some water. Can I get you something?"

I grab my glasses from the nightstand, then slide them on. "Water would be great. Thanks."

I watch him stroll to the kitchen, the globes of his ass cheeks flexing with each step. Oddly, the rubber ducky he has tattooed on his lower back seems to take his own step as the muscles beneath it flex. The effect is disconcerting, but also a little funny, so of course I giggle, which makes Nick turn toward me.

"Something funny?"

"That duck looks like it's walking." No sense in hiding what I'm laughing at. He has to have heard it before. Logically, I know I'm not the only of Nick's lovers to have noticed. That doesn't stop the frisson of jealousy that hits me when I think about it, though. I fight down the slight burn in my belly and continue. "With every step you take, he takes one too."

"If you think that's funny, you should hear him quack," he says, grinning, then blowing a raspberry at me before leaving the room.

A bark of laughter escapes me, my moment of jealousy forgotten as the memory of something my dad used to say pops into my head. Every time he passed gas, he'd look around in pretend shock and say, "Who let those ducks in here?". All us kids, and even my mom, would laugh at this joke every time he said it, despite knowing full well how stupid it was. And I think Nick...just made a similar joke.

"Did you-did you just make a fart joke?" I ask him.

"Farts are natural, babe. And also hilarious," he yells back from the kitchen. "I don't make the rules."

I'm still snickering when he comes back to the room carrying two glasses of water. He grins as I take in the slabs of muscle stacked on his chest before moving my perusal to his arms. Even under the minimal weight of the water he carries, the muscles in his arms pop, showcasing a fraction of the strength I know is in them. I allow my eyes to drift lower, to his abdomen. I love the slight roundness of his stomach. Instead of making him look like he's less in shape, it makes him look stronger, sturdier somehow. Dependable. And beneath that? If I hadn't already experienced the double extra large size of him, I wouldn't believe my eyes. But I have experienced it. Many wonderful, glorious, orgasmic times. And even so, on seeing the full length, the full girth, of his cock hanging there half hard between his muscular thighs, my breath catches...

And I choke on my own spit like a weirdo.

"Shit. Tina, are you alright?" Nick deposits the water glasses on the nightstand, and comes up next to me on the bed, helping me to a sitting position, before rubbing my back in soft circles. After a moment, he presses a glass into my hand. "Here, baby. Drink some water. It will help."

I take one sip, then another, the wild coughs eventually subsiding. "Thanks," I mutter, passing the glass back. "Well," I say, forcing out one final cough. "That was sexy of me, wasn't it?"

Nick drops his head to my shoulder, a feat of flexibility if there ever was one thanks to the difference in our heights, and sniggers. "So sexy. Probably almost as sexy as me making fart jokes immediately after making love to you for hours." He doesn't notice when my heart stops at his use of the word "love", instead moving on to his next thought without hesitation. "Care to tell me what prompted that oh-so-sexy coughing fit in the first place?" He trails his lips over the sport where my neck meets my shoulder, sending tingles shooting up my spine. Another kiss, more tingles, and the heat builds in my lower belly again. "What was it *exactly* that caused you to choke like that?"

He licks up the shell of my ear and I gasp. He drops a kiss to the hollow behind my ear, then sits back.

"Then again, maybe we should save that for later. I'll need a lot more water and at least an hour of sleep before I'm ready to go again." I eye his dick and raise an eyebrow. Nick huffs a laugh. "Yeah, he thinks he's invincible. But at my age, it pays to show some restraint."

I laugh. "Restraint? Like the restraint you showed these last few hours?"

He fakes a growl and bundles me up onto his lap, the hardness of his dick pressing into my hip. "I could go grab more condoms and be back in ten minutes, ready to go again, if that's what you want. But I have to warn you, if I come one more time tonight, I'll pass out in your bed and sleep for the next ten hours. If you don't want me spending the night, then it's best if you let me rest for a few minutes."

My body tenses when he mentions the possibility of not spending the night, and it's only then that I realize I don't want him to leave. I'd never say it out loud, but I was scared out of my mind earlier.

Coming upstairs after a long day of cooking to find my apartment door wide open and noises coming from my bedroom knocked about six years off my life. My heart was pounding so loudly as I crept to the doorway I was sure whoever was in my room could hear it. The fear coursing through my veins made time stretch to interminable lengths, and I swear the three-step journey to my bedroom door took at least an hour. When I flicked the light switch and saw Winston horns down in my underwear drawer, I nearly cried from relief. I'd never been happier to find someone rummaging through my panties. But even the relief I felt at seeing our town's unconventional mayor snacking on my unmentionables couldn't banish the fear altogether.

Chloe and Nick have gotten to me.

I am now someone who is afraid for my safety.

I kind of hate it. But at least when Nick's here, it's not quite as scary. Not that I want to admit that to him.

I force a laugh. "I know what you mean," I say with a yawn. "I'm exhausted, too. If you wanted to, I wouldn't object if you spent the night, though. Just sleeping, I mean. I think you broke my vagina with that last round. So you better not let your dick wander over to my side of the bed."

He laughs and buries his face in my neck again. "That was a hell of an invitation," he says with a laugh. "How could I possibly resist?"

"You can't." I climb off his lap and push his chest until he scoots up the bed and lays back. Seeing him relaxed like that, I'm hit with the certainty that I want nothing more than for him to stay the night. "It's probably best if you give in and get comfortable."

"Hmmm." His voice comes out as a deep rumble, and the heat in my belly rises again, but I'm content to wait. My vagina really could use a break. She's as unused to physical activity as the rest of me, and is suffering the effects of doing too much, too soon. "Come get comfy with me," he says, pulling me down next to him. "It might surprise you to know this about me, but I'm a bit of a snuggler."

I drop my glasses onto the nightstand before settling onto my side and resting my head on Nick's chest. He wraps his arms around me, pulling me in closer, then drops a kiss onto my head and blows out a breath. Comfortable in a way I'm not sure I've ever felt before, I tuck my face into his chest and inhale the scent of soap, and sweat, and man, and *Nick* a balm to my senses. Any remaining fear I was feeling floats away, leaving me thoroughly relaxed. I melt into Nick. He's even more cuddly than I thought he would be, and it's wonderful. I press myself a little closer, relishing the heat coming off him as he holds me.

"Thanks for letting me stay over," he mumbles into my hair. "I'm beat. I might not fall asleep on my feet while walking home, but why risk it? Even this semi I'm sporting is making me a little lightheaded."

I chuckle, placing a kiss on his chest before I can stop myself. It doesn't occur to me until after I've done it, that it's a little too much like something one would do with a boyfriend. As much as I enjoy having Nick around, and as much as he makes me feel safe, I shouldn't get used to this. *Right?*

"You think I'm joking? You wore me out, woman. I feel better since chugging water straight from your faucet, but some sleep would do me good. Especially sleep with you in my arms. I can't think of anything that would make me feel better than that."

I can't either, and I'm a little concerned at how much I like the thought of it. *Remember, Tina, you don't want a relationship. Don't get used to this.*

I wrap my arm around his chest and squeeze, then throw my leg over his thigh, breathing a contented sigh. I suppose it won't hurt to get used to it for a little while.

"So, Tina. Remember what I said earlier?" His breath is hot in my hair as he whispers the words. "You agreed to talk about dating."

My chest squeezes and butterflies flutter in my belly. Being with Nick has been fun so far, but that means nothing. I bet my dad was fun a long time ago, too. But these days all he does is sit in his recliner, and let my mother wait on him hand and foot. I want nothing to do with that kind of life. I'm too busy with my restaurant, with my friends and hobbies, for that kind of relationship.

"Whoa, slow down. Your heart is racing. What's going through your head right now?"

I suck in a breath, then blow it out, letting my lips make a flapping noise. "You're a nice guy, and this has been so much fun." I never knew sex could be so fun. "But I don't date. I thought I mentioned that the other day."

I feel more than hear him chuckle. "I recall you saying something about that, yes."

"So...you understand?"

Another chuckle. "Oh, no. Not at all."

"It's just..." I blow out a huge breath and continue, "I don't have time, you know? I work anywhere from ten to fourteen hours a day. I have hobbies I enjoy. I can't take on a responsibility like dating."

"Responsibility?" he scoffs. "Since when is dating a responsibility?"

"Ugh," I groan. "You know what I mean. Maybe it's more accurate to say I don't do relationships."

Nick tenses beneath me, and for some reason, it makes my stomach clench uncomfortably.

"Did someone hurt you, Tina?" He asks, his voice nearly a growl. "Was someone careless with your heart?"

My head snaps up and I take in the hard look on his face. "God no. It's nothing like that. No. No." He softens, and his lips turn up at the corners. "I've never let anyone get close enough."

"So, what is it, then?"

I lay my head back on his chest and wrap my arm around him. "A couple of things, I guess. My mom has been trying to get me married off since I turned eighteen. In my family, the women get married and have babies. They stay home and look after their husbands and their children until they drop dead. I want nothing to do with that."

"Okay?"

"All I ever wanted was to open my own restaurant, cook good food, and feed people."

He laughs. "You've done that. Demetrius thinks I can't tell, but he's put on a little weight in the last few days, thanks to your cooking. I'm pretty sure it's ninety percent cheese. He's making insane gains in his weightlifting thanks to all the extra calories, but it's making him slower in the ring."

I laugh and dig a finger into his ribs, making him wriggle. "Hey. That's not my fault. I asked him for healthy ideas, and he practically begged me to send over something cheesy."

"Oh, believe me, I know. He hasn't stopped talking about your food. I think he would move here if he thought he could eat your cooking all the time. He knows he'd have to retire from fighting to do that, though. He's not tall enough to move up a weight class."

"He proposed to me again when I dropped the food off yesterday," I say. "It was hilarious."

Nick's gruff voice coupled with the tightening of his arms around me floods me with warmth. "He shouldn't do that. It's not professional."

I shrug. "It's fine. I know he's joking."

We lay there wrapped up in each other for several minutes until I start to drift off. As everything gets fuzzy and the darkness settles over me, I think I hear Nick say through the fog of impending sleep, "When I do it, you'll know I'm not joking."

Chapter 20

HE LOOKS LIKE HE KNOWS WHAT HE'S DOING

Tina

NICK CRAWLED OUT OF bed early this morning to make it to a training session with one of his fighters, but not before making me come again with his mouth and fingers. He left me so thoroughly wrung out, I couldn't keep my eyes open long enough to say goodbye before falling back to sleep with a giant satisfied smile on my face. A few hours later, after I'd finally gotten myself up and ready for another day of work, he started texting me.

When the first message comes through, I grin wider than I have in years.

Happy last day of catering. What are we doing to celebrate?

I'm bringing your food over, then I'm coming straight back to work. I don't know what you're doing.

Booooo. That doesn't sound like much fun.

I have work to do.

Of course. But we can still celebrate. Do you ever take a day off?

Not really. I own my own business. I can't afford days off.

Can Chloe cover? Maybe I can send someone over to help. I think Demetrius knows his way around a kitchen well enough to follow orders.

Tina

Chloe is busy tonight. And if I let Demetrius in my kitchen, he'll eat all the cheese. I'll have to roll him out of here and be forced to close up shop.

Nick

The man loves his cheese.

Tina

More than anyone I know. And that's saying something, because my family literally thanks the lord for cheese when they say grace.

Nick

Maybe Demetrius is a long-lost relative of yours? It would explain the cheese thing.

Tina

Maybe. But how much weirder would that make the joke proposals?

Nick

Good point. Not that he should be doing that, anyway.

Tina

* eye-roll emoji *

"This is what you dragged me out here for?"

Nick lowers his binoculars and grins. "Yeah, isn't it awesome?" He's wearing tiny shorts again, bright orange ones this time, but today he's paired it with the official turquoise shirt of our local bird watching group, the Tit Peepers.

After arranging for Rhett to come work at Wings and Pizza for the evening, it appears Nick was busy planning the strangest outing I've ever been on. As soon as I'd delivered the food, he handed me an orange visor and hustled me onto the Spring Chickens' bus. The dirty look Stephen gave me as I walked up the steps added a little pep to my step. Pep that quickly waned as I realized what exactly Nick had in mind for a last day of catering celebration.

"You know, in my five years of living here, I have never been bird watching," I say, trying to muster up a little enthusiasm. When I was looking for a place to settle to open my restaurant, I chose Tuft Swallow because I liked the name. An interest in bird watching played no part in my choice.

"Me neither," he calls out, raising his binoculars and looking off into the woods. "I should have done this sooner. It's nice to be outside enjoying the scenery. Usually if I'm outside, it's because I'm out for a run. I didn't realize how much I liked nature." He turns to grin at me, gesturing to his chest with one hand. "Plus, I look amazing in turquoise."

I chuckle and shake my head as he turns back to look through his binoculars. He's right about it being nice to be outside. I walk wherever I need to go, and I'm on my feet all day, so I get plenty of exercise, but there's something to be said for actually being in the great outdoors in order to experience it, rather than pass through it as quickly as possible. It's peaceful.

The birdwatching, on the other hand, *that* I could probably do without. I wouldn't know a Blue Jay from a Blue-Footed Booby if one flew by and shat on my head. I'm pretty sure the only bird I could identify on sight is the one on the box of the fruity cereal I used to eat when I was a kid. And even then, I'd need the box for reference to be sure.

An icy breeze blows past me, and I pull my hood up before shoving my hands into my pockets. If I'd known we'd be walking outside near sunset, I would have dressed much warmer. No wonder the Tit Peepers wear bespoke turquoise windbreakers when they're out at this time of the year. I could use a windproof layer to stop the cool air from blowing right through my sweater.

Looking at Nick, though, you'd never even guess that it was cold out. The man is out here dressed for a hot summer day in what must be his shortest shorts, and a t-shirt that's at least two sizes too small. I guess the Tit Peepers didn't take a man of Nick's size into account when they ordered shirts for their club. Not that I mind. He makes for a much nicer view than any bird out here.

I'm lost in my head, admiring the flex of his thighs, recalling the way he moved underneath me in bed and how it felt to be lifted like that when he was buried inside me, when Miss Martha clears her throat behind me, causing me to jump several inches in the air. I land awkwardly, rolling my ankle and smashing to the trail flat on my ass.

"Ouch, that must've hurt," she says, a small smile playing at her bright pink painted lips. "I suppose that's bound to happen when you're too busy staring at a half-naked hunk to notice what's going on around you. I've been trying to get your attention for three whole minutes."

Groaning, I roll to a sitting position and rub my ankle. It's a little sore, but not terrible, so I get to my feet before Nick can notice I'm down. I'm not sure why, but I sense that if he saw what had happened, he'd be throwing me over his shoulder and marching my ass home to rest. And as much as I'd like the throwing me over his shoulder part, I don't think I'm ready for the celebrating part of the day to be over. I enjoy spending time with him. Which is weird. Because whatever else this little foray into birdwatching might be, it feels unmistakably date-like.

I dust the dirt and leaves from my ass and turn to Miss Martha. "I'm sorry, Miss Martha. What was it you wanted?"

The older woman scoffs and waves a hand. "It's too late now. I wanted you to confirm my identification of what I thought was a Lesser Tufted Kink, but he flew away while you were undressing Nick with your eyes." She chuckles. "You know, if you wait around a little while, he'll take that shirt off. Nick almost never wears a shirt. He begged us to give him that one when he asked if you two could join us tonight."

"It looks like it was made for a kid," I say with a laugh. "How'd he manage to get it on?"

Miss Martha shrugs, her windbreaker swishing with the movement. "He got it over his head and arms, then forced it down the rest of the way. I doubt he'll get it back off so easily. Come to think of it, you'll need to cut him out of it later. Lucky you." She waggles her thin, sharply arched eyebrows.

The heat rises in my cheeks. She's right. I am lucky.

Even though he's frequently shirtless, when we're alone, it seems more personal somehow. It's strange. It's the same skin, the same chiseled chest, the same slightly soft stomach, and the same muscular arms as when he's shirtless at the gym or out in public, but when it's just the two of us, it's so much...more.

"If I had a man like that between my thighs, I'd never let him out of my bed," Miss Martha whispers. "He looks like he knows what he's doing."

A pulse of warmth hits my lower belly, and a throb at that apex of my thighs catches me off guard. *Is that all it takes, Tina? Come on. Get it together.* I force myself to smile casually. "I wouldn't know," I lie.

Miss Martha cocks an eyebrow and leans in close. "Are you sure that's the answer you're going with? I've seen the way you look at him, and more importantly, I've seen the way he looks at you. Like he's devoured you before, and he's counting the seconds until he gets to do it again."

Just then, Nick turns to me and smiles, his grin crooked as he takes in the sight of Miss Martha whispering in my ear. He lowers his binoculars to his chest, letting the strap keep them around his neck, and walks over to join us. "When I see two beautiful women with their heads together, I know something interesting must be going on. Care to let me in on the secret?"

"It's nothi—"

"I was just telling the lovely Tina how every time you look at her, it's written on your face how badly you want to hold her down and lick every inch of her body."

Nick's eyes flare with lust, and he fixes me with a look so full of promise I swear my panties melt right there on the spot.

Later, he seems to say with that look. But before I can respond, he turns to Miss Martha and smiles. "I'd say you're not far off with that assessment, Miss Martha," he says, before leaning over and whispering to her behind his hand. "But you know what? I think I like it even better when she's the one holding me down."

Miss Martha barks a laugh. "Well now, I can see how you would. Tina here is a beautiful young woman. I imagine she has a lot to offer a big, strong fella like you."

Nick laces our fingers together and lifts my hand, pressing his lips to the back of it. "She sure does," he murmurs, with his lips still pressed to my skin. He lets our hands drop, keeping his fingers tangled with mine. "But I have a lot to offer her, too. And one day soon, I'll prove it to her."

"I bet you will, Odd Duck. I bet you will. Now, if you'll excuse me. The Woodcocks are just up ahead and I have an urgent matter to discuss with them." Miss Martha shakes her head as she walks away, giggling to herself the whole time.

"I like her," Nick says. "She always says exactly what's on her mind. My grandmother was nothing like that before she died. I don't think I ever heard that woman state an opinion that didn't come from my grandfather's mouth first." He shakes his head before turning to face me. "I'm sad that I never got the chance to know her. At least, not really. My mom is kind of the same way."

"That's... sad. I can't imagine my mom not saying exactly what's on her mind as soon as she thinks it. I think she would literally explode if she couldn't tell everyone what she thought about a situation. Our Sunday chats are mostly me listening as she tells me how she thinks I should run my life."

Nick chuckles under his breath, and starts walking. "Yeah, I sort of got that when I walked in on you talking to her that day."

My heart quickens. That was the day that Nick came to arrange the catering for the week. It's hard to believe that was only six days ago. I wonder what my mother would say if I told her about this little adventure in birdwatching when I call her tomorrow. Not that I plan on telling her. That would be insane. I'd find myself strapped into a wedding dress and walking down the aisle before I could say boo. Considering this isn't even a proper date, that might be a bit of an overreaction. So why does the thought of walking down the aisle to a smiling Nick not scare the shit out of me like it clearly should?

"So, what brings you to Tuft Swallow? You moved here, what, six months ago? How does a famous fighter come to settle in a town like this? I can't imagine there's much call for an MMA gym in a town as small as this. You'd probably have better luck in Spitz Hollow."

He laughs. "You're not the first person to tell me that. I had a meeting with a guy from that Spitz-Shein sportsplex in Spitz Hollow, and he seemed to think having my gym in this tiny town was a wasted opportunity. But I grew up here in Tuft Swallow. When my age started to adversely affect my fighting, I knew it was time to retire. This is the only place I ever felt at home, so it was a no-brainer to come back here."

I freeze in place, pulling Nick to a stop. "Wait a sec. You grew up here? In Tuft Swallow?" He nods. "How on earth did you become a fighter instead of a cornhole player? If my part-timer hadn't told me about a basketball camp he wants to do this summer, I would have thought cornhole was the only sport offered around here."

His face goes dark, and he scrubs a hand through his hair. "My parents drove me to Spitz Hollow for martial arts training in the beginning. When I showed a talent for it, I went to training camps all over the country."

"Alone?" The thought of a young Nick all alone on the other side of the country makes my heart heavy. A young kid like that needs someone looking out for him.

He shrugs. "I was a big kid. I could take care of myself. Besides, when I was fifteen, my whole family left Tuft Swallow and moved to Vegas. I trained out of a gym there for most of my career."

I turn back to the path and continue walking, still holding Nick's hand. "That sounds lonely."

"What about you? You're here all by yourself, aren't you? What brought you to Tuft Swallow?"

"I came to open the restaurant. After culinary school, and working in way too many kitchens that weren't mine, I decided it was time to follow my dream. I wanted a place that was near enough to Boston that I could visit my family, but far enough that my mom and aunts wouldn't be on my doorstep every day with a new man they wanted me to date." Nick's hand squeezes mine. "I looked at a map and saw Tuft Swallow. I figured a bird obsessed town was the perfect place for someone named Falcone."

I see him grin from the corner of my eye. "It does have a certain sense of poetry to it."

"Exactly. It's like it was fate. That was five years ago, and I'm still here, so I must've made the right choice." And now that I have a little boost from catering for Nick, I'll be able to stick around a little longer. With the slight increase in traffic I've seen in by-the-slice sales, thanks to the Spring Chickens, I think I might be okay.

"So, why pizza?"

"What do you mean?"

"You said you went to culinary school, right? So why pizza? Why not something fancier?"

It's not the first time I've been asked this, but it is the first time I didn't get a hint of derision from the person asking the question. "Some of my old acquaintances from culinary school and the restaurants I've worked in have asked me the same thing, all while looking down their noses at me. They could never understand why I'd want to make pizza in a hole in the wall town instead of working my way up to being the head chef in a Michelin starred restaurant. But this is what I've always wanted to do. It's a tradition in my family for the men to move to a new city and open a pizza place." I shrug. "I always wanted to do the same thing."

Nick stops walking and steps in front of me, taking both of my hands in his. "That's pretty amazing, Tina. You're living your dream. Your parents must be proud."

Disappointment settles over me. "You would think so, wouldn't you? But they're not. Not really. I didn't follow the pattern. It's the men who are supposed to move away and open pizza places. The women are supposed to get married, pop out some babies, and look after everyone else for the rest of their lives. And I can think of nothing I'd like to do less than take care of a grown ass man for the rest of my life."

Chapter 21

HIGH VALUE DUMPSTER DIVER

Nick

I DROP ANOTHER KISS to Tina's swollen lips and lower my forehead to hers, dragging a ragged breath into my lungs. "Are you sure you need to go in to close? We could sneak upstairs before they even know we're here."

Tina huffs a small laugh, her hands resting on my chest. "I'm sure. Besides, if we wanted to sneak upstairs without being caught, we probably shouldn't have stopped right in front of the restaurant to make out on the sidewalk."

A knock sounds on the window behind Tina and I look up to find a grinning Rhett waving at me through the glass. "You make a good point," I say, glaring at Rhett before looking back at Tina. "We should have gone to my place."

She sighs, the smile on her face lighting her eyes. "No. I need to close up. The kid who's working doesn't even have keys. And didn't you say you needed to go check on Jared?"

"Shit," I say with a groan. She's right. I need to go check on him. He's still pretty upset about his breakup, and I don't want to leave him completely alone. He's been at the gym with the other trainers for most of the night, but I still want to check on him before I spend the night at Tina's. "How about this? I'll check on Jared while you close the store, then I'll come by after. And we can continue where we left off." I take her lips in a quick kiss. "Half an hour," I murmur against her lips. "I'll be back in half an hour. Close quickly."

I turn from her lips, bang on the window and give a quick wave to Rhett, then take off running back to my place, the sound of Tina's laughter echoing along the storefronts as I go. The jog to my house is quick, and before I know it, I'm running upstairs to check on Jared.

When I get to his room, he's getting ready to go out and meet some friends.

"Hey, Jared. Nice to see you up and about."

He shrugs and continues fixing his hair in the mirror, arranging the long locks in the perfect disheveled swoop over his eyes. "I thought about what you said, and you were right. I need to focus on what I'm doing here if I want to be successful. Besides, I talked to Gloria, and she told me what's going on with my latest foster parents. Thanks for agreeing to let me stick around until she finds me some new ones. I'm sure I'll be out of here before you know it."

Gloria, Jared's caseworker, informed me earlier that Jared's foster parents don't want him back. Just like that. After he was here with me for a few weeks, they discovered they were pregnant, and removed themselves from the foster parent program altogether. The assholes didn't even have the decency to say goodbye to him. Even with knowing what they do about his history, about how many times he's had to move to new foster homes without notice, they still didn't write so much as a note. If I were the vengeful type, I'd pay them a visit. It's a good thing for them I'm more worried about how Jared feels than about delivering a bag of flaming goat turds to their front porch.

I might still do that, though. It's on the back burner for now.

Knowing he's facing yet another new foster home, I asked Gloria to take another crack at tracking down Jared's parents. Maybe they've been looking for him, but because he's moved around so much, they can't find him. If there's any possibility they could reconcile, now would be a great time.

"There's no rush, buddy. You can stay here as long as you need." I make a mental note to call Gloria on Monday. I don't want Jared to go to just anyone. He's a good kid who doesn't deserve to be shunted around any more than he already has. He can stay here until she finds him a good, permanent foster home. In fact, I might insist on it.

"That's nice of you, man, but it's cool. I'll stay here until the end of the school year like I was supposed to, and then I'll move on. Maybe I'll move to California and learn how to surf or something."

I scoff. "I doubt your new foster parents will be out of state. Not if reconciliation is still the goal."

Jared laughs dryly, turning to face me. "Reconciliation hasn't been on the table for a long time, Nick. I haven't seen my real parents since I was nine years old. For all I know, they died in a trap house or under a bridge somewhere."

My heart breaks for the kid. Behind his laughter is pain. It's there in his eyes, plain as day. "Jared, you don't know that. Your parents could be out there, working hard to get clean so they can get you back."

"You have no clue, do you?" Jared asks with a heavy sigh, his shoulders sagging under the weight of his thoughts. "Do you know why I went into foster care when I was nine? Did Gloria tell you?"

I nod. "She said your parents were addicts who couldn't take care of you properly. Child Protective Services placed you into temporary custody until they could sort themselves out."

"Exactly! Temporary custody. When I was nine. If they wanted me back, they would have gotten clean by now. I stopped hoping for that after the first couple of years. Do you know what I wished for after that? A permanent placement." He laughs. "But I couldn't even get that." He lists items on his fingers. "I worked my ass off. Got good grades. Mastered several martial arts. Was the perfect kid at home and at school. And still, here I am, about to be sent to yet another new foster home. So you'll forgive me for considering giving up on the whole system, and taking care of myself instead." His eyes fill with unshed tears. "I can't do a worse job than my parents did. I'm pretty sure I can keep myself away from the kinds of creeps and lowlifes they used to drag me around to, anyway."

I can't take the pain in his voice anymore, and before I know it, I'm wrapping him up in a tight hug, the tears streaming down my face matching the ones he's soaking my Tit Peepers shirt with. "That is not happening, you hear me? You're not going anywhere until you're eighteen, or something better comes along. This is your home for as long as you need it."

"You don't mean that." He sniffs through his tears and tries to push me away, but I squeeze him tighter.

"I do mean that, kid. You're not going anywhere." When his arms wrap around me, I know he's accepted my offer. He'll stay. I sniff back my tears and smile, feeling the rightness of this. This time, when he pushes away from me, I let him go. "Do we have a deal?"

He nods, swiping at his cheeks with the backs of his hands. He blows out a breath, then chuckles. "Yeah, we have a deal. Thanks, Nick."

"No problem, kid. I like having you around." I watch as he fixes his hair in the mirror again, perfecting that swoop one more time. "I, uh, didn't mean what I said about not going anywhere, though." His face drops and I realize my mistake. "No, no. Not like that. I mean that you can still go hang out with your friends and stuff. You're not confined to the house, or anything. You're just not moving out any time soon."

A smile creeps back onto his face, and he nods. "Yeah, of course. I knew that."

"Okay, then. So...yeah. Good talk." I punch his shoulder playfully, not sure what to do now.

He smothers a smile. "Can I go now? My friends are waiting."

I nod, the reality of what I've just done creeping into my consciousness. "Yes. Go. Have fun. Be home by midnight."

"Midnight? That won't work. The movie doesn't start until ten. There's no way we'll make it back from Spitz Hollow by midnight."

He's right. That's not enough time to make it back here. "Text me when you leave the movie theater, then. So I know you're on your way."

Jared smiles again. "Yes, *Dad,*" he jokes. "See you later."

I follow him out of the room and down the stairs, waving from the door as he gets into his friend's car and drives away.

I blow out a breath and leave the house, locking the door behind me. It's been more than the half an hour I said it would be, but I'm still going to see Tina.

After all, I have to find a way to share my big news. I'm basically a dad now.

I RUN BACK TO Tina's place, still wearing my orange shorts and the too-tight Tit Peepers shirt. It's a little uncomfortable, but the way Tina couldn't stop her eyes from devouring me earlier makes it worth it. Too bad I'll need to rip it to get it off.

The first thing I notice when I get to Tina's building is that all the lights are off, both in the restaurant and upstairs in her apartment. And I still haven't changed the lightbulb above the stairs for her, so the only light is from the streetlight at the police station a couple doors down. The next thing I notice is how quiet it is. I'm the only person out here. It's peaceful.

It's peaceful until a scream cuts through the air, shattering the silence like so much fragile glass.

I snicker to myself, and head for the side of the building where the stairs to Tina's apartment are located. Another scream drifts down the stairs. "You dirty son of a bitch." Tina sounds even angrier than she did the last time Winston got into her underwear. He must have gotten into the good stuff. I tighten my grip on the railing in anticipation of his inevitable departure from the apartment. The last thing I need is to be knocked down the stairs by a runaway goat strung with Tina's lingerie. "I can't believe you thought it was okay to come into my apartment. What is wrong with you?"

As I'm climbing the last few stairs to the unlit landing, I hear a man's voice mutter, "We had a date."

Now, I know for a fact that Tina doesn't date. I mean, she's told me often enough, hasn't she? So there's no way she has a date with whoever is talking to her right now. At least, I'm pretty sure she doesn't.

"Get the fuck out of my apartment, you asshole," I hear Tina scream. "I already told you, that wasn't me."

I jump the last two stairs and grip the doorknob to Tina's apartment, but it doesn't turn. It's locked, for once.

"Tina," I call through the door. "Are you okay?"

"Fine." There's a crashing sound followed by a loud thump that rumbles under my feet. "Be right there."

"You bitch," I hear the man reply. "Do you have any idea who I am?"

"I don't give a shit who you are." Another crash punctuates Tina's words. "All I care about is getting you out of my apartment without breaking every teapot I own." Another crash. "Now get out." Crash.

"You would be lucky to go out with me," the guy says. Another crash and another floor shaking thump rattles me. "I took pity on you when I made that date. A high value man like me would never be interested in someone like you."

"Oh, good grief. Can you hear yourself? High value? I can guarantee that any man who has to refer to himself as high value is anything but. Also," she says, her voice getting louder as footsteps sound like they're getting closer to the door. "I would shower more frequently if I were you. I don't know how long you were hiding up here, but thanks to you, my apartment now stinks like shitty body spray and b.o. It's disgusting." The door clicks and then opens. Tina gestures for me to come in but continues facing a strange man laying on the floor in front of her couch.

She's not kidding about the smell. I'm tempted to cover my nose, which is saying something since I work in a gym filled with sweaty fighters and senior citizens every day. A closer look shows that the man is lying in the middle of a ton of broken pottery in a rainbow of colors, with miniature trees, buildings, headstones, and greenery mixed in with the pieces. The cut on his forehead is trickling blood, and his eyes are a little wild when he looks from me to Tina.

"Looks like I missed all the fun." I hold a hand out to the guy on the floor. "I'm Nick. And you are?"

The guy snorts at me with a disgusted look on his face before scrambling to his feet and turning to Tina. "This guy? Really? You're turning me down for this guy?"

Tina laughs. "No, idiot. I'm turning you down because you're a reprehensible worm. Nick doesn't factor into my choice at all. Even if he weren't here, I still wouldn't date you. I have standards."

"You'll regret this," the guy says with a sneer. "You were lucky an alpha dom like me took pity on you once. I can guarantee it will never happen again. A high value alpha only wants a woman who can bring something to the table. All you bring is ugly glasses and a fat ass."

"Okay, that's enough, buddy." I say, crowding into his space, using my size to intimidate him. "Tin—"

"You little weasel." Tina steps around me and pokes a finger in the man's chest, pushing him back toward the door. "I was nice when you came into the restaurant last time, but I'm done with being nice." Quicker than some heavyweights I've fought over the course of my career, Tina winds up and throws a massive haymaker, hitting the guy square in the face, knocking him out on impact. I watch him crumple to the floor, too stunned to even laugh.

"Damn it," Tina complains, shaking out her fist as she looks down at the crumpled heap on the floor. "Now, how will I get him out of here?"

With a chuckle, I step forward, grab the man's arms, and hoist him into a fireman's carry. "That's where I come in. Can you get the door for me?"

Tina scrambles to open the door, her mouth wide as she watches me carry the man out of her apartment and down the stairs. I'm about to drop him on the sidewalk when a voice from the building next door catches my attention.

"Hey, Nick. I heard some concerning noises coming from Tina's place. You the cause of that ruckus just now?" I look over to see Wade Biddescombe standing in front of the door to his realty office. "Is that Milton Maguire you've got there?"

I adjust the dead weight I have slung over my shoulder. "I have no idea. Tina knocked him out because he was in her apartment uninvited. I'm just taking out the trash."

Wade's eyes light up, and the realtor takes a step closer. "Dumpster's around back. I'll get the lid." Without waiting, he walks past me and turns the corner. "Come on, Nick. After what he's done, being thrown into a dumpster is the least he deserves."

And try as hard as I might, I can't see any fault in Wade's logic. "Looks like you're going in the dumpster," I mutter to the unconscious man. I crack a grin and hurry to catch up to my new favorite realtor. "Wade, has anyone ever told you how smart you are? Because this is the best idea I've ever heard."

"Yeah, yeah. If I had my way, he'd get a lot worse than the dumpster treatment. Those days are long behind me, though. And besides, we're too close to the cop shop to get away with anything else."

The stench of sulfur burns my eyes as I flip the unconscious man into the dumpster, and I wonder to myself what Wade meant when he said those days were long behind him. Rumor has it he used to be in the mob, and with the way his eyes gleam as he slams the lid on the dumpster and threads the padlock through the loops to hold it closed, I believe it. It seems like he has a soft spot for Tina, though, which means no matter what he did in the past, he's alright with me.

"Good work, kid," Wade says as we walk back to the front of the building. "I better get back to bed. I have a showing first thing in the morning." He waves to me before going back into his realty office next door. As I lose sight of him, my phone rings.

It's Gloria. She never calls this late.

I press the answer call button and bring the phone to my ear, assuming she's calling to talk about Jared's parents. "Hi, Gloria. Did you find them?"

 Chapter 22

I Have A Plan

Tina

Nick didn't make it back inside after disposing of that asshole, Milton. Instead, about twenty minutes after he carried the intruder out for me, Nick sent me a text.

Nick

Something's come up. I'll call you later.

Despite my immediate reply asking if everything was okay, I still haven't heard from him. After cleaning up the broken pieces of my creepy teapot house collection, and getting mad about that idiot Milton all over again, I had nothing to do but wait. I've been sitting here freaking out for the last half hour, trying to work on a new teapot cemetery, while worrying that Milton somehow convinced Nick he was telling the truth, that I was supposed to go on a date with him. He probably showed Nick the dating app profile that's been making all these random dates. What if Nick believed him? What if he thinks I was blowing him off when I said I don't date? Maybe that's why he didn't bother coming back inside?

Before I can spiral any further, someone pounds on my door. Rather than throwing the door open like I normally would, I call out, "Who is it?"

"Valentina, it's Wade. Open up." What is my landlord doing here this late at night? It's after eleven. There's no way this is good.

I throw open the door to see Wade standing on my step in two-piece, pin-striped pajamas, looking like he's been woken from a dead sleep, his hair sticking up at odd angles. He's methodically cracking the knuckles on each hand, one after the other. *Crack. Crack. Crack.*

"I got a call. The kid's house burned down earlier today. He's okay, but his parents didn't make it."

My heart drops into my stomach as I fight back a sudden wave of nausea. Wade notices that I'm wavering on my feet, and takes my hand to lead me to the couch where I drop like a rock onto the closest cushion.

"They checked him over at the hospital already, and he's fine. He suffered mild burns on his hands and some smoke inhalation, but they're not concerned enough to keep him overnight."

Confusion settles in, along with a healthy dose of worry. I don't know what I would do if something happened to Carson. "He was at work tonight. H-how did he get hurt at all?"

Wade blows out a breath, looking more like Uncle Gianni from the old neighborhood than he ever has. "He went in after them."

"Shit," I mutter under my breath. Of course he went in after them. Carson is a good kid. The best kid. There's no way he'd walk up to the smoking ruin of his house and not try to help his parents. A thought occurs to me. "How do you know all this?"

"I know a guy." He shrugs and sits down beside me before continuing. "When I first figured out what Carson's life was like at home, I told this guy to let me know if Carson ever needed help. When the kid showed up at the hospital tonight, the guy called me. I was helping Nick with your unwanted guest when he called the first time, so he left a message. When I didn't show up at the hospital, he called me again after Carson left. He knew I'd want to know sooner rather than later."

"He left? But where did he go?" Will he have to go live with family now? I never even got the chance to say goodbye. Or give him the sneakers I ordered for him.

Wade shrugs, anger darkening his face. "A social worker picked him up, but my guy couldn't tell me who it was. Apparently, Carson's going to stay at some emergency placement for the next couple of days until they figure out something more permanent. Now that his worthless parents are dead, he doesn't have any living family. They'll probably end up dumping him into the system to rot until he turns eighteen."

My stomach turns to lead as an unknown fear races through me. "No way," I say, my voice taking an edge. "He can stay with me. I'll sleep on the couch until we find a bigger place. Where's my phone? I'll call him and tell him to come here." I pat my pockets and come up empty-handed. Where did I leave that thing?

"I already tried," Wade says, blowing out a breath. "It goes straight to voicemail."

I can't help but smile at the older man, despite the crisis we're currently facing. I knew he had a soft spot for Carson, like he does for all kids, but I didn't know how far he'd go to help when the shit hit the fan.

"Look at you, you old softie." I tease, welcoming the distraction. "Who knew you had it in you?"

He scoffs, his lip turning up at the corner. "Never mind that. What are we going to do about this? We can't let him get shipped off to some stranger's house. There's a chance he won't even end up in Tuft Swallow."

I pull my knee up onto the couch and turn to face him. "I don't know. What *can* we do? I'd say we should go get him, but we don't even know where he is."

"I'm not sure, Valentina. But we can't let him get shipped off to where he doesn't know anyone. And we probably shouldn't kidnap him either. If we want this to work, then we should probably do it the right way." He faces me, his eyes serious. "I'm not really in a position to take in a kid. But you could." He raises an eyebrow. "You'd probably need to get in touch with the social worker. I bet they could tell you what you'd need to do." With a sigh, Wade gets to his feet. "I'll leave you to think about that. I have an early showing in the morning, and I should probably get some sleep. I'll let you know if I hear from the kid. Or if my guy has any other news for me."

I stand and walk him to the door. "Thanks for coming right away to tell me about Carson," I say as he steps out onto the landing. "We'll get this figured out. He won't have to go anywhere if he doesn't want to."

Wade nods and heads down the stairs. "I'll come by and change the lightbulb tomorrow. Sorry I didn't notice before now." He stops on the last step. "And you better close and lock that door right now, too. Milton won't be a problem for a while yet, but he's not that far away."

"What do you mean?" The news about Carson pushed my earlier anger aside, and now it's replaced with irritation.

"We put him in the dumpster," he says with a chuckle. "It's the least he deserves. Goodnight, Valentina."

My mouth drops, and I snort a laugh. "Goodnight, Wade," I say, shaking my head at the thought of Wade and Nick teaming up to throw some guy in a dumpster. Is it weird that I find it heartwarming? Probably.

I close and lock the door, wedging a chair under the doorknob for good measure. The last thing Milton Maguire knew, he was in my apartment being a menace. If he's observant, which somehow I doubt, he might have seen my fist flying toward his face. When he wakes up in a dumpster, there's a chance he'll direct his anger this way. When the door seems like it will hold if he comes back, I set off in search of my phone.

I know Wade said he already tried calling Carson and got no answer, but I'm compelled to try it myself. I'm like the second person arriving at the elevator, pushing the button when it's obvious the first person already did. I need to be sure. After a quick search, I find my phone on the kitchen counter. I must've dropped it there when Milton surprised me. In the dark of the apartment, I didn't notice him sitting on my couch until he said something, at which point I nearly jumped out of my skin and dropped what I was holding.

Carson doesn't answer. The phone doesn't even ring, instead clicking directly over to voicemail. Knowing he hates listening to messages almost as much as I do, I hang up and send him a text instead.

There. It's not nearly enough considering what he's going through, but at least he knows I'm here for him. I don't want him to feel like he's alone in this. He won't be, if I have anything to say about it.

Too wired to sleep now, I dig out the laptop that I normally only use for restaurant stuff, and pull up a search engine. It's time to figure out exactly what I need to do to keep Carson here with me. I type in "how to become a child's guardian" and start reading.

After skimming the first few paragraphs, I settle in for a long night. I'll figure out how to keep Carson here before I go to sleep, even if it kills me.

Chapter 23

CONGRATULATIONS, IT'S A BOY!

Nick

"Hi, Gloria. Did you find them?"

"No, Nick. That's actually not why I'm calling. I'll cut right to the chase. We have an emergency and I need a huge favor. I need you to take in a kid for a few nights. I've called every foster parent in the surrounding area and no one will bring in a seventeen-year-old boy. With the whole Jared situation, I thought maybe you'd have room for one more teenage boy?"

To say I'm stunned is an understatement. I took the foster parent training because of Jared. The only reason I'm qualified is because he and his foster parents wanted him to have an opportunity to train with me for an extended period, effectively making me his caregiver for the duration of his stay. But am I willing to take in another kid? One who wouldn't be here because I'm Odd Duck D'Onofrio, MMA coach and former heavyweight champion. Instead, this kid would be here because I'm Nick D'Onofrio, responsible adult and qualified caregiver.

"I wouldn't ask if it weren't an emergency. I know you didn't set out to become a foster parent. But this kid's had it rough for a long time, Nick. I've been out to his place more times than I can count, but I've never had a reason to remove him from his parents, no matter how badly I wanted to. I'm pretty sure this kid's been looking after himself since he could walk, but I could never prove it."

"He's seventeen? Why doesn't he move out on his own?"

Gloria huffs a laugh. *"He's still in school. By all accounts, he's a great kid. I'm sure he could move out and take care of himself if he'd had time to prepare, but that's the thing. He didn't. He got home from work tonight to find his house on fire."* She pauses, blows out a heavy breath. *"His parents didn't make it."*

All the breath in my lungs leaves in a rush. "Shit."

"Shit is right. And you know what's wild? Even after all the years his parents neglected him, he still went in there trying to save them? There was nothing he could do, but that he tried after the life he's had? This kid deserves a shot, Nick. At least take him until I can somewhere halfway decent to place him."

I scrub a hand down my face. I don't know that I'm ready for the added responsibility of another kid. Sending Jared to the hospital for being drunk was a huge overreaction. What will I do if something happens to this kid? Call in the National Guard? Even if he has to leave town, I'm sure he'd be much better off with a relative. "Doesn't he have family who can take him in? Grandparents? Aunts and uncles?"

Gloria's heavy sigh reverberates through the phone. *"There's no family. His grandparents died before he was born, and the only uncle he has is serving time in a maximum security prison. And he won't be out for a long, long time. He's going to a group home if you can't take him tonight. And the only one that has space is basically a juvenile detention center. This kid would get eaten alive there."*

My heart breaks for the kid. The thought of him having no one at all in his life who could take him in on what has to be the worst day of his short life is enough to make my eyes burn with unshed tears. And it makes up my mind for me. I can't let this kid be shuffled off to some group home. Not when I'm able to do something about his situation right now.

"Okay, Gloria. What do I need to do?"

I can hear the smile in her voice when she speaks. *"I'll take care of everything,"* she says in a rush. *"We'll be at your place in twenty."*

"Sounds good. I'll get his bedroom ready."

As soon as I hang up, I send a text message to Tina.

I'll figure out how to explain this to her when I have a little more time. Right now, I need to run home and get a room ready for a kid I've never met. It's a good thing the trainers who were staying with me for the retreat left as soon as they'd finished dinner tonight, or else I wouldn't have anywhere to stash this kid.

After a quick jog through dark streets, I make it to my house with a few minutes to spare. I've just finished wrestling a clean fitted sheet onto the mattress when the doorbell rings. Leaving the bed unmade, I run down the stairs and throw open the door. Gloria looks at me with a sad smile. A young man stands next to her, a plastic bag slung over one arm as he inspects his shoes.

He smells faintly of smoke, with singe marks and burn holes decorating his jacket sleeves, the bandages wrapped around his hands, a stark reminder of what he's been through tonight.

He ran into a fire to save his parents. That's hero shit, right there, regardless of the outcome.

"Hi, Nick, meet Carson. Carson, this is Nick. You'll be staying with him for a while."

The kid nods without looking up. "Hey," he mumbles.

"Hi, Carson. Come on in." I step back and hold the door open, gesturing for Carson and Gloria to come inside.

"Thanks," Gloria says, her hand on Carson's back as she guides him inside. Other than the clothes on his back, all he has with him is a small plastic grocery sack from a pharmacy. If I'm right, that's the medication for his burns. "Thanks again for making room for Carson on such short notice."

I wave her off. "I have plenty of room. As it happens, all my spare rooms were vacated earlier today."

"You told your company to leave? I'm sorry, man. I can go somewhere else." Carson hurries to apologize, attempting to turn back to the door. I hate that he feels like a burden.

"No, no," I say, placing a hand on his shoulder. "It was a prearranged thing. They left before I even heard you needed somewhere to stay. I promise. The room is yours for as long as you need it." His shoulders slump as he relaxes, his breath leaving him in a steady stream. "I was putting fresh sheets on the bed when you guys got here," I add dumbly.

This kid lost everything tonight, and I'm here telling him about sheets like an asshole. But what could I possibly say to someone whose parents have just died that would help?

"Okay, thanks. Uh..." Carson hesitates, before blowing out another breath. "Do you think I could borrow some clothes for tonight?" He gestures to his body with a bandaged hand. "I'd love to get out of this stuff. It stinks like smoke." He holds his sleeve closer to his face. "And I just now noticed my jacket has burn holes in it. I don't..." His voice cracks slightly as emotion bubbles up. "I didn't get anything out of the house."

"Sure thing," I say with a nod. "You can borrow whatever you need for now, and when you're ready, we'll go shopping and get you some new clothes."

Gloria speaks up. "Oh, um...I don't have authorization to release emergency funds yet. I'm hoping to get that call soon, though."

I roll my eyes. Leave it to the bureaucracy to help without actually helping. "That's fine. I have more than enough."

"I have a little money in my bank account," Carson says. "I can pay you back."

"No way, kid. Gloria and the Department of Children and Families can pay their share and I'm happy to pitch in the rest. I'm sure you're saving up for something a lot better than some new clothes, anyway."

A small smile tugs at the corners of Carson's lips. "Well, I am saving up for some sick basketball shoes and basketball camp this summer."

"There you go," I say with a chuckle, briefly wondering if it's the same basketball camp Tina's part timer wants to attend. "Save your money for basketball and let us take care of the boring stuff."

The kid's eyes take on a faraway look as he nods in agreement. Just as he opens his mouth to say something, the front door swings open, and in walks Jared, home much earlier than expected.

"Hey, guys," he drawls, his voice laced with confusion. "Gloria? What are you doing here? Shit. I'm not leaving already, am I? I'm supposed to stay until school's over." His head swivels frantically between me and Gloria, panic written all over his face. If I ever doubted he wanted to stay here, the look on his face right now would cure me of that thought right quick.

Gloria fixes a friendly smile on her face and turns to Jared. "No, honey. I'm here on other business tonight. Have you met Carson? Maybe you've seen him at school?"

Jared gives Carson a head tip, and receives an answering, "hey."

"Carson's going to stay here with us for a while. Can you take him upstairs and show him his room? I've got him in the one beside yours." Jared nods, his eyes full of questions that he's dying to ask, but he's too polite to do it in front of the other boy. Without giving him any clues, I turn to Carson. "I'll be up soon to finish making the bed, and to get you something to wear. I need to talk to Gloria for a few minutes first."

Carson nods, the dazed look he was sporting when he first arrived here back on his face. He trudges up the stairs behind Jared, leaving me with Gloria.

"What did the doctor say about his hands?" I ask, worried about the bandages I'd seen wrapped around Carson's fingers. "Can he shower? Do I need to go pick up an ointment or something?"

Gloria shakes her head. "The doctor said he can shower right away. He said as long as he keeps the water at a cool temperature, and is gentle with his hands, everything will be fine. And Carson has the ointment and more bandages in the bag he was carrying. He needs to keep the burns covered for a few days, at least. And the doctor wants to see him in a few days, too. I'll text you the appointment information tomorrow when her receptionist sends it to me."

"Okay, yeah. That sounds good." I scrub a hand through my hair. The tightness of the Tit Peepers t-shirt I'm still wearing is more irritating now than it was earlier. "And how is he doing with the rest? With his parents?"

She blows out a heavy breath. "He's keeping it pretty close to the vest. Kids like Carson... sometimes they don't feel safe enough to express their emotions. He'll be seeing a therapist as soon as I can arrange it."

"That's probably a good idea. Can you add Jared to that, too? I have a feeling he's more upset about his foster parents disappearing than he's letting on." The poor kid's been shuffled out of more foster homes than he can count.

"Already on it," she says. "The therapist's office will call you to book an appointment sometime in the next week."

"Good. There's...there's one other thing I was hoping to talk to you about. I was actually planning to call you on Monday, but since you're here now..."

She nods, the smile on her face telling me she already has an idea of what I'm planning to say. "You're in luck. I have a minute to talk."

"I thought maybe we could make Jared's stay here a little more permanent? Since no one knows where his biological parents are, and since this latest set of foster parents appears to have ditched him... Maybe he could stay here? For good. Or, you know, until he goes off to college or whatever he decides to do after he turns eighteen." He's an excellent fighter, and I'll support him if that's what he decides he wants to do, but he's also one of the smartest kids I've ever met, and could do damn near anything else he set his mind to. "He can train with me if he wants to, but instead of this being an extended training camp, it could just be home."

The grin on Gloria's face grows to epic proportions, her genuine happiness shining from her features. "Nick, you have *no idea* how badly I was hoping you would suggest that. I think this would be the perfect place for Jared. I'll get the paperwork started as soon as I get back to the office."

The worry that had been weighing on me magically lifts, and my smile grows to match Gloria's. "Thanks, Gloria. I appreciate it."

She gives me an appraising look, claps me on the shoulder, and says, "You're a good guy, Nick. These boys are lucky to have you."

"Let's not get ahead of ourselves. I know there's a shit ton of paperwork we need to do before we can make any of this permanent. But I still want to get the ball rolling."

"You've already done the hard part. I'm confident I can push this through quickly."

She walks to the door without further preamble, and I watch as she gets into her car to drive away. I've heard some horror stories about social workers, especially those who work with kids and foster parents, but Gloria is one of the good ones. I've never doubted for a single second that she has Jared's best interests at heart, and she's never once made him, or me, feel like a burden for asking questions or needing help.

If she thinks it's a good idea for Jared to stay with me, then I'm confident I'll be able to pull it off.

For now, though, I need to focus on Carson and how I can help him settle in. And after that, how I'll support him as he grieves the death of his parents.

With a fortifying breath, I head upstairs to start on the first part of my task. When I get to Carson's room, I'm surprised to see Jared making the bed, and Carson nowhere to be found. Jared sees the confusion on my face.

"He's in the shower," he says, jerking his thumb toward the bathroom. "I gave him some of my clothes to change into and threw his old stuff into a trash bag until we can get it into the laundry. The smell of smoke was giving both of us a headache."

Yep. I made the right decision. Jared deserves to stay here until he's old enough to decide where he wants to go. It's time for him to have a home. I'm so glad I'm able to provide it.

"Thanks, kid. I appreciate it. How's he doing? Does he like the room alright?"

He shrugs. "He's not talking much. That's pretty standard when it's a kid's first time in foster care, though. No matter how they get there, it's almost like they can't believe it's really happening." He smooths the duvet over the bed and fluffs the pillows. "It's really nice of you to let him stay here. He said he didn't have anywhere to go now that his parents are dead."

I nod, scrubbing a hand down my face. "Yeah, that's what Gloria said, too. She said he doesn't have any family who could help. There's no way I wouldn't let him stay here. I got certified as a foster parent so you could stay for your training camp, but I guess it comes in pretty handy in this situation, too."

Jared barks a mirthless laugh. "I bet you never thought you'd get stuck looking after *two* kids that no one wants when you agreed to bring me here."

My stomach drops.

"Hey." I grab his shoulder and turn him to face me. "I want you here. Both of you. So enough of that 'kids no one wants' bullshit. Got it? You are welcome here for as long as you need." I rub a hand over my forehead. I think I have a headache coming on. "I can't believe I'm spilling the beans already, but I'm working it out with Gloria so that you don't have to leave here until you want to. If it were solely up to me, you could stay here until you're eighteen, or longer if you want. But you know better than anyone that we need to cross all the t's and dot all the i's on the paperwork before we can celebrate."

He swipes at his eyes with the backs of his hands, fighting back a smile the whole time. "You're serious? I can stay in Tuft Swallow?"

"Yes. As long as you promise me one thing."

"What?"

"That you drop the whole unwanted kid thing. Because I want you here."

He grins, sniffling back the tears I'm sure he wants me to ignore. "Yeah. Yeah, of course. I can do that."

"Well, then. Welcome home, Jared."

The kid wraps his arms around me so fast I don't even see it coming. "Thanks, Nick. You won't regret this."

I enfold him in a hug and squeeze. "I know I won't, kid. I'm pretty sure this is the best decision I ever made."

He lets me hug him for a few more seconds before extricating himself from my arms. "Carson, too?" he asks, shocking me. "Can he stay?"

I open my mouth to answer, but the words don't come. Instead, my brain reels with my own unanswered questions. Can Carson stay? Would he even want to? My heart tells me he's more than welcome to stay, if that's what he wants. I never planned on being a foster dad, but now that it's happening, I kind of love the idea.

But how will I ever tell Tina about my newly acquired instant family knowing her thoughts on responsibility and needing to look after people?

And more importantly, how will I go on when she refuses to have anything to do with me after she learns I'm now basically a dad to two teenage boys?

Chapter 24

Time To Talk To The Cops

Tina

After a long night spent reading and rereading everything I could find about becoming a guardian to a minor, I finally figured out what I'll need to do to make it happen. I even managed to sneak in a couple hours of sleep before the screeching of my alarm woke me up way too damn early.

The first thing I do after turning it off is check to see if Carson got back to me. I'm more than a little concerned when I see he hasn't.

With a body shaking stretch, I drag myself out of bed and head to the kitchen to make a pot of coffee before showering and getting dressed. I didn't die from the lack of sleep, but as the twentieth monster-sized yawn attempts to crack my jaw on its way out of my mouth, I regret staying up so late. I may know what I need to do, but it's not something easy or fast. Which is why I'm heading over to the police station as soon as the caffeine kicks in. The first step in my plan is to track down the social worker who picked up Carson, and if anyone would know how to do that, it's Chief Woodcock.

While the coffee is brewing, I take the fastest shower known to man, throw on my usual black leggings and t-shirt, then check my phone again. Still nothing.

I chug a cup of coffee, pour the rest of the pot into a giant travel mug, and head out, making doubly sure to lock the door behind me.

I'm not making the mistake of leaving it open ever again, not after what happened last night. I suppose I should mention that to Chief Woodcock, too. Whether there's something he can do about it or not, he should know that there's likely a man trapped in my dumpster.

Oh shit. The eggs. How could I forget about the six dozen rotten eggs that are still in that dumpster? A laugh bubbles up at the realization that, after spending the night laying on them, Milton will likely smell like rotten eggs for weeks. I refuse to allow myself to feel bad about that, though, because he totally deserves it after the way he acted last night. Maybe the lingering stench will remind him he's not such a catch after all.

I almost stop next door at Wade's to ask if wants to join me when I talk to the chief before I remember he said he had a showing this morning. That, and he probably isn't a huge fan of law enforcement thanks to his shady past. I wonder what happened to get him to move here under an alias? After spending the last few years getting to know him better, I bet it was something altruistic. I could see him turning on his bosses in a heartbeat if he found out they were doing anything to hurt kids. He's always had a soft spot for children of all ages.

Taking a fortifying sip of my coffee, I step into the police station, ready to plead my case to the chief. Not that he makes the decisions for this kind of thing, but he's the first obstacle to finding out where Carson is.

"Good morning, Anita." The secretary is already hard at work behind the reception desk, but she pauses in her typing to throw me a smile.

"Well, good morning to you, Tina. What brings you in so early?"

"Is the chief in yet? I have something important to talk to him about." I take another gulp of my coffee and add, "And if one of the other officers is around, I'd like it if they could check the dumpster behind my restaurant. I had some trouble last night with an unwanted houseguest and I have a sneaking suspicion he may have spent the night with the garbage." There. That should ensure Milton gets looked after, without snitching on Nick or Wade. I'd hate for them to get in trouble when all they did was help me out.

Anita draws her eyebrows in concern. "An unwanted houseguest? Are you alright? For a small town, Tuft Swallow sure isn't as safe as it used to be. If you ask me, a dumpster is too good for someone who intrudes on your space without being invited."

I cringe, scrunching my nose up. "Well, it's partly my fault. I left my door open. Or unlocked. Or open and unlocked, I can't quite remember which."

The secretary waves me off as she picks up the handset of the huge phone on her desk and presses a single button. She holds her hand over the mouthpiece and says, "It doesn't matter if you had it open or not. That's not an invitation for anyone to go traipsing in there." She removes her hand from the mouthpiece and holds a finger up, indicating that she wants me to wait. "Hey, Officer Johnson. I have Tina Falcone here. Uh huh. That's right. Well, she had a spot of trouble with an intruder last night. No, no. She says she's okay. But she would like you to check the dumpster out back of her restaurant... That's what I think, too. A dumpster is the perfect spot for someone like that."

"Psst," I whisper to get her attention. "Tell him to cover his nose when he opens it. I threw away six dozen rotten eggs the other day, and the garbage truck hasn't been by yet."

She nods, her eyes widening. "Oh, and you better use body recovery protocols. Oh no, he's fine, I'm sure. But Tina says she threw out a bunch of rotten eggs the other day, and she's sure you won't want to smell that." She nods as though he can see her, then hangs up and immediately picks up the receiver again. "He says thanks for the tip." She presses another button on the phone. "Chief? Tina Falcone is here to see you... Okay, will do, boss." She hangs up and points to a hallway. "He says you can go straight back."

"Thanks, Anita," I say with a nod, before heading back to the chief's office.

I pause in front of his open door, knocking on the frame to let him know I'm here. He looks away from his computer screen to grant me a welcoming smile. "Come on in, Tina. What brings you by?" He gestures to the chair across from his desk, and I take a seat.

"Thanks for seeing me." I take and blow out a deep breath. "I need a favor."

He cocks an eyebrow and leans back in his chair. "I'll help if I can, Tina, but you know there's not a lot I can do for anyone when it comes to favors. And it goes without saying that I can't help you with anything illegal."

I smother a laugh. "No, no. It's nothing like that. Well, I don't think it is. I need help with finding someone."

He narrows his eyes and gestures for me to go on.

"You know Carson Howe? The teenager who works for me?"

"Yeah, I know Carson. He's a good kid." He nods, steepling his fingers. "It's so sad, what happened."

"Yes, exactly." I nod, sliding forward in my chair. "And here's the thing; he has no living family. It was just him and his parents. I've filled out all the paperwork I could and registered for the classes, but I need to keep him out of the system until I get approved to become a foster parent. I can't let him be sent off to live with strangers, Chief. That wouldn't be right."

"I understand you care for your employee." The chief eyes me, as though trying to gauge what my actual interest is in Carson, and I can't help but feel a little offended, but also relieved. The more people Carson has looking out for his best interests, the better. "But you must realize, even if I knew where he was right now, I couldn't tell you. He's in a vulnerable position. I'm sure you get that."

"You're absolutely right, Chief. But like I said, I'm taking all the proper steps, and I will be a foster parent soon. There has to be something we can do to keep him nearby until that happens."

"Even if you become a foster parent, there's no guarantee that he would be placed with you. He's almost of age, isn't he?"

I nod. "He turned seventeen not that long ago."

"Then he might end up in a group home until his eighteenth birthday."

"We can't let that happen," I say a little louder than I intend to. Worry for Carson is making me careless. Yelling at the chief of police in his own office isn't the best idea. "He has people here who care about him. I care about him. Wade cares about him. We will do everything we can to keep him here with us."

Seeing that I won't be deterred, Chief Woodcock releases a heavy sigh, leans forward in his chair, and grabs a pen. He pulls a business card from the holder on his desk and proceeds to write on the back of it, before passing it to me. "This is who you'll need to call. Her name is Gloria, and she's the social worker who deals with all child welfare cases coming out of Tuft Swallow, and a few other surrounding areas. If anyone can help you track him down, it's her. If she doesn't answer, keep trying. She's a lot busier than you would think."

I huff a relieved breath. "Thank you, Chief. You don't know how much I appreciate this."

He gives me a non-committal nod. "Don't tell anyone I said this, but it's good that Carson has someone who cares as much as you seem to. I don't mean to speak ill of the dead, but his parents were worthless nobodies if I ever saw some. You didn't hear it from me, but we've been called out to their place on more than one occasion, and it's amazing to me it took this tragedy to get Carson out of that house. If it were left up to his parents, that place would have been a rundown shack. Carson is the only one who did anything to make that house a home." His eyes get serious as he stands. "And it didn't escape my notice that most of the time the only food in that place was from Wings and Pizza. It was kind of you to keep him fed like that."

My eyes get a little misty as he confirms my earlier suspicions. Carson only ate what I fed him. I'm extra thankful that I started sending him home with food after every shift, besides what I made him eat every time he showed up for work. He's still too skinny, but I can work on that when he comes to live with me. I know I can't make up for the life that he's lived so far, but I'm going to do everything in my power to make sure the rest of it is a thousand times better.

I don't trust my voice to hold out, so after another quick thank you to Chief Woodcock, I say goodbye and leave his office. I'll give myself a few minutes to calm my emotions, but then I'm calling this Gloria person.

I may not have Carson with me yet, but I will do everything I can to make that happen. Because no matter how much I said I didn't want to look after a bunch of kids, I can't think of anyone more deserving of care than him. And strangely enough, I can't bear the thought of anyone taking care of him but me.

After walking back to Wings and Pizza, I've calmed down enough to give this Gloria woman a call. I'm not letting Carson stay with a stranger any longer than absolutely necessary.

Without bothering to turn on any lights, I sit at my usual table and dial the number the chief gave me, prepared to leave a heartfelt message explaining my situation.

Imagine my surprise when I hear a short, business-like, "*Glorian Freeman,*" come through the phone.

I stutter a moment after the shock of getting a real person instead of a voicemail service. "Oh, um, yes. Hello. My name is Tina Falcone. I own Wings and Pizza in Tuft Swallow?"

Why did I say that like a question? It's not like owning a restaurant will help me in this situation.

"*How can I help you, Tina?*"

To the point. I like her already. Now if she can help me find Carson, I'll like her even more.

"I'm hoping you *can* help me. You see, I'm looking for someone and Chief Woodcock mentioned you might be able to help me track him down. Carson Howe?"

The other woman hesitates before answering. "*I'm acquainted with the young man. But I'm afraid I can't tell you more than that.*"

I blow out a breath. Maybe I don't like this woman after all. "Carson works for me at the restaurant," I say, hoping that will grant me some leeway. "I've been calling and texting him since

I heard about what happened last night, but I haven't heard anything from him yet."

"He doesn't have his phone. He said he dropped it last night. At the house."

Shit. If that's what happened, he won't have a phone at all. And I doubt this social worker will be able to get him a replacement. But I bet that's the kind of thing a guardian would take care of.

"I'll go to Spitz Hollow and pick him up a new one today. Just tell me where to find him and I'll deliver it myself."

The woman blows out a breath, sounding both exasperated and exhausted. *"I can't tell you that. But if you really want to get him a new phone, you can drop it off at my office in city hall. I'm almost never there, but I'll swing by as soon as I can and make sure he gets it. That's the best I can do. Now, if that's all…"*

"No! Wait. I spent all night on my computer last night figuring out how to become a legal guardian. I've filled out the form on the website and now I need to wait for someone to contact me. I was hoping you could help me speed that along? I'm sure you're incredibly busy, but I thought maybe you could send me the application to fill out and then we could set up a meeting for when you have a little free time?"

Silence greets me from the other end of the phone. *"You want to become Carson's legal guardian? Because he works for you?"*

"Well, not only that, no. He works for me because my friend, Wade Biddescombe, found him eating out of my dumpster and brought him in for a meal. I hired him so I could make sure he ate regularly, and so we could keep an eye on him. I want to become his guardian because he's a great kid who deserves a better shake than life has given him so far. And because I would hate for him to have to move away from everything he's ever known when he's so close to finishing high school, you know?" I know I'm rambling, but I can't seem to stop myself. The more

I say these things out loud, the more I realize I need Carson to stay in Tuft Swallow, the more I need to be the one who makes sure he's okay. "And he has that basketball camp this summer that he's been so excited for, too. It would be so unfair if he had to leave before he had the chance to do it. He's been saving up for it. And the basketball shoes he's been drooling over should be here any day. I ordered them as soon as he told me about them."

"Tina, slow down. Take a breath. I understand your feelings of urgency, but there are legal ways to go about this, and I have to follow the law. So how about this? When we hang up, you text your email address to this number. I'll send you that application. I'll come by the restaurant when I have some time over the next couple of days, and we can have our meeting then. In the meantime, you make sure you have everything you need to be eligible to take custody of Carson. I'll send the list of requirements along with the application, okay?"

My heart beats a giddy rhythm as excitement takes over. She'll help me!

"Yes! Oh my God. Thank you so much, Gloria. You do not know how much this means to me."

"Don't get too excited. I can't make any promises. But I happen to have a soft spot for this kid, and I'm willing to wait to find him the best possible placement. And you're right; keeping him in Tuft Swallow is a priority. He's been through a lot in his life, and I'll do everything in my power to make sure he has a great head start as he moves into adulthood."

"I completely understand. That's what I want for him, too."

"Good. I hope you do. Send me that email address and I'll talk to you soon."

She hangs up without saying goodbye, and as soon as the call disconnects, I text her my email address.

So far, things are going better than I planned. I just hope I can maintain this momentum. For Carson's sake.

Chapter 25

DIPPY EGGS AND TOAST SOLDIERS

Nick

THE FIRST NIGHT WITH two boys in the house passes more quietly than I would have expected.

Jared went to bed immediately after our chat. I'm guessing to hide the evidence of his tears from Carson. I don't know of any teenage boy who'd want to be seen crying by another teenage boy, no matter the circumstance. With the way most kids are, that's like asking to be mocked. Hopefully, I can set them straight while they're here with me. Being in touch with your emotions is the only way to be a strong man. You can't expect anyone to feel safe around you if you're constantly pushing everything down until one day you can't handle your emotions

218

and you explode in anger all over the ones you love. Handling your shit starts with handling your own feelings.

Carson kept his feelings locked up pretty tight last night. When he came back from his shower, I helped him apply the burn ointment to his hands, then wrapped them in gauze. Even when I offered to talk, he begged off, claiming he was too tired to do much more than collapse into bed and fall asleep. I wasn't about to force him to talk to me about what he went through, so I said goodnight and left him to it. The lights went out as soon as I closed the door, and I heard him falling into bed like he'd said he would.

Now, it's after noon, and both boys are still sleeping. I figure after such an emotional night, they both needed the extra sleep, so I've been tiptoeing around the house, finishing up some chores and trying to keep the noise to a minimum. For Carson especially, today is will be hard.

He lost his parents last night, and I'm sure that knowledge didn't fully sink in with everything that happened after the fire. Running into a burning house and needing to be rescued would make it hard to focus on anything, I would imagine. Never mind that, Gloria has already called to let me know the coroner has already released Carson's parents, and as their only living relative, Carson is now in charge of arranging for their funeral. I've already called the funeral home to have them collect the bodies, and now I'm waiting to see how Carson wants to move forward.

So yeah, I expect today to be pretty shitty, overall.

But I know one thing that can make it a little better. A home cooked meal from the best chef I know. Even though her last day of catering has already passed, I doubt she'll have a problem doing one more dinner, especially since there will be fewer people to feed. Before I can talk myself out of it, I send her a message.

> Hi Tina, sorry about bailing on you so suddenly last night. There was an emergency at home that I had to deal with, and by the time I was done, it was so late I didn't want to wake you.

Not exactly a lie, but not the full truth, either. I can't tell her about the boys in a text message, though. Partly because it's not the kind of information that you tell someone over text, and partly because I know she'll want nothing more to do with me once she knows. If I insist on telling her in person, at least I'll get to see her one more time. At least she can break my heart to my face.

> Anyway, I was hoping I could order a meal from you for dinner tonight? And maybe you could deliver it to my house, instead of the gym? I need to see you, but I can't leave home for the next while. I promise I'll explain everything when you come over.

I linger over my phone for a few minutes, waiting for the dots to show me she's writing her response. When nothing happens, I slide my phone into my pocket and head into the kitchen to make lunch. I may not be as talented in the kitchen as Tina, but I know my way around a plate of bacon and eggs, so that's what

I make. When the bacon is crispy, I turn to get eggs from the fridge to find two teenage boys lurching into the room, eyes half closed, rumpled pajamas hanging from their bodies.

"Is that bacon?" Jared asks.

"And eggs?" Carson adds.

They grin at each other and each take a seat at the table, swiping the plate of bacon from the counter on their way by.

I shake my head and laugh as they stuff several pieces in their mouths at once, making a plan to cook up some more bacon after I finish the eggs. "How do you like your eggs, Carson?"

His eyes widen as he rushes to chew before roughly swallowing the pile of bacon. "Umm, however you make them, I guess?"

I reduce the temperature of the induction burner and look at him. "You don't have a preference?"

He shrugs. "Never really ate a lot of eggs. My parents never made them for me and it wasn't something I ever considered learning to make for myself."

An audible gasp drops from my lips as my mouth drops open. I cannot let this injustice stand. "That's not right. You hold on a minute then, kid. You're getting the kind of eggs every kid has to have at least once in their life." I push the lever on the toaster before cracking six eggs into the pan. "And you're getting some too, Jared."

The boys scarf down the rest of the bacon while I cook up a modified version of my favorite breakfast from when I was a little kid. The look on their faces when I pass each of them a plate holding three sunny-side up eggs with a pile of toast cut into sticks beside them is one of utter confusion. Jared's had bacon and eggs with toast many times in this house, but I think this is the first time he's seen me cut the toast this way.

"It's my version of dippy eggs and soldiers. See? The toast sticks are like little soldiers and you dip them into the egg yolk before taking a bite. Traditionally, you're supposed to use soft-boiled eggs for the dippy eggs, but I've always preferred it this way. If you guys want to try it with the soft-boiled eggs, though, I can pick up some egg cups next time I go shopping." Maybe. Now that I'm thinking about it, I can't remember ever seeing egg cups at the store. I might have to order those online. Thank God for online shopping.

Both boys look at me with confusion, their eyebrows scrunched up in identical grimaces that say, "what is with this guy?".

"Just try it. Dip your toast into the egg. It's a silly way to eat eggs and toast. It's not that serious."

One by one, they each pick up a stick, dip it into an egg yolk, and take a bite. The matching smiles they wear as they immediately begin to shovel down the rest of their breakfasts tell me I made the right call. I know dippy eggs with toast soldiers is a dish usually served to little kids, but neither of these boys had the luxury of having normal childhoods. They didn't have anyone in their life who cared enough to cook eggs and cut toast into strips, and I needed to fix that. I care enough that I will make them dippy eggs and toast every day if that's what it takes to show them how much I care.

While they finish their breakfast, I cook some more bacon, then make myself some eggs and toast and join them. As soon as the plate of bacon touches the tables, they both grab several more pieces. We eat in a companionable silence for a few minutes, each of us enjoying our breakfasts. But the silence can't last, not with two teenage boys in the house, and not with so many things we need to get done as soon as possible.

"So...what the heck is an egg cup?" Jared asks.

Carson stifles a laugh. "I thought he made that up."

I grin at the two of them. After everything they've been through, especially with Carson's recent loss, that they can sit here with me and laugh at something as silly as an egg cup, well, it's truly a blessing. I know things won't always be easy, but if I can give them moments like this, moments where they eat a big breakfast and laugh at something ridiculous, everything will be alright.

"Egg cups are exactly what they sound like. Cups for eggs."

The boys both snicker, fighting hard to contain their laughter. "But why?" Carson asks.

"So you can eat your soft-boiled egg, of course. First you have to chop a bit of the top of the shell off, then you use a spoon, or your toast soldier, to scoop out the inside of the egg. If you didn't have a special cup to hold your egg, it would be pretty hard to do any of that."

They burst into laughter, the loud, gleeful sounds echoing off the walls of the mostly bare kitchen, and my heart swells. I came to Tuft Swallow hoping to start a family, and here all I had to do was wait for one to find me.

After they calm themselves, Carson looks over at me, a small smile on his face. "You know, I think I might like to try the traditional style of dippy eggs after all."

I smile. "Okay. I'll track down some egg cups and we'll have traditional dippy eggs and soldiers."

When we've all finished our food, the boys clean up the plates and load the dishwasher before heading back upstairs. Jared is helping Rhett with the Spring Chickens movement class today, which leaves me with some time to talk to Carson about how he's doing.

I don't really understand it, but he doesn't seem very broken up about the fact his parents died last night. Although, if what Gloria was saying is true, and this kid raised himself for most of his life, then he probably mourned his parents long before they ever died. I don't know much about what it's like to be raised by alcoholics, but it makes sense that he wouldn't have a powerful reaction to their passing if they weren't there for him much to begin with. It makes sense, but that doesn't make it any less sad.

I've just finished ordering egg cups in several ridiculous styles when my phone dings with a message from Tina.

Swing by? Doesn't she have to work?

I snort a laugh.

"That has to be your girlfriend to have you grinning like that." Carson walks into the room wearing some clothes he obviously borrowed from Jared. Carson has a good six inches on the other kid, so the jogging pants are several inches too short, but at least they fit around the waist. I hadn't thought it through when I offered him my clothes, but there's no way anything I own would stay on this kid's body, at least not without some serious belting.

"Oh, uh…" I hesitate, unsure of how to respond. Tina could have eventually been my girlfriend before I agreed to take on the raising of two teenage boys, but now I doubt she'll want that kind of relationship with me. I could easily prove that I wouldn't need looking after, but I don't think the same could be said about two kids. And I'd never expect her to compromise her life for my sake. "As much as I'd like her to be, I don't think that's going to work out like I'd hoped."

He nods more sagely than a kid his age has a right to. "I hear you. Unrequited love is the worst."

I smother a chuckle. "Oh, yeah? You have a lot of experience with that, do you?"

"Not in the way you'd think," he says with a heavy sigh. "But unrequited is unrequited, no matter who it is, right? So I know a thing or two."

Shit. He's talking about his parents. He's talking about loving his parents and them not loving him back, and now I'm going to cry in front of this teenage boy and he'll think I'm too much of a baby to take care of him properly. Why did I think I could do this? How can I support this kid when the mere mention of his parents makes me cry?

"So…" he says, breaking my runaway train of thought. "Can you help me with something?"

I school my features, swallow my sadness, and say in my most competent sounding voice, "Of course. What do you need?"

"I think I need to deal with my parents. With their bodies, I mean."

My mouth drops open at his casual tone. Even now, he doesn't seem that upset.

"You think I'm weird, don't you?" he asks when he sees the look on my face. "Because I'm not completely fucked up over my parents' death?"

"I mean, something like that crossed my mind. Not that I think you're weird, but that you're handling this a lot differently than I would if it were my parents."

He nods. "Yeah. I think if I had a different relationship, or any relationship, with mine, things would be different. But they chose alcohol over me a long time ago. I've been dreaming of getting out of that mess for as long as I can remember. You know, I couldn't tell you the last time I even spoke to them. Most days, I'd go straight to my room and lock the door as soon as I got home. I doubt they would even remember I lived there if it weren't for that social worker showing up a couple of times a year. They were strangers to me, like I was to them. It's hard to miss something you never had."

The silence that settles around us should be uncomfortable, but instead, it feels more like acceptance. After a few moments, I lean forward and say, "Okay. Then let's get started on the funeral arrangements."

 Chapter 26

TOM SELLECK'S MUSTACHE

Tina

"So he'll be able to transfer all his contacts and stuff over?"

"You bet, ma'am. And if he has trouble, bring him in and we can help him figure it out." The young man working at the cell phone store assures me that Carson won't have an issue recovering his contacts. I've never tried to set up a new phone without having the old one right next to it, so I'm not so sure, but this guy seems confident.

I pay for the phone and tuck the box into the bag of clothes I also picked up for Carson. I realized when I was driving into Spitz Hollow that Carson most likely lost all his clothes in the fire, along with all of his other belongings, so I picked up a few things for him before I came to get the phone. Well, I picked up several things that took far too long to find, but it's not a big deal. It's not that many clothes, but it's enough to get him through a few days until we have time to take him shopping. I'm sure he has so much on his mind right now that he's not worried about the clothes he's wearing, but it's not like I can do much else for him right now. I'll leave the clothes at Gloria's office when I drop off the phone and she can make sure he gets them.

Since I left the chief's office earlier, all I've been doing is checking tasks off a list. Pick up new phone. Check. Buy some clothes. Check. Call Wade about finding me a new place with an extra bedroom for Carson. Check. Get groceries for dinner at Nick's. Doing that now.

It only takes a few minutes to find what I need in the grocery store, and within fifteen minutes, I'm back in my car with a back seat full of bags. I'm about to pull out of the lot and head back to Tuft Swallow when the phone rings with a number I don't recognize. My heart races as I stab the answer call button without lightning speed and shout into the receiver.

"Hello? Carson? Is that you?"

"*Carson? Who's Carson? This is your mother. Did you forget we had a call today?*"

"Mom? Whose phone are you calling from? I don't recognize this number." I hear a commotion in the call's background, which is a sure sign she's with my aunts. But I have all of their phone numbers and this number is not one of them.

"*Oh, it's—what's your name, young man?*" There's some indistinct mumbling in the background. "*Well, I never. Do you kiss your mother with that mouth?*" More mumbling, a little louder this time. "*Ohhhh, Woodcock. I thought you said Hardcock. You know, like an innuendo? I thought you were plonking me. What's that? Plunking? Punking? No, I'm pretty*" *sure it's plonking.*" Even louder mumbling from the background while my mother laughs. "*Yes, Woodcock is a very respectable name. I'm so sorry for the misunderstanding. Valentina? Are you still there?*"

"Yes, Mom." I drop my head back, bumping my messy bun on the headrest. "I'm still here."

"*Oh. Good. The young man said his name is Jay Woodcock.*"

Jay Woodcock? Why does that sound so familiar... Oh, shit. I shoot forward in my seat, back ramrod straight. No, no, no. Please tell me this is a horrifying coincidence, and she's not where I think she is.

"Mom?" I pinch the bridge of my nose under my glasses, rubbing at the headache that is forming between my eyes. "Are you-are you and the aunts in Tuft Swallow right now?"

"*Yes, we are. And your father and Nonna Mona are here, too. Say hello, you two.*" I hear my dad and Nonna yell hello in the background. "*When we didn't hear from you earlier, we thought it would be fun to drive out and surprise you. But wouldn't you know it? When we got out of the car, we locked the keys, and all our phones, inside. Can you believe that? This nice Chief Woodcock happened along just as your father was about to climb into your dumpster to find something to use as a... what did you call it, Stan? A skinny Jerry? A thin Tim? A who? A slim Jim? Are you sure? That doesn't sound right.*" My dad's muffled words echo in the background. "*Okay, you don't have to get huffy about it. He was trying to find something to use as a slim Jim to pop the door locks. Did you know your dumpster smells like the gates of hell? And why aren't you at the restaurant? It's getting close to dinnertime and I don't even smell any sauce.*"

The headache becomes a sharp stab behind my eyes as I listen to my mother's barrage of questions. But there's no way around this visit now. They're already in Tuft Swallow. There's nothing for it but to have Nick bring his guests to the restaurant, where

I'll subject all three of them to my overbearing family. This should be...fun.

"I'm over in Spitz Hollow. I had to pick up some stuff for a friend, but I was about to head back."

"Ooh, a friend. Which friend? Is this a boyfriend?"

"No, Mom. It's not stuff for a boyfriend. It's for the kid that works for me. I'll tell you about when I see you, okay? It's complicated. And you'll probably think I'm crazy for what I'm planning."

"I doubt that, sweetheart. Nothing could be crazier than moving away from your entire family to open this pizza restaurant in a tiny town none of us had ever even heard of before. Now that was crazy."

"Okay, Mom." I rush to derail that line of conversation because otherwise I'll be here in this parking lot for the rest of the night. "Listen, I'll be home in about twenty minutes. Why don't you go have a drink at the Crow Bar next door? I'll explain everything when I get back."

She hums into the phone, and I can tell I've piqued her curiosity. *"Alright, Valentina. We'll see you soon. Drive safely. Wear your seatbelt."*

I roll my eyes at her reminder to wear a seatbelt, because for my entire life, it's literally the first thing I do when I sit in a vehicle. She drilled it into all of us when we were kids, but somehow seems to think we all still need reminders. I love my mom, but sometimes she can be a bit much.

"You bet, Mom. See you soon."

I hang up and quickly pull up Nick's contact information so I can tell him about the change of plans.

I snort a laugh when I read his reply.

I totally understand if you don't want to come. I can deliver some food from the restaurant if you prefer. We're still closed today, but I'll be cooking for all my crazy relatives anyway, so you're more than welcome to join us there.

Having my family here will give me something other than Carson to worry about, at least for a little while.

He doesn't answer right away, so my mind runs away with itself. Why would he want to meet my family so soon? Or ever. We're not together. It makes sense that he wouldn't want to know any more about me than he already does. We slept together a few times and went for a walk. And laughed. And talked. And he carried an intruder out of my apartment. And he's the best snuggler.

Damn it. I really like him. I probably more than like him, if I'm being honest. Now is not a good time for this. Not while trying to get this situation with Carson sorted out. But I can't seem to get him out of my head, no matter how inconvenient the timing is.

We'll be there. Want me to bring anything?

The breath leaves my lungs in a rush of air as my shoulders slump with relief. *That was a stressful couple of minutes.*

I tuck my phone away, take a deep breath, and start the car. Time to get this over with so I can get back to what's really important. Finding Carson. And maybe after that, figuring out what this thing with Nick is.

"Hi, Honey." My dad jumps off his barstool and throws an arm over my shoulder before planting a sloppy kiss on my cheek. "I've missed you so much."

"Hey, Dad. Where is everyone else?" I swivel my head around, looking for my mother and aunts. However, they're nowhere to be seen.

He rolls his eyes. "Nonna Mona saw a bus full of old folks and demanded they follow it. Before I knew what was happening, your mother had handed me a twenty and steered me toward this bar. They all piled in the minivan and left me here to drink by myself."

Charlene tips her chin up at me from behind the bar. "Hey, Tina. Stan's your dad?"

I smile as I glance back at my father. He's been here ten minutes and is already on a first name basis with the bartender. "Yeah, Charlene. Sounds like he drove a van full of women over an hour to come visit me, then they ditched him as soon as they could."

She shrugs. "He seems nice."

"This wonderful young lady put on the sports channel while I waited for you. She wouldn't let me watch anything other than last year's American Cornhole League Superhole championship, though."

"It's like I already told you, Stan. We take our cornhole seriously here in Tuft Swallow. If we're watching sports highlights, it's cornhole or nothing."

Dad nods, grabbing his beer from the bar top and taking a swig. "You make a valid point, Charlene. When in Rome, and all that. Maybe I should learn how to play?"

"I bet you'd like it, Dad. They probably even have a seniors' league in Boston if you really got into it."

He grins as he chugs the rest of his beer. "You think I could meet that Shemar Moore fella?" He nods at the TV where, sure enough, the actor Shemar Moore is winding up to toss a bean bag at a cornhole board while his ACL Pro partner looks on with confidence. "He's been number one on my hall pass list since his Derek Morgan days." He swipes at his mouth with the back of his hand, pulls a twenty-dollar bill from the front pocket of his shirt, and drops it on the bar top. "Charlene, honey. It has been a real pleasure." He raps his knuckles on top of the twenty. "Keep the change."

Charlene stares after him, mouth and eyes wide, watching as he walks out of the bar. "Did your dad just...?"

"Did my sixty-seven-year-old father say he has a handsome male actor at the top of his hall pass list?" I grin, loving the fact that my father has always been more comfortable with his sexuality than many other men his age. "He sure did. That's pretty standard for him. What I'd like to know is, when did Shemar Moore take the top spot? Because last I heard, Tom

Selleck and his magnificent mustache were permanent residents of the number one position."

Charlene barks a laugh. "I kind of love your dad."

"Yeah. I kind of love him, too." I smile and follow my dad out the door. No matter how helpless my father might be around the house, he's a decent man.

The sight that greets me when I get back to the street makes me freeze. There, standing in front of my restaurant, talking to my dad, is Wade Biddescombe. And I'm just now realizing I forgot to call him and warn him about my family being here so he'd be able to keep his real identity private. And from the look on my dad's face right now, he recognizes him.

Then, as if that weren't enough to knock me off my feet, a familiar voice calls out from behind me.

"Tina!"

I spin around to find Carson a few storefronts away and the worry about Dad and Wade drifts away. The relief is immediate and immense, making my knees wobble. "Carson! Oh my God, where have you been?" When he reaches me, I throw my arms around him, squeezing him tightly as the tears well up and sting my eyes. I hold him away from me, scanning his body from head to toe, taking in his too-short pants and bandaged hands with a sob. "Are you okay?"

He gives me a sad smile, knowing I'm not asking about just the hands. He swallows roughly, and nods. "I am, Tina. It's... hard. And weird. But I'm okay."

I choke out a relieved sob and wrap him in another hug. "I was so scared we wouldn't see you again. When Wade came over and told me what happened, and then said a social worker had picked you up, well... I thought she'd take you away from Tuft Swallow before I could find a way to keep you here with us."

He chuckles and fidgets, clumsily working his way out of my hug. "Come on, Tina. I have a shift today. You know I'd never no-call, no-show on you."

My mouth drops open, and I have to fight to stop from smacking my palm into my face. I can't believe I didn't think of that. I've been running myself ragged trying to find Carson when all I had to do was wait for him to show up for his shift. I shake my head and grin. "Come on, then, kid. We're closed today, but I can still use your help. My family showed up and I have a friend bringing a couple of people in for dinner. We need to start right away if we have any chance of making food before my mother gets back. That woman has taken over every kitchen she's ever been in."

And I need to talk to my father so he knows not to go home and blow Wade's cover. Because no matter who he used to be in the past, the Wade Biddescombe of today is a decent man and a good friend.

Chapter 27

MOM'S FRIED CATFISH

Tina

"Hey, *Wade*," I say, placing extra emphasis on his name for my dad's benefit. "Got any news for me?"

Wade's grateful smile tells me he's happy for the interruption. Whatever my dad was saying to him must have been making him uncomfortable. "Not exactly, Valentina. But let's talk about that later," he says, tipping his head in greeting before turning to Carson, his smile widening and becoming sad all at the same time. "Carson. Good to see you, kid. How're you doing?"

"Hey, Mr. Biddescombe." Carson rocks back on his heels, his hands shoved deep into the pockets of his too-short jogging pants. "I'm okay, I guess."

My dad shoots me a confused look before darting a glance at Wade. I know he's trying to ask me about the man's identity, but Carson mistakes his look to be a question for him instead.

"I...uh...my parents died last night," he says in a rush. "But they weren't good people. And maybe I'm not a good person either, because I'm not that upset about the whole thing."

My heart breaks to hear him say that he's not a good person, but before I can pull him into a hug and smother him with reassurances, my dad intervenes.

My dad's face softens, and he steps up to wrap Carson in a hug. "Even if they weren't good people, they were your parents. However you feel about it is okay. And not being upset doesn't make you a bad person. It makes you human." He smooths Carson's hair before kissing him on the top of the head. "Grieving is a very personal thing, and you get to do it however you want."

Carson freezes at the head kiss, but sinks into the hug a moment later, and I can feel the tension seep from his shoulders.

"Hey, Dad? I know Carson appreciates the sentiment, but maybe next time we can try doing the introductions before we throw in the hugging and kissing?" I say, steering the conversation to something less depressing for now. "Carson, this is my dad, Stan Falcone. Dad, this is Carson. He works for me in the restaurant."

Dad chuckles and releases Carson from the hug, holding a hand out for a shake. "Nice to meet you, Carson."

Carson takes my dad's hand. "Nice to meet you, too, sir."

I unlock the door to Wings and Pizza and hold it open. "Carson, can you get started on some prep? I need to talk to my dad for a second."

"I'll come keep you company," Wade says to Carson. "I have something I wanted to ask you."

As soon as they're out of earshot, my father turns to me, his eyes wide. "Do you know who that is, Tina?" He asks in a harsh whisper.

I give him a pointed look. "That's Wade Biddescombe, Dad. The best realtor in Tuft Swallow, and my landlord and neighbor." I point to Wade's office next door. "As for who he used to be... well, that doesn't matter to me. And I can only hope it doesn't matter to you, either."

"You can't be serious, Tina."

"I am so fucking serious right now, Dad." Panic wells in my chest as I worry that my dad's going to say something to the wrong person and Wade will pay the price. "Wade has done nothing but look out for me since I got here. If it weren't for him charging me so little rent, my restaurant would have closed years ago. I will never forgive you if you go blabbing your mouth and get him killed."

My dad recoils, pulling his hands to his chest as he sucks in a gasp of indignation. "I would *never,*" he hisses, his eyes narrowing. "Stanley Falcone is no snitch."

I shake my head, unsure of what I'm hearing. If he's not ratting him out, why does he care if Wade Biddescombe is who he says he is? "What am I missing here?"

Dad chuckles and rolls his eyes. "Come on, Tina. Don't you remember anything about the man I've obviously mistaken your friend for?" He winks, and I release a breath. He'll keep Wade's secret. But why? "Your friend, Wade, looks a little like someone who used to come to the old neighborhood from time to time. He disappeared several years ago, after many of his associates were arrested for their involvement in a sex trafficking ring. It seems someone didn't agree with their treatment of children and turned them, and a lot of very damning evidence, over to the FBI."

I stare dumbfounded at my father, his face filling with glee as he tells the story. Holy shit. It's like I thought. I knew it had something to do with helping kids.

"I think I got a little carried away when I thought I recognized him, hoping maybe I'd get the chance to shake the hand of the man who single-handedly saved the lives of so many people." He blows out a happy breath and shows me a brilliant grin. "But I would be just as happy to shake the hand of the man who helped my youngest daughter achieve her dream. Come on," he says, opening the door with one hand, and looping his other arm through mine. "Come introduce me properly. I want to thank him for giving you a helping hand when you needed it."

The sound of a roaring engine and squealing tires makes me jump, drawing my attention away from my father and the door. I spin around just in time to see my parents' minivan screeching to a sliding stop by the curb. It rocks as it settles into position after stopping so abruptly, then every door opens and an army of black-haired women streams out, every one of them talking at once.

"Valentina." My mother smiles at me with love in her eyes, running over to hug me. "I've missed you, sweetheart."

"You'll never believe what we found." My aunt Vera says.

"It's too good to be true," Aunt Maude adds. "I love this town."

"That's the place for me." Nonna Mona says, waving a handful of brochures in my direction. "They call themselves Spring Chickens, if you can believe it. My new friend Martha said she'd bring me to her gym so I can see the hot piece of ass they got running the place over there. She says his shorts are so short you can almost see his ding—"

"Ma!" my dad yells. "No one wants to hear that."

"And she said the other guys they got running around there aren't bad to look at, either. I can't wait." Nonna rubs her hands together, a gleam in her eye.

My dad cocks an eyebrow at my mother, who can only nod and smile. "She really enjoyed her visit," she says. "The rooms are nice and the people living there seemed like they were having a great time."

"But Mom," my dad says, interrupting Nonna as she tries to continue her earlier statement about someone's short shorts. *I wonder if Nick knows exactly what those shorts do to all the women who see him wearing them? What they do to me?* "I thought you didn't want to move into a home."

Nonna waves him off. "Eh," she says with a shrug. "I didn't before, but you should see this place, Stanley. It's like living with a group of friends in college. Did I tell you they have a cornhole team? And they said I could join. It's been a long time since I had my hands on a quality bag. I haven't even thought about it since your father passed. Rest his soul."

I snort a laugh, faking a cough to hide it, just as the familiar dinging sound of a brass bell gets my attention.

"Oh, what a sweet boy you are. Aren't you the cutest little thing?" Aunt Vera's voice carries over Nonna's continuing talk of getting her hands on weighty bag, mercifully distracting me from (what I'm hoping are) Nonna's unintentional innuendos.

I look past my grandmother as she squeezes the fingers of her empty upturned hands, demonstrating her method of testing a bean bag's heft, to find Aunt Vera, Aunt Bernice, Aunt Dorothy, and Aunt Maude all cooing at none other than Mayor Winston, who somehow manages to look smug as he climbs out of the minivan. *What the hell?*

"Uh…" I screw up my eyebrows in confusion. "Why did you have a goat in the van?"

Aunt Vera answers without looking away from the goat in question. "This poor goat was walking in the middle of the road, Valentina. It's not safe."

"That is not a poor goat. That is Winston. He is an unrepentant underwear thief, and a general menace." Winston looks directly at me with his creepy sideways pupils and licks his lips. The nerve of him!

"Nevertheless, he shouldn't be walking around on his own. Anything could happen."

"So your solution was to put a two hundred pound farm animal into a minivan? How did you even get him in there?"

She shrugs. "We had snacks."

"You had snacks?" This group of ladies lured a farm animal into their vehicle with snacks, and they see nothing wrong with that? Worry races through me at the thought of Winston's hot daddy finding out about this goatnapping because my crazy family fed his goat something toxic. "Please tell me you didn't feed him anything that would be bad for him."

Aunt Bernice laughs. "Oh no, dear. Of course not. We just gave him a few little peppermints."

I blow out a relieved breath. I've witnessed countless people using peppermints to lure Winston away from things he shouldn't be getting into. In fact, deputy mayor Verona uses them when she needs Winston to make a public appearance as the mayor. Apparently, the soft peppermints are his favorite. "Thank goodness that's all you gave him. His owner won't be happy that you kidnapped his goat, but I have a feeling he'd be even less happy if you'd poisoned him."

"His owner? This goat was wandering in the middle of the street. I doubt his owner cares much about what happens to him."

I swivel my head around, expecting to see Winston's hot daddy storming up any minute. "He loves that goat like it's his own child." Or at least I assume he does. Winston's hot daddy is notoriously hard to read. "This is a small town, and this particular goat just so happens to be the mayor. He's allowed to go wherever he wants."

I'm expecting laughter at my announcement, which is the usual reaction when outsiders learn of Winston's mayoral status, but instead I'm met with silent mouths and widening eyes.

"What's wro—" I'm interrupted by a firm tap on the shoulder, and it's only then that I notice Winston's mounting excitement. I turn my head ever so slowly, looking up and up until I spy the scowling face of Tuft Swallow's favorite mechanic... also known as Winston's Hot Daddy. "Oh, hey... you." I've lived in Tuft Swallow for five years and I've yet to ferret out the name of the man standing in front of me. I know he's lived here for years too, so someone around town has to know it, but most of us, women and men alike, refer to him as Winston's Hot Daddy. Not to his face, of course.

He points at Winston, saying nothing.

"Yeah, I know. I'm sorry about that. My family showed up for a surprise visit and when they saw Winston wandering around town, they were worried something might happen to him. So they... so they brought him here."

His expression doesn't change throughout the course of my little speech, but I can sense that he softens, becoming less angry as I go on.

"They had no idea that Winston goes wherever he wants." My mother and aunts all murmur their agreement. "They're all very sorry for the inconvenience."

The slight upturn at the corner of his mouth makes me think we're in the clear. That is, until with a tip of his chin, he has me turning around just in time to catch sight of Winston attempting to sneak around the corner to the stairs that go up to my apartment. I spin back to see Winston's dad and his cocked eyebrow, and I can feel it in my bones that he knows of Winston's little underwear stealing escapades. Knows and thinks it's hilarious.

"You sneaky bastard, Winston," I yell, before pointing a finger in the goat's dad's face. "And you. You owe me new underwear."

The man chuckles, which for Winston's Hot Daddy is about the same as bursting into laughter, while my family members watch me run after the thieving goat. I'm halfway up the stairs before I realize my door is closed and locked, leaving Winston with no way to get inside. My underwear drawer is safe. I chuckle when I see the goat standing at my door, with something like consternation coloring his features. Who knew goats could be so expressive?

"Serves you right, you old goat. Try to steal my underwear now."

I'm in the middle of staring him down when a loud whistle sends him flying down the stairs. I'm forced to hoist myself onto the railing to avoid being trampled by two hundred pounds of stampeding goat. By the time I climb down and make my way back to the front of the store, Winston and his hot daddy are already halfway back to Impeckable Auto.

"Valentina, did I hear you tell that man he owes you new underwear? Is he the reason you forgot to call me today?" My mother can't contain her excitement, her eyebrows waggling even as a massive grin takes over her face. "He's *very* handsome. And you can tell he'd be a wonderful father because of how much he cares for that goat."

I squeeze my eyes shut to stop them from rolling. "Weren't you all *just* complaining about him letting Winston wander wherever he pleases?"

My mother huffs. "Well, that's before I knew the goat was the mayor of this town. The constituents need to have access to their mayor, so it makes sense to let him go where he pleases."

I don't tell her it would make more sense if he stayed in one spot so people knew where to find him, because even that is ridiculous. Having a goat as a mayor is a silly thing, and no matter where the goat is, it's not like he can actually perform any of his mayoral duties. Except for ribbon-cutting ceremonies. He chews the ribbon instead of cutting it, and no one seems to mind. Except Verona, but she's still mad about the whole losing-an-election-to-a-goat thing.

That's neither here nor there, though, because the only reason my mother is making so many excuses for Winston is that she thinks I'm involved with his daddy. And as much as I'm sure he's a catch, my heart belongs to another.

I smile. "Actually, Mom. I'm seeing someone else."

My mother and aunts all begin to chatter excitedly, their voices getting higher and louder as they compete to speak over each other.

"Oh, what's his name?"

"When do we get to meet him?"

"Which one was it?"

"I can't wait to spoil your children."

"Does he have a pet goat too?"

"Hi Tina, are you ready for our date?"

Hold up.

That last voice didn't belong to one of my relatives. I spin around and spot Mr. Landon straightening his brown corduroy suit with one hand and holding a single yellow rose out to me with the other.

"Mr. Landon?" I ask, my voice laced with confusion. It's the only thing I can think of to say. *A date? With Mr. Landon? He's got to be twenty years older than me. And if he isn't, he sure dresses that way.*

"Please call me Leonard, Tina. It wouldn't be proper of you to call me Mr. Landon on our date." He notices I've not taken the rose, so he tucks it into a buttonhole on his jacket, turning it into an oddly placed and overly long boutonniere. "Are you ready? I can wait if you'd like to change." He glances down at my black t-shirt and leggings. "You look beautiful the way you are, but if you'd like to dress up, I'm happy to wait while you get ready."

I shake off the confusion enough to say, "Mr. Landon? We don't have a date."

How is this still happening? I really need to figure out who is making these men think I've agreed to go out with them. Although, I suppose I should be thankful that Mr. Landon isn't another one of those incel douchebros from that tech place in Spitz Hollow. Seriously, did that place only hire raging misogynists on purpose, or was that some sort of unfortunate accident?

He pulls a cell phone from his pocket, looking confused. "Yes, we do. I suggested tonight we could make up for the date that was ruined by the unfortunate sauce incident and you agreed. See? it's right here." He points to a spot on the screen and passes his phone to me.

Sure enough, there I am in a text message agreeing to a do over date for a date that I hadn't agreed to in the first place. And poor Mr. Landon seems so excited at the idea of going on a date with me, I actually feel a little guilty about having to let him down. The other guys who showed up expecting dates were dicks, so I didn't much care if I hurt their feelings, but Mr. Landon has always been nothing but kind to me.

"Mr. Landon," I begin, softening my voice.

"Please, call me Leonard."

"Leonard," I say with a nod. "I am so sorry, but I did not make that date with you. Someone has been impersonating me on dating sites. Several men have shown up here claiming to have made a date with me when I knew nothing about it. It appears you've fallen victim to someone's catfishing scheme. You seem nice, and if things were different, I would probably enjoy going on a date with you, but I'm afraid I'm already seeing someone."

The brown-suited man sighs, his shoulders slumping. "It's Nick, isn't it?" he asks, with resignation in his voice. "I could tell that day with the sauce. The way you two looked at each other was electric."

"Who's Nick?" comes a harsh whisper from behind me, a stark reminder that Mr. Landon and I have an audience. "Is that the man with the goat?"

"I should get going, Tina. Sorry to have bothered you. Let me know if things don't work out with Nick. I'd love to tell you all about my work with documentary films." True to form, he trips over his own feet as he turns around, but catches himself before he crashes to the sidewalk. "I'll see you around." He says without looking back.

"Where are these guys coming from?" I mutter through my teeth. "I don't even use dating sites. This makes no sense. And whoever is doing this does not understand catfishing at all."

My mother steps forward from the gaggle of women, each of them staring at me with a serious expression. "I think I might know something about that," she says without looking me in the eye.

My stomach turns as a lump of suspicion grows in my chest. "Mom. *What did you do?*"

"Shit"

Tina

As I scroll through fake Tina Falcone profiles on dating app after dating app, from the phones of my mother and my aunts, anger burns hotter in my belly. So *this* is where all the dates have been coming from.

My meddling family took it upon themselves to create these profiles, scroll through the available men, and start conversations with them. As far as I can tell, their only requirement for accepting dates was that the man be interested, and willing to pick me up at work. Nothing else. There was no vetting process in place, at least not one that made itself apparent with a quick read of the messages they'd exchanged.

If they asked "me" out, the owner of the phone, and apparently the administrator of that phone's dating app, would accept and set the date, ensuring they knew to meet me at the restaurant.

I'm so pissed off I don't even want to tell them they could have added more than one app per phone. It's not like there's a limit.

"I can't believe you," I whisper, dropping the last phone into the pile of discarded phones on the coffee table. "What the hell were you thinking?"

My mother wrings her hands and pulls her lips between her teeth, but says nothing, sensing I'm not really looking for an answer to that. I shoot a glare at my aunts, who are crowded into the tiny kitchen of my apartment, looking embarrassed. Good. They should be ashamed after what they've done.

As soon as my mother confessed to knowing something about the random men showing up to date me, everything clicked into place. The older pictures of me, the dates, the confirmation texts the men received. Everything. Before she'd even confessed, I knew this problem would be traced back to my mother. She's been begging me to let her be my matchmaker for years. I guess she was tired of my refusals, because she decided to go ahead and do it anyway, using the power of modern technology and my aunts as willing accomplices. I'm a little disappointed that it took this long for me to figure it out, actually.

Nonna sits on my couch, making the odd tsk noise as she reads through her Spring Chickens brochures. She, at least, had no part in this scheme.

"This has gone too far, Mom. You can see that, can't you?" I wait for an answer this time, but only get the barest of nods from her. "Never mind that this scheme was a huge overstep on your part. Do you even know what kinds of men you've been sending my way? Mr. Landon was the best of the bunch, and the only one I'd ever *consider* even speaking to. I mean, literally everything about him screams boring, but at least he's nice, and treats women like they're human beings. The other guys...Gah!" I splutter and throw up my hands. I take a different tack, thinking some definitions might be helpful in helping her understand. "Do you know what *incel* means, Mom? Or *red-pill*? Or what about *alpha male*?" She shakes her head. "Well, you must know what misogyny is, right?" A nod. Okay, good. Now we're getting somewhere. "Well, basically, the men you sent were raging misogynists. The kind of guys who believe that women should literally be barefoot and pregnant in the kitchen. That women are here to serve men and nothing more. Is that the kind of man you would choose for me? Is that who you think dad is?"

Her head shoots up, and she gives it a vehement shake. "No. No way, Valentina. Your dad isn't like that. And that's not what I would want for you, either."

My aunts all mutter their agreements, confirming their belief that my dad is a good man, and that they'd never choose the kind of man I'd just described to be my partner.

"I had a man waiting for me in my apartment last night. One of the men *you all* chose." A collective gasp is the only response. "Don't worry. I took care of it. But it could have been a lot worse. And that happened even though I'm two doors down from the police station. Dating is different these days. A man doesn't get to know where you live until he proves he is safe. This man was not safe."

I hear a sniffle and look over to see my aunts all swiping at their eyes and noses, trying not to look directly at me. Then I look at my mother. Tears stream down her face and she makes no attempt to wipe them away. "Oh, Valentina. I'm so sorry. I had no idea. We were so worried that you would be lonely living here all by yourself. After five years here, you still haven't found anyone, so we thought we'd help you."

"I've told you countless times, Mom, I'm happy with my life the way it is." At least, I was before I met Nick. Now I'm not so sure I want to be alone for the rest of my life. Not only that, now I have Carson to worry about. I've been looking out for him for so long that it's only natural for me to continue. He's practically family already. "I didn't meet anyone because I wasn't looking. I saw the way you were with dad and I didn't want that for myself."

Her head snaps up, cheeks still wet, but her eyes are steely. "What do you mean *how I was with dad*?"

I shrug, rolling my eyes. "I know he's a good man, but I also know he's practically helpless around the house."

She scoffs. "Your father is anything but helpless, Valentina. What on earth makes you think that?"

Less sure of myself now, I say, "Because he's never set foot in the kitchen? Because I've never seen him clean anything?"

My mother barks a laugh, and my aunts giggle along with her. I have the distinct feeling I'm about to get schooled, and I'm not sure I'm ready for it.

"Really? That's your issue? Your father never set foot in the kitchen because I never allowed it. I told him before we ever got married, if he ever tried to interfere with my cooking, he'd get nothing but peanut butter sandwiches for the rest of his life. He has a tendency to cut himself, and I had no interest in driving to the hospital because he couldn't figure out how to use a knife. But the cleaning thing? Tell me this, in your entire life have you ever seen me clean the bathrooms? Mop a floor?"

My mouth drops open as I realize with a start that no, I have never seen those things. "Wait. You're saying all these years, Dad cleaned the bathrooms? He's the one who mopped the floors?"

She nods, her grin just a little smug. "Do you really think your Nonna would allow her son to grow up thinking he didn't have to take part in caring for his home? For his family?"

I shake my head, knowing she's right.

"Damn right, I wouldn't," Nonna says, without looking up from her reading. "No son of mine was going to grow up to be some useless layabout."

"But-but how? When? How could he do all this without me noticing?"

My mother shrugs. "Your father has always been an early riser. And he's quiet as a cat. You never saw it, because he always cleaned in the very early mornings. He said it was the only way to make sure none of you kids walked on his clean floors before they dried."

I shake my head, trying to reconcile this new image of my father as a cleaning maven with what I'd thought to be true my entire life. All I'd seen was my father coming home from work, then sitting on the couch watching sports highlights until my mother called him for dinner. It never crossed my mind that he was up in the early morning hours scrubbing toilets and mopping floors.

"And that's not all he did. He also folded laundry at night before he went to bed. I have always had a nasty habit of dumping clean laundry all over the bed because I hate folding it. Your father noticed that and took it upon himself to fold it so I wouldn't have to. He also does any ironing that needs doing and takes care of all the dry-cleaning."

After a moment of silence, I say the only thing I can. "Shit."

Mom and my aunts burst into laughter.

"I had no idea you didn't know that about him, Valentina," Mom says. "And you're saying that's why you don't want to date? Don't want to find a partner?"

I raise my eyebrows and grimace. "Kind of? I mean, there are plenty of examples of men who don't do their share around the house, and I guess I assumed Dad was one of them. To me, that proved that good men weren't real, they were fairy tales."

Mom's eyes go soft. "Your father is my Prince Charming, but he's no fairy tale. Even the good men drive you crazy sometimes."

"Amen to that," Aunt Bernice says with a chuckle. "Sometimes I want to strangle your uncle Paul with the socks he leaves lying around the house, but every Friday he brings me my favorite flowers and takes me out to dinner. There's always a balance. Plus, he does all the dishes."

Aunt Vera nods her agreement. "Uncle Richard is the same. He leaves his beard trimmings in the sink when he shaves, but he does all the dusting and vacuuming. And he does the grocery shopping, too."

Aunt Dorothy and Aunt Maude chime in with variations on the same theme, even though Aunt Dorothy is a widow and Aunt Maude never married, and I realize that most of the men in my life are actually pretty good guys. I've had nothing but examples of what real partnership looks like but couldn't look past my own bias to see it. I think... I think I've been an asshole.

"But none of that matters. We've been horrible, Valentina. I am so, so sorry for overstepping like this. I wanted you to be as happy as I am with your father. And yes, maybe a little, I wanted you to have someone to look after." I shoot her a look that has her chuckling. "Don't give me that look. Out of all my kids, you've always been the most nurturing. Even when you were a kid, you're the one who made sure everyone in the neighborhood knew they had a meal at our house if they needed it. You insisted on bringing an extra lunch to school for years, in case one of your classmates forgot theirs that day. You've been looking after people for years, Valentina. Your heart is so big, you can't help it."

Holy. Shit.

Is she right?

"But I think I understand now why you've avoided dating. If you thought even your father was taking advantage of the woman he loved, I can see why you'd be hesitant to become involved with any man when there was a chance he would do the same. You're such a natural nurturer that you worried a man like that would suck you dry."

I shake my head again. "I don't think I ever thought that, Mom. I didn't even realize until right now that I...that I *like* to take care of people."

She purses her lips, then smiles. "Oh, really? What about the young man you hired? Didn't you tell me you hired him so you could look out for him? To make sure he got enough to eat?"

I can only nod. I did tell her that. "Okay, but that's one kid."

"Uh huh. Okay. Didn't you also tell me you started making off menu items because you wanted your landlord to have more variety in his food?"

"He's literally my only customer some days, Ma. And he gives me such a great deal on my rent that making him special food is the least I can do. Besides, he's not getting any younger. He needs to watch his cholesterol levels. I would feel so guilty if the amount of cheese in my food were to cause him to have a major coronary event."

Her grin widens, and her eyes take on a knowing gleam. "And why are you responsible for watching a grown man's cholesterol levels?" Her eyes light up as I realize she's got me there. "Then there's Chloe. Don't you let her work split shifts and keep her on full-time, even though you don't really need that much help?"

I open my mouth to answer, but the words don't come. Damn it. She's right. I do take care of people. For the second time during this conversation, I say the only thing I can, "Shit."

How did I not notice it before? I love taking care of Carson. I love making sure Chloe can continue doing the art that she loves. Heck, I became a chef so I can feed people, and that's one of the most nurturing careers I can think of. Well, other than nurse or daycare educator, but both of those involve way more poop than I'm comfortable with.

She laughs. "You're a nurturing person, sweetheart. There's nothing wrong with that."

"This is…" I blow out a breath and push my glasses up my nose. "This is a lot of information for one day."

"Oh, honey." She takes a step closer and pulls me into a hug. "You don't need to explore all that today. For now, I just want to make sure you know how completely, utterly sorry I am. How sorry we all are." My aunts voice their agreements with assorted yeses and mm hmm noises. "We'll cancel the other dates, delete the apps, and never bother you about it again."

I slowly pull back. "There are more dates? How many?"

Mom's eyes shift to the women still huddled in my tiny kitchen.

"Um, six. I think," Aunt Vera says. "But we'll cancel them right now."

"Please do." I step out of my mother's arms and rub the bridge of my nose.

Aunt Vera tiptoes out of the kitchen, grabbing the stack of phones from the coffee table before heading back to the rest of my aunts. She distributes the phones and, to their credit, it looks like they get started with canceling dates and deleting accounts right away. My shoulders sag in relief. Thank goodness that's over. I wonder if I should tell them more about Nick before he shows up, or let them sweat it out? After all the trouble they've caused, I'm inclined to let them sweat. Besides, I have more pressing matters to explain to them right now.

"So, should we go down and get dinner started?" My mother asks, rubbing her hands together in excitement. She loves cooking in commercial kitchens.

"Before that, I have a couple of things to talk to you about."

The look of surprise on their faces as I explain about Wade looking like someone they'll recognize and how they, under no circumstances, are to mention it to anyone, pales in comparison to the excited grins they give me when I tell them about Carson. Because hiring him to help him out is the least of the ways I hope to take care of him. When I tell them he's downstairs right now, I can't contain them any longer. As one, they burst from my apartment and run down the stairs, where I assume they storm into the restaurant and demand to see him.

I can't help but smile a little at their excitement as I watch them go.

Chapter 29

LESSER KNOWN DANGERS OF CORNHOLE

Nick

"WHERE DOES CARSON WORK, anyway?" Jared asks, tying his wet hair up on top of his head. When I interrupted his workout to tell him about our dinner plans, I asked him to shower early so we could talk about the living situation. I still need to tell him I'm planning to extend the offer of a permanent place to live to Carson, too. Not that I think he'll have an issue with it, but if we're going to be a family, we need to talk about things. Just like Carson and I talked a little about his parents earlier today.

And when I say we talked a little, I mean *a little*.

It took Carson less than five minutes to settle on cremation and the least expensive urns the funeral home had. Rather than choosing interment, he's keeping their remains until he finds somewhere meaningful to spread the ashes. Our conversation led me to the conclusion that aside from their love of drinking, Carson knew very little about his parents. He had no idea what they would have wanted as their final resting place, and he wasn't ready to make that decision today. But he did what he could. And damn it, I am so proud of him for that.

Shortly after we finished talking about his parents, Carson informed me about the shift he has at work this evening. He said he was sorry, but that he couldn't let his boss down and wouldn't be joining us for dinner. No matter how much I tried, I couldn't talk him out of going. The kid lost his parents last night, and he still feels so much loyalty to his boss that he's going to work.

When he left the house, I came into the gym to get in a little cornhole practice before heading over to Tina's place. Peter might think I'd be better off to focus on my love life, but now that being with Tina is no longer a possibility, mastering cornhole is back on the agenda. Well... sucking *less* at cornhole is back on the agenda, anyway. I know my limits. Just like I know cornhole is no substitute for Tina. But it's what I've got, so it will have to do.

"I didn't ask." I shrug, pulling my practice cornhole board out of storage, forcing my brain to focus on anything other than Tina. "I was so stunned that he was thinking about going to work so soon after last night, it didn't even occur to me to find out where. Bring the bean bags for me, would you?"

Jared grabs the bags off the shelf and jogs along behind me. He watches me set up the board, then walks with me to the line taped on the floor that marks the twenty-seven foot regulation distance before passing me the bean bags. Peter says there's no point in practicing if you're not practicing to competition standards.

"Wherever it is, he'll have a hard time doing much with his hands all messed up," Jared says, holding his hands up and rotating them at the wrists. "He should have taken a few days off, at least. I get why he didn't, though. He was telling me last night that his boss has been better to him than his parents ever were."

"I got that feeling, too, when he insisted on going to work today. Seems like whoever this boss is, they're one of the few people who ever looked out for Carson."

"Until now," Jared says with a grin. "Until you."

I scrub a hand over my face. "You already know, don't you?"

"Know what? That you're a big softie?" I cock an eyebrow at him, but that only encourages him. "That you're going to be my new daddy? And Carson's new daddy?" He says in a baby voice, then laughs. "I knew as soon as I walked in last night. That stunned look on Carson's face? The way Gloria rushed to reassure me I wasn't being sent to yet another new foster home? Yeah, I know."

"And you're fine with that?" I take my spot behind the line, then gently lob a bean bag toward the board, overshooting my mark by a good 5 feet. "You'll be okay with another kid in the house?"

Jared laughs. "You serious, dude? Am I okay with another kid in the house? It's one guy, and he's older than I am." He shakes his head, like he can't believe I would ask him such a ridiculous question. "Do you know how many shitty diapers I've changed over the years I've lived in foster care? How many crying babies I rocked to sleep at night because their lazy parents couldn't be bothered to wake up when they had a free nanny, excuse me, I mean grateful foster kid, living in their house?" He barks another laugh. "Coach, this is the best situation I've ever lived in. Carson living there won't make that any less true."

Jesus, this kid. My heart breaks for him. "Okay." I nod, turning away so he can't see the emotion on my face. "Good to know." I lob another bean bag, this time landing short by at least eight feet. "Shit," I whisper harshly. "How am I getting worse?"

"I don't know," Jared says, grabbing a bean bag from me and tossing it in the air. "Were you standing closer to the board the last time you played?" He tosses the bean bag, and it lands in the hole without even touching the board. He claps me on the shoulder and says, "Keep trying. You'll get there."

He walks into the staff room as I stare after him with my mouth hanging open. How did he do that?

I bounce the last bean bag in my hand, visualizing the trajectory I want it to take when it leaves my hand. Over and over in my mind, I picture myself winding my arm back, before gracefully swinging it forward, then letting the bean bag go at the end of the arc. I watch the bean bag leave my hand. I watch it sail through the air. I imagine how it will feel to watch it land on the board before sliding into the hole. When I've visualized the sequence several times, I open my eyes, take a deep breath, then perform the action precisely like I've done it in my mind, expecting to see it land on the board in the same way.

But that's not what happens.

Not. Even. Close.

This time, instead of the bean bag flying in a perfect arc toward the cornhole board like it does in my visualization exercise, it catches on a finger, leaves my hand at an awkward angle, then swerves off to the right, traveling faster than a projectile thrown by underhanded lob has any right to.

All I can do is hold my breath and watch in horror as it flies past the reception desk and smashes into my trophy case. The front shatters, sending a shower of glass shards, championship belts, and rubber ducks crashing to the floor in a heap.

"No!" I scream, my hands flying to my cheeks. "My babies." My heart races as I sprint to the wreckage and drop to my knees, palms to the sky. "No, no, no. Not my innocent little duckies."

"Coach," Jared yells as he runs out of the staff room. "Are you okay? What was that crash? Oh shit! Not the ducks. I'll get a broom."

I crawl as close to the pile of glass as I dare, and begin gingerly picking my duckies out of the mess, pinching them between two fingers to shake off any stray shards before placing them onto the reception desk.

As I grab each one, a memory flashes in my brain as I remember how I got it. *This referee one was a gift from Rhett. This vampire one I bought in a market in New Orleans. This luchador one was left on my pillow in a hotel room in Mexico with a note from the maid saying her husband was a big fan.* One after another, I pick up my ducks, and one after another, the memory of how I acquired it comes back to me. *I got the one who's holding a little bell from an opponent after I knocked him out in the first round.*

Jared comes back with a broom and some boxes. "Here, put them in the box. I'll get your belts, then sweep up the glass."

Together, Jared and I get the worst of the mess cleaned up, and soon I'm left with a box of championship belts, another, bigger box full of my favorite duckies, and an empty wall where my trophy case used to be.

"I bet you're glad most of your duckies are back at the house, huh?"

"Yeah." I nod. "I tried cramming them all in that trophy case, but I guess I'm lucky that so much of my collection didn't fit."

Jared shrugs. "It could have been worse," he says, inspecting the contents of the ducky box. "At least they're waterproof. A quick rinse should take care of any mess."

"I guess I should spring for the bulletproof glass on the next case." I should have done it in the first place, but at the time, I couldn't think of any reason I'd need to take that kind of precaution. Who knew cornhole could cause so much destruction?

"Or you could move your cornholing to another location. Outside, maybe?"

I shudder. "Oh no. I learned my lesson. No more cornhole for me. That sport is way too hazardous. From now on, I'll stick to something safe, like full-contact combat sports. Or defusing explosives with the military."

Jared chuckles, then picks up the box of championship belts. "Come on, Coach. Let's put these boxes in your office so we can finish cleaning the floor. We need to get all this glass up before we can open the gym again."

"Shit. You're right. I've done enough damage with my terrible cornhole skills. I couldn't live with myself if someone got hurt because I can't throw a bean bag in a straight line." I grab the other box and follow Jared to the office, stopping on my way back to get the vacuum from the cleaning supplies closet.

After I vacuum each section thoroughly, Jared uses a flashlight and a damp paper towel to wipe up any stray glass that is too small to see. When we've done the entire area three times, and we're confident the glass is all gone, we put the cleaning supplies away and begin our walk to Tina's.

We're on our way to Wings and Pizza, walking past the town square, where a group of people are playing a game at the permanent cornhole court. I watch as player after player throws a perfect lob onto the opposite board and the realization that I smashed my trophy case hits me hard, live and in full color. I still can't believe I nearly destroyed so much of my duck collection in my ill-advised attempt at learning to play cornhole. I should have never strayed from my natural talents.

Peter was right. I am not made for cornhole. Something about my body makes it impossible for me to throw that damn bean bag with the finesse required to make it to the board. And I don't think it's my lat muscles, no matter what Peter keeps trying to tell me. I guess it's time to accept the fact that I'm the only Swallower in history who can't get his bag near a hole.

I'm a disgrace. Not only that, now that I can't in good conscience continue with cornhole, I have nothing to distract me from my failed-before-it-could-begin relationship with Tina. After dinner tonight, when I tell her about the boys living with me permanently, I'll have nothing to do but wallow in my misery.

I blow out a heavy sigh, getting some serious side-eye from Jared for it.

"It's not that big a deal, Coach. Not everyone can be good at cornhole. It's a lot harder than it looks."

"I know, kid. I'll be alright." I won't be one of those adults who burdens his kids with their adult problems. But I will call Rhett later to ask if he knows any reliable distraction techniques. Because I'm damn sure going to need something, considering Tina lives right down the street from the gym and I'm already having problems staying away from her. And if there's one thing I won't be doing with Jared and Carson living with me, it's drowning my sorrows in alcohol. They deserve better than the life their parents gave them, and I'll do everything in my power to give it to them.

Even if that means I lose Tina forever.

Chapter 30

WE NEED TO TALK

Tina

"I CAN'T BELIEVE HOW good you are at this, Dad."

My dad smiles up at me from where he's dicing vegetables. "I'm surprised I still know how," he says with a laugh. "Forty years is a long time to go without practicing my knife skills."

"I heard that." My mom is at the back prep table, fawning over Carson like he's her favorite grandchild. She hasn't left the poor kid alone since she stormed out of my apartment earlier. After I told her about trying to become a foster parent so I can get custody of him, she was determined to get to know him better. "I remember very well what your knife skills were like. I didn't let you practice because I couldn't bear the thought of scraping your fingers into a plastic baggie full of ice before racing you to the hospital to have them sewn back on."

Dad rolls his eyes and laughs. "Whatever you say, honey."

Mom doesn't even hear him, though, since she's back to peppering Carson with questions about school, basketball, and anything else she can think of to keep his mind off his parents. She tried to talk me out of letting him work, insisting he needed more time to mourn, but he's old enough to know what he wants to do. I know he has complicated feelings about his parents, and I won't force him to think about this until he's ready.

But when he's ready, I'll be here to listen. For now, I think he's enjoying my mother's chatter.

When I first came down from my apartment to see Carson's face poking out the top of a hug made almost entirely of matronly bosoms and slightly wobbly upper arms, I laughed so hard I nearly peed myself. Even now, thinking about the shock in his eyes as he looked down at the tops of their heads and all that fluffy, overly-teased, black hair tickled his nose because he's at least six inches taller than the tallest of them, I can't stop myself from snickering.

"He's a good kid," Dad says, drawing my attention away from Carson and my mother. "He'll be alright, you know."

"Yeah. He's a great kid," I say before turning my attention to my father. "You think it's okay that he's not very upset?" I've been worrying about how Carson was taking the knowledge of his parents' passing ever since Wade banged on my door late last night to tell me the news. I thought he'd put on a brave face, but this seems like more than that. It almost seems like he doesn't care.

My dad shrugs. "Who's to say he isn't upset? Give him some time. And get him some professional help."

Dad goes back to his vegetables, leaving me with my thoughts.

Does Carson need someone to talk to? A therapist? I sneak a look at where he's now regaling my mother and aunts with a tale that has them all laughing, and determine that talking to a therapist couldn't hurt. Because even if he's not upset, the situation with him running into the house to find them has to be weighing on him.

"Valentina? You got a second?" Wade speaks quietly, his voice barely audible over my family's laughter. "Outside." He walks down the back hallway, past the walk-in fridge and freezer, and out the door to the alley, not bothering to see if I follow.

I'm barely out the door when he asks, "Why didn't you tell me your family was coming?"

In the past, when my family decided they hadn't seen enough of me, they would warn me before coming out to Tuft Swallow, giving me time to warn Wade. He's tolerated my presence all these years, no doubt because he trusted I would never rat him out. But he's never had to extend that trust to my family, because I've always given him warning of their visit. Seeing my dad on the sidewalk today must've scared the crap out of him.

"I'm so sorry, Wade." I stoop, setting the doorstop to ensure it doesn't close and lock us out here. "I didn't know they were coming until they were already here. I had so much on my mind today that when my mom called to say they were standing in front of the restaurant, it didn't even occur to me to warn you about it."

Wade huffs, then tugs the wide lapels of his sport coat. "Your Nonna winks at me every time she calls me Wade," he says, the corner of his mouth turning up despite the irritated tone of his voice. "And one of your aunts said I remind her of someone she used to know. She said if she ever saw him again, she'd tell him how proud she was that he walked away from his life to save so many people."

"For what it's worth, I think everyone from the old neighborhood feels the same way about that man."

He nods absently, his mind clearly somewhere else. "You might be right." He claps his hands against his legs before turning his attention back to me. "That's not really what I wanted to talk to you about. I came here to tell you... Shit, Valentina. I'm sorry, but there's nothing available with two bedrooms in Tuft Swallow right now. I can probably get you into something reasonably priced in Spitz Hollow, but it would mean a longer commute for you. And it wouldn't be anywhere as cheap as this place." He tips his chin toward the back window of my tiny upstairs apartment. "I'd swap apartments with you, but my place is even smaller than yours, if you can believe it."

I feel myself deflate, the positive thoughts I'd been having about getting custody of Carson gone in an instant as panic takes over. Finding the wall of the alley, I lean against it for support. If we have nowhere to live, he'll have to go somewhere else. And I can't let that happen. I won't let that happen. And that means I know what I have to do.

"Set up some viewings. If moving to Spitz Hollow is my only option, then that's what I'm doing."

Wade nods, giving me a sad smile. "I figured you'd say that. I have a few viewings set up for tomorrow. I'll send you the addresses and times later."

I take a deep breath, attempting to calm my racing heart. "Okay. Okay, that's fine. Even with a commute of twenty minutes, I'm still working fewer hours than I did in the city. And I can cut back a little if I need to. It's fine. Everything is fine." I drag in another deep breath, still not convinced that everything will be okay. There's so much that could still go wrong.

"I'll help you however I can. After you find a new place, we can talk about the rent on the restaurant. We'll get this figured out."

"What?" I snap my head up and look at Wade. "No. I can't let you do that. You already charge me next to nothing." And that's the only reason I can afford to keep my restaurant, but still. It's not fair for Wade to foot the bill. Besides, business is picking up. I've seen the Spring Chickens a couple of times this week since explaining that they can order by the slice at the walk-up window. And since they've been hitting the walking trails with their hands full of pizza, a steady trickle of curious birdwatchers has been visiting me as well. It's too early to say with certainty, but it feels like Wings and Pizza might make it after all. On top of that, if Nick orders catering a few times a year, I'll have nothing to worry about.

He shrugs. "Too bad."

"Wade..."

"Valentina?"

"I can't ask you to do that."

"I suppose it's a good thing you're not asking then, isn't it?" He grants me a rare grin, and I get a glimpse of the Uncle Gianni I remember from the old neighborhood. The one who used to pay the ice cream man so every kid could get a treat. The one who made sure none of us kids saw anything that could scare us when his associates tended to the mob business they'd come to town to conduct.

I can't stop the answering grin from creeping onto my face. "Fine. We can talk about it." I won't accept it unless I have no other choice, but I have to admit, it's nice to have a back-up plan.

"Good." He takes a step toward the back door. "Now, if you don't mind, I think I'll head back inside and see if your Aunt Maude wants to tell me more about this fella she used to know.

It sounds like she was pretty fond of him." He steps inside, hands in his pockets, while he whistles a cheerful tune like he doesn't have a care in the world. Like his real identity isn't now known by seven more people than knew it this morning when he started this day. Seven people who have the potential to blow the life he's created here to smithereens.

As I watch the door drift close behind him, I realize he's whistling like... like a man who thinks he's about to get some.

"Ew," I say out loud when realization dawns on me. "Wade and Aunt Maude?" Is that why she never got married? Has she been pining after Wade—Gianni Scibetta—for all these years? Maybe my family's surprise visit won't be such a bad thing after all.

I look at the back door of the restaurant. Shit. I'm locked out here now. Good thing I can walk around the building and go in the front door. I've locked myself out back on more than one occasion, but that was back when I was leaving my apartment door open and I could just go up and get my spare restaurant keys. I'll need to be extra vigilant now that I'm keeping it closed and locked when I'm not home. At the very least, I need to keep my keys in my pocket, like they are now.

As I reach the front corner of the building, I see Nick and Jared crossing the street in front of me and can't stop the grin from taking over my face. Jared waves and jogs over to me.

"Tina," he says with a smile. "I'm starving. What's for dinner?"

My face scrunches up as I realize I have no idea what's for dinner. I mean, I can guess what's cooking because I bought the groceries, but after leaving my mom in there with Carson and my dad doing prep work, Jared's guess is as good as mine. "You know, Jared, I'm not sure. Why don't you go in and find out? Be careful, though. My mom and my aunts will definitely try to hug you. They surrounded my part timer in a group hug not long ago, and it took him a while to escape."

Jared's eyes light up. "Hugs? I love hugs." He runs to the door and throws it open, yelling, "Get your free hugs."

Nick gets to me as I'm laughing at Jared's announcement. "I didn't know he loved hugs that much," he says with a shake of his head. "I'll have to be sure to hug him more." He turns to me, the smile dropping from his face, and I can tell something's wrong. Then he says it. Those four dreaded words. "We need to talk."

Shit, shit, shit. There's no way this day could possibly get any worse. I open my mouth to make an excuse, because I can't handle any more bad news today, when my phone rings. I hold a finger up for Nick to give me a minute, then look at my caller ID. *Gloria Freeman.* My heart jumps into my throat. *Holy shit, this is it.* I can't tell if I'm more excited or scared.

"Hello?" My voice shakes when I answer.

"Tina. It's Gloria Freeman calling. I got your application paperwork."

"Did I get everything you needed?" My heart pounds in my ears.

"Yes, everything is filled out properly. I will need confirmation of suitable housing, of course, but assuming you get that, and pass the background check, you'll be able to take the foster parent classes."

Relief floods me, and I exhale with a whoosh. "Thank God. I was worried that he'd have to move somewhere else."

"Wait a minute, Tina. I said you'll be eligible to take the classes, not that he'd come to live with you now. That could take up to six months—"

"Six months?" I interrupt Gloria with a yell, making Nick look at me with concern. I wave him off and turn away, not wanting him to be involved in this conversation. Not wanting him to see me cry tears of frustration. Tears of anger. I'm about to fly apart with worry. "Six months? Will he… where will he go for six months?"

"That's actually why I was calling you," Gloria says, her voice sounding more cheerful that I think this situation calls for. I kind of want to punch her in her cheerful face. *"For privacy reasons, I can't give you any details, but given how concerned you were that Carson would have to leave town, I wanted to let you know I found a place for him right in Tuft Swallow. He won't have to switch schools. He'll be around just as much as he was before."*

I look at the sky, one hand pressed to my chest as I force myself to breathe. He won't be with me, but he'll still be in town. I can still look after him. "You had me worried for a second there, I won't lie. Pretty sure this has been the most stressful two minutes of my life."

Gloria's laugh tinkles through the phone. *"Sorry about that. I didn't want to leave you hanging. I could tell the first time we spoke how much you care about Carson."*

"Well… thank you. I appreciate the head's up." I pause for a moment, then add, "This place he's going to? It's good? He'll-he'll be okay?"

I can almost hear her smile through the phone. *"He'll be fine, Tina. In fact, he stayed there last night. I have another client staying there right now, too. It was supposed to be temporary, but the foster dad recently gave me the okay to start work on placing the kid permanently. While he's there, Carson will have a foster brother who's about the same age. And before you ask, yes, that kid is a good kid, like Carson. He's been in the system a long time, but has somehow managed to hang on to all of his kindness. I think Carson is really going to like it there."*

"I'm happy to hear that. Thank you for calling me." A heaviness weighs on my shoulders, a new worry caused by this new information. *Would Carson be better off with this new family than with me?* I hold the phone away to hide my sniffle. "I should get going, unless you have anything else for me?" I need to get off the phone before I burst into tears. This day has been one thing after another, and I don't know how much more I can take.

"That was it. I didn't want to leave you hanging until I'm back in the office tomorrow."

"I appreciate that. I guess we'll talk soon?"

"I'll call you when I have more information. Bye, Tina." Gloria hangs up before I can return her goodbye. Just in time, too, because the first tears spill down my cheeks as I pull the phone away from my face.

"Tina? Is everything alright?"

Shit. I forgot about Nick and his four stupid words. *We need to talk.*

"Come upstairs. We can talk there."

 Chapter 31

I'm Not Ready

Nick

As Jared and I cross the street to get to Wings and Pizza, he spots Tina coming around the side of the building before I do.

"Tina," he says, jogging over to her. "I'm starving. What's for dinner?"

I can't hear her reply, but they both smile before Jared runs into the restaurant yelling something about hugs.

"I didn't know he loved hugs that much," I say. "I'll have to be sure to hug him more." I take a deep breath and turn to face Tina. I can't put this off any longer. I'll tell her about the kids, then give her some privacy. I'm sure she won't mind if I leave

Jared here to eat dinner, even though I'm sure she won't want me around after I tell her my news. "We need to talk."

Her face drops, and I instinctively know why. No one likes to hear those words. Nothing good ever comes after someone says "we need to talk" and this is no different. She's about to say something when her phone rings and she holds up a finger, telling me to wait.

I only hear one side of the conversation, and it sounds like she's getting bad news that's maybe also good news. Or good news that's also bad news. I'm still trying to figure out which it is, when she gets off the phone and turns back to me, the tears welling in her eyes confirming that it's more bad news than good. Whatever she learned in that phone call, it distracted her enough that she seems surprised to see I'm still there.

"Come upstairs. We can talk there," she says, pulling keys from her pocket and leading me back around the side of the building.

"Nice to see you're locking your door," I say, attempting to lighten the mood. "I bet your underwear drawer is relieved."

She grants me a small huff of a laugh as she lets us inside, but that's it.

"Well?" She stands near her couch, face turned down to the floor, hands on her hips as she waits for me to talk. I hate that she's not looking at me.

Suddenly, the last thing in the world I want is to have this conversation that ends whatever it is we have before it starts. My heart screams at me to put it off a little while longer. To take a few more minutes to enjoy the possibility before throwing it away for the good of the boys. I step forward into her space and pull her into my arms, dipping my head down and breathing in the scent of her hair, a mixture of coconut shampoo and fresh bread. *Is there a better smell in the world?*

I hold her a moment before she relents and wraps her arms around my waist, melting against me, her breath hot as she presses her cheek to my chest. *I don't want to let go. I don't want to give her up.* I blow out a breath and unwind my arms from around her, allowing her to step back. "Want to tell me what's wrong?" I ask. "It might help to talk about it."

She backs up until her legs hit the couch, then flops down and tucks her legs beneath her. "It's been a long day, Nick. A long shit-show of a day."

I walk around the coffee table and lower myself onto the couch next to her. "What happened?"

She exhales, the sound a long-suffering sigh, and drops her head to the back of the couch, letting her knees flop to the sides before crossing her legs criss-cross applesauce style. "Well, my family showed up to surprise me, for one." She raises a finger in the air, then lets her arm drop back to her side. "And that's an issue for Wade."

"Why is that an issue for Wade?" The real estate agent has always been a bit of a question mark in my mind, but it's obvious how much he cares for Tina. And how much he means to her. *Shit.* Is there something...*more* than friendship there?

She glances at me without turning her head. "You've heard the rumors? About Wade, I mean."

I nod, unsure where she's heading with this.

"Well, my family knows who he was *before* he was Wade." My eyes widen in shock. *Holy shit.* Was Wade *really* in the mob? That guy is so lucky he only got thrown in the dumpster last night. "And I usually warn him before they visit, so he can make himself scarce. I didn't get the chance to do that today, though. And I feel like shit about it."

"He can't possibly expect you to keep his secret forever? You've done it until now, haven't you?"

"*Everyone* needs to keep his secret. I'm pretty sure he's in witness protection." She glares at me. "You better not say anything."

"What the hell? What did he do?"

She shrugs. "The guy people *mistake* him for," she says, emphasizing the word *mistake,* narrowing her eyes at me until I nod to let her know I get her meaning, "may have taken down a sex trafficking ring and saved a bunch of kids. And sent a bunch of very dangerous people to jail in the process."

"Jesus."

"Yeah."

She narrows her eyes at me again.

"My lips are sealed."

"Good."

We sit in silence for a couple of minutes before she speaks again. "I also found out I've been selling my dad short my whole life. I thought he was some kind of deadbeat husband around the house, and even though I loved him, it colored the way I thought about men. Turns out he's an early riser who does all his household chores when everyone else is still asleep. That man cleaned the bathrooms in the dead of night the entire time I was growing up, and I never knew a thing about it."

"That must've been quite the eye opener." I chuckle, picturing an older man in two-piece pajamas scrubbing toilets in the dark.

She huffs a laugh. "You have no idea. I was so sure that he was helpless because I'd never seen him clean a thing, never mind cook a meal." She lets out a full laugh, the smile finally reaching her eyes. "But it's not that he didn't know how to cook. It's that my mom banned him from the kitchen because she thought he was a danger to himself and she didn't want to bring him to the hospital with a plastic baggie full of his own fingers."

I snort a laugh at that. "I wouldn't want to do that either. It doesn't sound like a good time."

"That's the whole reason I didn't date, you know. I was positive I wanted nothing to do with the kind of relationship my parents had, where I'd have to do everything for my partner, and it turns out I wasn't seeing things clearly. My mother didn't do everything. She was just the only one who did stuff while I was watching. How could I be so stupid?"

My stomach clenches at her confession. If only the timing were on our side. "For what it's worth, I'm an excellent housekeeper. I can fold a fitted sheet like nobody's business."

She heaves an enormous sigh. "You said we needed to talk..."

"What was the phone call about?" I ask, changing the subject. I'm not ready for this thing with Tina to be over yet, and if extending our last conversation is the only way to hold on a little longer, then that's what I'll do. "Who made you cry?"

She pulls her knees back up to her chest. "Just some paper pusher. She's trying to help me out, but there's only so much she can do." Tina rolls her eyes. "There are laws she has to follow, apparently."

I bark a laugh at the air quotes she puts around the word *laws* before I can rein it in. Tina shoots me another glare, and I snort another laugh. "Sorry."

"It's fine." She blows out a breath. "I mean, I get where she's coming from. This is her job, and I don't expect her to bend the rules for me. But I was hoping things would go more smoothly, you know? I need to find a bigger place to live, and it looks like unless I want that dumpster-diving idiot from last night to be my landlord, I'll need to look in Spitz Hollow for that. And that means I'll have to pay a lot more in rent than what Wade charges me for this entire building. Not to mention my one-minute walk to work will become a twenty minute commute. It's crap all around."

I mull over her words in my mind, getting stuck on one part in particular. "You're moving?"

She nods. "That's the plan."

"Why?" Did the run in with that guy last night scare her that much? Maybe I should ask Wade how to best dispose of a body and get rid of that idiot once and for all. I've never killed anyone before, but for Tina, I'd be willing to try.

"I need a bigger place."

I look around her tiny apartment. The whole thing could fit in the kitchen at my house, so I can understand why she might want something a little bigger. But if she's been living here for five years already, why is she now so eager for a larger space that she'd be willing to leave town to get it? "I think I'm missing something here."

She laughs, the sound brittle. "More of the shit show," she says. "I got some news last night after you left without warning, and it made me rethink my entire stance on having a family. On having someone to take care of. Then, after talking to my mother today, I realized I *enjoy* taking care of people. I've been doing it my whole life, and I had no idea. Who knew?"

Thinking of the way she took everyone's needs into consideration when catering for me and the other trainers, and the way she talks about Wade, Chloe, and her part-time worker, I'm surprised I didn't see it sooner. There's a giddiness in my chest that feels a lot like hope. She looks at me for a response, but all I have for her is a cocked eyebrow, which makes her laugh.

"Fine. So everyone knew but me."

"No," I say with a laugh. "I'm messing with you. I believed you when you said you didn't want to take care of anyone." I take in her sad answering smile. "So, does this mean you've changed your mind, then? You want a husband and kids? The whole nine yards?" *Please say yes, please say yes.*

She snorts a laugh. "I think I could do without shooting a human being out of my vagina, thanks." Tina shakes her head and sighs. "I honestly don't know how to answer that right now. I've spent my entire life avoiding those kinds of relationships because I didn't want to be responsible for another human being. I mean, look at this place." She swings her arm out, gesturing to her apartment. "It barely counts as a one bedroom, and I still have a hard time looking after it. I can't be responsible for an entire house full of people who can't take care of themselves. That's crazy."

When I hear that, my stomach drops straight to my feet. So much for the hope that something still might come of our... whatever this is. "I get that. But you know you wouldn't be responsible for everything, right? The other people in the house would be responsible for some of it, too. Besides, this place is nice." I laugh at the face she makes. "It is. It's perfect for a single person who works as much as you do. How much are you even home?"

She looks down at her knees. "Not much."

"Exactly. With how much you work, and how much you're home, this place is perfect for you. I'm sure if you decided you wanted a family, you'd find a bigger place and make it a home."

She sighs. "That's the idea."

My phone buzzes in my back pocket before I can ask what she means. A quick look at the screen shows me a message from Jared.

Jared

Where are you, Coach? You need to get in here. You're never going to believe who's here.

I stand up and turn to Tina. "Are you going to be alright if I go downstairs? Jared needs something." I hold my phone up before putting it back in my pocket and jerking a thumb toward the door. I hate to leave her right now, but something tells me she could use some time alone to think. "You coming down now, or do you need a minute?"

She drops her head to the back of the couch again, and blows out a long breath. "I'll be down in a few."

"Sure." I nod, and turn to the door. "I'll see you in a bit."

Tina's attention is already turned inward, so I leave, closing the door behind me. I hope whatever she's worried about, she has what she needs to figure it out. And if she doesn't, I hope she knows she can ask me for help.

Chapter 32

My Knight In... White Fleeced Glory?

Tina

AFTER NICK LEAVES MY apartment, I snuggle into the couch to allow myself a few minutes to cry.

I know Gloria said Carson has somewhere to stay until I get the foster parent stuff squared away, but six months is a long time to live with a stranger. Even if Gloria says she knows them personally, I'm still worried. I mean, how many kids does she see every day? She can't possibly have enough room in her heart to care about each and every one of those kids, can she? Not the way I care about Carson. And I'm sure getting his situation sorted out as quickly as she did was a tremendous weight off her shoulders.

But that doesn't mean I have to be happy about it.

The tears course down my cheeks as I allow myself to settle into the disappointment.

I thought I'd finally found the nurturing side of me. And what about my mother and aunts? They're downstairs right now, smothering Carson with all their love, so eager to welcome him to our family. How can I tell them it's not happening now? How can I disappoint them again, after I've been disappointing them my whole life?

Shit. I still need to go downstairs and face them all.

At least I avoided Nick's "we need to talk" conversation. That, on top of everything, would have been too much to bear. A sob tears free from my throat and I slam my fist into the couch cushion. And why was he so being so fucking nice if he's planning to break up with me? Or stop seeing me? Or whatever he's doing to end whatever this is?

Shit.

I'm not ready for it to end. I don't want it to end. Who says he gets to decide things are over? That's bullshit. I refuse to sit back and let it happen. I have a say in this too, damn it.

I unfold myself from the couch and head into the bathroom to clean up before going downstairs. One look at my splotchy face in the mirror tells me I made the right choice. I can't come clean to my family about Carson, and demand that Nick give me another chance while resembling a defective tomato. My family won't care, but I don't think it would help my position with Nick all that much.

After splashing my face with water and fixing the bun on top of my head, a noise in the living room gets my attention. Shit, Did Nick come back to have that conversation after all?

"Nick? I don't want to stop whatever this is we're doing," I blurt as I quickly wash my hands. "I've never had a relationship, but I want to try with you."

What I see when I step out of the bathroom has me freezing in my tracks. No. Not what. Who.

Milton. Fucking. Maguire.

"What the fuck are you doing in my apartment again?" How dare this guy come back here?

"Is that any way to greet the man who's here to take you out?"

My eyes roll so far back I think I see my brain. "Not that shit again." I am not in the mood. My mother and aunts assured me they had this dating app fiasco taken care of. So what is this idiot doing back here? Maybe he's confused? Against my better judgment, I try the polite approach. "Listen, you should have received a message canceling any date we may have had. My mother and my aunts set up profiles without my knowledge. We do not have a date."

He shrugs and bares his teeth in a menacing smile. "Not my problem. I was promised a date, and I'm here to collect."

Okay. Looks like the polite approach isn't going to work. "Are you insane? What is the matter with you that you want to date someone who clearly wants nothing to do with you?"

He takes a step forward, and I instinctively step back. The predatory gleam in his eyes makes my gut clench. "A real man isn't afraid of a little fight from a woman. A true alpha male relishes the opportunity to"—he slicks a yellow-coated tongue over his chapped lips—"*overcome* resistance to show a woman what she really wants." His wolfish grin is back.

My skin crawls as he takes another deliberate step. "Ew, are you fucking for real, dude? *Show a woman what she really wants*? Newsflash, dickhead. I can guarantee that *you*"—I jab a finger in his direction—"are not on *any* woman's wishlist."

The smile drops from Milton's face, and he snarls. "*You fat fucking bitch.* How dare you talk to me like that?"

"You're in my apartment uninvited. *Again.* I'll talk to you however the fuck I want." Jesus, this guy must be allergic to getting a fucking clue. And what is it with these misogynists and all the body shaming? It's exhausting to listen to.

He barks a cruel laugh. "Keep at it, Tina. You'll see what happens when your big guy friend isn't here to knock me out and throw me in a dumpster."

I can't stop myself from snickering. "You dumbass. Nick didn't knock you out. *I did.* And I'll do it again if you don't get the fuck out of here." Seriously, what is with this guy? "But if you really want him to take a turn, he'll be back any minute." I doubt he will be, but if this idiot is afraid of Nick, then I'm willing to use that fear to get him the hell out of here.

"Nice try," he says with another cruel laugh. "I watched him walk into your restaurant five minutes ago, where several older women with butts even larger than yours swarmed him. I think he'll be busy for quite a while." He takes another step forward, forcing my back against the wall. "Plenty of time for you to get on your knees and apologize to me properly."

My heartbeat ramps up several notches as the rage within me builds. I try to draw in a calming breath, but Milton smells like old cheese and too much body spray, and it's all I can do not to gag. He must sense my disgust, though, because he laughs.

"I don't think you understand the situation you're in here, Tina. I'm here to collect on the date I was promised." He steps back and I seize the opportunity to take a breath free from his stench. "Now, why don't you go change into something a little nicer? I'm taking you to dinner in Spitz Hollow. Lord knows there aren't any decent restaurants in this town." He sneers at me. "No offense."

This is crazy. Is this negging? That's what he's doing, right? He's trying to make me feel bad about myself so that he can swoop in with a half-assed compliment that I'll then swoon over so he can take me to bed. What a fucking moron.

"You're insane," I mutter. "That's the only explanation."

"No," he says, that creepy smile plastered on his face again. "I'm a high value man. And you're lucky I'm willing to give you another chance. Now. Go get changed so we can go. I don't want to be in Tuft Swallow a minute longer than I have to be." He looks around my tiny living space. "And we'll be staying in my apartment tonight."

Heavy footsteps on the stairs outside my apartment have me breathing an enormous sigh of relief. Milton, on the other hand, suddenly looks much less relaxed.

"What was that you were saying about Nick not coming back? Because it sure as hell sounds to me like he's coming up the stairs right now."

Milton's eyes go comically wide as he looks from me to the apartment door. The apartment door he left wide open when he walked in here.

"Yeah, that's a lesson I learned the hard way, too. When you leave your door open, sometimes you get unwanted guests."

"Shit," He mutters as he lunges for the open door, his fingers barely grazing the edge before my hero arrives in all his... *white fleeced glory*?

"Winston?" The name falls from my mouth in confusion as the goat bursts through the door with a triumphant screaming bleat.

"MAAAAAA!" he bleats as he rams his head horns first into Milton's crotch. "Maaaa," he bleats again before ramming Milton a second time.

"*Mommy.*" Milton's high-pitched squeal is feeble as he crumples to the floor with his hands over his mashed testicles, the sound barely audible over Winston's continued cries of triumph.

Winston looks at me with his sideways slitted eyes, offering a slight tilt of his head and one last, short bleat that seems to convey a sense of "you're welcome." He then tramples over Milton's body, his hooves digging into all the prone man's softest parts, as he makes his way to my bedroom, no doubt to ransack my underwear drawer again.

"Help yourself, Winston," I call out, without taking my eyes off Milton. "I owe you. Take whatever you want. And I take it back, you totally have my vote in the next election."

I watch as Milton continues mewling while he rocks side to side, my attention so fully occupied that I don't hear the footsteps coming up the stairs until Nick and Chief Woodcock come bursting into my apartment, followed closely by Winston's hot daddy. The sight of the three men almost tripping over Milton's body as they frantically scan the room is enough to send me flying into a fit of giggles.

"Hey, Tina. I was walking into the station and heard a ruckus coming from over here. Is everything okay?" Chief Woodcock's voice takes on the calming tone one uses when they're talking someone down off a ledge. Placating. Soft.

I nod through my tears of laughter, forcing out, "Winston...Winston...he..." before succumbing to the giggles again, and waving my hand toward my bedroom. "Take it all, Winston," I blurt between laughs. "You deserve it. I'll buy more and you can take those, too."

Nick's eyes are wild with worry as he steps over Milton's body, kicking him as he goes by, forcing another little squeal from the so-called "high value alpha dom". He wraps me in his arms and leads me to the couch, sitting down before pulling me into his lap. He smooths his hands up and down my back, whispering in my ear that everything will be okay, that he's here now. Once the giggles are under control, I sag in his arms, the adrenaline of the last several minutes leaving me in a rush.

"Hey, Chief?" Nick says without taking his eyes off of me. "Can you do me a favor and get rid of that guy? And make sure he doesn't come back to bother Tina again?"

I look up to see Chief Woodcock smiling down at Milton. "Oh, I think that could be arranged. Tina? Before I take him out of here, I need to know, will you be pressing charges?"

I stare at Milton. His eyes are wide, and somehow I can sense he's finally scared enough that he won't be back. Turning my attention to the chief, I shake my head. "No. I think we're good here." A snort of laughter works its way free. "You might want to get him some medical attention, though. Winston did a real number on his testicles."

A single huff of deep laughter comes from Winston's hot daddy, so short I might have imagined it. His eyes have a slight crinkle at the corners when I look at him, though, so maybe not?

"I think that can be arranged. I'll have Dr. Cratchett meet us at the clinic." He pulls a pair of handcuffs from his belt, rolls Milton to his stomach, then cuffs him. "Come on. Up you go," he says, as he hoists Milton to his feet and shoves him toward the door. "Let me know if you change your mind about pressing charges, Tina. I'll have him in custody for a little while, at least until he can see Dr. Cratchett."

I nod, and he takes Milton out. Winston's hot daddy gives a low whistle and Winston comes trotting out of my bedroom, a half-eaten pair of panties in his mouth and a bra hanging from a horn. Nick leans over to remove the panties before nodding to Winston's owner and waving them both off. As soon as they're out the door, Nick slides me off his lap, gets up, and locks the door behind them.

He looks at me, head tilted as his eyes fill with concern. He blows out a breath, allowing his shoulders to relax. "Jesus, Tina. Are you okay?" he asks, his voice low. "Tell me everything."

The weight of everything that's happened today, never mind just in the last twenty minutes, comes crashing down, and I burst into tears. Nick rushes back to the couch, dragging me back onto his lap, and encouraging me to rest my head on his shoulder. I cry, and cry, great hiccuping sobs that would be embarrassing if I had the capacity to feel shame right now. Nick lets me cry all over him, seemingly oblivious to the mess soaking his shirt, and it makes me like him even more.

There's no way I'm giving him up without a fight now. But so much for cleaning myself up before begging Nick to give us a chance. Looks like he's getting the defective tomato version of me, after all.

Chapter 33

DAISY DUCK DOESN'T EVEN WEAR SHORTS

Nick

MY HEART TRIES TO claw its way out of my chest as I sit with Tina cuddled on my lap mere minutes after finding her standing over that Milton asshole. After what happened last night, I can't believe he'd have it in him to come back. That guy is lucky he only has goat-inflicted groin injuries to contend with. If I'd gotten here before Winston, and if the chief of police hadn't followed me in, I guarantee he wouldn't have been so lucky. And he would have done more than spend the night in a dumpster this time, too.

As Tina relays the story to me, starting with her mistaking the sound of Milton coming up the stairs for me coming back, the anger grows until it threatens to burn a hole in my stomach. When she repeats what he said about her getting on her knees and apologizing properly, I'm ready to track the asshole down at the clinic and smash his face with my fists until it matches his balls, Chief Woodcock or no Chief Woodcock.

What pisses me off the most is this is my fault. I should kick my own ass for what happened. Better yet, maybe I should get Winston back here to teach me a lesson. Why didn't I insist she lock the door behind me when I left? Instead, I closed it and trusted nothing bad would happen. And look where that got us.

I can tell Tina senses the direction my thoughts are heading when she places a hand on my cheek and turns my face to hers.

"Hey. It's okay. Nothing happened." She chuckles, the sunny sound a direct contrast to the tears that still dry on her cheeks. "Well, maybe not nothing. Milton might have some trouble conceiving children after what Winston did to his junk."

I snigger at the thought of the busted-nut butter situation in Milton's pants, before burying my face in Tina's neck, breathing in her sweet and savory scent. Shit. She is perfect. The sound of her voice is a balm to my ears. Her ass in my lap is fucking heaven.

I can't give this up. It's been two weeks since I crashed into her on the sidewalk and I'm already so obsessed with this woman I can't think straight. My brain spins with thoughts of how I can get her to agree to be with me, even with the boys in the picture. They're both teenagers now, so it shouldn't be as daunting as it would be if they were little. In a couple of years, they'll both legally be adults. We could even keep our dating separate from my family for a while, if that helps her accept it. Not that I want her to be separate, but if she has serious reservations about having a family, I would wait. For her, I would wait.

But would that be enough for her?

I think she might come around. You can tell her family already loves Jared. I couldn't even get close to him when I went down to the restaurant because Tina's grandmother was talking his ear off. And then, while I was waiting for him, Tina's mother and aunts swarmed me with questions. How did you meet Tina? Are you the one from the video? Are you the man she's dating? I shudder when I remember that I almost didn't hear the commotion from Tina's apartment over their barrage of questions.

Not that I helped much. Winston had already taken care of it by the time I made it up here.

I squeeze Tina tighter, my mind flashing to the sight of Milton writhing in agony on the floor.

I owe Winston so much. How does one properly thank a goat for saving the woman you love?

Love? We just met, so I'm not sure I'm quite there yet, but as I hold Tina on my lap and think about what a disaster the situation could have been if Winston hadn't been here, I know I'm not far off. Which is insane, obviously. But I'm a grown man with a rubber duck collection, so I doubt anyone would blink twice if I said I loved a woman after knowing her for a week. I wouldn't say that, though. If there's anything that would scare Tina off for sure, it would be that.

But I need to say something, before I drive myself crazy thinking about the possibilities. With a deep breath, I gather up my courage and begin. "Tina, I need to tell you something."

In a flash, she's off my lap, standing on the floor by the couch with a look of panic on her reddened face. "No. Not until I say something first." She wrings her hands, pacing in front of the coffee table.

Shit. I'm too late. She's calling the whole thing off right now, before I can explain. "Tina, baby. Please, let me say something before you do this." I can't keep the pleading tone from my voice, the panic I feel at losing her before I can really get to know her clawing at my chest.

"No, Nick. I know you came here today intending to break up with me, but you will sit there and listen to me first."

Excuse me? Did I hear that correctly?

"So much has happened since you left last night, Nick. So much."

"Okay?" I drawl, still not sure I heard her correctly.

"And it gave me a chance to think. I want to try this with you. With everything I have going on, it's probably the wrong time, but I'd never forgive myself if I didn't give it a shot, you know?"

My eyes go wide as my mouth drops open. So many words are on the tip of my tongue, the things I want to say all fighting for dominance, so instead of saying a thing, I jump off the couch. Tina watches me stalk toward her, her eyes going glassy as I wrap her in my arms and lower my lips to hers. The feel of her melting into my arms has blood rushing to my dick.

"Holy shit, Tina. That's...that's amazing," I say on a breath, tasting her lips before continuing. "But there's still something I need to tell you." I rush to the next part without giving her the chance to protest again. "Jared is moving in with me permanently, but that's not all."

She steps back, her eyes lowering. "Shit. I'm too late, aren't I? I knew it." She shakes her head and turns away. "Stupid, Tina. You waited too long to realize you like people, and now you're paying for it by losing the best guy you've ever met. Stupid, stupid." She tucks a loose strand of hair behind her ear, and pushes her glasses up her nose, her shoulders rising and falling with each breath. When she faces me again, she squares her shoulders, looks me right in the eyes, and says, "Alright. Let me have it. Rip this bandaid off so I can focus on fulfilling the foster parent requirements so I can get Carson out of that stranger's house as soon as possible."

"No, Tina. That's not what I'm saying. I want nothing more than to try this with you. It's just that..." I slowly stop speaking as her words sink in. Foster parent requirements? Get Carson out of a stranger's house? He can't be the same Carson, can he? "Tina?"

She huffs. "What, Nick?"

"Did you say *Carson*?"

She narrows her eyes at me. "Yeah. And?"

"How do you know Carson?"

She scoffs. "He's worked for me for the last three years."

"And what was that you said about foster parent requirements?"

"I'm becoming a foster parent so Carson can come live with me. I love that kid, and can't bear the thought of never seeing him again. The social worker said he has somewhere to stay here in town, but who knows how long that will last? I need to find a new apartment and take all the classes so I can get custody of him."

Holy shit. It's the same Carson. It has to be. I snort a laugh before I can stop myself.

"Why is that funny? You think it's funny for a kid to lose his sorry excuses for parents, then have to rely on a stranger for help on top of that? That's sick, Nick. Maybe you're not who I thought you were."

"No, Tina. That's not what I was laugh—"

Her answering chuckle is dry, humorless. "You know what? I really don't give a shit what you were laughing at. Maybe it's better that we call this off now. I can't be with someone who thinks a kid losing his parents is funny."

"For fuck's sake, Tina. Will you please shut up for a minute and let me explain?"

She crosses her arms over her chest and gives me a look so dark I have to will my body not to tremble. Why does this remind me of what she told me about butchering pigs and cleaning blood? I'm fucking this up. Badly.

I wonder if Wade's already taught her how to dispose of a body without being caught.

"I'm sorry," she says, the calm tone of her voice unnerving. "Please, continue. Explain to me why it's funny that Carson lost his parents."

Fuck. That's not what I meant. That's the least funny thing about all this.

I release a strangled breath as I think over how to say this. I don't want to trivialize her worries about Carson. Just because I'm the stranger he'll be living with doesn't mean her feelings are any less valid. I only hope when I tell her, she's relieved.

"When I first spoke with Jared's foster parents and his caseworker about having him come to an extended training camp, they said there were courses I'd need to take and certifications I'd need to get. Because he'd be staying here with me for so long, they had to be sure I'd be a suitable temporary guardian for him."

Tina widens her eyes and dips her head slightly, in a "yes, and?" motion, like she's telling me to get on with it.

"There wasn't really anything that fit our particular situation, so Gloria, Jared's caseworker, came up with a plan for me to take a certain training. Foster parent training, Tina."

Her mouth opens, and she looks to the sky. "You've taken the foster parent training?"

I nod. "Yes. And now that Jared's foster parents have disappeared, he will be living with me full time, at least until he turns eighteen." I shrug. "He's welcome to stay with me after, of course, but I assume he'll want to go to college or something. Or continue with fighting. I'll support him either way."

Her face softens as she takes me in. "That's nice of you, Nick. But I don't really know why you're telling me this. I admit I don't know much about it, but I don't think there's any way to cheat the training. You can't give me your crib notes to help me get through foster parent training faster." She chuckles. "What am I missing here?"

She's so worried she can't get the pieces to fit together, so I take a deep breath and say it. "Carson is staying with me."

"Shut up." Her mouth works, but nothing further comes out.

"That was my emergency last night. Gloria called after Wade and I threw that asshole into the dumpster. I had to leave so I could meet her at my house to get Carson settled in."

"No. What?" She shakes her head like she doesn't believe what she's hearing. "Wait. *What?* Why didn't he say anything to me when he showed up for work?"

"You'd have to ask him that. I didn't see him when I went downstairs earlier, but I bet that's what Jared meant when he messaged me 'you'll never guess who's here'. I assume he's in the restaurant somewhere."

I can see the tension seep from her body, the muscles in her neck and shoulders loosening in front of my eyes, and I can't help but to relax a little myself. I might be mistaken, but I think hearing that Carson will stay helped her. And fuck if that doesn't make me proud.

"He's living with you?"

I risk taking a step forward, wanting to wrap her in my arms again, but understanding she may still need some space. "Yes," I say, my voice a soft whisper.

"And that's why you wanted to talk?"

I nod.

"Holy shit," she says on a breath, walking back to the couch before flopping down onto the middle cushion. "Holy shit, Nick. Didn't anyone ever teach you that the words 'we need to talk' should never be uttered unless you're breaking up with someone? You scared me half to death." She pats the seat next to her and gives me a tired smile before sinking against the back of the couch. "I decide to give this dating thing a shot with you, and then you bust out the 'we need to talk'. After what was happening with Carson, I nearly died from the stress. And *that* stressed me out even more, because if I died, where would Carson go?"

I lower myself onto the couch next to her and drape an arm over her shoulder, my heart still racing. "I thought you would decide I wasn't worth the trouble, now that I'm basically a father to two teenage boys. I figured that would be a lot to ask of someone who swore off dating because she never wanted to have to look after another person."

I see her cringe from the corner of my eye.

"Until recently, you probably would have been right. But with meeting you, and with Carson, and with finally coming to terms with the idea that I've always taken care of people, I think I'm coming around." She shifts, throwing an arm over my belly and resting her head on my chest. "These last twenty-four hours have been a lot." She releases a heavy sigh that develops into an enormous yawn. "I'm exhausted."

I pull her closer and drop a kiss on the top of her head. "I bet you are. Unfortunately, you can't nap right now."

She rolls her head to the side to scowl at me, and even when she's exhausted and angry, she's adorable. I still can't quite believe I didn't ruin this.

"I know," I say with a chuckle. "But you have a restaurant full of people downstairs, and I can't face them by myself. I haven't talked to her yet, but I'm pretty sure I heard your grandmother saying something about 'short shorts' and 'hot buns' when I was down there the first time."

Tina snorts a laugh and forces herself to sit up. "Nonna took a tour of the Spring Chickens facility today. Someone told her about the physical activity classes at the local gym, and they mentioned the tiny shorts the owner likes to wear."

Recognition dawns on me, having heard similar phrasing every couple of days since I started the seniors' fitness classes. "Miss Martha. The woman can't get enough of my hot buns." I shake my head. "My shorts aren't even that short."

Her eyes go comically wide and she looks side to side. "Okay, Daisy. You keep telling yourself that." She places a hand on my knee and pushes herself up to standing. "Let's go before my family breaks down the door. The curiosity has to be eating them alive by now."

She's unlocking the deadbolt before I take in what she's said. "Wait a minute. Are you calling me Daisy Duke? From the *Dukes of Hazzard*? That's not even accurate, Tina. Daisy wore denim cut-offs. My shorts are a breathable blend of polyester and spandex. They're specially designed for running and other athletic activities."

She shakes her head and walks to the door, waiting for me to catch up before heading out of the apartment. My brain is occupied with one thought as I follow her down the stairs. When we reach the door to the restaurant, I can't hold it in any longer. There's something I desperately need to know. I stop her with a hand on her arm.

"Tina?"

"Yes, Nick?" She cocks an eyebrow in question, sending a rush of blood to my dick. God, I love her eyebrows.

"Are we talking Jessica Simpson's Daisy Duke, or Catherine Bach's? Because that's a pretty important distinction."

When she bursts into laughter before pulling the door open, my heart soars. I love hearing her laugh. It's almost enough to distract me from the question at hand. I say almost, because I still need to know.

Jessica or Catherine?

Oh, shit. She doesn't mean Daisy *Duck*, does she?

Nah. That can't be it.

Daisy Duck doesn't even wear shorts.

 Chapter 34

"CALL ME THE NICKMOBILE"

Tina

"THAT WAS DELICIOUS, DAD. I didn't know you could cook like that. And look," I add with a laugh. "You still have all your fingers."

My father and I are in the back of Wings and Pizza washing up the last of the dinner dishes while the rest of our group heads across the street to the cornhole pitch. He keeps casting longing looks over there, but insists he wants to help me finish in the kitchen before trying his hand at cornhole. I think that Superhole footage he watched at Crow Bar earlier motivated him to add some activity to his life. And I'm at least sixty percent sure it's not only because his number one hall pass plays the sport.

Dad chuckles and lifts his hands from the soapy water, giving his fingers a wiggle before submerging them again. "Thanks, sweetheart. It's been so long since I cooked, I wasn't sure I could pull it off. But when your mother, Nonna, and aunts couldn't tear themselves away from those young men, and you and that Nick fella were nowhere to be found, Wade and I realized we'd need to step in and get it done if we wanted to eat today." He shoots me a sly glance before adding, "I thanked him for all the help he's given you over the years. You and everyone else."

I sigh.

I suppose that's the best I can hope for when it comes to keeping Wade's real identity a secret. Most everyone in Tuft Swallow knows he's not exactly who he says he is, anyway. If his old gang were going to find him, I bet they'd have had no trouble doing it before now. Besides, despite his mild-mannered realtor persona, he's still the old Gianni Scibetta underneath, and I have no doubt he could take care of himself if needed.

"Hey, Stan. Why don't you let me help Tina finish up in here while you go play cornhole? I called my coach, former world cornhole champion Peter Harrelson, and he's agreed to come give you all some pointers. I had to promise to never touch a bean bag again to get him to come, but after the disaster I made of my trophy case earlier, that's an easy promise to keep."

My dad's eyes light up at the mention of Nick's cornhole coach, and after dropping a quick kiss on my cheek, he's out the door. Surprisingly, my dad is more impressed with the former world champion cornholer than he is with Nick, despite admitting to watching all of his fights *and* his stint as a professional wrestler. Stan Falcone is full of surprises today.

During dinner, Nick told us all about how his cornhole lessons culminated in the near destruction of some of his most treasured rubber ducks. Jared said Nick was almost ready to rush the little rubber guys to the hospital in Spitz Hollow for medical attention before he reminded him they're not real. Nick threatened to increase Jared's training if he didn't confess to making that part up.

It was the first family dinner I'd attended in years where I wasn't singled out for being the only Falcone child bucking tradition to follow her own path. Could the two teenage boys present have had something to do with that? Most definitely. Mom spent most of dinner convincing them to call her Nonna.

My own grandmother was giddy with the knowledge she finally had a great-grandchild old enough to call her Bisnonna, which she says sounds just enough like *BitchNonna* to be funny. She was a little sad that my grandfather wouldn't get to enjoy being called Bisnonno, but when she realized the two boys are old enough now that she may still be alive when they have kids, and she'd get to see my father called *BitchNonno*, she cheered up. Did any of them care that Jared and Carson aren't my kids, or even my foster kids? Not in the slightest. As soon as my family caught on that I'm seeing Nick (which he made a lot easier for them by pulling me into a passionate kiss the second we walked back into the restaurant), and that Nick is the boys' guardian, my family brought them fully into the fold. As far as my mother is concerned, those two boys are Falcones now.

"You knew how much he would love that, didn't you?" I ask Nick while placing the last of the dishes on the rack before sending them through the dish sanitizer. "Did you see his eyes when you first mentioned Peter during dinner? It wouldn't surprise me if Peter took first place on my dad's hall pass. You know, if it weren't already laminated, that is."

Nick narrows his eyes at me. "Do I want to know who his current number one is?"

I shrug. "Apparently, Shemar Moore has that honor. What I'd like to know is, when did Shemar oust Tom Selleck from the top spot? My dad's been obsessed with that man's mustache for literal decades."

Nick shakes his head, then grins. "I kind of love your dad. I have Shemar's number if he wants it."

"That's going around today," I say with a chuckle. "Charlene at Crow Bar said the same thing. And after seeing what he can do in the kitchen, I have a new appreciation for him, too. But don't you dare give my dad Shemar Moore's number. Leave that poor man alone."

I undo my apron and pull it over my head, making the look in Nick's eyes morph from playful to hungry in an instant.

"As much as I'd love to stand here and talk about the men on your dad's hall pass list—"

"He has women, too," I interrupt. "Not just men."

He smiles. "As much as I want to talk about the men *and women* on your dad's hall pass list, I've been waiting to get you alone. It's like I haven't seen you in weeks." He wraps a hand around the back of my neck and drags me closer, sending a flood of butterflies rushing through me. "I need to remember what your kiss tastes like." He presses his lips to mine, parting them with a slip of his tongue. He pulls back too soon. "Delicious."

The butterflies in my belly are in full on riot mode now, and with the heat flooding my core, I'm about to lose all sense of decorum. I throw my arms around Nick's neck, smashing my lips to his as I thrust my tongue in his mouth, deepening the kiss as I attempt to get closer than the laws of physical space will allow. My body presses closer and Nick, being the genius that he is, grabs me under my thighs and lifts me from the floor in one smooth motion. I sense movement as he carries me, but I'm too busy kissing him, and rubbing myself against the hard ridge in his jeans to care where we're going. All I want is to quench this burning need, and the only thing that will work is Nick.

He pushes me against the wall and grinds his erection against my core, driving me closer to the edge. The throbbing need between my legs forces a long moan from me when Nick breaks our kiss and bends his lips to my neck to leave a sucking kiss along my collarbone. He pins me to the wall with his hips, while nipping and grazing his teeth along the flesh at the base of my throat as he works to push my shirt and bra up with one hand.

"Fuck, baby. Look at your gorgeous tits." He rubs his thumb over my nipple, forcing me to make a mewling sound I've never heard before. "You're so sensitive for me." He pinches me lightly, making my hips buck, and he drives his hips forward in response, grinding that hard length against me again. His lips brush my ear. "I can feel how hot you are through your clothes, Tina. How wet are you for me?"

"So wet," I whisper, my need for him suddenly overwhelming.

My breath comes in panting gasps as I scramble for purchase, for leverage, for any way to grind against him harder so I can get some relief from this growing tension, but Nick is in control. He yanks my shirt down, covering me yet leaving my bra shoved up above my breasts, and lifts me away from the wall.

"Tell me there's a fucking back door in this place, Tina. Because if there isn't, I'm marching you out the front door in full view of everyone in Tuft Swallow, and the top story in tomorrow's Nosy Pecker will be all about how I manhandled you into your apartment in a fog of lust."

I wrap my arms around his neck more tightly and point down the back hallway. "There. That leads to the back lane. No one will see us there." Except the apartments that line the opposite side of the street, but I can't care about them. Not when I'm already so close.

He wastes no time getting us out the back door as we devour each other's kisses and bump blindly into every wall along the way. My face is buried in his neck as I suck and lick the salty skin, when I hear him growl a warning.

"Not a fucking word, Rhett. If you call their attention over here, I will kill you in your sleep."

I keep my face hidden, but hear Rhett chuckle. "Sure thing, Boss. Carry on."

"Hold on tight, kitten," Nick says a second later. "Stairs."

Somehow, during the climb, Nick fumbles the keys out of my pocket, and he's able to unlock my apartment to let us inside without putting me down. He kicks the door shut behind him, stopping only to lock the deadbolt again before carrying me to my bed, where he promptly drops me on my ass.

"Hey," I complain, more at the loss of contact than anything else. "I was enjoying that."

"Sorry," he says, moving to stand between my legs. "It's too hard to get undressed when I'm carrying you. I promise I'll pick you up again after. Fuck, if you want, I'll carry you anywhere you want to go. Call me the Nickmobile, because you'll never have to walk again." His breathing is heavy as he pulls my shirt over my head before reaching around my back to undo my bra. He drags the lace down my arms, his pupils darkening as he takes me in. "You are so fucking beautiful, Tina." He leans forward to drop a quick kiss on my lips, then pushes my shoulder until my back is flat on the bed. "But if you don't get these pants off so I can taste you in the next five seconds, I'm pretty sure I'll die." He grabs my pants and underwear at the waist and drags them down and off my legs, dropping them to the floor. "*Fuck, yes,*" he groans, then drops to his knees and drags me to the edge of the bed.

I prop myself up on my elbows in time to see him lick his lips before diving forward and burying his face between my legs.

With one slow, dragging lick up my center, stars ignite in my vision, but I can't drag my eyes away from his. He stares at me while he circles my clit with his tongue, his eyes becoming more molten with each mewling gasp I make. He pins my legs down with his rough hands, holding me steady as he devours me. With each lick, he drives me higher, the tension building in my core as I get closer and closer to careening over that edge into bliss.

Then he stops.

"What the fuck?" I ask, more than a hint of irritation in my voice. "Why'd you stop?"

He says nothing, just grins down at me with that lopsided smile of his before reaching over his head and pulling his shirt off in one clean motion, exposing the chiseled pecs and slightly rounded belly that both drive me wild with lust. He pulls a condom out of his pocket and places it on the bed before shucking his jeans and underwear.

"I'm guessing we have maybe ten more minutes before your family comes looking for us." He rips the condom open and rolls it down over his length. "And I'll be damned if you don't come all over my cock before I have to go out there and show you my terrible cornhole skills. There's an excellent chance you won't want me anymore after you see the kind of havoc I can cause with a bean bag." He lifts a knee onto the bed, notches his cock at my entrance, and slides in with a sinfully delicious groan. "*Fuuuck, babe.* You feel so damn good." He pulls out, then slams back in with another groan. "I'm sorry, Tina. I'll take my time with you later, but I think this time needs to be fast and rough." He pulls out and thrusts in again, his hands digging into my hips so hard I'm sure they'll leave a mark. "This last day has been torture. I thought I'd never be with you like this again."

When he reaches between us and presses a thumb to my clit, I can't hold back any longer. The orgasm rockets through me, sending spasms of bliss through my core, my arms, my legs, my hands, and my feet, like the sensation is too big for it to stay in just one part of my body. I'm powerless as I twitch and tremble beneath him.

Nick groans and stills, seating himself in me so fully I can feel each throb of his orgasm as he pulses, filling the condom. "Jesus. Oh, fuck. You're squeezing me so good, baby." He lowers himself over me, careful not to crush me, and presses his forehead to mine.

I sling my boneless arms around his neck, forcing him to lower his body, loving the weight of this enormous man pressing me into my bed. "Shut up and kiss me, Nick," I whisper before bringing my lips to his.

He peppers my lips with tiny kisses, then pulls back and looks down at me with a grin. "You're fucking amazing. You know that?"

I shrug, forcing an air of nonchalance even though his words make me giddy. "You're not so bad yourself."

Nick smiles and presses his lips to mine, kissing me softly but deeply until he begins to stiffen once more, the heat in my core rising in response, before he pulls away and sighs. "As much as I'd love to stay here and make love to you again, I think we'd better get out on that cornhole pitch before your family notices our absence." He slides out of me with a moan, and I already miss the feel of him. He ties off the condom and drops it in the wastebasket next to my bed before grabbing my hands and pulling me up. "Come on. Let's get this over with."

He picks my clothes up from the floor and helps me get dressed, pausing a few times to stroke my body and sigh wistfully, making me laugh each time. "Don't laugh. All I want is to stay here with you so I can worship you properly. A few minutes with my mouth on your body was not enough. Next time we're making sure neither of us has anywhere to go." He gets on his knees to slide my feet back into my socks.

"A girl could get used to this," I say as he finishes with getting me dressed and moves on to find his own clothes. "I've never been treated like a queen before."

I watch as he pulls his shirt back over his head, wishing we'd had a few more minutes to cuddle before having to get dressed again. I was right that first night. He is the best cuddler.

"Well, go ahead and get used to it," Nick says while pulling up and fastening his jeans. "I knew from the moment I met you that you'd be someone special in my life. And you should know right now that I intend to marry you some day. Not right now, of course. But it'll happen someday."

My heart races at his mention of marriage. *He wants to marry me?*

The funny thing is, even though I'm not there yet, I could actually see myself marrying Nick one day.

Huh.

Who knew?

I Now Pronounce You...

Tina

Six Months Later

I REACH UP TO straighten the bow tie around Carson's neck, then smooth the lapels of his navy three-piece suit and fix the boutonniere. Standing back, I take a long look at the young man before me. In the last six months, he's grown so much, and I'm not just talking about his height. Though he's grown taller too, I'm talking more about the emotional growth he's worked so hard for. He's put in the hours with a therapist learning how to cope with his parents' death. We had a rough couple of months when the reality of their passing hit him the hardest; when his anger at both his parents and the system that allowed them to neglect him for all those years sparked a rage that was frightening for me to witness, and even harder for him to experience. Watching him put in the work, though? That was a privilege.

I have never been more proud, and the tears welling in my eyes prove it.

"Aw, Tina. Not again. You promised you wouldn't cry any more today, remember?" he says, placing a hand on my shoulder as he does his best to comfort me. "This is supposed to be a happy day. You don't have to go through with it if it upsets you this much, you know. There's still time to get out of it." He hunches his shoulders and swivels his head, looking around with exaggerated sneakiness. He holds up a hand and whispers behind it. "We can run out those doors and forget about the whole thing."

I slap him playfully on the arm. "I will do no such thing, young man. Do you know how upset Nick would be if we ran out of this courthouse right now?"

Carson nods once. "You're right. He'd be devastated." He snickers. "Actually, I think he's cried more happy tears today than you have."

Warmth floods my chest when I think about Nick. The last six months with him have been amazing. I never could have guessed how right it would feel to fall in love with a man who isn't afraid of his own emotions. One who tells me how much he loves me every day. One who tells the boys how much he loves them.

One who does his fair share and more around the house.

After all those years of thinking I didn't want a family, I'm thrilled to admit how wrong I was. Turns out I just needed to find the right family.

"Where is he? I know they got back a little late last night after the fight, but they were up before we left this morning."

When Nick crawled into bed late last night, he was practically vibrating with excitement. Jared's first time as part of the corner team during a fight couldn't have gone better, with Demetrius knocking his opponent out in the second round. Nick said he could tell the exact moment when Jared lost his heart to fighting. It wasn't when the ring girl came out after the first round like I thought. Instead, it was when he got to see Demetrius hugging his opponent, and hear the compliments he had to say about the man's skills during his post fight interview. Nick was almost glowing when he told me how proud he was that Jared focused on the art and athleticism of the sport, instead of letting himself get caught up in the drama that sometimes follows fighters. My dad told me Nick always had the utmost respect for his opponents, and for Jared to follow in those footsteps? Well, let's just say Nick is thrilled by it, and not because being sportsmanlike is the right thing to do. He won't admit it, but I know it's because it makes him feel like he's making a difference as a father. It reinforces the decision he made to offer Jared a permanent home.

It makes him feel like a dad.

Carson puts his phone in selfie mode and starts fussing with his hair, trying to get that flipped up at the ends look that so many teenage boys are doing these days. If he'd let me flat iron it back at the house like I offered, he would have the look he wants, but he refuses to believe that's the method the other boys are using to get it. Since my hair is usually up in a knot on top of my head, he thinks I don't know what I'm talking about. "They said something about Jared's suit," he says as he attempts to curl the strands up with his fingers. "I think it ripped or something. I'm not sure. I wasn't really listening when Jared explained where they were going."

I chuckle, shaking my head. Jared and Carson settled into life at Nick's house faster than anyone could have expected. Now, a mere six months later, you'd never believe they aren't biological brothers. Which means the teasing and fighting never stops. Almost, anyway.

When Carson was at his worst after his parents' death, Jared would take him to Put Up Your Ducks and get in the ring with him. He'd suit up in full protective gear and let Carson take his frustrations out on him. And Carson returned the favor. When Jared's old girlfriend popped back up and started messing with his emotions, Carson would take him to the basketball court and they'd run drills together until neither boy had the energy to talk, let alone worry about a girl who'd already proven she wasn't worth Jared's time. Okay, I may be a little biased because I know Jared is one of the best kids ever, but that doesn't mean I'm wrong. And that little girl better stay away from my boy if she knows what's good for her. (And yes, I'm aware I'm being overprotective, but I don't care. These boys haven't had anyone looking out for them for most of their lives, so I'll be as overprotective as I want.) But other than having each other's backs in times of emotional turmoil, the boys are at each other's throats like actual siblings, and I couldn't love it more. But even in those first couple of months, when they supported each other, Nick and I had a couple of exhausted and bruised boys on our hands.

"We had the last fitting for your suits two days ago. How on earth could he have ripped it already?"

Carson shrugs, shoving his phone back into his pocket, satisfied with his hair at last. "Who knows? It's Jared. He probably decided to practice his high kicks after he put it on. I bet you ten bucks he comes in here wearing new pants."

"You're on," I say with a laugh. "I seriously doubt Jared would put on a three-piece suit, then start throwing kicks." He has impulse control issues on occasion, like any teenage boy, but I can't see him doing something this silly on such a big day.

The doors at the end of the hall fly open with a bang, drawing my attention away from Carson's too-confident smile.

"Sorry we're late," Nick says, rushing over to kiss my cheek. He's wearing his own three-piece suit, the light gray plaid stretching over his muscles enticingly, his pink tie a perfect color match the heels I have strapped on my feet. I love his normal uniform of tiny shorts with no shirt, but this look is really doing it for me. *I wonder if we have time to sneak away before the ceremony starts.* "This knucklehead ripped his suit pants practicing high kicks, so we had to find a seamstress to do a rush repair," he adds with an indulgent smile, interrupting my increasingly naughty thoughts.

My mouth drops open and I swing my head back to Carson, who is now chuckling and shaking his head. "You knew before we made that bet, didn't you?"

He nods, still laughing. "You owe me ten bucks."

I narrow my eyes at him, making him laugh even more. I swivel my head back to Jared. "Did you get them fixed? Or did you buy new pants?"

He looks from me to Carson, his eyes clouded with confusion. "We lucked out and the Dirty Hookers were meeting on Mrs. Woodcock's front porch when we went by." He turns and flips up his suit jacket, showing me where the seat of his pants has been repaired with a multicolored, knitted yarn patch. "They whipped up this patch and stitched it on while I waited in their bathroom."

I snort a laugh. Only in Tuft Swallow will a rogue knitting group come to your rescue when you least expect it.

"Oh, and they wanted me to ask if they should bring anything to the reception later? I told them we had it covered, but you know how Mrs. Woodcock gets."

"I told her to bring wine," Nick says. "I had to say something to get us out of there."

I nod. "Good thinking. You'd have never made it on time if you hadn't come up with something. Besides, with my entire family coming, we could always use more wine."

Nick grimaces, no doubt remembering the time my family came to help my Nonna get settled into her new home at Spring Chickens, and he tried to have a friendly drink with my mother and my aunts.

Did you know a hangover can last for three days? Yeah, I didn't know either until that day. And Nick didn't come close to drinking as much as my family did. I'm surprised he drank at all in front of the boys, to tell the truth. But after the celebration, both Carson and Jared expressed surprise that people can have a few drinks without going to excess. They'd only ever been exposed to problem drinking in the past, and I think it did some good to see responsible drinking in action. I imagine it feels different when you see adults having a couple glasses of wine while enjoying each other's company than it does to see them drink to get drunk and pass out.

I turn to Carson, remembering what Jared just admitted. "That sounds to me like he's wearing the same pants, not new pants. Looks like you owe me ten bucks."

"Hmmm," he says, rubbing his chin. "But he was practicing high kicks like I guessed, so I think this might still be my win."

Jared cocks an eyebrow at Carson. "You watched me do it, bro. I told you Nick was coming with me to get it fixed."

"So, is everyone here?" Nick asks, changing the subject when he sees my mouth drop.

That little shit, Carson. I can't believe he tried to hustle me.

I stuff down my irritation. It was a little funny, I suppose. "Yeah, I think so," I say. "I haven't peeked inside to check, but I know my family was planning on arriving early to get the best seats. They didn't trust there would be room for everyone."

He nods, his eyes getting misty. Uh oh. He can't cry. If he cries, then I'll cry, then we'll both look like defective tomatoes which will make for terrible pictures. And I want so many pictures to remember this day.

"Guys?" I say, getting Jared and Carson's attention in the nick of time. They looked to be five seconds away from engaging in a wrestling match to settle their budding argument. "Can you head inside and make sure everyone is ready? I need to talk to Nick for a second, and then we'll get started."

The boys quickly disengage. Carson grumbles an "okay" before heading into the courtroom, but Jared stops in front of me. He throws his arms around me and squeezes until my own eyes get misty with emotion.

"This is the best day ever," he whispers before letting me go and following Carson into the courtroom.

"Damn it," I whisper, fanning at my tear-filled eyes with my hands. "I can't cry again today."

Nick nods his agreement. "I know. Do you know how hard it was to fight back my tears while the Dirty Hookers were patching up Jared's pants?"

I choke out a laugh. "Why would he do that?"

Nick shakes his head, chuckling. "It's Jared. His reasons are his own."

"And that patch?" I snort another laugh. "It's huge. Why didn't you go get new pants? "

His shoulders shake with laughter as he wraps his arms around me. "Jared said no. He said he couldn't bear to hurt their feelings after they jumped into action to help him out. He knows every person in that knitting group will be at our reception later, and he'd feel terrible if they thought he didn't like their patch job."

I relax into Nick's embrace, our laughter dying down as we enjoy the comfort of each other's arms before heading into the courtroom ourselves to start the ceremony.

"Are you ready for this?" he asks, dropping a kiss on my forehead before stepping back. "It's not too late to turn back."

"Are you kidding me? There's no way I'd turn back now. Of course, we're going through with this. It took way too long to admit it, but there's nothing I want more."

His grin lights up his entire face. "I know exactly what you mean, Tina. Let's get in there." Nick holds his arm up and I wrap my hand around his elbow, tucking in close to him.

"Let's do this." Together we grab the handles and swing the double doors open wide, stepping into the room to sounds of scattered applause.

A quick look around shows our closest family and friends filling the seats of the tiny courtroom, watching with teary eyes and giant smiles as we make our way to the small judge's bench. A kind looking older woman introduces herself as Judge Miller before granting us a glimpse of pearly dentures with a wide grin.

"Well, it's so nice to see you all here today," Judge Miller begins, her smile never faltering. "I'm sure you understand if I don't stand on circumstance here today as we celebrate this joyous occasion." Her grin grows even larger. "Gloria has filled me in on all the details, and of course I've followed your story in the Nosy Pecker since the beginning, so I don't think we need to ask all the questions and do all the other mumbo jumbo that goes along with this, do you? The paperwork is in order, so what say we get right to the fun part?"

Nick and I both shake our heads in agreement. I know I, for one, am a little stunned at how casual Judge Miller is being about this, but she's the judge, so I'm sure she knows what she's doing. After all, she's done this before. I haven't.

"Good, good," she says, stepping out from behind her dark-paneled bench to approach us. "Then let's get this show on the road, shall we?" she whispers before giving us a wink. She takes another step forward and addresses our assembled families. "Good afternoon, folks," she says. "Thank you so much for joining us today. Before we get started, I'll let you in on a little secret."

My hand tightens on Nick's arm as we look at each other with concern. This wasn't part of the plan. What's this judge doing?

"I hear there's a party in town square after this," she says with a wink. "So what do you say we finalize the adoption of Jared Unsworth and Carson Howe by Nick D'Onofrio and Tina Falcone, then we can head over there to celebrate this new family properly?"

I can't hear what she says next over the cheers of our assembled families, but one look at Nick and the boys tells me the only thing I need to know. Judge Miller is making us a family, officially. The rest is only details.

When Nick grabs my hand and drags me over to the boys before wrapping us all up in a massive hug, I can't contain it any longer. I burst into the happiest tears of my life. I've never been happier to take responsibility for another human than I am at this moment. And no, the irony of it being one overgrown man-child, and two literal man-children hasn't escaped me, but you know what? I don't care.

My mom was right. I *do* love taking care of people, and I *am* happier now that I have a family.

It's not all sunshine and rainbows, though. I still have to call a handyman when I need gas range repairs, but maybe my mother was right about that too, and Nick and I need to tie the knot before all my gas range problems disappear.

Chapter 36

FINALLY GOT MY DUCKS IN A ROW

Nick

"I THINK MY MOM was hoping we'd surprise her with a wedding," Tina says, an exhausted but happy smile on her face. "But with everything else that's going on, I think that would have been overkill."

We're hiding on the steps of the pavilion in the town square, taking a break from the adoption celebration and the well-meaning congratulations from the party-goers. I feel a little weird about accepting congratulations when the reasons we have the boys are so awful. It's like we're saying it's a good thing Carson's parents died, or that we're glad Jared's parents are addicts who, when Gloria finally tracked them down, signed away their parental rights in a heartbeat. As happy as our little family is, we know what the boys had to lose to get us here. It makes this party seem a little like it's in poor taste coming so soon after all that.

Not that we aren't ecstatic that we've adopted the boys. It's just that neither of us wanted a party of this size. But when the Tit Peepers heard we were finalizing our adoption of Jared and Carson, they insisted they be in charge of the reception. What was supposed to be a small celebration with only our closest family and friends has turned into a town wide party. Luckily, most of the people in attendance assume it's another impromptu cornhole tournament, so we're spared from having to endure too many conversations with kindhearted but misguided townsfolk. Besides, I'm pretty sure you can't call yourself a real Tuft Swallower until your party turns into a cornhole tournament. It's a Swallowers' rite of passage.

After Milton Maguire found us at the party, and offered yet another apology for what he likes to refer to as the "misunderstanding" that day at Tina's apartment, I took Tina's hand and led her to the pavilion so we could have a few minutes to breathe. Tina may be willing to forgive and forget when it comes to that asshole, but I'm not as kind as she is, at least not when Milton is involved. I have a hard time not throwing him back in the dumpster every time I see his stupid face. Or better yet, letting Mayor Winston have another go at him.

"She did make a snarky comment about not seeing a ring on your finger." I pull Tina closer to me, breathing in her comforting sweet and savory scent. "Nonna Mona giggled the whole time your mom was giving me shit."

Tina laughs. "Letting Nonna in on the secret was a brilliant idea. My mom's going crazy because she knows something's up, but she can't figure it out."

I chuckle. I don't enjoy keeping the secret from Tina's parents, but I know it's for the best. If they knew I'd proposed months ago, her mother would have been here every chance she got to help plan the wedding. We'd have never had time to get the adoption sorted out. Plus, we've *really* been enjoying our mornings alone together after the boys head off to school, *if you know what I mean.*

I've never been more confident in my decision to hire Rhett as a manager than when I'm buried balls deep in my fiancée. Which I admit is a weird thing to say, but if it weren't for Rhett, I wouldn't have the luxury of staying home with Tina in the mornings, so I stand by it.

I grab Tina's left hand and play with her empty ring finger. "I have to say, it's a little weird to see you without your ring."

The simple gold band is tucked in a ring box on our nightstand, right next to the giant container we keep fully stocked with the brand of XXL condoms we prefer. Tina and I decided together not long after I convinced her to move in with me and the boys (which wasn't until after my kitchen renovation was finished, because I couldn't in good conscience invite a chef into that mess), that we won't be having any biological kids of our own. We're both thrilled to call Carson and Jared our sons, and have discussed the possibility of fostering more teens in the future, but for now, our family is complete.

She laughs. "You know what? It feels weird." She shifts her body until she's leaning into me, then rubs her hand along the scruff on my jaw. "But I'm sure one of the nosy nellies from the Tit Peepers will spill the beans any minute, so we won't have to hide it anymore. Or that damn Nosy Pecker will put it in their gossip rag while my parents are visiting, and they'll learn of it that way."

Tina still isn't a fan of the Nosy Pecker. She hates not knowing who's writing about us. In the last couple of months, she's confronted every Tit Peeper and Spring Chicken in town, but none of them will fess up. Either they're telling the truth, and they don't know who writes the Nosy Pecker, or they have better poker faces than anyone I've ever met. We avoid playing cards with any of them, just to be on the safe side.

In the last few months, we've graced the front page of the Nosy Pecker a few times, thanks to our whirlwind romance and quick adoption of the boys. I'm actually looking forward to tomorrow's edition. I already have a place for it in the adoption scrapbook I'm making about our little family. I call it the boys' baby book, which some might say is too tongue in cheek, considering we haven't been able to track down any baby photos of either of the boys, but they both think it's funny and theirs are the only opinions that matter. Believe me, though, if I could punch their parents for not preserving anything from the boys' childhoods, I would do it in a heartbeat. But considering Jared's parents disappeared again as soon as they signed their rights away, and Carson's parents are still in their urns in Carson's closet at home, I'll have to settle for being pissed off instead.

I take her chin in my hand and tilt her head so I can look into her eyes. "What if we tell her now?"

She relaxes against my chest, wrapping her arms around my waist. "Maybe you're right. We should probably ask the boys what they think first, though. This is their day, too, after all."

"Ask us what?" Carson strolls around the corner of the pavilion, Jared hot on his heels. "What are you guys talking about?"

Carson sits on the step next to Tina, and Jared stays standing. No doubt that has something to do with the yarn patch currently holding the seat of his pants together. Mrs. Woodcock showed it to me before they stitched it on, and the thing looked lumpy. I bet sitting on it is uncomfortable. Serves him right for practicing kicks in a suit.

"We're thinking of telling Tina's parents about the engagement today."

"But we wanted to know what you two thought about it," Tina says, looking between the two boys. "This is your day, after all. We don't want to steal your thunder."

Jared laughs. "Steal our thunder. Please."

"Yeah. I have no problem with that. This party feels a little weird."

Jared nods his agreement. "Right? It's like 'congratulations for having alcoholic junkie parents who died or didn't want you. Here's Tina and Nick as consolation'." He snorts a laugh. "I mean, you guys are great and all, but still...it's a weird thing. And we're nearly eighteen, anyway. You guys didn't really need to adopt us."

It's a conversation we've already had, but both Carson and Jared like to remind us every so often that we didn't need to adopt them. It's taken a while, but we've almost convinced them it's what we wanted. They still sometimes have a hard time believing that anyone actually wants them, after what both their parents put them through. It's something they're working on it in therapy.

Tina gasps, clutching imaginary pearls. "You shut your mouth," she teases. "Of course we needed to adopt you. This is the only way we can leave our legacy for the next generation. If it weren't for you two, I'd have no one to bequeath my creepy teapot collection to."

Carson shakes his head and chuckles. "I can't believe you convinced Jared to help you with those. Coming into the house to see you two hunched over the coffee table while you craft tiny corpses and headstones is so weird. The only thing weirder is the murder podcasts you listen to while you're doing it."

Jared scoffs. "That's not weird. What's weird is you helping Nick with his duck collection every weekend."

"Hey." I interject. "I'll have you know he's not just helping me with my collection. We're out there spreading the ducky love while running other errands."

After the boys moved in, I realized I'd need a bigger vehicle. I drove a regular sized sedan at the time, but with two growing boys, and Tina, we needed something bigger. That's when Carson introduced me to the wonder that is Jeep ducking, and convinced me I needed a Jeep so I could get in on the action. Now, when we go out in the new Jeep, we bring a selection of brand new ducks (because besides that one I gifted to Chief Woodcock for reasons no one but the two of us will ever know, I would never give away one of my babies), hoping we'll find other Jeeps to leave them on. And sometimes, when we're lucky, we get ducked back. It's become one of my favorite things, especially since it's something that I can do with Carson. I still train with Jared every day, but my basketball skills are almost as bad as my cornhole skills, so it's harder to find things to do with Carson. Driving around putting ducks on Jeeps is something we can do while spending time together.

Jared rolls his eyes, then grins. "Yeah, I know. I'm actually surprised you didn't already own a Jeep. This duck, duck, Jeep thing has been around for a few years. You should have been all over that."

He's not wrong. I've lamented the missed duck opportunities many times since Carson told me about the game. Imagine if I'd had a Jeep while I was still traveling for fights? I could have ducks from so many places. I'm working on a plan to fix that, though. When the boys are off to college, I plan to take Tina on a road trip to places important for both of our hobbies.

She can visit some of the oldest graveyards in the country to get inspiration for her creepy teapots, and I can collect and dispense ducks everywhere we go.

"That's what I like to see." Wade strolls around the corner, hands in his pockets and a rare smile on his face. "The Falcone-D'Onofrio family enjoying a little quality time away from the madness of this crazy little town."

Tina sits up and smiles. She and Wade have a strange relationship. She still won't tell me all the details, but from what I gather, she knew Wade a long time ago, and they reconnected when she moved to Tuft Swallow. Despite his reputation around Tuft Swallow for being a little rough around the edges, he's always been nothing but kind to her. I've asked her a few times what exactly she knows about his former ties to the mob, but she keeps that information pretty close to the vest. No doubt that's one reason Wade likes her so much. I imagine a man with ties to a criminal organization values discretion. But really, it doesn't matter to me who he used to be, because I like the man he is today. He's good to Tina and the boys, that's all I care about.

"Wade, you know Jared and Carson are keeping their last names," Tina says, still smiling at him. "Besides, Falcone-D'Onofrio is a bit of a mouthful, don't you think?"

The older man shrugs. "No worse than Biddescombe. But never mind that. I ain't here to talk surnames." He reaches a hand into his jacket, pulling two envelopes from the inside pocket. "I have a gift for you," he says, handing one envelope to Carson. "And for you." He gives the other envelope to Jared.

The boys tear into the envelopes, their faces becoming twin masks of bewilderment when they see what's inside.

"The address of a used car lot?" Jared asks, his brows drawn in confusion.

"Wade. But-but...what?" Carson says.

Wade shrugs and shoves his hands back into his pockets. "I've known kids from rough backgrounds who didn't get out. You have that chance now, with Tina and Nick, and I wanted to do my part to make sure you both have a good future ahead of you. It's not a lot, but…" he shrugs again. "Go there and tell him I sent you. He'll hook you up with anything on the lot. It'll help with getting around while you're in school. Or with whatever the hell else you decide to do with the rest of your life. You'll still have to work damn hard at whatever you do, but this will help you get there."

Tina jumps up and wraps Wade in a hug. "I knew you had a soft heart behind that grumpy exterior."

The older man fights back a grin and gives Tina one pat on the back before clearing his throat and stepping out of her embrace. "I'd appreciate if you don't tell anyone else about this," he says, schooling his features into his usual frown. "I've got a reputation to maintain."

Tina purses her lips and gives him a tight nod. "Of course. Your secret's safe with me."

He shakes his head and narrows his eyes at her. "Right. Okay. That's enough sappy shit. "

He turns to leave, but before he takes two steps, Jared and Carson launch themselves toward him and wrap him in another hug. The way Wade's eyes widen at the contact is almost comical.

"Thanks, Wade. I won't let you down," Carson says.

"Me neither," Jared adds. "Thanks for believing in me."

I can't stop the grin from creeping onto my face as I watch Wade try to fight back his tears while the two teenage boys hug him tightly. I wonder what he'd think about being called Poppa? Kids can't have too many grandparent figures in their lives, especially those who care as much as Wade evidently does. I'll have to ask Tina what she thinks about it later.

"Okay, boys. Let Mr. Biddescombe go. You're cramping his style." I call the boys off. "I'm sure he has other places he needs to be."

The boys reluctantly let Wade go, offering more thanks as they watch him walk off.

"Why don't we go put those in the office at the gym? You wouldn't want to lose a business card that will turn itself into a car of your choice."

The boys take off at a run, leaving Tina and me to follow at our own pace.

I stand up, holding a hand out to Tina. "Walk with me?"

She slides a warm hand into mine. "I would love nothing more."

As we walk hand in hand across the town square, I realize I feel the same as she does. There's nothing I love more than this. More than her. More than the little family we created here in Tuft Swallow.

I knew moving back here was a fantastic idea. Everything has turned out perfectly.

Well, almost.

Looking across the square, I spy a familiar white-fleeced menace and narrow my eyes. I know I owe Winston so much after he rescued Tina that day, and he'll have my vote in the next election. But still, it would be nice if he'd leave Tina and her underwear alone. To be fair, though, he's only broken into our house once. I have a feeling his days of stealing Tina's underwear are coming to an end. Now, if he would quit looking at my fiancée like he's about to run up and snatch the underwear off her body right this minute, everything would be perfect.

THE END?

THE PANTY THIEF

Mayor Winston aka the GOAT

(a not at all accurate representation of what the darn goat is thinking)

THE BIG ONE IS on to me. I see it in his weird, round pupils when he thinks I don't notice him staring at me.

I can always tell when they figure out what I'm up to by the way they watch me. It doesn't matter, though. Nothing will prevent me from reaching my goals. I've already become the mayor of Tuft Swallow. Up next? Take over the world. After that? I'll finally get to eat all the snacks I want, including that pizza woman's clothes.

Actually, scratch that last one. Ever since she moved in with the big guy, her clothes don't smell nearly as tasty. I went to all that trouble getting into her new house and had to leave my snack at the side of the road because it didn't taste a thing like pizza or chicken wings. I haven't been back since.

That pink-haired paint woman who moved into her old place, though? Her clothes are smelling more and more delicious these days. And thankfully, her underwear doesn't have a hint of paint smell, unlike the rest of her clothes. She never leaves the door open for me like the pizza woman did, but I have my ways. No one can keep Mayor Winston from his snacks for long.

THE END (OR MAYBE A NEW BEGINNING?)

THANK YOU SO MUCH for reading Tit Me With Your Best Shot. I'd love it you left a review on your favorite social media platform or book buying site.

When I first learned of the opportunity to join this group of authors to write a romantic comedy as part of a shared world, I promptly talked myself out of it. *Heck No!* I said to myself. *You're not good enough for that.* Luckily for me, I suck at taking my own advice, and I filled out the interest form, anyway. And I'm so glad I did. This has been the best experience. While I still don't think I'm good enough (seriously, I have issues with perfectionism), working with this group of writers has been a blast and I would do it again in a heartbeat. I encourage you to read the other books in the world of Tuft Swallow (they're listed on the next page for you) as soon as possible. You'll laugh, scream, and cry (and if you're anything like me, maybe pee your pants a little) when you read about this bird obsessed town and its quirky residents.

Be prepared, though. No matter how many bird puns you think you'll encounter, I promise it's more.

<3 Chantal Roome

Other Books From The Shared World Of Tuft Swallow

That's Cockatoo Much - Kristin MacQueen
Flock and Roll - Vicki Hilton
Don't Give A Cluck - Karigan Hale
Fowl Play - Cassandra Medcalf
This Is Hawkward - Joelle Evans
No Egrets - Susan Renee

*Scan the QR code to go
directly to the books page on
Chantal Roome's website*

About the Author

Chantal Roome writes contemporary romantic comedies and is the author of the Sleeping Dogs series of cinnamon roll rock star rom-coms, the hilarious holiday rom-com, Santa's Baby, and the small town rom-com, Tit Me With Your Best Shot (from the shared world of Tuft Swallow). She loves writing love stories with just the right mix of sweetness, humor, and sex. When she isn't writing, she's drinking way too much coffee, binge reading romance, and living out her own second chance romance with her husband. She's also a mediocre mom to two frustrating, but hilarious and endlessly loveable kids, one seizure-prone dog who has eaten every toy he's ever been given, and another dog who wants nothing more to use her tiny puppy shark teeth on any exposed flesh she can find.

Keep in touch with Chantal on social media

visit the website at chantalroome.com
get the Roomie Review Newsletter at
chantalroome.com/newsletter

join the readers' group at
facebook.com/groups/theromcomroome

facebook.com/chantalroomeauthor

instagram.com/chantalroomeauthor

pinterest.com/chantalroome

tiktok.com/chantalroomeauthor

goodreads.com/chantalroome

bookbub.com/authors/chantal-roome